BUNNYMAN BRIDGE

A Novel

by

Ronald J Van Wynsberg

Order this book online at www.trafford.com
or email orders@trafford.com

Most Trafford titles are also available at major online book retailers.

Printed in the United States of America.

ISBN: 978-1-4269-1420-1 (sc)
ISBN: 978-1-4269-1421-8 (hc)
ISBN: 978-1-4269-3768-2 (e)

Library of Congress Control Number: 2009931992

Trafford rev. 03/05/2014

 www.trafford.com

North America & international
toll-free: 1 888 232 4444 (USA & Canada)
fax: 812 355 4082

For my Wife of Twenty Years.

For being patient when patience was needed. For love when love was needed. For hope when this project felt hopeless. For being the best wife a man could ask for.

Acknowledgments

There are several people to whom I feel made this dream of mine a reality. First and foremost, my wife Marie, who has shown me enduring love and patience during the six years it took me to write this book.

Thanks and praise also goes to a dear friend, Jacqueline Bell, with who I badgered relentlessly about proper vernacular uses and whose vocabulary is beyond words. She also taught me when and when not to use the word then.

I would also like to thank the first editor of this book, John Reed, for pointing out that there is such a thing as being, well, wordy.

Thanks to the staff at Trafford Publishing for making the transition into publishing less scary.

And a special thanks to all veterans, past, present, and the fallen, and to all of their families. Without their unselfish heroism, we would be living in a totally different world today. Thank You Armed Forces of the United States!

Chapter 1

Thursday, 6:00 p.m.

Kiersten woke up groggy and disoriented. Her head throbbed. Her blonde hair was matted with blood. Every muscle in her body felt as if someone had pummeled her. She was unable to see anything but the blackness that engulfed her. Was she blind due to the knock she had taken on the head? Her eyes were open; she could blink, move them from side to side, so no, at least she didn't think so. Wherever she was, the darkness–was absolute.

She was cold and scared completely out of her wits. Her memory failed to produce answers to questions that she desperately needed answered. How had she gotten here? Where, exactly, was here? And who was it that had taken her against her will to bring her to—where ever here was.

Everything in her memory seemed a blur. She felt as if she had just awakened from a nightmare. But this was no nightmare, this she knew. It felt too damn real to be anything but a terrifying reality.

After several minutes had passed, the grogginess had finally started to dissipate. As it did, blurred reflections started to return. Bit by bit at first, and then the flood gates of her memory opened. She remembered waiting outside her mother's antique shop; All Thing's Old and New, for her boyfriend Todd to pick her up. He never showed. She remembered calling home for a ride, the phone was busy. She remembered that she started to walk home alone, or—was she? She remembered being startled, frightened by something in the woods. She recalled thinking that in the hopes of self-preservation she had better run. She ran hard and fast. She remembered the feeling of being pursued. She ran faster. She remembered the sight of her home—at how welcoming it had looked. Then she remembered a blurred face, a sharp pain on her head, and seeing the contents of her purse emptied out on the road beside her before everything went black.

The cold earth against her skin told her that most of her clothes had been removed. All that remained were her bra, panties, and socks. It did not tell her, however, where she was.

A cellar?

A cave?

She tried hard to sit up, but her hands and feet had been bound together, and with the unevenness of the ground, she found it impossible to keep her balance. *A cave*, she thought. Home in bed sleeping, dreaming this tale of frightening lunacy would have been the answer of choice, but she knew it was not.

Then, as if on cue, she felt it, a feeling of something lurking, staring—watching—waiting, somewhere in the darkness, for what, she had no clue.

"Who are you?" she asked, her voice quivering. "Why have you brought me here?"

Silence.

"What do you want with me? Please, just tell me what you want."

All she heard, however, was silence shouting back through the unending blackness.

Fear coursed through her body. Fear of what was going to happen to her, of not knowing who or why. But in the eyes of this sixteen-year-old girl who had really never known the true definition of the word fear in concrete terms until now, she feared not knowing when more than anything.

Her mind devoured the horrific possibility that maybe she had been kidnapped. And if so, what could they possibly want? Money? She and her mom weren't poor or destitute, but by no means were they rich. And what happens, she thought, if her mother couldn't come up with the cash?

Torture?

Murder?

Or could it be something even more horrifying?

Rape?

Kiersten was, after all, a sixteen old who had a firm belief that one's appearance is reflective in the efforts put forth in their own health and self respect; she was beautiful.

"Oh, God!" she said quivering, the thought now etched in the back of her mind, letter by letter.

The thought of being kidnapped was terrifying in and of itself, but the thought of having her virginity breached by someone unknown to her, being touched by a complete stranger whose idea of a good time was to violate young women; she would sooner welcome death.

And it was then, as she thought of unknown strangers rubbing their hands across her half- naked body, that she became even more aware of just what little clothing she had on. A thin layer of cotton was all that was left between the persons who had brought her here, and her virginity, her sanity.

As rape, a word that though spoken softly or even whispered, roared through her mind, a single—haunting, one word question kept repeating itself.

When?

She wouldn't be able to see it coming. All she could do was lie there and let her imagination manifest terror after terror.

2

5:10 p.m.

Sheriff Joan Fortune leaned back in her chair with her legs stretched out over her desk; her feet crossed at the ankles, and watched over the quiet streets of her town.

Her office was small, cramped, and held three desks and a jail cell in an alcove in the rear of the police station. Nothing like the office she had shared with 40 or so other fellow officers in her precinct in the upper Manhattan district of New York City, but it served its purpose.

And except for a call from Mrs. Zachary, a local elderly resident, it had been another uneventful day. Just the kind she liked.

Her view was that of just about the entire town. She admired just how much the town had grown since her tenure as Sheriff began. There were new streets, new street signs, shops, restaurants, and hotels. These changes made Milford what it was today—a successful tourist town.

Joan had started her career in law enforcement in New York City. She was a good hardnosed cop and was rewarded by a quick move up the pay grade. It had only taken her seven years to go from walking the beat to making detective. Some had said it was because of her more than generous feminine beauty, accompanied with her long dark brown hair and penetrating green eyes. But her arrest record simply spoke for itself.

From the time she was 5 years old, she had dreamed of being part of the N.Y.P.D. She had wanted to follow in her father's footsteps, and follow she did. It was in her blood, and she missed it. Joan also missed what the city had taken from her, a fellow officer and husband, John Fortune. And in an ensuing fall upon hearing the news of his murder, she lost their unborn child. She would more than likely still be carrying out her dream as a New York City detective if not for an abandoned three-year-old girl.

The girl, Caitlin, had been left at an old church in upper Manhattan. She had been found by an aging, well-rounded priest named Father Malloy. Upon finding her, he called Joan's precinct. Everyone was amazed by the remarkable strength and poise the little girl showed. Joan, being the only woman on the floor when Caitlin arrived, was asked to escort the little girl to the locker room. She was in need of a little cleaning up before child care services arrived. Joan took the little girl's hand, and led her down the hall.

Caitlin had been wearing rags for clothes and had no shoes. Dirt covered her face. Joan leaned toward the child, and with a wet paper towel, wiped away the dirt. As the dirt melted into the wetness of the towel, a tiny angelic face emerged. Joan was heartsick for the little girl whose world seemed to be in complete shambles, though one could not tell by her demeanor. She knelt down to Caitlin's level and hugged the child to her. "Everything will be alright," Joan whispered in her ear.

"I know," the little girl replied, "In the end, everything will be fine and dandy, better than a bowl of candy." Caitlin stretched out her arms and wrapped them around Joan's neck. Joan's heart melted. She spent the next six months trying to adopt Caitlin. Finally, in May of 1996, she was awarded sole custody. It was then that Joan started looking for a less hectic place to live. She found and accepted the position of 'Sheriff of Milford' in March of 1997.

3

The door to the police station flew open and slammed up against the file cabinets. Joan, engrossed in the events of her past, didn't hear her deputy, Gage Jensen, coming until it was too late. "Hey, what gives?" he asked within seconds of the door slamming. Joan's entire body jolted in cadence with the broken silence. Her cup of coffee ended up in her lap.

"Damn it, Gage!" she said, standing up from her chair, coffee dripping down her uniform and onto the floor.

"Sorry!" He said half grinning, "Really, I had no idea you were still here."

"Yeah, yeah," she said, adding "Asshole," under her breath after seeing his grin. She reached for the napkins next to the coffeepot.

Joan and Gage were actually very good friends. They had arrived in town just a few weeks apart. Shortly after Joan had taken over the position of sheriff, her deputy, Henry Turner, decided to follow the former sheriff and retired leaving the town's two person police force with a vacancy. Gage applied for the position and was hired. His file from the Dallas Texas Police Department showed that he was a good cop with good instincts. He had a pleasant look about him: brown eyes and hair to match, no discernable features that would make him stand out in a crowd. *He'd be perfect for undercover work*, Joan had thought. But he also, as Joan had discovered through the years, could be obnoxious.

"Where's Ed?" Gage asked.

"Mrs. Zachary's place." Joan replied, still wiping off her uniform. "I sent him out there about an hour ago. He'll be back shortly."

"Her? Again?" Gage was no longer smiling. He walked over to the coffeepot and poured himself a cup. "Do I even want to venture a guess as to why she called this time?" Before Joan could answer, Gage added, "You have heard the story about '*The little boy who cried wolf*', right?"

"Yes I have. And I've seen the movie bearing a similar title."

"That's my point. She's wasting our time."

"No, I think you're missing the point."

"Which is?"

"Let me put it in a way that your southern upbringing can understand. Be it the story or the movie, someone got dead."

Gage thought about that as he looked down at the steam rolling off his coffee. "Okay, okay. You win, but I still think it's a waste of time."

"It's not a waste of time. It's our job. Besides, she sounded—almost frightened.

"Frightened?"

"Yes, frightened."

Gage took a sip of his coffee as he gave Joan a questioning glare.

"You know the woman," Joan said, "She's not the sort that scares all that easy."

"So?"

"So, when someone calls, we go out. Protect and serve, Gage. It's what we do."

Gage made a face. "Well, did she at least manage to say what it was she was afraid of?"

"Not exactly." Joan threw the coffee soaked napkins in the trash. "She did say that something, or as she put it, that someone was roaming around her property."

"That's it?"

"Isn't that enough?"

Gage shifted his eyes towards the window, to the darkening skyline.

"She also said that whatever it was ran off with four of her rabbits."

"Four? Yeah, right. Like she knows how many rabbits she had to start with. Those things breed faster than she can count." Gage's remark was underlined by a short pause, then, "So, what do you make of it?"

"Not sure. But like I said, she's tough as nails and isn't one to get scared over nothing. And as for her rabbits, you can think what you want. She may be old, but she still has all her wits. And you better believe she not only knows how many rabbits she had, she knows their names and can tell you which ones are missing."

Gage took another sip of coffee. "It was probably a bunch of kids out for a cheap thrill. Like you said, she lives out in the middle of nowhere," he said, setting his coffee down. "Yeah, I'm sure that's all it is."

"Sure of what?"

"That it was just kids out having a little fun at the old woman's expense. You know how it is. It's not like they have much else to do around here." Gage took a seat at his desk. "I can just picture those little punk bastards sitting back behind a bush just out of sight petting the damn rabbits and laughing their collective asses off watching her give Ed an earful."

"You're probably right." Joan replied. "And if you are, that could turn out to be a problem."

"Problem? No. Funny as shit, yes."

Joan sat back down. "No, Gage, it will be a problem because she still thinks it was a bunch of kids that shook her cabin a couple of days ago."

"But that was a…"

"I know what it was," Joan replied, cutting Gage off, "But try telling her that."

"How could she not know? I mean, it's all over the news. It's not like tremors are commonplace around here. I can't remember the last, no, scratch that, I don't ever remember having heard of one around these parts before. Do you?"

"No, can't say that I do," Joan replied. "And to answer your question, apparently Mrs. Zachary doesn't own a TV or a radio."

"Well, in that case, I hope it wasn't kids. Can you imagine what she'd do if she caught one of them messing around with her precious rabbits?"

"Yet another reason why I sent Ed out there." Joan glanced out the window just as the streetlights flickered and came to full glow. "If it was just kids, maybe seeing Ed scared them off." Joan grabbed her jacket and ball cap. "Well, Gage, I'm calling it a day. You should do the same."

"I will," Gage replied, "But––I think I'll just hang out here for awhile to see if ole Ed makes it back in one piece." He paused and smiled at Joan. "Besides, I'm dying to find out what had Mrs. Zachary's panties all tied up in a knot."

"Gage, you are a real piece of work."

4

5:05 p.m.

Ed Cross was the last member of the Milford police force. At fifty-three years of age, he was still a formidable looking man standing nearly six foot two and weighed a healthy 225 lbs. He wore glasses and had a slight gap between his front teeth. His eyes were charcoal-colored and went well with his full head of graying hair.

Ed's personality was the opposite of Gage's. He took a more serious approach to things. He could, however, always be loosened up with a few screwdrivers over at Jackie's Bar-n-Grill, the local hot spot.

Joan hired Ed three years earlier, in June of 1999. As the town continued to grow, additional security was needed. Ed spent the better part of his military career working as a part of the Military Police Unit after doing two tours in Vietnam. Joan found him well suited for the position.

"Mrs. Zachary," Deputy Ed Cross said, holding back a regretful look, "I've searched the entire perimeter of your property. There's nothing out there for you to worry about."

Mrs. Zachary frowned at Ed, "Bullshit! I saw what I saw."

"Tell me again, Mrs. Zachary, what it was you thought you saw."

She hesitated, "I donno." Her eyes shifted to the dense layers of trees to the west. "But damn it, I saw somethin. So don't go tellin me I didn't," she said as she flicked her eyes back to Ed, "And don't go lookin' at me like I's crazy, cuz I isn't. I saw somethin. I did!"

"Well, if you see it again," Ed said, "Give the sheriff's office a call—day or night." He gave Mrs. Zachary a quick smile and tipped his hat before returning to his truck. While reaching for the door handle, Ed turned his head and peered out into the woods in the direction in which he had discovered the old lady's four dead rabbits. As he swung open the door, a sudden unnerving feeling swept over him. He felt like he was being watched. But as suddenly as it had come, it was gone. Ed jumped into his truck and chalked the feeling up to the gruesome mess of the de-skinned rabbits whose bodies had been mangled and ripped apart. He had discovered them in the woods twenty yards outside Mrs. Zachary's property line. He had wanted to tell her, but she was already genuinely upset and definitely angry, and he saw no point in adding to either emotion.

He glanced in his rearview mirror as he pulled away. He found Mrs. Zachary with her right arm held up in the air, her hand fisted. She was waving it as if she were taunting some invisible presence. He noticed that it was in the same direction that he himself had just been looking, the same direction in which an eerie feeling had momentarily claimed his body, and the same direction in which he had found the rabbits.

5

After the deputy had left, Mrs. Zachary glared out at the woods. "You stay the hell off my property, ya bastard from hell!" She yelled.

In the past, yelling and cursing at a wrongdoer would have made her feel better. But as she started the walk down to the barn where she kept her furry little friends, she didn't feel any better. If anything she was even angrier because she knew that after she counted her rabbits again, she was still going to be four short.

Arriving at the rabbits' pen, she could tell they were still spooked. They had all gathered in the furthest corner from the barn door; their ears pinned down, their eyes wide open as if sensing danger. "Don't worry," she said in the softest voice. "Mama's not gunna let anythin else bad happen to my precious babies." She left the barn with the doors shut and padlocked behind her.

On the way up the slow-rising hill to her log cabin, her eyes did not once waver from the direction of the woods that she had earlier, *saw what she saw.*

Inside her house, she grabbed the shotgun off the rack above the stone fireplace and loaded it. Her mind was set on protecting her remaining rabbits at any cost. She leaned the shotgun against the wall next to the solid oak door that led out to the back yard, the safety off. "Come mess with my rabbits now!" she said, the softness in her voice gone.

6

Marie Shae pulled into her driveway noticing the enormous amount of leaves that seemed to have fallen since she left for work that morning. "A leaf-raking weekend, I guess," she muttered under her breath.

Marie was a forty-one year old divorcee. She could have gone on to do just about anything she wanted after college, but she met Mark Shae, fell in love, and got married. Big mistake. The only good thing to come out of that marriage was her daughter, Kiersten. She was her pride and joy.

Inside, Marie started dinner. She decided to fix one of her daughter's favorites: meatloaf, garlic mashed-potatoes, and green beans simmering in butter sauce. She put the meatloaf into the oven and decided to give an old friend a call with the time she normally would have spent picking up her daughter.

"Hello?" Mickey answered.

<h1 style="text-align:center">7</h1>

Deputy Cross turned off Pine Hill Road onto Route 517. He was heading back into town. The clock on the dashboard read 5:40 p.m. He should have been back at the station long ago. But tell that to an eighty-year-old lady who would swear on the *Good Book* itself that she *saw what she saw*, which in the end, still left Ed clueless as to what she did, in fact, see. He knew she hadn't seen the slaughtered rabbits, and he knew she hadn't done the slaughtering. *Still*, he thought, *those rabbits didn't butcher themselves.* Something was definitely off about the whole situation. He just couldn't wrap his head around the cruelty involved in doing — whatever it was that was done to those poor creatures.

He turned the corner and parked in front of the municipal building. He climbed the stairs to the police station where he found Gage slumped over in Joan's chair nodding off. "Earning your paycheck, I see."

Gage slowly raised his head, swung out his arms, stretched, yawned, and replied, "Not much else to do around here."

"Thought you'd be gone by now."

"Yeah well, I just couldn't wait till morning to find out what Mrs. Zachary was complaining about this time." He paused, waiting for a response that did not come. "Joan mentioned something about missing rabbits, and, well, you know me, I just knew I wouldn't be able to sleep tonight without knowing whether or not she ate the damn things and forgot about it, or if maybe she just miscounted the little critters."

Ed hung his hat and coat on the rack by the door.

"Or," Gage said, grinning as he stood up, "It could be that the old gal called to arrange a booty call, and you just had to oblige. Is that it?"

"You're a funny guy," Ed replied.

"If that's not it, then what?

Ed grabbed a formal complaint form from the file cabinet, and took a seat at his desk.

"Ed!"

Ed put the form in the typewriter, and then stared blankly at it before his fingers typed in the NAME, ADDRESS, TIME OF CALL…

"Come on man, you know I was just kidding around about you and Mrs. Z. No need to go and get all quiet on me." Gage stood and moved over and sat on the edge of Ed's desk. "Seriously, what was it?"

Ed's fingers hovered above the typewriter keys when he reached the part of the form marked Nature of Incident. His mind revisited the scene. When he had been in Nam and happened upon a gruesome scene of body parts, the who, what, why and how had been obvious. Now, staring at the form, he was reluctant to type what was on his mind fearing it might come off sounding like an excerpt out of a Stephen King Novel.

Ed finally looked up at Gage and said, "As it turns out, some of her rabbits were, in fact, missing. And no, she did not eat them. That, I can guarantee!"

"So basically, what you're telling me is that I waited around for you to tell me about a few missing fur balls, is that right?"

"Four," Ed pointed out.

"Huh?"

"You waited around for four missing fur balls," Ed replied, the words escaping his lips without his voice rising or falling.

Ed had always displayed a certain amount of seriousness in his work. Gage knew this and was used to it. But this was different. The look in his eyes and his monotone voice suggested that there was something more than missing rabbits on his mind.

"Okay. So what happened?" Gage asked. "Dog's gone wild?"

"I don't think it was any animal."

"So, a couple of kids then, you know, trying to spook the ole gal. Or maybe a couple of hungry hunters happen by and said, hey Earl, look, dinner?

A moment of silence passed. Ed again found himself to be at a loss for words. As a matter of fact, he wasn't at all sure he was ready to finish the report, let alone able to.

"Well?" Gage asked.

Silence.

Ed moved to the window and looked out past the glow of the street lamps, past the town, and into the woods. And though he could not see the Zachary residence, in the back of his mind, he saw it perfectly, and that raised the hairs on the nape of his neck. "It's nothing that can't wait till morning," he said.

8

Todd Chandler gawked at his watch in between passing a red Lamborghini and a black Ferrari during an extreme, Three-D racing arcade game in which he had control of a burnt orange Porsche. It was hard to believe that time had slipped by so quickly. It was 5:05 p.m. If he left now, he would still be, at best, twenty minutes late. Surely, this was something that she would not let him forget about easily. This was something that she would hold over his head. Especially since tonight was to be a momentous occasion; it was to be the first time he could take her out on a real date. He would be able to pick her up from her mother's shop in his very own car.

Todd had chestnut eyes and short ash-brown hair, the tips bleached blonde. His five-foot eleven-inch, 170 lb. frame was perfect for the starting running-back position he played on the Milford High School football team. He was an outstanding student who was thought as much of off the field, as he was on. He was cool and hip, and very reliable, until now.

He had turned seventeen just two days earlier on October 13th, and as all teenagers do, eagerly waited for the opportunity to get his driver's license. His mistake was bringing his two buds along for a little celebration at the Rainbow Arcade inside the Dixon City Mall. Video games were a luxury Milford didn't offer outside of the Ms. Pacman game at Jackie's.

"Damn it you guys!" Todd said, clearly irritated.

"What?" Mike asked.

"It's 5:00, that's what! I was supposed to pick Kiersten up at 5:00."

Todd jumped up and bolted out of the arcade to the nearest pay phone. Mike and Chad followed.

The phone rang and rang. Each ring seemed longer and louder than the last. When no one answered, he tried her house.

"Great! The line's busy," he said. "How stupid am I? I keep telling Kiersten she can trust me, and what do I do when I get my first real opportunity? I find a way to muck it up, that's what."

Todd looked at his two friends, and took off running, this time for his car. Mike and Chad could barely keep up. Todd reached his car and started it just as the other two vaulted over the doors. Todd nearly struck another car as he floored it out of the parking lot.

"Todd! Dude, take it easy," Chad said, "We're already late. What difference is a few more minutes going to make?"

"That's easy for you to say," Todd said, his eyes shifting to the rearview mirror, to Chad. "I need to get back and try to save a little face."

Chapter 2

1

Joan arrived home to an empty house. Her home, a modest styled ranch, was located one-hundred yards off of Route 517, four miles west of town. A towering stand of blue spruce surrounded the perimeter of her property.

As she reached to open her front door, she heard a noise stemming from the rear of the house. She stepped quietly off the porch and headed for the back yard.

She crept down the left side of the house with her right hand on her holster, her thumb instinctively unsnapping the leather strap. Reaching the rear, she peeked around the corner. "Jesus, Charlie," she said.

"Oh, hey, Joan," Charlie answered, eyeing Joan's hand lowering from her holster. "Hope I didn't spook ya none."

"No, not spooked, just wasn't... it doesn't matter, Charlie. Why are you delivering wood this time of night?" Joan asked, stopping at Charlie's truck.

Charlie was sixty-eight years old, had a pitted, dried-out face with a reddened, round nose. He had once been about 80 lbs heavier, but now, his skin just seemed to hang on his bones. He had once been a town congressman, a strong community leader, but for the last twenty plus years, Charlie worked for the township in a much different capacity. He was the town's handyman.

"No reason. I just happen to have a load and noticed ya was a bit low, and well, it ain't gettin any warmer."

"Well, thank you, Charlie, I appreciate it. Stop by my office tomorrow and I'll write you out a check to even us out."

"That sounds right fine, Joan." Charlie said, jumping into his truck. "I'll see ya tomorrow."

Joan returned to the front of her house. She grabbed her mail as she entered. Mostly bills, she noted. She threw them on the kitchen table. That's when she saw the note on the fridge.

Joan,
Caitlin and I went into Richmond to
see a movie. Don't worry, no school
tomorrow, teacher's conference.
There's a plate for you in the fridge.
Love, Mom & Caitlin
Love you, Mom.
P.S. Don't wait up, might be back late.

Joan sat down at the kitchen table and reread "Love you, Mom," aloud, remembering the first time Caitlin had ever used those three words.

*   *   *

Joan had been awarded temporary custody of Caitlin during the legal proceedings, and wanted to throw her a big birthday party, the likes of which she was sure the little girl had never seen.

The doctors that had checked her out from head to toe during her stay with the State Child Care Services were quite sure she was nearing, if not already, three years of age. Since no one knew the official date of her birthday, Joan let Caitlin pick one. She had chosen Easter Sunday. When asked why, she simply said, "Because I love rabbits."

More than likely, this party would be the first normal thing she would have ever experienced in her young life. And Joan wanted to make sure it was one she would always remember.

The day turned out to be magical. Caitlin was running around with the kids of Joan's friends; kids she had just met. They all seemed to want to be around her, and not just the kids, the parents too. It was as if Caitlin had become a magnet.

It was obvious to Joan by the ever-present smile on Caitlin's face that no matter how the adoption proceedings went, somehow, this beautiful young girl would make it in this harsh world. Joan wasn't sure in the end how the courts would view a gun-toting single woman wanting to adopt a child, but she steeled herself against any negative thoughts.

She watched Caitlin run around and play like any other normal three year old would. Caitlin, however, was not normal. Not in the sense that she had a normal upbringing. Being dumped off at a church, abandoned by idiotic parents who apparently decided that they would be better off without a child, is not what you would call normal. And, in Joan's eyes, being abandoned by such parents made Caitlin the fortunate one.

She wondered, however, as she continued to watch Caitlin play, how this amazing, articulate, beautiful three-year-old girl could show such strength with all she had gone through. But she did, and she did it smiling all the way.

It was on that same day, as she continued to watch Caitlin, that Joan prayed that the courts would rule in her favor, granting her full custody so that she would one day be able to call Caitlin her daughter, and that Caitlin—would call her Mommy.

When the party was over and all the guests had gone, Caitlin came to Joan. She somehow knew how she could make Joan feel as happy as she was at that very moment. "Joan," she said with perfect clarity, "Would it be all right if," she paused, purposely, "If I were to call you Mommy?"

It had caught Joan completely off guard at the time, and for a brief moment, she was left speechless. Joan sat down at the kitchen table and looked into Caitlin's eyes. She grabbed her tiny hands and held them gently in hers.

"Caitlin, it would mean the world to me if you were to call me Mommy," she said, her eyes filling instantly with tears.

"Why are you crying then, Mommy?"

"I'm crying because I love you so much, and for you to want to call me your Mommy—God, for you to want me to be your Mommy, well——it's just the most special gift that anyone could have ever given me." She reached out and hugged Caitlin close.

"*I love you* too, Mommy!" Caitlin said, hugging her new mother back.

$$*\qquad*\qquad*$$

Joan wiped away the tears that came with the memory and walked over to the fridge, grabbed the plate of food: pork chops, corn and a baked potato, and tossed it into the microwave.

After eating, Joan poured herself a glass of red wine and took it into the master bathroom. *All I need now,* she thought, *is a nice—long—soak.*

Chapter 3

1

Todd passed a break in the trees and caught a quick glimpse of Lake Andrea ten minutes outside Milford. For a brief moment, he daydreamed of the romantic evening that he had planned by that lake with Kiersten—plans that were now undoubtedly history—ruined by his own sheer ignorance.

"I can't believe it," Todd muddled. "What the hell was I thinking? Why didn't I just go straight home after the test?"

"Dude," Mike said, grinning, "what's the big deal? It's not like you won't see her tomorrow."

"I know. It's just that tonight was supposed to be," his voice trailed off for a moment, "Ah, forget it, it's over now anyway."

"Todd," Mike said, "Just tell her you had a flat tire. We'll back you up."

"Yeah, Todd, that's the ticket," Chad replied from the back seat.

"Guys, think about it," Todd said, keeping his eyes on the road. "Kiersten's not stupid. She's going to want to know why I didn't at least call her to let her know I was going to be late. Besides," Todd added, "Nothing good ever comes from a lie."

Mike smirked and looked back at Chad. They simultaneously wiggled their pinkies at Todd to insinuate that Kiersten had Todd wrapped around her little finger.

"Knock it off!" Todd exclaimed.

"Okay, sorry," Mike said, lowering his arm, "But I'm telling ya, lying works for me. But if you insist on taking the high road, it's your grave."

"Whatever." Todd said with a sigh. "You two may not give a shit, but I happen to like Kiersten——a lot. I've made one mistake tonight, and I'm not going to add to it by lying to her."

They arrived in Milford a little after six. The town looked deserted except for Jackie's, where five cars were parked out on the street with another ten or so in the lot behind the establishment.

Todd drove past the bar and went straight over to All Things Old and New. Kiersten, as he had expected, was nowhere to be found. He sat in his car with his eyes fixed straight ahead, wondering where she was. *Had she gone home? Did she call her Mom to come and pick her up, or maybe one of her friends, or worse, an old boyfriend?*

2

Leaning against the window jam for the better part of ten minutes, gazing out over the lamp-lit streets of Milford, Ed had but one thing on his mind—a plausible explanation for what he had seen at Mrs. Zachary's. He kept telling himself that it had only been rabbits. And though it was a singular incident and would more than likely not be repeated, what bothered him, what kept jabbing at his mind, was how they were killed.

As the images resurfaced in his mind, he kept telling himself that it was getting dark, and that maybe what he saw was exaggerated by the hardening glow of his flashlight melding with the shadows, but…

"Hey," Gage said, glancing at the report. But Ed did not answer. "Hey Mr. By the Book," Gage said grinning, ignoring Ed's silence, "You finishing this tonight? I mean, it's not like you to go and leave things half done."

"Yeah, well, it's not like me to put any ole thing down on a report either."

"What's that supposed to mean?"

"It means that it was dark and tomorrow's another day. After I take another look around Mrs. Zachary's property, I'll finish the report. Besides, I'm supposed to meet Barb over at Jackie's, and it's getting late."Ed said glancing at Gage as he walked to the coat rack.

"Are you honestly going to stand there and tell me that you have no idea what it was you saw? What? No flashlight? It's not like you to go off unprepared, Ed. Now, come on, out with it."

"Out with what?"

"Whatever it is that has you spooked."

"I'm not spooked, now leave it alone. You're fishing without bait again," Ed said, glaring at the report in Gage's hands, "I said I'd finish it in the morning, and I will. Now come on. I'll buy you a beer before you head home."

"Works for me," Gage replied. "I still think something has you spooked, but as long as you're buying, it can wait a day. Hell, for two beers, it can wait a whole week. Just let me give the wife a call and I'll meet you over there."

"Fine," Ed replied, snatching his coat off the rack as he headed out.

3

"Well," Chad said from the back seat, "She's obviously not here, and seeing how the lights are off inside the store, my guess is she got tired of waiting for your sorry ass, and called her mother to come and pick her up."

"No shit, Sherlock," Todd exclaimed.

Of the many consequences of being late, Todd knew that his reputation for always being responsible and on time, attributes strongly admired by his parents, coaches, teachers and friends, would now be blighted at the hands of a stupid video game. But that's not what was bothering him. Not even close. In fact, his now tarnished record hadn't even crossed his mind. What bothered him the most, what had him gripping the steering wheel firm enough to make the sound of rung leather, was knowing that he had let his girl down, that he, like her father, had failed her.

"I know she left, damn it, I'm not blind," Todd said hesitating for a second before continuing, "But something's just not right."

"And what would that be?" Mike asked.

"I, I don't know, but I can feel it."

Mike and Chad looked at Todd with 'what the' looks on their faces.

"Todd, are you alright?" Mike asked.

"I'm not sure. I mean, I just have this weird feeling that something's wrong, and it just won't go away. To be honest with you, it's kinda creeping me out." As the words left his mouth, his stomach began to feel ominous. Not nauseous, it was more of a creeping sensation, as if millions of spider eggs had been laid in the pit of his stomach and were all simultaneously trying to hatch.

"So, now what?" Mike asked.

"A phone, I need a phone. I need to make sure that she got home. I need to know that she's okay."

From the back seat, Chad said, "That weird feeling you're having."

"What about it?"

"It's just your body's way of letting you know that you screwed the pooch, dude. And now your mind is making you feel guilty. Forget about it. What's done is done." Although Chad had yet to find the right girl, had yet to experience love and all that goes with it, he knew from Todd's glare, however, that *love* is a lunatic's world, and the best thing he could do right now, was to shut up.

Sensing hostility between Chad and Todd, Mike said, "Jackie's has pay phones, you can call her from there."

"Fine," Todd said, and floored it.

Jackie's was only a few blocks away. Two turns and a traffic light, and they'd be there. Todd's mind focused on the fact that he was the one male in Kiersten's life that she had learned to trust since her father had abandoned her, and now that trust was in jeopardy. He so wished he had the power to go back in time, to have the opportunity to not take Chad and Mike with him, to come straight home after he had taken his driving test, but that, he knew, wasn't possible.

Todd parked in front of Jackie's and they exited the car. "You guys go on in," Todd said, gazing up at the dark clouds that threatened the night sky with rain. "I'd better put the top up. It looks like it could start pouring any minute." Todd flicked his eyes back to his Mustang, which, as he looked at it now, seemed somehow tainted and not as flashy as it did that morning.

Mike and Chad went inside after opening the door for Deputy Ed, who was walking over from the municipal building as they pulled up.

"Thank you, gentlemen," Ed said as he passed by.

"Evening, Deputy," they responded back.

After putting the top up, Todd entered the bar and grill, but didn't bother looking for his two friends; he went straight to the phones in the rear of the building. He could feel his palms start to sweat as his body grew tense with anticipation of getting an earful from Kiersten. Still, it was an earful he'd more than willingly take if it meant knowing that she'd gotten home safely, which in return, would alleviate the feeling of *spiders gone wild* in his stomach. He picked up the receiver.

He dialed Kiersten's number, but the line was busy. The spidery feeling intensified. Something was wrong and he knew it. He didn't know how he knew, he just did. Todd picked up the phone again, still busy. He dialed 0 for the operator in hopes that they could tell whether the phone had been taken off the hook on purpose, or if someone was actually using it.

The seconds that passed seemed unending. As Todd's eyes paced the room waiting for the operator, he saw his friends shooting a game of pool, having fun. But his attention and his eyes flicked back to the phone at the sound of the operator's voice. "Someone's on that line, sir. Is there anything else I can do for..."

Todd hung up the phone. *At least the phone hadn't been taken off the hook on purpose,* he thought. But if it had been, it would have meant that Kiersten was home; pissed, but home. All he really knew now was that her line was busy. He had no clue who it was using the phone.

Todd walked over to his friends, his mind spinning. "Line's busy, guys," he told them, "I'm gunna head over to her house. I have to know that she's ok," Todd said, with a look of despair and worry written all over his face.

"I'll swing by and pick you guys up on my way back."

"Yeah," Mike said, "like we'd trust you to pick us up."

"Dude, that was totally called for," Chad said smiling. "Don't worry about us though, my mom's here with Deputy Ed; she'll give us a ride."

"O.K. then," Todd said. "Thanks. I guess I'll see you both tomorrow at practice."

Todd turned and walked purposely towards the front door. He tried to think of the words that he would use to explain. He smiled for a moment as a line from a movie he once saw came to mind, *"I don't know, but I'm sure that at some point, there'll be some groveling involved."*

Todd jumped into his car and sped off to Kiersten's.

4

Marie sat on the loveseat adjacent to the sofa in the living room. She had been talking to her friend, Mickey, for a little over an hour. From the sofa, she could see all oncoming traffic through the picture window that overlooked the front yard. She thought she would have seen Todd dropping off her daughter by now, but in the eyes of today's teens, it was still early.

With the cordless phone in tow, her friend chatting in her ear, Marie checked on dinner every now and then. The last thing she wanted was a burnt meatloaf.

A few minutes later, she said goodbye and hung up the phone. With Kiersten still not home, Marie decided to start collecting the laundry, and maybe throw a load in the washer. She went from room to room, purposely leaving her daughter's for last. She had hoped that Kiersten would have returned home before she had to enter the room that was branded with a sign, THE DANGER ZONE. The waiting, however, was for naught.

The sign on her door lived up to the billing. There were clothes scattered all over the floor, on and under her unmade bed, and behind the closet door that had been left open.

Marie moved from one end of the room to the other several times before managing to retrieve all of Kiersten's clothes.

Outside Kiersten's shaded windows, the wind shifted direction. It was now blowing straight out of the east, and was far gustier. Marie stopped for a second to listen to the howling wind. She could hear the shuffling of the leaves. *Hopefully,* she thought, *the wind will put them in a nice neat pile to one end of the yard.*

5

Todd stopped and took in a deep breath at the entrance to Kiersten's driveway. The light to Kiersten's room popped on just as he put the car in park. He hesitated to go any further when he saw her shadow moving about as if she were pacing in anger; anger that had been established because she had been stood up, and worse, because it had been Todd who stood her up.

Better to leave things alone for the night, he thought, *and return in the morning with a bouquet of fresh-cut flowers, and with it, a picnic- style breakfast.*

Todd backed out of the driveway and paused. He glanced at Kiersten's window one last time. In his mind, he could see the disappointment on her face; hear the anger in her voice. For now, he could only hope that he was doing the right thing. He was hoping that with time, her anger would diminish.

6

Marie walked over to the window to see if the westerly winds were indeed doing the work she would otherwise have to do on Saturday. As she pulled the tassel and raised the mini-blinds, she could see taillights from a car bouncing off a low-lying fog that had crept in. The car was heading back toward town.

Her daughter was home.

She hurried down the hall, anxious to see her daughter, to hear how her first real date had gone. The front door, however, never opened, and Kiersten never entered.

7

The first thing Todd noticed when he arrived home was that his mother's car was not in the driveway. He was hoping to get another woman's opinion—his mother's opinion—on how to handle his unfortunate moment of ignorance. He was pretty sure—no, he was positive that his father had goofed in the past, and his mother, after a brief overnight turf war over who would be sleeping in the spare bedroom, had always forgiven him. This inside information would have been helpful if she had been home to dispense it.

Todd went to his room and switched on his stereo. But his mind quickly flashed back to the image of Kiersten pacing across her bedroom. He could see her as clear as the night was dark, walking back and forth, her lips more than likely moving in sync to words like, *asshole,* and *inconsiderate dipshit.*

Even though he had seen her, his stomach had still not relinquished the spidery sensation. It had now, in fact, manifested throughout his entire body. *Nerves,* he told himself, *nerves and guilt,* like Chad had suggested.

His eyes flicked down the hall to the phone on the desk. It was ringing. Todd bolted out of his room with the speed and agility of a cat hoping that he would hear Kiersten's voice on the other end. At this point, he didn't much care if all she did was curse him out. He just wanted to hear her voice—mad or not. No matter what she said, she would sound like an angel saying them.

"Hello!" Todd answered, anxiously.

"Todd, it's me, Mike."

"Oh, what's up?" Todd replied, disappointed.

"Glad to hear your voice too, pal," Mike said sarcastically.

"Sorry. I was just hoping that you were Kiersten."

"Well, big boy, I'm not Kiersten, but I am kinda cute," Mike said jokingly. "Will I do?"

"Yeah, sure, you'll do alright," Todd replied, half-smiling, "As a date to a Halloween party."

"Funny," Mike said, "No, seriously, I just wanted to find out how things turned out with you and Kiersten. Was she pissed, or what?"

"Well, I know she got home all right. I mean, I saw her shadow pacing back and forth through her window in that *I'm pissed off* sort of way, but I didn't actually talk to her."

"Chicken shit!"

"Bite me! I'm not chicken. I just thought it best to wait till tomorrow, that's all."

"Yeah, yeah," Mike said, still chuckling. "Just don't forget we have football practice at noon."

"Don't worry, I'll be there. I plan on surprising Kiersten in the morning."

Todd set the phone back down on the desk and returned to his room. He cranked up the stereo and jumped onto the bed fully dressed. He stretched out his legs and tucked his interlocked fingers behind his head. AC-DC's *Back in Black* blasted through the speakers. As he closed his eyes, he could see her lying on her bed, holding a daisy with her right hand, plucking the soft white petals off one by one with her left. *"Can I trust him? Can I trust him not?"* Ending on the inevitable, *Can I trust him not?*

Unable to bear that unpleasant thought, Todd flushed it from his mind, and fell off to sleep.

8

By the time Marie finished the laundry, it was 9:15 p.m., and her daughter was still not home. Kiersten was a very responsible person who would normally call if she were going to be late. But the phone remained silent.

Marie was now getting worried as her head started filling with the '*what ifs*'. *What if they had been stranded? What if they had been in an accident? What if Todd had taken her back to his place?*

Marie reached for the phone and dialed Todd's number, but the phone just rang repeatedly. She hung up and walked over to the front door, opened it, and peered out onto the lit lawn. The fog had all but faded away and Marie could now see that her lawn had indeed been brushed clean of leaves by the wind. Mother Nature's handiwork, however, was now the furthest thing from her mind. She was now thinking about the call she had made earlier to her friend Mickey. During the call they had relived a lifetime of memories—one memory in particular that was funny back then—and was even funnier during the call, but now…

*   *   *

One night, when they were twelve, the two had worried their parents to death by staying out way past midnight with no attempt at letting them know that they were okay, where they were, or whom they were with.

Their parents had called the police, friends and neighbors to help search for them. Her parents, and Mickey's, were livid, and they had a right to be.

She had never seen her father so mad; his face so cold; his eyes so reddened with fury. And she remembered how scared her mother had looked—her whole body frozen stiff and rigid. And if it had not been for the untouched tears that fell, she would have thought her dead.

*   *   *

A slight smile came to Marie as she again recalled the incident. They were found behind a barn playing an innocent game of show and tell with two neighborhood boys. But the smile quickly faded. It was now after ten, and Kiersten was still not home, or had yet to call.

"She knows better than this! She knows she's supposed to call. Damn it, Kiersten, where the hell are you?"

She glanced at the phone, and before she knew it, the receiver was at her ear, listening to a constant ring that again went unanswered.

Chapter 4

1

Vanessa Chandler arrived home at 10:20 p.m. She stood at the front door with two bags of groceries in her arms as she blindly searched through a ring of keys to find the right one. It was during those few seconds of search that the phone had started to ring. This made her hasten her pace to find the key, which in retrospect only hindered her efforts. Five rings had passed before her fingers found the key to the front door. She stabbed the key at the cylinder; two more rings echoed through the air. The key slid easily in. She turned the knob and entered. By the time she set the bags down in the kitchen, the phone fell silent.

Vanessa turned her attention to the music blaring from Todd's room. "Todd," she yelled, "Turn down that music." She quickly put the groceries away and exited the kitchen toward her son's room where the music was still blasting away at the same volume. She found Todd sound asleep. She turned off the stereo and gazed at her son who was oblivious to her presence. She wondered how on earth anybody could possibly fall asleep with all that noise blasting through the speakers.

2

Marie sat on her living room sofa with her legs drawn in close, her arms wrapped around them. Steam rolled off an untouched cup of tea that sat on the end table. The meatloaf she had prepared had grown cold. It was still sitting in the oven. The T.V. was on out of habit, blaring away.

A quick glance at the clock revealed it to be 10:30 p.m. Her mind sifted through reasons for why her daughter was not yet home. But what worried her most was the fact that she had not even called. *It was inconsiderate and selfish,* Marie thought, *and it sure as hell wasn't the way I raised her.*

Being a half-hour late may have slipped by unnoticed. An hour could have been excused with a reasonable explanation. *But two?* She was supposed to have been home by 8:00 p.m.—8:30 p.m. at the latest. Kiersten was now treading on the edge of a mother's patience. And though she tried to steel herself against daunting feelings of worry and fear by remembering her daughter's responsible traits, in the end, it only made her worry even more.

3

Somewhere on the other side of Kiersten's pitch-black quarters, an unknown distance away, the wind howled like a pack of wolves in front of a stark white moon. To Kiersten, it sounded more like bits and pieces of disturbed silence that had been stitched together and made to sound like muffled voices whispering in foreign-tongues. This only added to her fear. Her body had already failed her, as she was unable to maintain dominance over her bodily functions: her panties were drenched in urine.

Having been knocked unconscious and left in blackness, deprived of food, water, and human contact, her mind was left with no clear conception of time.

Being alone in the dark gave her a bitter taste of what it would be like to be blind, which in turn gave her a new appreciation of sight. The darkness also heightened her sense of hearing. Other senses had been heightened as well, and though they did not make her feel any less terrified, those senses told her that the shadowy presence that had left her here had not yet returned.

For now, at least, she was alone.

From the moment Kiersten realized that her hands and feet were bound, she had been lying in one place. The right side of her body ached while the left side felt numb. Her wrists and ankles were worn raw from her attempts to free herself from the nylon rope. Her beautiful blonde hair was matted with dried blood, and her head continued to throb from the blow she had received at the onset of this horrible nightmare. She was physically and emotionally drained. Her eyes wanted to close, but fear kept them open.

Left with nothing more than a sense of hopelessness and dread, her mind painted pictures of regret. One such picture was that of her estranged father. It brought out feelings of remorse for having wished him dead, a fate that she now believed to be her own. She came to the realization that she still loved him even though he may not have warranted it. But as time slipped away, hour-by-hour, the less likely it seemed that she would ever have the opportunity of telling him so.

At that moment, she felt more alone than she had ever felt before. But then a thought crossed her terrified mind. *Was she, in fact, alone?* She felt the prickly hairs stand up on the nape of her neck. She started to shake again. Not because she no longer felt alone, but because of the question that entered her mind. Was she the first one, or just one of many?

"Hello," she said in nothing more than a whisper. "Is anyone there?" But silence yelled back, and in its same breath said, *If there were anyone here, don't you think you'd hear them crying, screaming; don't you think you'd hear something?*

She listened to the stillness—the quiet—and found even less comfort in it than if she *had* heard something. Now, she would have to believe that if by some chance there had been someone else there, they were probably dead.

Chapter 5

1

Caitlin and her grandmother, Jesse, were heading home from an evening of shopping, the movies, and dinner. The normal drive back from Dixon should have only taken twenty five minutes or so. But as the night progressed, the thick fog that had started to dissipate, reemerged, embracing the area as a mother would a child.

Jesse glanced over at a pair of eyes that struggled to remain open. "Tired, Caitlin?" She asked.

"No. Well, maybe a little," Caitlin replied as she yawned, and then asked, "Grandma?"

"What, sweetie?"

"Do you think Mom will be awake when we get home?"

Jesse again glanced over at Caitlin and then flicked her eyes back to the road. "I told your mother not to wait up for us, kiddo. But— knowing her as well as I do, yes, it's a fair assumption to think that she'll be waiting up, probably just to give you the world's biggest hug." Caitlin smiled.

As Jesse pulled into the driveway, Caitlin yawned again and then asked, "Grandma, do you think Mom will take me up to Mrs. Zachary's place tomorrow? I haven't seen her or her rabbits since school started." Caitlin yawned a third time before continuing, "I bet the little one has gotten big."

"Well, Caitlin, it looks like we may get the chance to ask her," Jesse said, smiling. "Your mother is at the front door waiting for us. So, what do you say we go find out?"

"Okay," Caitlin said with a smile, "But I already know what she'll say."

"Then, why ask?"

"It has to get brought up, otherwise, how is she to know that I want to go?"

"Well, you got me there, kiddo."

"Thanks for asking for me, Grandma," Caitlin said bouncing out of the car and up the steps.

Joan reached down and snatched Caitlin up and hugged her just like Grandma had said. Joan glanced at Jesse. "Hi Mom," she said, holding Caitlin close and tight. "Hi sweetie. How was your day?" She asked in the middle of the hug.

"We, I mean, Grandma and I had lots of fun," Caitlin answered back in a sweet innocent voice. "We went shopping, saw a funny movie, and we had dinner at Pizza Hut."

"Wow. You did have a good time. And I can see that you went shopping by the amount of bags Grandma is carrying," Joan replied, setting Caitlin back down. "What did you buy?"

"We can't tell you that, silly," Caitlin said, laughing, "We did some early Christmas shopping."

Joan looked at her daughter with loving eyes and smiled. "Well, let us get inside before we freeze." To Caitlin, Joan said as she turned the knob to the deadbolt, "I know there's no school tomorrow, but it is getting late, so why don't you go and get ready for bed. Okay? And don't forget to brush your teeth."

"Okay, Mommy," Caitlin said, and then scampered down the hall. As she neared her bedroom door, she stopped, and turned around. She waved at her grandma until she had her attention. When she did, she extended her two pointer fingers and put them on the top of her head. Grandma Jesse saw the rabbit ear gesture and gave her granddaughter a quick wink.

"Joan?" Jesse asked, after Caitlin disappeared into her bedroom, "Do you have to work tomorrow?"

"Why? Is something wrong?"

"No, no, there's nothing wrong. It's just that I think Caitlin would like to spend a little more time with you," Jesse continued as they headed for the kitchen. "And, tomorrow, being that there's a teacher's conference, it's kind of a perfect opportunity."

"Did she say something to indicate that I haven't been spending enough time with her?" Joan asked. As she asked the question, a sudden feeling of guilt overwhelmed her as she thought of the times that the two had made plans only to have those mother-daughter moments disrupted by her job.

"No!" Jesse replied as she started to make a cup of instant coffee, "Do you want a cup?"

"No thanks." Joan paused for a second as she glanced at her mother. "What was it, exactly, that she did say?"

"Well, she asked me about tomorrow. Specifically, she asked whether or not I thought you would take her over to Mrs. Zachary's place so that she could play with the rabbits." Joan sat at the kitchen table and thought about her schedule for the following day. "Now, Joan, you know I wouldn't have a problem taking her myself if you're busy, but I got the distinct impression that she wanted you to take her. I think she would like to have a mother-daughter day," Jessie said, her eyes focusing on Joan.

"Okay, I brushed my teeth and I'm dressed for bed, but I'm not at all tired," Caitlin said, yawning, hoping that Grandma had already spoken to her mother about the rabbit situation.

"Well, I'll make a deal with you, sweetie," Joan replied as she reached out for Caitlin's hand. "If you go on to bed and get a good night's sleep, we'll go up to Mrs. Zachary's tomorrow to see her and her rabbits. How would you like that?"

"I'd say that would be just fine and dandy, better than a bowl of candy," Caitlin blurted, finishing with a big smile.

"Okay, then, little miss poet. Go on along now, and I'll be there in a minute to tuck you in," Joan said, smiling back at her daughter. Caitlin gave her grandma a goodnight hug and hurried off to bed full of anticipation of the next day.

Joan gave her mother a kiss on the cheek and whispered a thank-you in her ear before leaving the kitchen. She walked softly into Caitlin's room, sat down on the side of the bed and stroked Caitlin's beautiful blonde hair that lay across her pillow. Caitlin turned toward her mother as she felt the caress of her hand. "Thanks, Mom," she said softly, "For spending the day with me tomorrow."

"Sweetie, I hope you know that I wish I could spend every day with you," Joan said tenderly. "You are my whole world. I can't even imagine what my life would be like without you in it."

"You'd still be a great cop in the Big Apple," Caitlin replied tiredly.

Joan leaned over and kissed her daughter on the tip of her nose. "Well, aren't you my little optimistic gift from the heavens?" They looked at each other for a moment, and broke out into a case of the giggles as Joan tickled Caitlin's belly. "God, I love you so much. Don't ever question that, okay?"

"I won't, Mommy. I love you too."

Joan continued to stroke Caitlin's hair until she fell asleep. She kissed Caitlin gently on the forehead before leaving her room, and then went to bed herself.

2

Marie glanced at the clock on the living room wall. "11:20," she said under her breath. "Where in the hell are they?" She stood up from the sofa and began to pace, glancing at the phone as if willing it to ring.

She went into the kitchen to make a pot of coffee, and while it brewed, made another attempt at Todd's number. On the fifth ring, she slammed the receiver down in frustration.

The scent of the coffee filled the kitchen as she poured herself a cup. After a few sips, she again called Todd's house.

On the second ring, a female voice answered, "Hello?" Vanessa was busy putting on her bathrobe as she answered the phone.

"Thank God you're there!" Marie said in a feverish tone, her heart pounding. "This is Marie Shae, Kiersten's mother."

"Oh, hey, God, it's been a long time since we've talked."

"Yes it has, and I don't want to start off sounding rude, but all I want to do is talk to my daughter. Is she there? Can I speak to her please?"

Vanessa knew straight away that something was wrong. There was insistence in Marie's tone. "Your daughter?" She answered back.

"Yes, Kiersten, can I speak with her?" She paused. Her words reared with frustration and concern. "*Now,* please." Her plea was answered by silence. "Hello? Vanessa, are you still there?"

"Yes, it's just," Vanessa hesitated, "I'm sorry, it's just that—I'm not exactly sure what you're talking about. Todd's here, has been since I arrived home over an hour ago. But I haven't seen Kiersten. I just... What was that?" Vanessa asked, "Are you alright?"

Marie's cup of coffee had slipped from her limp fingers and shattered on impact. The words "I haven't seen Kiersten" echoed in her head like shouted words through a canyon. "Damn it," Marie yelled.

"Marie, are you alright?"

"I'm fine," she said, wiping the hot coffee from her legs. "What do you mean you haven't seen her? She was supposed to be getting a ride home from your son, wasn't she?"

"As far as I know, I mean that's what Todd told me this morning."

"Then put her on the phone."

"Mrs. Shae—Marie, I'm sorry," Vanessa said, quickly realizing that no matter what she said, it would not be what Marie wanted to hear, "I really am, but the fact still remains that your daughter isn't here."

"Vanessa," Marie asked, her voice hardening. "What aren't you telling me? Did something happen? Is she O.K.? Tell me now, damn it. I have a right to know."

"Marie, the first thing you need to do, is calm down. There's…"

"Calm down my ass," Marie shouted. "I'm trying to locate my sixteen year old daughter, and you want me to calm down? Have you lost your mind?"

"Marie, I'm not trying to minimize your concern, it's just that I don't know where she is. All I know is that she isn't here."

"Well, where the hell is she, then?" Marie blasted. "Todd was supposed to pick her up at the store at 5:00."

"I don't know."

"Can I talk to him?" Marie replied as she wiped away tears of worry from her angered face.

"Uh, yeah, hold on, I'll, uh—go and get him."

Vanessa lowered the cordless phone to her side and made haste toward Todd's room. She wondered if her son knew anything about Kiersten's whereabouts.

"Todd, honey, wake up."

Todd rolled over slowly, his eyes squinted, "Mom, you're home," he muttered. "What's up?"

"Where's Kiersten? Her mother's on the phone asking me questions about where she is. Do you know?" she asked, handing Todd the phone.

Todd shrugged his shoulders as he took the phone. "Hello," Todd said, and then yawned.

"Todd, where's Kiersten? Isn't she with you?"

"Mrs. Shae, I haven't seen Kiersten at all tonight. I..." Before Todd could finish, Marie cut him off.

"What do you mean you haven't seen her? Didn't you tell her you would be picking her up at the antique store? Didn't you promise to take her out for a drive and then bring her home? That is what you told her, isn't it? *Isn't it?*"

Todd had never heard Mrs. Shae this angry, or upset. In fact, he couldn't remember a single time when she had ever raised her voice in anger, and he had known her since he was a young boy.

"Isn't it?" she asked again.

"Whoa, whoa." Todd said, still groggy. "Would you please tell me what the hell's going on before you start blasting me with the third degree routine?"

"Where's Kiersten?"

"Mrs. Shae," Todd said, the spidery feeling returning, "I can tell you're upset, but I really don't have a clue as to what it is you're talking about."

Marie took a second to collect herself before speaking. "Okay, Kiersten isn't home yet, and I don't know where she is. She hasn't called, and that's not like her. I'm scared that something is wrong," Marie hesitated for a second as her voice started quivering, "I'm scared that maybe she's hurt, or worse."

"Kiersten hasn't been home all night—are you sure?" Todd asked, sitting up as he comprehended what she was saying.

"I'm positive," Marie exclaimed. Marie stopped momentarily to grab another tissue, and continued, "I mean, I saw a car pull into the drive hours ago and I thought it was you dropping her off. I waited for her at the front door, but she never came in."

"Mrs. Shae, I'm coming over. I'll be there in twenty. Don't worry, we'll sort this out."

3

Mrs. Zachary woke to a thumping sound. Not a sound inside her house, at least she didn't think so. Again, thump. It was dull and almost hollow sounding, like a boat thumping against a wooden dock. Thump. Thump. She groggily sat up in bed as she struggled to fight off the drowsiness of a deep sleep. She cocked her head and listened. Thump. Thump. Each thump seemed in cadence with a gusting wind. Thump. Thump. Now, wide awake, she knew the sound was coming from her backyard. Her thoughts went immediately to her rabbits.

She cast aside the covers and reached for her housecoat. She walked blindly out of her bedroom towards the rear door by the kitchen where she had positioned the shotgun. She grabbed it, and glanced out the back door window. The night was dark and she could barely see the numerous lawn ornaments of wooden rabbits dressed like children doing various outdoor activities. Anything beyond that fell off into a malevolent darkness.

She moved to the front door to glance outside. Nothing moved. She turned and headed back to the kitchen. Her heart thumped hard and fast; not from fear, no, her heart was thumping out of anger. She reached out with her left hand and flicked on the outside floodlights, and without a second look outside, made her way out the back door and down the three steps towards the barn.

She stopped near the tall oak that grew between her house and the barn. From there she could now see what was making the thumping sound. Banging against the side of the barn with each gust of wind was the fourteen by eight-foot barn doors. Mrs. Zachary hesitated to go forward. She was positive she had put a padlock on the doors earlier. As she stood there, gun still in tow, she made her mind up. No way was she letting anyone take anymore of her babies. She took a deep breath and whispered, "I've got you now, you rabbit-thievin' bastard from hell."

Mrs. Zachary raised the gun to her shoulder and crept towards the thumping barn doors. The closer she got, the slower she walked. With twenty feet left to the entrance, she could hear the rabbits scuffling around. In her mind, she could picture them with their ears pinned back and their eyes wide open, almost to the point where they protruded from the sockets, all of them trying desperately to get out of the pen.

This vision made her even angrier, and she moved closer.

It wasn't until she saw her own shadow on the barn door that she stopped. She stood there, listening, her old arms trembling. Her ability to keep the gun steady had now gone. The scuffling noise from the pen had stopped.

"Damn it," she whispered to herself. Mrs. Zachary moved as quickly as her old legs would take her to the front corner of the barn. She leaned against it with a thud of exhaustion. She stood there for a moment as she felt her eighty-year-old heart palpitating. She was now officially frightened. Not just for her rabbits, but for herself.

Nevertheless, fear had never stopped her before, and she wasn't about to let it stop her now. After her breathing had subsided to as close to normal as she could get it under the circumstances, she began to creep along the front of the barn, stopping just short of the entrance. She took another deep breath, reached in and flipped on the lights. "All right, you bastard from hell, come on out." she yelled, stepping in as the lights lit up the barn. But no one was there.

But how could that be? The doors didn't open by themselves.

Confused, she moved to the left side of the barn, toward her penned rabbits. Three steps away from the pen, she felt a presence behind her. She stopped. Her heart raced hard and fast. She could almost hear it thumping against her breast plate like her barn doors against the side of the barn. She was afraid to turn around. But what else could she do? What choice did she have? With a long deep breath, she belted out, "Who's there?" Steeling against fear, she said, "Whoever the hell you are, you'd better answer up, cuz this here gun is loaded, and I ain't afraid to use it." Mrs. Zachary listened for a response. All she heard, however, was the howling wind rustling the leaves outside the barn, and her heart beating faster and faster. She took one last look at her rabbits. They were exactly how she had pictured them, but silent and as motionless as a tomb. Her body started to shake uncontrollably.

"All right," she yelled as she spun herself around, "You asked for…" A flash of pain sent her to the ground. As she fell, the butt of the gun slammed to the barn floor, her finger depressed the trigger, discharging a round before coming to rest several feet away. Mrs. Zachary laid there as the wound on her head bled down across her forehead and into her eyes. She tried to raise her right hand to wipe away the blood, but could not find the strength to do so. With every ounce of resolve she could muster, she whimpered, "Help! Somebody, please, God, help me," and then passed out.

Chapter 6

1

Todd put down the receiver. The spidery sensation intensified. He grabbed his jacket from off the bedpost, and in doing so, saw the picture that he and Kiersten had taken only two weeks earlier out of the corner of his eye. *She was so beautiful*, he thought; *perfect blonde hair, blue-green eyes, and a smile larger than life.* He had once told her that she looked like Marilyn Monroe with straight hair. She never believed him. In fact, she never really thought herself to be all that cute, which, in Todd's eyes, made her even more beautiful.

Other pictures of Kiersten were scattered around the room, but this one was special; it was the only one in which the two of them were together as a couple, as boyfriend and girlfriend. Kiersten had picked out the perfect frame from her mother's antique shop for an early birthday present. It was made of pewter colored stone with but a single word etched across the top. 'FOREVER'.

Todd slipped on his jacket and then picked up the picture. He sat for a moment on the edge of his bed. He was so involved with the image of her face that he didn't hear his mother enter the room.

"Is everything all right?" she asked, putting her hand on his shoulder. He jumped at her touch. "Todd, it's just me. What's wrong? Why are you so jumpy all of the sudden?"

"Nothing! Everything! Hell, I don't know Mom. I just don't know."

Todd rubbed his hand over the picture as if to caress Kiersten's face. "Mrs. Shae hasn't seen Kiersten tonight," Todd said quietly, almost whispering. "I was supposed to pick her up, give her a ride home. But I got caught up in some stupid arcade game, and I didn't make it back in time, and now—now it looks like she's missing." Todd took a deep breath and looked toward his mother. "Mom, if anything happened…" Todd's voice trailed off, "Anyway, I told Mrs. Shae that I was coming over. I need to find out what's going on."

"I'm sure she's fine," his mother replied. "She's probably over at a friend's house right now badmouthing you because you didn't pick her up," she paused for a second. "The problem is that gossiping girls lose track of time just like arcade playing boys. I'm sure that's all it is."

"I hope you're right," Todd replied as he stood, "But if you're not, if anything has happened to her, it'll be my fault." The spider eggs were multiplying faster by the minute. He felt now more than ever that something was wrong, *very wrong.*

2

Deputy Ed took Mike McVain home and headed back to the police station; he was on duty for the night. He was accompanied by the uneasy feeling that had been with him all night. It wasn't just the dead rabbits that bothered him; it was the way he found them that was disturbing. They had been mutilated, a word that barely touched the essence of the horrific footage that kept repeating itself in his mind.

Ed had seen his share of blood and carnage in Vietnam, but there at least, one expected to see it. And even though this imagery brought back memories that he seriously wanted to forget, the slaughtered rabbits and the missing pelts weren't all that was bothering him, the overwhelming feeling of being watched before leaving the Zachary residence didn't sit well with him either. He now wondered if whatever it was watching him—if anything at all—had been waiting for him to leave.

After parking his truck, he hurried into the police station. He grabbed the report he had started earlier from off his desk. But even now the words he needed to finish the report eluded him.

How could he write down what he couldn't explain?

Ed laid the report back on his desk and glanced over to the file cabinets. *I wonder,* he thought. He opened the top drawer and pulled out the first file in the unsolved cases section.

He sat at his desk and went through each file diligently, searching for anything that might be remotely similar. The only thing that jumped out at him as he went through each file was that there seemed to be a sequence of missing dates. And by no means were the missing dates random; the same dates were missing in every file during the same time period, April 67 - October 69. At first, the absent files bothered him, but then he remembered how Sheriff Fortune had described the way the office was organized when she first took over.

He convinced himself it was nothing, but left a note of his findings on Sheriff Fortune's desk.

Ed leaned back in his chair with his hands clasped behind his head. With his eyes closed, the footage of the bloodied carnage repeated over and over in his mind. He began to feel that what he had seen had a—humanistic feel to it, not just because of the missing pelts, but because of what *wasn't* missing: the meat, entrails, and the fact that the exposed bones hadn't displayed any signs of being gnawed or chewed. He could no longer wait until morning for another look; he needed to see it now, tonight.

With less than a mile left before reaching the entrance to the Zachary residence, Ed heard a sound that echoed through the night as distinctive to him as a child's cry was to a mother.

A shotgun.

3

Marie hung up the phone and sat for a moment on the edge of the sofa. Her eyes blearily stared at the mess the fallen cup of coffee had made. Though she didn't have the desire to clean it up, she went to the kitchen to get the items necessary in which to do so.

4

Todd walked briskly out to his car. After talking to Mrs. Shae on the phone, hearing the fear in her voice, he felt a chill run through the entire length of his body, but it wasn't from the cold eastern wind—the chill was internal. Something was wrong. He had had the same feeling earlier. Something was indeed wrong.

He put the car in drive and pulled out of the circle shaped driveway.

"No!" He said aloud. "Kiersten is fine. Why am I even questioning it? She's fine. She has to be. I saw her. She *is* fine."

5

Marie went to the window and pushed back the curtain to look outside. The fog had thickened, but with the outside lights on, she was able to make out Todd's car at the end of her driveway. She moved to the front door and from there, she thought she could see the silhouette of someone, of Todd, sitting inside the car staring endlessly at the dashboard. She watched him for several minutes before heading out to see what was wrong.

The cold wind whipped past her as she ran out to the car. She tapped the window, "Todd? Todd, you okay?"

Todd powered the window down. He looked relieved to find Mrs. Shae outside his car, bending to look in.

"Todd, are you alright? You've been sitting out here for almost ten minutes."

Todd looked at her strangely as he realized that he didn't remember anything past putting the car in drive and pulling out of his own driveway.

"Come on, let's get inside," Marie said.

Inside, Todd took a seat on one side of the sofa. Marie took the other. The silence was deafening and the tension thick as the two sat separated by the center cushion.

"Mrs. Shae," Todd asked warily, "Are you sure Kiersten hasn't been home? I mean, I know I screwed up, I know that I was supposed to pick her up and bring her home. And I know that I have no justifiable excuse as to why I didn't. But I'm only asking because, even though I knew she would be mad at the sight of me, I still needed to make sure she got home safely, so I drove by. I parked at the end of your driveway for a few minutes. The blinds were drawn shut in her room, but I could see her shadow. She looked as if she were—pacing, you know, as if she were mad."

Marie gave him a hardened, water-eyed stare, and then spoke. "Todd that was me, I was in her room picking up laundry. Your car must have been the one I saw pulling away. I thought it was you dropping off Kiersten."

The tension thickened.

Todd's eyes panned around the room. His eyes stopped at a recent photo of Kiersten. He remembered the day it was taken; it was the same day they officially became a couple, the day they decided to extend their relationship beyond that of friendship. His hand moved to his cheek where she had gently kissed him, then to his lips where she all but took his breath away with a passionate kiss. His eyes watered at the memory.

Marie could clearly see the pain in his eyes.

"I never should have—I mean—I should have came straight home after taking that damn driving test," Todd said. "I know sorry isn't what you want to hear, but…"

Todd peered at the clock on the wall. He heard every tick and every tock in crystal clarity. "Have you called the police yet?" He asked. "Her friends?"

"A few of her friends, the ones I have numbers for anyway. No one I've talked to has seen her."

"And the police?"

"No." Marie answered weakly, "I wanted to make sure she wasn't with you first, but now…"

"I'm pretty sure Deputy Ed is on duty tonight. I know it's not my place, but I think we should head into town and tell him what's going on, that Kiersten is missing."

"Fine, okay" Marie said, sounding as broken as she looked, "I should leave Kiersten a note, just in case she shows up.

Marie put down the pen and left the note taped to the front door. She walked to the closet to retrieve her coat, and followed Todd out the door.

He walked to the passenger side and opened the door for Mrs. Shae. Just as he was about to jump in the driver's side, he glanced into the tree line on the far side of the road with the feeling that something was there, watching; something unexplainable, yet…

"Todd, what is it? What's the matter?" Marie asked.

"I don't know," he replied as he got into the car. "Probably nothing. Just a weird feeling, that's all."

Todd put the car in reverse and backed out of the drive and headed towards town.

Marie flew forward as Todd slammed on the brakes.

"Jesus, Todd, what the hell did you do that for?"

"Didn't you hear that?"

"Hear what?"

"That noise a second ago, it sounded like a shotgun." He paused and looked at her, "You didn't hear it?"

"No. And I don't know how you could either with all this wind. Now, let's get going."

Todd rolled down his window and stuck his head out and listened; he heard nothing.

"Todd, let's go. There was no gun."

Todd rolled up the window and released the brakes. About three hundred yards from her house, Marie yelled for Todd to stop. "What?" Todd asked, "Did you see something?"

"Todd, just back up the damn car," Marie yelled. Todd put the car in reverse, and backed up until she again yelled for him to stop.

Before the car had stopped completely, Marie was out the door. Todd pulled a flashlight from the glove box and exited. "Let's stay together," Todd said, as he flicked on the flashlight.

They panned the side of the road, sweeping the light from side to side. Ten feet further back from where they had stopped, Marie halted and told Todd to stop. The flashlight's beam pierced through the thin layer of fog and onto the object that had caught Marie's eye. It was her daughter's handbag. Marie fell to her knees. "It's Kiersten's," Marie managed to get out before bursting into tears. She bent down, reached for the bag, and clutched it to her chest.

Todd searched the surrounding area with the flashlight. He saw several other items that he had known to be Kiersten's: A blue Parker pen, a lipstick case, and an address book that had the initials K.S on the front. Just as he picked up the three items, Mrs. Shae let out an ear-piercing scream.

"Mrs. Shae, what is it?" Todd asked, shining the flashlight in her direction.

Though she knew it was her daughter's handbag, she held it out in front of her, praying that it was not. She lost her balance and fell from her knees to her right hip. Todd grabbed her coat to keep her from falling further, but Marie shrugged off his hold. She again embraced the bag and started sobbing uncontrollably. Todd then saw why she had screamed. A dark red stain stood out prominently against the off-white color of the handbag.

"Blood." Todd gasped.

Mrs. Shae fell to her side and curled up into a fetal position.

The flashlight in Todd's hand waved aimlessly into the looming darkness as he stumbled backwards. He realized then that his worst fears were upon him. The constant feelings of something being wrong, the feeling of being watched, the sound of a shotgun, and now, and perhaps the most substantial, finding Kiersten's handbag on the side of the road stained with blood. All these events together had trapped Todd into a nightmare from which he could not wake up, a nightmare from which the millions of spider eggs that had seemed embedded in his stomach had finally hatched and were now all simultaneously wreaking havoc throughout his body, each one shouting "Kiersten's missing."

Todd circled the road as he yelled out her name, *"Kiersten. Kiersten."* When he heard no reply, he became desperate and took off running into the woods in search of her.

6

Deputy Ed Cross floored the gas pedal and whipped his truck into the driveway of the Zachary residence. The sound of a shotgun was still fresh in his mind. He jumped out of the truck with his right hand firmly gripping the .45 at his side. He took a quick look around the area.

Silence.

At first glance, everything seemed normal. He grabbed the flashlight from the backseat and started walking slowly towards the house, circling as he went. He backed up the stairs and onto the porch and knocked. When no one answered, he stepped off the porch and moved to the front window to peek inside. The flickering glow from the oversized fireplace provided the only light, but it was adequate enough to see into the living room and most of the kitchen. Everywhere he looked, he saw the evidence of Mrs. Zachary's love of rabbits. Pictures, paintings, and brass wall hangings filled the walls, while figurines filled just about every flat surface in the room. What he didn't see was Mrs. Zachary. *Probably in bed sleeping,* he thought.

He moved towards the rear of the house where the entire yard was lit up by flood lights. Glancing down towards the barn, he could see that the barn doors were open. *Odd,* he thought. He turned the corner of the house and saw that the back door leading to the kitchen had also been left hanging wide open.

Mrs. Zachary had been adamant about seeing whatever it was that took her rabbits, and because of that, Ed knew there was no way she would have gone off to bed leaving the barn doors wide open. And she definitely would not have left her back door open. She would have made sure that everything had been locked up nice and tight.

Ed then remembered the shotgun he had heard only minutes ago.

He pulled out his gun and crept into the house. "Mrs. Zachary? Elli? Are you in here?"

Silence.

The glow of the fireplace glistened off the silver-plated forty-five held out in front of him with both hands as he maneuvered himself further into the house in standard police format.

He moved quickly and quietly through the house. He checked all the rooms, behind doors, and in closets. He found nothing: no Mrs. Zachary, no intruders, and no rabbit butchering sons-a-bitches.

Ed went back out the door, his gun still drawn, and jogged down to the barn. He stopped just to the left side of the entrance. With his back up against the barn, Ed held out his arms, bent at the elbows, with his gun pointed into the sky.

"Mrs. Zachary, are you in there?" Ed thought he heard a moaning sound, and asked again. "Mrs. Zachary, is that you? Elli?" This time he heard a voice. It was weak, but it sounded like Mrs. Zachary.

"Help..."

Ed entered the barn thrusting forward his .45. The first thing he saw was Mrs. Zachary lying on the ground, moving slightly, and bleeding from her head. He rushed to her, "Elli, oh God, Elli, what the hell happened to you?"

After making sure the barn was secure, he holstered his gun and slipped his arm under her shoulders. "Elli. Elli, talk to me. Who did this to you?"

Elli looked up at Ed. Her eyes looked like motionless water filled caverns. Her lips shivered in silence. Ed couldn't tell if she was just cold or if she was trying to tell him something.

"Elli, please try and concentrate. Who did this to you? Who would want to hurt you like this?"

Ed could only sit and hold her while he waited to see if words would form from her trembling lips.

Then, "Bun…nan," she muttered weakly, "Buuunnyman, bunnyman…" She passed out and fell limp in his arms.

"Bunny man?" Ed said. "What in the hell is a bunny man?"

Gently laying her head down in his lap, he retrieved a pocketknife from his rear pocket and quickly removed his jacket, and then his chamois shirt. He cut off the sleeve of his shirt and tied it around her head, covering the gash, and then slipped his jacket back on. "Mrs. Zachary, what did you mean by bunny man?"

Silence.

"Mrs. Zachary, if you can hear me, I need to leave you alone for a few minutes. I'm just going to run to the house to make a call to get some help out here." He laid her head softly to the ground using the rest of his shirt as a pillow, and ran out of the barn.

7

Todd had lost his bearing's and had no idea where he was until he reached a clearing past the tree line and realized that he was at the Zachary residence. As he got closer to the house he noticed Deputy Ed's truck in the driveway, and then saw him coming up from the barn. "Hey! Over here!" Todd yelled.

Ed had almost reached the truck when he heard someone yelling. He flicked his flashlight in the direction in which he heard the voice calling, and pulled out his weapon. When he saw that it was Todd, he holstered his .45 and took a deep breath.

"Deputy Ed," Todd said. "Thank God it's you."

"Why?" He watched Todd slump over, the palms of his hands resting on his knees. "What's going on? And just what the hell are you doing out here this time of night?"

"It's Kiersten. She's missing. Mrs. Shae and I, we—we found her handbag lying in the road. There was blood on it." Todd was panting, trying to catch his breath and talk at the same time.

Ed handed Todd the keys to his truck. "Grab the first-aid kit from the glove compartment, and my radio from the front seat. I'll be inside making a phone call." He turned toward the house.

"Haven't you heard a word I've said? Kiersten—she's missing." Todd exclaimed.

Ed stopped, his shoulders slumping a little. He couldn't remember when he had so much going on at the same time. But the military had taught him how to keep things in perspective and to prioritize. "Yes Todd, I did, every word, and I'm sorry, but right now I need to tend to Mrs. Zachary who is lying in her barn in a puddle of her own blood with a gash in her head the size of Texas, so do what I asked. The sooner you do, the sooner I can tend to your needs, and to Kiersten's."

Ed watched Todd run to the truck for a second and then made his way inside the house to call Barbara Williams, the town doctor.

"This had better be pretty damn important whoever the hell you are," he heard the voice from the other end say.

"If I were you, I'd probably say the same thing."

"Oh, Ed, I'm sorry. I didn't mean to come off sounding like a bitch."

"Don't worry about it. I would have probably sounded the same way. Listen, I'm sorry I had to wake you, but Mrs. Zachary has been attacked in her barn and I could really use your help out here. I'd bring her to you, but I'm not sure if I should move her."

"How bad is it?"

"I risked life and limb by calling you, didn't I?"

"I'll be there in a few."

"If I'm not here, Todd Chandler will be."

"Todd?"

"Yeah, long story, I'll explain later, I just need you out here as soon as possible."

Ed put down the receiver and saw Todd as he entered the house with the first-aid kit tucked under his right arm, the radio in his left hand. He looked confused.

Ed went to the sofa in the living room, grabbed the blanket that was draped over the back of a throw pillow and then tapped Todd on the arm.

"Come on. Let's get back to the barn and tend to Mrs. Z." Todd nodded, and they headed out the rear door towards the barn.

"Now, why don't you explain to me what's going on," Ed said in a calm tone.

"Kiersten, she's missing…"

"I gathered that much."

"But it's my fault."

"Todd, you're not making any sense. Why don't you start from the beginning," Ed replied as he spread the blanket out over Mrs. Zachary, and checked her pulse.

"Is she going to be all right?" Todd asked.

"Yeah, I think she'll pull through. But––that gash on her head's going to hurt when she wakes up." Ed replied, looking at Todd, "But judging from the look on your face, you need to finish telling me what's going on."

Todd did just that. He explained in detail the events as they happened. "Moments before we found Kiersten's handbag, I would have sworn I heard a shotgun going off. The next thing I knew, I was running through the woods. I ended up not knowing where I was until I hit the clearing in the trees. That's when I noticed your truck, and I saw you."

"Well, that would explain that look of worry," Ed said, pausing for a second before asking, "You said you thought you heard a shotgun?"

"Pretty sure that's what it was. I heard it just as I was pulling out of Mrs. Shae's driveway. It was windy though, it could have been..."

"No, it was a shotgun. I can only assume that it was Mrs. Zachary's. Guess the feisty ole gal got off a round before she got knocked out," Ed said looking out at the night through the open barn doors. "Where's Marie now?"

"We found the bag less then a quarter mile from her house," Todd said. "The last time I saw her, she was lying on the ground next to my car, crying—hysterically. I know I shouldn't have left her there like that. I guess I freaked a little, what with seeing the blood and all. I had to go look for her, I had to."

"Todd, listen, this has been a long day, and a lot of weird stuff has gone down. I can see that you're upset and that you're worried about Kiersten. I am too. But right now, what we need to do is remain calm, and keep a positive attitude. Can you do that?"

Todd looked down at Mrs. Zachary, and then peered out into the night.

"Can you?" Ed repeated.

"Yeah, yeah, I hear you," he answered with fearful eyes. The fear he felt was not for himself, but for not knowing where Kiersten was. And if finding her, uninjured and unharmed, meant that she would never again talk to him or even look at him, then it was a sacrifice he'd be willing to make.

"Good," Ed replied, "I want you to run up to the house and call Mrs. Shae at home. If she answers, tell her I'm on my way. If she doesn't, just hang up. Don't bother leaving a message. Okay? Can you handle that?"

Todd nodded and ran out of the barn.

"And be careful," Ed yelled.

After Todd left, Ed bent over the injured woman, tucking the blanket around her.

"Bunny man? What the hell is that supposed to mean? Bunny man..." he cut himself off as he thought of the four missing rabbits, the four slaughtered rabbits he had found in the woods, and wondered if she was trying to tell him that who or what had taken her rabbits, had come back.

"Bet they weren't expecting to find you waiting for them with a loaded gun, were they, Mrs. Z?" Ed said, half smiling. "Guess they don't know you too well."

Mrs. Zachary stirred and blinked her eyes.

"Mrs. Zachary, can you hear me?" Ed asked as she moved her head slightly and moaned. "Hold on, Mrs. Z, hold on."

Todd had returned to the barn. He had no luck reaching Mrs. Shae. "So now what?" Todd asked. "What are we going to do about Kiersten and Mrs. Shae?"

"You—you're not going to do anything except stay here and wait for Doc Williams." He paused to make sure Todd understood him. "You know how to handle one of those, don't you?" he asked motioning his head towards Mrs. Zachary's shotgun.

"Yeah, sure."

"Good. That's a Remington 870. If I no Mrs. Zachary, she'll have kept that thing fully loaded, which means there should be three rounds left."

Todd reached for the gun and cracked the breech. "There's at least one."

"That'll have to do."

He paused then, as if thinking of his next move. With some whacko on the loose, Mrs. Zachary bludgeoned unconscious, and Kiersten missing, he couldn't afford not to at least try and find Mrs. Shae. He didn't, however, relish the idea of leaving Todd alone; especially knowing that whoever attacked Mrs. Zachary could still be in the area.

"Listen, Todd, we don't have a lot of time. I need to contact the sheriff and locate Mrs. Shae. I don't much like the idea of leaving you here, but I like your chances better here armed with a gun than that of Mrs. Shae's. In all likelihood, she's probably still crying on the side of the road. I'm trusting you here, Todd," Ed said with a stern tone in his voice. "Don't let me down. Are you okay with this?"

"I think so."

"No time to think here, Todd, either you are or…"

"I'm fine. I'll be okay."

"I'm only going to be gone for fifteen maybe twenty minutes. Now, you have that gun. Use it only if you have to, but please, make sure of what you're shooting at before you pull the trigger. If it's a wild animal, go for a kill shot; if it's a man and he's threatening to come at you, lay that buckshot across his legs; that should keep him at bay until I get back. No warning shots, Todd. If you have to shoot, make it count." Ed paused, uneasy about the situation. He looked down at Mrs. Zachary. "I also need for you to look after her."

"I can do that."

"One more thing," Ed said dryly, "The only way into this barn is through that rear window, and the barn doors. Now the window is a stretch because it's so high off the ground, so position yourself so that you're facing the barn entrance."

"Anything else?"

"Yeah, be careful."

Ed glanced around the barn one last time, grabbed the hand held radio. "I'll ah—holler before I come back in," he said. "I don't need you getting all trigger happy."

"Good idea."

Todd pulled back the pump action of the shotgun, expelling the empty shell on to the barn floor. It was now ready to shoot again. He planted the butt firmly against his inner thigh for support, his finger all but pressing the trigger.

Deputy Ed reached into his truck, put the radio on the seat and pulled a rag out of the glove compartment to wipe the blood off his hands. He threw the rag into the back of his truck and picked up the radio. "Hope your radio's on tonight, Joan," he said in a low whisper, then, "Break for Sheriff Fortune, over." No reply. "Break for Sheriff Fortune, this is Deputy Ed Cross, do you have a copy? Over."

"Go ahead, over," a yawning voice replied.

"Sorry about waking you Sheriff, but I have a situation here, and I could use some assistance."

"What do you have, Ed?"

After filling in the sheriff, Ed jumped into his truck and sped off to find Mrs. Shae. It only took him a few minutes to reach the area in which Todd said his car would be, only— there was no car, and there was no Mrs. Shae. He looked towards Mrs. Shae's house, but could only see the outline of one car in the driveway. It was not Todd's Mustang.

Just as he was about to get out for a quick look around, Joan squawked in on the radio, "Ed, this is Joan, do you have a copy? Over."

"Go for Ed, over."

"Just wanted to let you know that Marie Shae is here with me."

"Is she okay?"

"She's scared out of her mind about her daughter, but physically, she's fine. I guess after trying the station and finding no one there, she said she didn't know where else to go, so she came here. I think we'll meet you at the town clinic. It might not be a bad idea to have Barb look her over, maybe give her a sedative to calm her down."

"Copy that, see you there, over and out."

He had no sooner put the radio down when, out of the corner of his eye, he thought he saw something moving in the trees. Whatever it was, was tall and upright, like a man, but oddly shaped. And then it was gone.

Chapter 7

1

Sheriff Fortune and Deputy Ed sat outside the examining room as Barbara treated Mrs. Zachary, Marie, and Todd. They stood as the doctor came out. "Well, Ed, you were right, that was one nasty cut; took eleven stitches."

"What's her prognosis?" Joan asked.

"Well, I don't want to speculate quite yet, least not till I get some tests run on her tomorrow. I can tell you this though," Barbara said, "You won't be getting anything out of her tonight; she's down for the count. I've made arrangements for her transfer to Dixon Memorial in the morning. I'll be able to run more tests there. They should be here around 7:00 a.m. to pick her up."

"And Marie Shae?" Ed asked. "How's she doing?"

"Marie, she's fine, worried as hell, of course, and for good reason. She doesn't know yet about those poor rabbits you found all bloodied and butchered, does she?" Barbara asked.

The words had barely left Barbara's vocal cords when Joan answered. "No. Thank God, and I don't want her to know either."

"Well, you don't have to worry about her finding out about it tonight. I gave her something to help her sleep; she'll be out of it till morning. If I were you, I'd be more inclined to worry about Todd."

"Why?" Ed asked.

"He refused to take anything, for one. I mean, it was a struggle just getting him to let me clean up the scratches on his face. All he could talk about was getting back out there to look for Kiersten. He's hell bent on it."

"Well," Ed stated, "He won't be going anywhere but home tonight. Has anyone called his mother yet?"

"Not that I'm aware of," Joan said.

"I'll take him home," Ed offered, "And I'll fill his mother in on what's going on; ask her to try and keep an eye on him."

Joan nodded and said, "I know enough to start the report for you Ed, but you'll have to proof it, make changes if need be and then sign it."

"Sounds good, thanks."

Just then, a noise coming from the examining room caught all of their attention. The noise was the sound of a door opening and closing followed by a very annoying high pitched alarm. They knew before entering that it was Todd sneaking out the back.

"Shit!" Joan said. "Ed, you'd better call the Dixon Fire Department and let them know it's a false alarm."

2

After the doctor had stepped out of the room, Todd moved as close to the door as possible so that he could listen in on the conversation between Ed, Joan, and the good doctor. Having heard the bulk of their conversation, he felt the urgent need to find Kiersten, and find her now.

Todd tiptoed back to where Mrs. Shae was lying in a drug-induced sleep and rifled through her purse. It only took a few seconds to find what he was looking for. He grabbed the keys to his car.

With keys in hand, Todd turned slowly in place, looking for another exit. The main door was not in play as Doc. Williams, Sheriff Fortune and Deputy Ed were right outside the door in the hall, and he knew by their conversation that his going back out was not an option, especially with some kind of rabbit-killing lunatic on the loose.

The windows looked inviting, but when he tried to open them, they would not budge. They hadn't been opened in years. The combination of wood swelling over time and the many coats of paint had seemingly sealed them for good. In the far back corner of the room, he saw a door that looked familiar; a gray metal door with a push bar across the front. *A fire exit*, he thought. He opened the door without hesitation and exited the room. He found himself in a dark shallow hallway with an exit sign lit above another door. He opened it and was now outside in the rear of the building. It was an unlit alleyway used for additional parking. But he was not afraid of the dark, and even if he were, it would not have prevented him from walking through it. Finding his girl was the only thing on his mind.

He darted through the darkness to the corner of the building. He stopped and peaked around. *Good,* he thought, *no one in sight.* On the move again, his pace increased as his mind revisited the grisly conversation he had overheard. Certain unnerving words stuck out like an old man in a room full of newborn babies; words that were now embedded into his memory and not easily forgotten. The words *'bloodied'* and *'butchered'* created unwelcome images in his mind.

"No," he said aloud. "She's fine. She has to be." But even as his mind tried to conjure up positive thoughts, doubt still lingered. It was in that instance where reality, being what it was, heightened his need to find Kiersten. A couple of unsettling words were by far more fueling than his guilt for not being there to pick her up on time.

As he neared his car, Todd knew he had to get back to the place where Kiersten had last been; he somehow felt drawn to that place by an invisible fear that grabs you by the guts and twists them into knots. He knew he messed up by being late, but this, he never expected this: to have a half-crazed, knife-wielding psychopath running around town butchering rabbits, lashing out at old women, or worse, his girlfriend. He had to find her. He had to.

Chapter 8

1

"That's all we need," Joan said looking out the window, glaring into the gloomy moonless night. "Is a seventeen-year old pumped full of reckless emotions out looking for his girl with some ludicrous psycho on the loose."

"I'll catch up to him," Ed said. "Don't worry."

"No," Joan replied. "You stay here, maybe try and catch a little shuteye. Keep the radio close by though, just in case."

Joan sprinted out the door and caught up with Todd just as he was backing up. "Todd!" She yelled, "Hold up a minute." Joan stopped at the curb just as Todd eased his car back into place. "Just where is it you think you're going? It's dark, it's cold, and you don't know jack-shit about what you're about to do."

"I don't care about what I do or don't know. All I care about is finding Kiersten before she ends up like Mrs. Zachary, or worse, like one of those rabbits."

Joan could see the intensity in Todd's eyes. She could hear it in his voice. He was going back out no matter what, and she knew that short of arresting the kid, she had about as much chance of talking him out of it as Todd did in finding Kiersten on his own.

"We'll have a better chance finding her at first light," Joan said sympathetically.

"Yeah, and if that's true, then it will be just as easy for that rabbit-killing psycho, if he hasn't found her already."

Joan saw the glare from Todd; she could actually feel Todd's eyes pushing against her face. "Oh, for God sakes, what were you doing? Listening in on a private conversation?"

"I had to find out what was going on."

"Yeah, right," Joan said with a sigh. "Christ Almighty, I can't believe I'm doing this. I must be getting soft," Joan continued, knowing full well that if it had been her daughter, Caitlin, she'd be doing the same thing.

Standing in another's shoes can often redirect one's perspective on any given situation.

"Alright, but if we're going to do this, then we're going to do it my way, or not at all. We don't know what we're dealing with, so what I say goes. Is that clear?"

"Fine, let's just go already."

Joan knew that trying to find someone in these woods during the day was a challenge, but at night, it would be nearly impossible. She decided, however, that if they were going to do this, it would be done with proper gear.

"Let's go back inside, grab a couple of jackets, four fresh flashlights..."

"And a couple of shotguns," Todd said, interrupting Joan.

"One shotgun and some extra shells."

"But..."

"But nothing!"

Although Joan wasn't pleased about them going out, it was better than the alternative of Todd going out alone. Besides, it was her best friend's daughter. If anything did happen to her, she wouldn't be able to forgive herself if she didn't at least try.

Upon reaching the office, Joan added an additional radio to her list of gear.

"Okay then," Joan announced, "let's do this, but let's do it smartly."

2

The crying had stopped. The throbbing headache had gone. Her wrists and ankles burned and were nearly rubbed raw. But Kirsten was done fighting the ropes. It was useless. She wasn't going to loosen them, and she knew it. She almost felt complacent in the fact that she was going to die. For now, however, all she wanted to do was close her eyes and drift off to sleep; to somehow dream away this nightmare that had become her reality. She wanted to dream of happy things, of home, her mother, of preparing for the upcoming homecoming dance. She wanted to remember shopping with her friends to find the perfect dress. She wanted to imagine Todd driving up in front of her house in his shiny new Mustang, decked out in a black Christian-Dior tuxedo carrying a nosegay filled with huge red Benjamin Britten roses.

Her last thought before drifting off was that of her and Todd dancing around a balloon-filled gymnasium as if no one else were there; everything was wonderful, magical, an evening that they would never forget.

Kiersten's eyes, however, opened as fast as they had closed to a sound she heard somewhere off in the distance. Her body jerked and quivered. The moment of peace was shattered, her body seemed robbed of breath, as if fear itself had reached out and seized her throat. She tried to scream, but no sound came out.

"There. There it is again," she mouthed in silence. Kiersten just sat there. She had come to the realization that her death was near.

The sound drew closer and more frequent, and as it did, it grew somehow familiar; it sounded like a voice calling out as if in search of someone, but with all the wind hissing in the background, she couldn't be sure. She wanted to yell out, draw attention to herself in case it was someone looking for her. The chance, however, was too great. *What if it was that thing, that same horrible thing that had brought her here to begin with?*

After a few daunting moments of silence, she heard it again. It was closer now. The sound was indeed a voice, and it was calling her name. She could hear it clearly now.

"Kiersten? Kiersten, where are you?"

Todd's voice.

"Todd, I'm over here," she yelled.

The light from Todd's flashlight penetrated the darkness, moving in circles.

"Todd, over here!"

"Holy shit, Kiersten," Todd said. "Are you alright?"

"I think so. I'm freezing though."

"What happened to your clothes?"

"I don't know. Just untie me and let's get the hell out of here!"

Todd pulled out his pocketknife and cut the ropes. She grabbed him and hugged him close. "Oh, Todd, I was so scared. Thank God you're here!"

"Kiersten, I'm so sorry I was late picking you up."

"It's okay, you're here now and that's all that matters."

He wrapped his arm around her shoulders and helped her up.

As soon as Kiersten stood, every muscle in her body froze with fear. "Todd," she whispered, pulling Todd closer to her side. "Can you smell that?" Then she screamed, "Todd! Oh, God, Todd. Watch out!"

Todd slipped from her grasp and she fell back to the ground. She was again smothered in darkness as the flashlight flew through the air and the light disappeared. She struck the ground and could do nothing but lay there and listen, hoping that Todd was okay, that he would call out for her again, but he never did.

"Todd? Todd, are you all right?" Her eyes filled with tears, as silence crept through the blackness. "Todd? Todd!" she yelled again, but still nothing. And though the silence was deafening and made her want to do nothing but sit there and cower, her hands and feet were untied, and therefore, she was free. Free to find Todd. Free to find her way out of this macabre place.

She reached out blindly, grabbing at the black nothingness before her, hoping to find Todd's flashlight. That hope, however, came to an abrupt halt as a wave of pain surged through her wrist and ankles. The ropes that had bound her were still around her wrist and ankles.

Had she ever been untied?

Had Todd really been there at all?

Kiersten was confused. She had only closed her eyes for a few seconds, but now there was no evidence to support that he had ever been there at all. There was no Todd, no flashlight, and the ropes had never been untied. She wept as she realized it had all been a dream, and yet, there was still something there that was real. It was as real now as it was during her dream. A foul stench.

The dark figure moved through the blackness with ease. It moved swiftly around Kiersten like a rogue shark gearing to strike its prey, yet, it felt tormented at the deed it must do.

That putrid stench, coupled with a sudden and uneasy feeling of being watched, told Kiersten, as in her dream, she was no longer alone.

She knew this, yet she felt even more alone than she had earlier, and more frightened.

"God, please help me," she cried.

Whatever it was made no sound, but it was moving, she was sure of it. Her head moved from side to side, her nose following the raunchy scent. "Please let me go. I just want to go home, please," she pleaded.

The figure heard her pleas, which only added to its torment. Its heart, though pure, was filled with guilt and pain, and was weak to its mind's ravenous urge to kill in order to rid itself of the memories it harbored deep within.

Finally, Kiersten was able to see the vague outline of a human-shaped figure that was blacker than the impenetrable darkness she had been peering into.

"Who are you?" she shrieked. "Please, just let me go. I won't say anything. Please!"

The stench and darker shade of black continue to circle the room as if contemplating its next move.

"I hope you know," Kiersten said angrily and scared with words quivering as they left her lips, "My dad's coming for me, so you better let me go, you sick freak!"

But again, all she heard was a frightening silence.

The creature, the man, the dark-figured freak, or whatever it was, maintained its ghostly silence. It did not utter a single word, or a syllable, not even a grunt. *Could it even talk?* She tried to recall that microsecond of time just prior to being struck on the head and passing out. Though blurry, she thought she had seen a mouth, a nose, and what appeared to be black, cavernous eyes. What she had thought she saw was a dark shadowed face, but—in the end, she just couldn't be sure of anything. But she did remember the smell, the same smell that was upon her now. It was ghastly and reminded her of the time she had found a dead, half-eaten raccoon in her backyard; its flesh had been moldering in the heat of the sun for days. It was the worst smell she had ever encountered—until now.

As cold as she was, she could feel the air around her growing colder. She could see the black man-shaped mass moving slowly towards her.

Kiersten cried out as the dark figure moved even closer in a death-like silence, stopping within inches of her shivering half-naked body. It reached down and grabbed her by the hair, lifting her off the ground with super-human strength. She let out a scream of pain as her body dangled in mid-air, her hands and feet still bound together. She felt a momentary pain explode on the right side of her head, and then nothing, as her body went limp.

3

With fresh flashlights in hand, Sheriff Fortune and Todd pressed on through a thin layer of fog. Their starting point had been the last place they had known Kiersten to be, the place where they had found her handbag.

"So," Todd said, "What do we do now, spread out? Isn't that what they say in the movies?"

"This isn't the movies."

"Don't you think I know that," Todd said in an agitated tone. "I was just asking. You were quick to point out that I don't know jack about this stuff." He paused. "All I want is to find Kiersten."

"I know you do. So do I. And you can bet that Marie is praying that we find her. So yes, we spread out. But I want to be able to hear you breathe.

Joan had her .38 in her right hand, the flashlight in her left, wrists crossed. She tried to keep both eyes glued to Todd as much as possible.

The night was eerily silent. They moved through the woods that seemed devoid of familiar life. All that could be heard was the rustling of the debris beneath their feet, deadened by the fog. The swaying of the trees created moving shadows, sparking a strange and unpleasant sensation of presence that stayed with them as they moved through the woods. In front of them, behind them, in arm's reach beside them, they looked, and saw no one, but the awareness of that presence was mirrored in the hollows of their own faces. Joan began questioning her lack of thought in leaving the second weapon, the shotgun, in her truck. God help them if Todd needed it.

Ninety minutes later, the only thing they had to show for their efforts was thorn snagged clothing and scratched hands and faces. Like Velcro, however, the feeling of being watched still clung to them.

To Todd, Joan said, "We need to be realistic here. With every step we take, we could be destroying crucial evidence. And if we don't…"

"If? What the hell do you mean if?" Todd snapped back. "What, you want to just quit? Leave Kiersten out here? Well, bye. See ya. There's nothing between you and your truck but trees and air. No one's stopping you. But get this," Todd continued angrily, "Don't expect me to disappoint Kiersten again tonight. No way that's happening. I'm not going anywhere."

"That's not what I'm saying, and you damn well know it," Joan fired back, "What I'm trying to get through your thick head, is that there comes a point when we're not helping the situation. I don't want to stop looking. Kiersten is my best friend's daughter. The last thing in the world I want is to stop looking for her."

Silence grew between the two, but their body language, like two mimes, were as loud as clashing cymbals.

Todd, with his flashlight pointing toward the ground, kicked at a rock, sending it further into the woods. The spidery feeling that had invaded his body, moved inside him with an even greater urge to get out.

Joan stood there staring, her patience wearing thin.

"I'm sorry," Todd finally said, "It's just that she's out here, somewhere, close, I can feel it. She's alone and scared. I'm scared that something…"

"Todd, don't even go there. I'm scared too, but we have to believe that she's fine. We have to have faith in knowing that she's a smart kid. I know it's not much, but for now, it's what we have, it's all we have."

Maybe it was her reassuring tone, or maybe Todd was just too tired to argue any further, but Joan could see the change in his eyes. Not that he was giving up, only giving in to the fact that maybe she was right; that maybe with a little luck, and the light of a new day, something would be found that would lead them to Kiersten.

"Listen," Joan said, seeing disappointment looming over Todd's face, "I've already made arrangements to have a search party out here at first light, which isn't all that far off. We'll find her Todd, we will. But right now, we're doing the right thing."

They made their way back to the truck and jumped in. Joan started the engine and turned the truck back towards town. At least that's where Todd thought they were going. Joan turned down Frog Pond Road towards Mrs. Zachary's place.

"Why are we heading for Mrs. Z's place?" Todd asked.

"With all that was going on there earlier, Ed didn't have a chance to cordon off the area. It'll only take a few minutes."

4

The sun would be up in less than an hour's time, and the sky would slowly relinquish its hold on darkness to the first hint of light; the dark figure had to move fast.

It cut free the ropes and tossed Kiersten's limp body up onto its shoulder and started walking. She could see and hear everything, but could not move a muscle as it carried her for miles through the woods, her arms and legs dangling.

The dark figure stopped at an abandoned bridge and dropped her down on the dried creek bed. Kiersten winced as she hit the ground.

Though her eyes were motionless, they were open, and she could see the clothes that she had worn at the time of her abduction. They were now lying on the ground underneath the bridge. They had been neatly folded on top of each other as if sitting in a chest of drawers after a wash. Her boots lay next to the pile of clothes.

A few seconds later, the dark figure again lifted her up by her hair. They were face to face. His eyes were dark and seemed almost lifeless, as if nothing were behind them, yet, somewhere in the midst of all that darkness she saw remorse within them for what it, no, for what *he* was about to do. She, however, could do nothing to stop it. With tear filled eyes, she could do no more than watch as a rope was slipped around her neck. She could feel the noose as he let her body's weight sink deep into the rope. She could feel the noose tighten, could feel the strain on her lungs as they labored for air. In her weakened and exposed state, she could do nothing but stare at her killer as the very essence of life slipped through the fibers of the rope. As her last tear fell, she tried one last time to scream, but all her motionless lips could summon was a last exhale of breath. And as everything went forever dark, death—came for her.

5

It was around 5:00 a.m., when Joan and Todd reached the Zachary residence. Joan parked the truck, and they both jumped out. She radioed in their position and told Ed to head home, which—he rejected.

Joan then pushed her seat forward, and ducked inside the rear cab, reemerging with a roll of police crime scene tape.

"Like I said, this should have been done ear—lier..." Joan's last word dragged through her lips as she noticed Todd was paying her no mind. His attention was directed toward the East end of the property. "Todd, what is it?" she asked.

"Not sure," Todd replied, his eyes glued to the tree line, "I'm having that same feeling again—like we're being watched. It's creeping me out."

"I'm having the same feeling, but there's no sense in letting them know it."

"Them? So you think there's more than one?"

"It's just a figure of speech, now come on."

Joan slammed her truck door and started toward the barn. Todd followed. Halfway there, Joan stopped dead in her tracks and stretched out her arm to stop Todd; it caught him in the chest. Todd shot her a befuddled look, but her attention was on the barn doors that she distinctly remembered Ed saying he had tied shut before leaving. The doors to the barn were now wide open, the rope was gone. A faint stench of death lingered in the air.

"Get back in the truck and lock the doors," Joan whispered.

"But what..."

"But nothing. Move it. Now!"

Todd glared at Joan as he turned to leave. Looking back over his shoulder, he watched as Joan unsnapped her holster and pulled out her .38. She brought it to eye level, her left hand cupped under the butt for support.

Joan turned around momentarily before moving on, only to see Todd standing beside the truck, not inside as he was instructed. She gave Todd a piercing stare, and he finally did as he was told.

Joan crept forward, the stench growing stronger the closer she got. Upon reaching the barn's entrance, she leaned back against the doorframe. Slowly, she reached inside the barn and fumbled for the light switch.

The lights came on and lit up the barn in a reddish tint.

Though the stench was almost unbearable, she resumed the position with the barrel of her gun pointing down her line of sight. She crouched down and slipped into the barn, aiming left, then right, ready to shoot.

The only thing moving, however, was her shadow as she duck-walked further into the barn.

It took Joan a few moments to wrap her mind around what she was looking at. She stood and blinked several times just to make sure her eyes weren't deceiving her. The only time she could ever remember seeing so much blood was nearly twenty years ago while she was still walking the beat as a New York City Police Officer; she was still a rookie at the time. It was a drive-by shooting that ended the lives of seven rival gang bangers and four innocent kids. She did then what she was doing now, standing and staring in disbelief at the grotesque view of all the carnage that surrounded her.

It was a jumbled mess of rabbit legs, torsos, and heads strewn about everywhere. The pieces of rabbits weren't cut apart; the raggedness of the limbs and necks indicated they had been savagely ripped from their sockets and slung aimlessly. The walls, the bales of hay stacked a few feet away from the rabbit pen, and the floor, were all covered with half dried blood and entrails. The closer to the rabbit pen she got, the more blood and gore there was. One glance up toward the light told Joan why the light had not been as bright. It was now covered with dried blood with small pieces of fur stuck to the bulb.

The smell, coupled with the sheer hideousness of what she was seeing, made Joan feel as though she were going to vomit. She cupped her hand over her mouth. At that same moment, something dripped onto the left shoulder of her jacket that felt like rain, only heavier, thicker. She turned and focused her eyes on her shoulder. What she saw was several drops of blood that had fallen from above. Looking up, she saw what appeared to be the hind legs of a rabbit hanging from a nail on one of the rafters.

"My God," Joan said, closing her eyes and dropping her weapon to waist level. "What in God's name would possess someone to be so…" Her voice trailed off.

Todd appeared at the barn entrance. All it took was one quick look at the carnage, and he threw up. The sound caught Joan off guard. As Todd hurled, she snapped around, her gun back at eye level. When she saw Todd hunched over, heaving violently, she let out a sigh of relief and holstered her weapon.

"Damn it, Todd. What the hell are you…" She stopped as Todd vomited again. "You scared the shit out of me. You're lucky I didn't turn around firing."

"I'm sorry," Todd said, wiping off the vomit from his mouth, "But I waited and I didn't see you come out, and…"

"And what? You thought you'd come and rescue me?"

"O.K., I wasn't thinking. But, if something did happen to you, what good would it have done for me to stay in the truck? You have the keys."

"At least you'd be in the truck with the doors locked, where it's safe."

"Safe?" Todd asked. "You don't think that whatever did all this, couldn't break a window and do that to me?"

By the look on Todd's face, Joan knew what his next question would almost certainly be.

"Don't go there, Todd," Joan said, looking away as she talked. "There's nothing to prove that any of this has to do with Kiersten. Nothing."

But Todd had already seen the uncomfortable look on Joan's face. It was a look that displayed more than just concern; it was a look that spoke the words she didn't want to say. She was horror-stricken. It was hard to hide.

"What I need right now," Joan said, "is the camera and the extra roll of film that's in the glove compartment of my truck. Are you up to getting that while I look for something to lock up the barn?" Todd nodded and took off for the truck, returning with the camera. He waited outside while Joan took picture after picture, trying to capture the evil that she knew would be beyond her ability to describe in words. She took thirty-two shots in all. When finished, Joan grabbed the chain and padlock she found hanging on the back wall, turned off the lights, locked the barn doors and placed a strip of crime scene tape across the chained doors.

"Now, the house and then we're out of here."

"But what about Kiersten? Don't you think we should try and find her before whatever did that, finds her first." He said, motioning his hand towards the barn." A brief pause, then, "If it hasn't already."

The worry that had been present in Todd's voice all night was now filled with fear.

"Listen, I want to find her more now than ever, just like you do, but let's be realistic here. After what we just saw, do you really want to head back out there, back into those woods, take a chance of running into whatever the hell it was that did that to those rabbits? Because, I can tell you without hesitation, I don't. At least not without proper backup, and a whole lot bigger gun," Joan said returning her .38 to her holster. "Besides, right now, you're my main priority. I need to get you back safe and sound. We already have one missing teen, and we sure as hell don't need another. Now come on and stay close. We'll check out the house, lock it up, and call it a night."

Todd nodded, and did as she asked. Together, they entered Mrs. Zachary's house through the back door that was now left ajar, not closed and locked as Ed had left it. Everything appeared normal, as Ed had said earlier.

The appearance of normalcy, however, disappeared after they caught a glimpse of the living room. Her love of rabbits that had been so neatly displayed on the walls, on the mantle over the fireplace, and the tables, had now been ripped, shattered and thrown about. Pieces of porcelain, shredded photos and paintings littered the floor.

The one thing that caught Joan's eye, were the two paintings that still hung untouched by whatever evil had ransacked the rest of the room. One was of the Nantucket coastline, and the other, an unknown town in the old west.

"Someone," Todd said, "has a serious animosity toward rabbits."

"You can say that again," Joan said as she snapped off what was left of the second roll of film. "Alright then, we've done what we came to do, so let's lock up this place and go home. It's been a long night, and I feel as tired as you look."

Before leaving, they placed yellow crime scene tape across both the back and front doors of Mrs. Zachary's residence, and a strip across the entrance of her driveway using two trees flanking each side. After tying off the ends, they headed back to town.

Chapter 9

1

At 5:45 a.m., Joan walked into the police station looking like anything but a respected officer of the law. She was tired, and in desperate need of a shower, but knew that was not in her immediate future. She settled for the closest chair, and collapsed into Ed's.

Gage arrived a few minutes after she had taken a seat. "You know," he said walking in, "If you're going to call someone in early, the least you could do is have a fresh pot of coffee brewing."

Joan shot him a look, her left eyebrow raised. "Please Gage, I'm not in the mood for your shit today," she said, sounding every bit as irritable as she looked. She rubbed the back of her neck in an effort to relieve the stiffness that ensued from a tension filled night that resulted in nothing more than disappointment.

She stood then and slowly made her way to her own desk. She leaned over and opened the bottom drawer, pulled out a spare pressed uniform and headed for the bathroom. As she splashed cold water to her face, she thought of the countless missing person cases that had crossed her desk in New York City. Some had been standard everyday runaways, and some had been abducted and utilized in various child pornography rings, or worse, used in human trafficking rings and shipped off to God knows where. She had also had some that had been raped and left for dead, and some raped and flat out murdered, not necessarily in that order. She remembered the tormented faces of the families as she told them of their loved one's fate, each time thinking that it would get easier, but it never did. In fact, it was just the opposite.

But Joan didn't want to think about murder. She wanted to have her vocabulary stripped of the word. But she'd be remiss if she didn't at least think of rape. Kiersten was, after all, a very attractive young woman.

As the word rape permeated through her mind, she realized that she could be faced with the possibility of having to tell her best friend the same type of horrific news. *How hard would that be?*

When she returned, Gage had just finished making coffee. She glared at him briefly and sat down at her desk.

"We're a bit moody today, aren't we?" He said.

Joan was too tired to comment.

"Fine, leave me in the dark. Personally, I like the dark. I find it soothing."

Before Joan could make a comment, the door to the office sprung open. In marched four big, brawny men. They formed a straight line as they came to a stop in front of Gage and Joan.

Each one was decked out in pressed dark blue pants, a light blue long sleeved shirt, and a wide-brimmed dark blue hat. Polished chrome badges that read *Virginia State Trooper* covered the left breast pocket flap of their shirts. Black leather gun belts outfitted with a .45 caliber pistol, two pistol magazine pouches and a pouch containing handcuffs hung from each of their hips.

"Sheriff Fortune?" Randy Hoister asked.

"That would be me," Joan replied. She watched the four men as they exchanged glances with each other as if they weren't sure they were in the right place.

"What?" Joan asked harshly. "Is there going to be a problem with me being a woman?" The four men again glanced at one another. The man closest to Joan spoke up, "Ah, no, Ma'am. There's no problem, and please forgive us, there was no offense intended. We knew that you were a woman." Randy glanced at his men, and then back to Joan, "I'm Randy, Sergeant Randy Hoister of the Virginia State Trooper's office. I'm the one you spoke with late last night."

"And?" Her voice edged toward anger.

"How do I say this?"

"Most educated people would just open their mouth and speak." Joan replied with the same tone.

"Well, to be completely honest, we ah, well—let's just say we had you pictured—differently, that's all. And I, I mean we, apologize if we made you feel at all uncomfortable."

"Oh, please," Joan said and walked to her desk.

The four troopers turned to Gage.

"Don't look at me, boys," Gage said, grinning. "I just arrived myself. Hell, I don't even know why you're here."

Joan returned, holding a pen and tablet.

"They're here because I asked them to be here," she said. "There's a lot going on that you don't know about yet, so all of you need to listen up." Joan's eyes flicked toward Gage for a second, and then back to the four state troopers. "Before I start, let me apologize if I sounded a little harsh. I was out all night searching for a missing teen, a girl named Kiersten Shae. Unfortunately, I didn't have any luck in finding her. So, if you don't mind, let's say we start over, shall we?" They responded with a nod and a yes ma'am.

Joan walked over to the men. The closer she got to them, the smaller she felt. Each one stood more than six feet tall, and they were all well built.

"I take it by the rank on your sleeve that you're in charge?" Joan asked the smallest of the four men, using a friendlier tone. Although he was the smallest, the sandy brown haired, hazel-eyed man still towered over Joan as she stood in front of him.

"I am, Ma'am!" Randy said, "And to my left here is, Ben Stevenson, an excellent tracker. To my right is, Donnie Campbell, or D.C., as he likes to be called. Standing next to him is my younger brother, Tony."

Joan acknowledged each with a quick glance and a nod, writing down their names as Randy rattled them off. She walked back to her desk and dropped off the writing tablet and pen. She turned to face Gage and the four troopers. After taking a moment to gather her thoughts, she spoke with a firm, but receptive tone, "O.K., let's cut through all the formalities. First, let me thank you for your time. Secondly, I know your jurisdiction outweighs a small town sheriff like myself, but I know the town, I know the people, and I know the surrounding areas, so if it's O.K. with you, I'd like to stay in charge and call the shots. I'm sure that any contact made with the locals would be more forthright if they knew I was handling things. Are we agreed?"

"Ma'am, that sounds more than reasonable, unless for some reason the investigation leads us outside your local jurisdiction, then I'd be forced to take over the case."

"Noted," Joan replied. "And one more thing. I would appreciate it if we cut the Ma'am crap—Joan will do just fine."

Joan leaned against her desk, and for a second, said nothing. She was wishing that this whole mess had been nothing more than a horrible misguided nightmare that just seemed real, but it wasn't. It was real, and that made her skin crawl.

Joan swallowed a lump that formed in her throat before she spoke, as she again thought about her best friend's daughter.

"As I said earlier, I was out most of the night searching for Kiersten Shae. She's a sixteen-year-old white female. She was reported missing around midnight, although it has been determined that she has been missing since around 6:00 p.m. yesterday."

Joan took several minutes to fill them in on the events as they had taken place.

When she was finished, several seconds passed in silence, then, "Rabbits?" Tony Hoister asked. "Why would anyone want to hurt an old woman for a few rabbits?

"To be quite honest with you," Joan said, her gaze shifting toward Tony, "we're not quite sure. We haven't had the opportunity to question Mrs. Zachary. She is still unconscious. However, there were four rabbits found yesterday afternoon just outside of her property. They appeared to have been slaughtered and skinned."

Joan felt five pairs of eyes staring at her.

"Now I know that none of this makes any sense, and that dead rabbits in and of themselves aren't all that important. What is important, is that we remain focused on finding Kiersten, and at the same time, remember that there's an old woman with a gash on the right side of her head, and that those rabbits were savagely killed by someone or something that is still on the loose." Joan took a deep breath and added, "That's all I have. So if anyone has any questions, now would be a good time."

"I have a few," Ben Stevenson said, stepping forward. "Are there any leads on the girl? Where was she last seen? Was she having any problems at school? Was anyone taunting her or her family—that sort of thing?"

Joan took another deep breath, and again rubbed the back of her neck. "We have two leads," she replied. "She was last seen sitting outside her mother's antique shop at or around 5:20 p.m. by me. And, we have a handbag—Kiersten's handbag, identified by her mother, Marie Shae, and Kiersten's boyfriend, Todd. It was found last night approximately three hundred yards from her own house. The bag itself has what appears to be a bloodstain on one side. I will be sending it to the state forensic lab in Richmond this morning. We should know the blood type later today, but as we all know, a positive DNA match will take longer. Because this is a missing teen, I'm sending it out as a priority rush and I hope to hear something tomorrow. As far as school goes, she's one of the most liked kids: very personable, not a mean streak in her, so I would have to say that there was no school issues, taunting or otherwise."

Joan answered the remaining questions with short, direct answers. She grabbed the picture of Kiersten from off her desk and handed it to the troopers. After allowing each ample time to look at the picture, they split up into pairs. Randy and his brother, Tony, volunteered to search the northwest section of Milford up around Lake Andrea. The other two, Ben and D.C., took the northeast section, leaving Joan and Gage with the southeast, which covered the area around the coalmines and the Zachary residence.

Joan asked them to report in by radio every half-hour, or if they found anything out of the ordinary.

The four troopers left for their respective search areas.

Joan and Gage were about to head out themselves when Ed walked into the office after taking Todd home. He looked as tired as Joan. "Man, that kid is stubborn––and ballsy too. Can you believe he tried to get me to go back out again? He said he knew I had a .45 and a shotgun. I'm tellin ya, that is one strong-headed kid."

"Thanks for taking him home," Joan, replied.

He walked straight over to his desk and plopped down in his chair. "God, what a long night!" He said rubbing his hands over his face, and yawned. "Is there any coffee?"

Gage poured him a cup. "Just made it." Gage said.

"Thanks." He took a sip. "Anyway, Todd's car is still out front, so if he does want to go back out, he'll have to hoof it to town first. I told his mother to keep an eye on him, and to make sure he didn't leave the house, and if he did, I'd have him arrested."

Chapter 10

1

At 6:30 a.m., an hour outside of Richmond, Virginia, Dr. Brandon Nelson walked down his brick walkway outside of his home located in the Branymill section of the southern Richmond suburbs.

His breath rolled out into the chilled air of the morning as he reached for the paper, after which he hastily retreated back to the warm confines of his house. The automatic coffee maker had just finished brewing a pot of coffee. With the TV droning in the background, he poured a cup as he glanced over an article on the front page about his expert testimony in a murder case the day before. The defendant was copping a temporary insanity plea. Dr. Nelson, a well-known and respected psychiatrist, had been used by the prosecution to rebut the quack hired by the defense.

As he put the paper aside, smirking at the comments made by the defense attacking his character, he heard his home town of Milford mentioned on the morning news. He turned up the volume and listened.

The story involved the sending of four Virginia State troopers to Milford to help in the search of a missing teen, Kiersten Shae. The station had promised to keep updating as information was reported.

At first, Brandon didn't react to the news. But then a memory pricked at his mind of how several teens had turned up missing shortly after he had left the Virginia Mental Institute for the Criminally Insane located just outside of Milford. He had been an intern there 32 years ago. And though the memory still pricked his thoughts, he was convinced that there was no connection.

2

Ed leaned back in the chair, stretched his legs out under his desk and took in a deep breath. "So, Joan," he said, "You radioed in saying that you were going to stop by the Zachary place and cordon it off. Did you have any problems?"

"Problems? No. Will I have nightmares? Probably."

Ed's legs retracted back, and he sat up straight. "What do you mean?"

"Remember that gruesome little scene you happened to find yesterday?"

"Yeah."

"Well, I got you beat a hundredfold."

"What do you mean?"

"I mean that when I got to the Zachary place, I noticed that the barn doors were wide open, just like you said you found them. I remembered you saying that you tied them shut, so I went for a look-see. When I walked in," she paused as a taste of puke crossed her pallet, "God, I'm glad I took the pictures, cause trying to describe what I saw, I mean, the place literally looked like a slaughter house. Someone had untied the ropes, went in, and ripped apart every rabbit Mrs. Zachary had." Joan's words were followed by silence, then, "Oh God, the rabbits—Caitlin..." her voice trailed off as she practically ran to her desk and grabbed the phone. When Jessie answered, Joan told her under no circumstances was she to take Caitlin up to Mrs. Zachary's place, and that she would explain later.

"Joan, you sound scared, what's going on?" Jessie asked.

"Mom, all I can tell you right now is that Mrs. Zachary was injured last night, and apparently so were some of her rabbits. I'll tell you the rest later. Right now I need to get moving, so I'll see you tonight. And Mom," Joan said as a tear fell across her cheek, "Tell Caitlin that I'm sorry, and that I love her."

"She knows that, Joan," Jessie replied.

"Just tell her for me, please, and give her a big hug."

Joan hung up and took a moment to gather her thoughts before returning to face Gage and Ed.

"Everything alright?" Gage asked.

"For now," Joan replied. "My daughter wanted to visit Mrs. Zachary today. She wanted to play with the rabbits. I was supposed to take her myself, but after the news on Kiersten… anyway my mother was going to take her. Thank God I remembered to call and tell her not to. *God what a mess that would have been,* she thought, *her little girl seeing all that blood and carnage.* She shuddered at the thought.

"Why in the hell would anybody want to kill, let alone mutilate, rabbits in the first place? Gage asked "Not to mention bashing an old woman's head in."

"It doesn't make any sense to me either." Ed replied, wiping his hands over his eyes revealing more of his tiredness. He yawned and then asked, "Joan, you said you took pictures?"

"Yeah, although right now I have no desire to see them." She tossed the two rolls of film on Ed's desk. "I need to get them developed."

"Want me to take care of that?" Ed asked.

"No, I want you to go home and get some sleep."

"You sure?"

"Positive."

"Alright then, but there was one other thing I wanted to mention, well, ask really," Ed said just as Charlie Malloy entered the office, whistling *Zippity do dah.*

"Hey there people," Charlie said, smiling. "What's with all the extra activity today? Did yah know u-all had an ambulance down in front of the buildin?"

Joan and Gage looked at Ed.

"Mrs. Zachary isn't doing too well. Coma," Ed whispered.

Silence, then, "Yeah Charlie, we know," Joan replied, "Have a seat. I'll be with you in a minute." Charlie took a seat on the other side of Joan's desk. From there, he could see the EMTs emerge from the building with someone on a stretcher. They loaded the stretcher into the back of the ambulance and pulled away with the lights flashing.

"Now, Ed, you were saying?"

"A name," Ed replied.

Joan's eyes widened, as she wondered why he had not mentioned that last night.

"Well, sort of a name anyway," Ed continued, sounding a little hesitant, "Have either of you ever heard of someone or something called 'Bunnyman'?"

"Bunnyman? No, why?" Joan asked.

"It was the last thing that Mrs. Zachary said to me before passing out. I didn't think anymore about it until just now when you threw the film on my desk. Now that I think back on it, it was like she was trying to tell me who it was that had attacked her. Could be that the same sick-o that slapped her around came back deciding it wasn't enough just to crack open some old woman's head, he had to rip apart a bunch of defenseless rabbits too?"

Charlie, who pretended not to be listening, stood up. He began to pace nervously. The smile and happy disposition that he had displayed when he entered the office was now gone, leaving his face to age dramatically within seconds. He tried to hide his sudden uneasiness by turning his back to them. But Joan had already noticed the change in his mood and in his movement. The change came within seconds of Ed saying the name, *Bunnyman.*

Joan turned back to Ed. "Anything else?"

"Well, now that you mention it, I did mean to ask you about some missing files."

"Missing files?" Joan asked, her eyes again on Charlie.

"Yeah, it's the main reason I headed back out to Mrs. Zachary's place."

"Go on."

"After leaving Jackie's last night, I came back here to try and finish my report. But even after having time to think about what to put down, I was still drawing a blank. I just couldn't wrap my mind around why someone would do that to those rabbits. Anyway, I started thinking about past events. You know—things that happened before the three of us arrived. I was hoping to find something, anything that might have explained what the hell was going on, but all I found was a gap in the files that dated between April of '67, and October of '69. I mean, I know this town doesn't see a lot of action, but come on, there had to have been something, a brawl at Jackie's, or at the very least, some sort of vandalism."

Joan was listening to every word Ed was saying, but her focus was on Charlie Malloy. She couldn't help but notice his persistent agitation. Gage was watching him as well, she noticed.

"And, if you ask me," Ed continued, "That seems a bit strange, don't…"

"Hey, ah, guys," Charlie, muttered, "I've got to, ah, I've gotta run. Besides, u-all are busy, so I'll be a seein ya."

"Hold on there, Charlie," Joan said, hearing fear and distress in his voice. "Don't leave just yet. I've got a job for you. Have a seat and I'll be with you in a few minutes."

Charlie shuffled his way back to the chair. He removed his worn-out ball cap as he sat down. He fidgeted with the cap, rubbing the rim with both thumbs.

"Anything else, Ed, or does that about sum it up?" Joan asked.

"That's it, but what about the files?" Ed countered.

"I'll look into it," Joan replied. "Go on home now and get some sleep. I'll call if I need you."

"Yeah, buddy," Gage said. "Get some sleep, you look like shit."

"Thanks pal," Ed replied. "It's nice to know we can always count on you for your opinion—whether we want it or not."

Joan reached out and patted Ed on the back as he got ready to leave. She then asked Gage to run down and check in on Marie Shae.

After Ed and Gage left the office, Joan glanced for a second at Charlie. He was still fidgety, glancing around the room, shifting his head nervously.

Joan picked up the rolls of film off Ed's desk, and walked over to Charlie, who stood up at her approach.

"Oh, Char-lie," Joan said, drawing his name out. He stood there with his shoulders slumped over and his head down, his hands still fidgeting with his cap. "Charlie," she said again, "Today, you're working for the township."

"Doin what?" he asked.

Though Joan wanted to question him right then and there about his reaction to the name *Bunnyman*, she knew that finding Kiersten was her main priority.

"What I need Charlie, is for you to take this film to the one hour photo shop in Dixon, the one on Madison Drive." Joan put the two rolls of film into Charlie's hand. "I want you to wait for it no matter how long it takes."

"What's the pictures of?" he asked.

"Just some kids vandalizing some property, nothing for you to worry about. Just take the film, get it developed, and come straight back here. Do you think you can handle that?"

"Um, yes, Ma'am," Charlie replied.

"And Charlie, I don't want you looking at the pictures when you get them back. They have nothing to do with you. Is that clear?" Charlie answered with a quick nod. Joan reached into her pocket, pulled out a twenty-dollar bill, and handed it to Charlie. "Here," she said, looking at the old man with suspicious eyes. "This is for the pictures and your gas. Don't forget to bring back the receipts."

Charlie took the money from Joan's hand. He was so nervous at that point, mostly from Joan's penetrating stare, that it took him several attempts to stick his hand into his pocket to put the money away.

"Oh, and Charlie," she said, looking him straight in the eye, "Don't forget to come back. We need to talk—you and I."

"Yes Ma'am," he replied skittishly, his hands shaking as he put on his cap. He then turned away and left the office.

As Charlie left, Gage returned. "What in the hell did you say to Charlie?" Gage asked. "He looks as confused as a newborn at a topless bar."

"Nothing," Joan replied. "Not yet anyway, but I intend to. He seemed way too jittery about what Ed was saying—almost like he knew something, or maybe he had heard that name, 'Bunnyman' before."

"You noticed that too, did you?" Gage asked.

"Kind of hard not to."

"Do you think he knows anything about Kiersten's disappearance?"

"I doubt it. You know how drunks can be, fine one moment, unglued the next. He probably just needs a drink. Anyway, what'd you find out?"

"Well," Gage said, "Ed was right, Mrs. Zachary is in some kind of coma, and is now on her way to Richmond Memorial, and apparently, Marie is still sleeping."

"Let's get moving then. We have a lot of ground to cover." Joan grabbed her gun belt from the safe and buckled it around her waist. Both Joan and Gage grabbed a shotgun and a box of shells before leaving the office.

Chapter 11

1

Caitlin woke to find her Grandma Jessie peering out of her bedroom window. She lay there quietly and watched her. She somehow sensed that something was bothering her grandmother.

Caitlin had always had an uncanny ability to sense things from the first day she was born. Things like whether or not her mom would hear her cry; when her mom would be in a good mood, or a bad one. As she grew, her abilities grew with her. She just started knowing things without knowing why she knew them. And because she didn't know, and because she didn't want to be different, she kept it a secret, never telling anyone, not even her stuffed rabbits.

Caitlin had heard the phone ring earlier and knew that it was her mother saying she wouldn't be able to take her to Mrs. Zachary's. She had so looked forward to going, even dreamt about it. She dreamt of holding the cute cuddly rabbits up to her neck. She liked the feel of the rabbit's soft fur against her skin.

She wasn't, however, upset, or even mad. Caitlin didn't know why the anger wasn't there, it just wasn't. She had a right to at least be upset. Her mother, after all, had promised to take her, but once again, work had taken her away. But that was okay, because Caitlin knew why.

"Grandma," Caitlin said in a soft voice, "its okay. I know Mommy's busy trying to find her."

Jessie turned to Caitlin, surprised at her comment. *Who could she be talking about?* Jessie wondered. Jessie then thought of the phone call she had received earlier. She remembered Joan mentioning how someone had attacked Mrs. Zachary. She also remembered how worried Joan had sounded, scared even. But Jessie couldn't recollect Joan saying anything about someone being missing. Even if there were, how could Caitlin have known, and how would she have known the missing person, if there was one at all, was a female? Jessie had taken the call in the kitchen, and if by some chance Caitlin had not been sleeping, there was still no way she would have been able to hear the conversation. *She may have heard the phone ringing, sure,* Jessie thought, *but the conversation, no way.*

"Whatever do you mean, sweetheart?" Jessie finally asked as she neared her granddaughter's bed. "Find who?"

"I'm not sure of the name. I just know there's a girl missing, and Mommy's going to find her. That's what she does," Caitlin said with a smile. "She'll find her by an old bridge." Jessie sat on the edge of Caitlin's bed. She reached out and brushed back Caitlin's tousled hair.

"Sweetie," Jessie said, sounding a little confused, "I don't know what it is you're talking about. Are you sure you weren't just dreaming?"

Caitlin shook her head back and forth. "Sure, I was dreaming, but not about that. I was dreaming of Mrs. Zachary's rabbits, but. . ." She hesitated. Jessie saw a strange look running across Caitlin's face.

"But what, sweetie?"

Caitlin looked over to her right, and grabbed her little brown stuffed rabbit, Suzanne. She laid it on her stomach, facing her.

"I've seen a lot of different kinds of rabbits," she said, glancing up at her grandmother, "White ones, brown ones, black ones, even spotted ones. But, all the rabbits in my dream, well..." She stopped for a brief second to hold up her stuffed rabbit, "All the rabbits were red. Have you ever seen a red rabbit before, Grandma?"

Jessie stood up as she again remembered what Joan had said about Mrs. Zachary's rabbits, that some had been hurt. What Joan hadn't said, was how bad.

Jessie snatched the rabbit from her granddaughter's hand and tickled her nose with it. "You know how dreams work, sweetie," she said with a broad smile, "They're not real. You probably just saw a stuffed red rabbit while we were out shopping yesterday, that's all." Jessie hated having to lie, especially to her own granddaughter. But what else was she to do? Joan, after all had said that some of Mrs. Zachary's rabbits had been injured. What if some of the rabbits were in fact red—reddened with their own blood. And if Caitlin were by some chance right about the rabbits, could she also be right about the missing girl?

2

Joan and Gage had made good time. Their plan was to cover the woods east of Mrs. Zachary's place. By mid morning they had reached the historic coalmines of Milford; an area Joan had not been all too familiar with. She did know that there were a few rundown buildings around the main mineshaft. They weren't big, but she knew they could be used as a holding area by a kidnapper, or worse, a rapist.

They followed what looked like an old road covered over with layers of leaves, pine needles, and other forest debris that a dirt road has a habit of collecting over time. The road came to an abrupt halt in front of a vine wall that seemed to scale at least ten feet in height. Gage reached blindly into the vines and took hold of what felt like a fence. He pushed the greenery aside revealing a gate. Birds fluttered in the trees as they ripped down the vines that encapsulated the gate. There was a heavily rusted chain hanging loose, but no lock.

"Probably kids," Gage said aloud, "They probably threw the lock into the woods."

"Ya think?"

A screeching sound made the hair on their arms stand up as they pushed open the gate. They could see that the dirt road kept going straight into the woods for several hundred yards before bending hard to the right. Wild autumn flowers lined the path on either side.

"You take the right, I'll take the left," Joan said staring into the woods. Twenty feet in, Joan heard a noise that was all too familiar. Looking up through a gap in the trees she saw a flock of geese flying in the typical V formation.

"Must be nice," she said.

"What?"

"To be able to just pick up and go on a whim, travel carefree, follow the warmth of the seasons."

"Ya think?" Gage said and then snickered.

Joan shot him a look and he turned to continue the search of his side of the road.

The day had turned out to be a spectacular one with the temperature reaching near seventy degrees. The sun was out in an almost cloudless sky with a light breeze whispering in from the West. *A far cry from last night,* Joan thought.

They continued walking their respected sides of the debris-riddled road until it opened up to a vast gap, stopping momentarily to take in the sheer size of what used to be the main source of revenue for their humble little town. They could see three buildings a hundred yards to the left. Just in front of the buildings they could see the train tracks that ran all the way to Richmond. Joan's eyes followed the train tracks in both directions until they disappeared back into the woods where they eventually reconnected to the main tracks a mile or so away. The system, for its time, had been more than adequate.

"I'm going to head up that way," Joan said pointing towards the tracks, "Those tracks make for easy travel through the woods. You check out the buildings."

"You got it."

"And make sure the mineshafts are still sealed. Give me a holler if you find anything."

"You too."

Joan moved methodically along the tracks for almost ten minutes. She didn't want to miss anything. She came to an abrupt halt when she caught sight of a rotting carcass. As best she could tell, it was the body of a rabbit that had been killed in the same fashion as the initial four that Ed had found, and the twenty or more she had discovered in Mrs. Zachary's barn. The stench made her stomach churn. She looked up and scanned the trees hoping for a gust of wind to rid her senses of the smell. Three hundred yards or so away, the sun was pouring through an opening in the trees onto what appeared to be an old bridge.

Coming from a big city like New York, and being of the female persuasion wearing a police officer's uniform, and later, a detective shield, Joan was prone to people looking at her, watching her, or just downright staring. She learned when to worry about it, and when not to. As she was looking toward the bridge, the worried feeling crept in hard and fast. She was being watched by someone or something, and she knew it.

But from where?

Moving forward, she slipped her right hand to her gun and unsnapped the holster. She eased the gun half way out. At that same moment, Ben Stevenson squawked in on the two-way radio. She jumped and had drawn her gun completely out of its holster before realizing what the sound was.

"Joan, this is Ben, over."

Joan answered the call and listened as Ben told her all was clear. Seconds later, Randy Hoister radioed in the same. Joan keyed the mike and told them of her findings.

3

Gage finished checking the three buildings. Other than broken windows, two busted-down doors, rotting furniture, dust, debris, and animal scat on pretty much everything, there were no signs of any recent activity. Next, he made his way to the main mineshaft which appeared to have been sealed shut by way of explosives.

Near the top of the onetime opening, he discovered a hole that appeared to be about one, maybe one and a half feet high by two feet wide. *Just big enough to crawl out of,* he thought, *or into.* Just as he was about to climb up the rocky incline for a look see, his radio squawked. Ben and Randy had kept to the sheriff's orders of checking in every half hour. They reported nothing out of the ordinary. He listened intently as Joan's voice took over the airway telling them about the dead rabbit she had come across.

He looked back up at the opening in the caved in mineshaft as Joan finished her report. "Really Gage, really," he said to himself, "What are you, an idiot? You really want to risk breaking your neck climbing up there?" he paused. "Good. Glad that's settled." He turned and made a beeline for the tracks that led Joan into the woods, grabbing his radio as he did so. "Sheriff this is Gage, over."

"I read you Gage. What do you have?"

"Nothing of interest, well, except for a small opening in the mine; probably caused by the tremor the other day. I'm heading your way."

"Copy that, over and out."

4

Joan holstered her gun and drew closer to the bridge. Her peripheral vision caught what looked like a shadow—*a human shaped shadow,* she thought, swaying in the wind. It was silhouetted against the backdrop of the tunnel wall under the bridge a hundred and fifty yards away.

Joan's pace quickened, but the distance between her and the shadow seemed unwilling to close even though she knew she was moving closer. She stayed on the tracks, unwilling to take her eyes off the shadow. Halfway to the crest of the bridge, she realized why the bridge had to be built in the first place. Glancing down for a second to check her footing, she noticed that while the tracks remained level, the ground had sunk quickly into a gully. She knew that she needed to jump down the embankment in order to get to the base of the bridge.

And she did.

Six feet down.

She landed on her feet, but her momentum caused her to fall forward and roll. She landed hard on her chest and stomach, and for a second, lost her breath.

Once she regained her bearings, she glanced up and saw the silhouette, but in much greater detail. Now, only thirty yards separated her from the base of the bridge. But each yard seemed infinitely longer as she reanalyzed exactly what the shadow was. It was a body—the half-naked body of a young girl dangling by the neck from a rope, her feet just clearing the ground as she swayed. In her heart, Joan knew it was Kiersten.

Ignoring the dirt and debris that was on her uniform, she sprinted the thirty yards left to the tunnel entrance beneath the bridge and stopped.

Her first instincts were to rush over and cut the rope that had been placed around Kiersten's neck. She knew however, that she could not. She crept along the tunnel wall, careful not to disturb or contaminate the crime scene. When she was within an arm's reach of the teen that she had watched grow up for the last five years, Joan turned and fell against the tunnel wall. For the next few minutes, everything around her seemed to move in slow motion.

"Why? For God sakes, why?" Joan yelled, looking upwards to the sky as if asking God for answers. Instead of God, she saw a dozen or more large turkey buzzards perched high on the surrounding tree limbs overhanging the bridge looking greedily down as if they've spotted their next meal. Joan pulled out her gun and fired several shots aimlessly into the trees. "Get the hell out of here." She yelled, and then fired several more shots. And with last shot fired, all that could be heard was the fluttering of wings as the big ugly birds took flight; abandoning the hopes of their feast.

Joan felt paralyzed. She could do nothing more than stand with her arms down at her sides, her gun hanging limply from her right hand, and stare. This ungodly display of violence, that, in her eyes, seemed so disproportionate for a town the size of Milford, made her feel fragile, small, and helpless. She could not believe what she was seeing, could not wrap logical thinking around it. Yet, there it was, the true ugliness of the world staring right back at her in the form of a half-naked teen strung up by the neck, dead. *Dead.* It was that very essence of evil that she tried to get her own daughter, Caitlin, away from; the very reason she moved away from New York City.

Hours ago Joan had shuttered at the thought that she may have had to tell her best friend that Kiersten had been raped. Now she was faced with telling her that her daughter was dead.

Joan holstered her gun and tried to regain her composure. She knew she had to inform the other officers that were out looking for the missing teen, but when she reached for her two-way radio, all she felt was an empty pouch on her belt where the radio had been. "Damn it! Where the hell…" her voice trailed off as she remembered her fall. Her mind raced backwards to another fall she had taken years ago, a fall that had caused her to lose her unborn child. *How frail life was*, she remembered thinking, *and how quickly it can all be taken from you.*

5

Gage followed the train tracks for a couple hundred yards before hearing the gunfire. He stopped and looked around. Joan was nowhere in sight. He grabbed his two-way to try and reach her. She did not answer. He started moving again but with a quicker pace only to find himself stopping when he saw the bridge. He tried Joan again on the radio, but instead of the sheriff, Ben Stevenson squawked in to find out what was going on. Gage thought he could hear a faint echoing of another radio somewhere in the ravine six feet or so down. He looked searchingly into the surrounding woods, but there was still no sign of Joan.

"I'm not sure," Gage answered back. "I've lost sight of Joan, but I can hear her radio, hold on a minute." Gage scrambled down the side of the embankment. "Ben, you have a copy?" Gage asked reaching the bottom.

"Yeah, go ahead."

"Do me a favor and keep talking."

"Keep talking—about what?" Ben replied.

"About anything you damn well please, just keep talking!"

Gage turned off his radio and followed Ben's voice emitting from Joan's radio as he rattled on about how he used to fish up around Lake Andrea. Within minutes, he found the radio lying next to a log covered with dirt and debris. He picked it up and keyed the mike, "O.K., Ben, I've got it, but I still don't. . ." he stopped in mid-sentence when he caught sight of Joan leaning against the tunnel wall beneath the bridge. There was a body hanging only a few feet away. "Oh God, no. Not like this. This can't be…"

"Deputy Gage?" Ben Stevenson asked over the radio, "Is everything okay? Have you located the sheriff?"

"Yes to the sheriff question, and no, everything is not okay," Gage said in a cryptic tone, "Listen, you guys sit tight. I think Joan may have found our missing girl. Over and out."

Gage jogged to the tunnel entrance. When he arrived, Joan was on her knees hunched over and leaning against the tunnel wall, her hands beside her on the ground, her body trembling. Next he glanced up at the body and saw that it was indeed, Kiersten. *Oh, God,* he thought.

"Joan, you all right?" he asked.

"Stay next to the wall," she said.

Gage could hear the despair in her voice. "Joan, I'm so sorry that you had to be the one to find her like this. I know how close you and Marie are." Gage put his hand on her shoulder and gave a gentle squeeze.

She turned and grabbed his hand. "Thanks," was all she managed to say. It was at that moment that she noticed the clothes folded neatly and lying on the ground inches from Kiersten's dangling toes. "Gage," Joan said, "Look, there under the leaves. Those are her clothes!"

"Are you sure?" he asked as he bent down for a closer look.

"Yeah, I'm sure. That's the same top I saw her wearing yesterday on my way home." Gage went to remove the leaves that covered the clothes.

"Don't! Don't move or touch anything. The last thing I want is to contaminate any evidence," Joan said, her voice now cold and hard.

"I'm only moving the leaves."

"I don't care. I don't want anything touched, and that's an order."

Gage stood up. This was a side of Joan that he had not seen before, cold and unnerved.

"Gage," she said in a calmer voice, "Get hold of the other two search parties. Let them know we've found her. Thank them for their help, and tell them I'll forward a copy of the report to their chief as soon as I can."

"Don't you think we could use them up here to help us with the crime scene?"

To Gage, Joan said, "No. I don't want that many people up here stepping on evidence. And," Joan paused, "And I don't want them to see her like this."

She paused again as she tried to collect her thoughts.

"Gage," she said finally, "You're not going to like this, but I need you to go back to town and call the State Police headquarters in Richmond. Tell them to put their best forensics person on standby. Let them know what we have, and that whatever evidence is collected, I want it worked yesterday. Then I want you to pick up Barbara and tell her to dust off her C.S.I kit and get up here as soon as possible."

"Barb's a C.S.I.?"

"She hasn't actually had the opportunity to practice since moving here a few years ago, but she keeps up her State Certified License by attending whatever training seminars are required. She's up-to-date."

Joan stared out into the woods thinking that this shouldn't be happening; that she should be with her daughter right now watching her as she played with Mrs. Zachary's rabbits. "I also need you to tell Barbara to bring a. . ." Joan's voice trailed off as she found the words difficult to say "A body bag, she managed to get out, tears reemerging. "I'm staying here. I don't want to leave her here alone."

"You're right," Gage replied, "I don't like it. The whole thing sucks. I don't like the idea of you being out here alone, especially with the state of mind you're in. Not to mention, that whoever did this could still be in the area. Who knows, he could be watching us right now waiting for me to do exactly what you want me to do, to leave."

I hope so, Joan thought.

"I'm fine," she said, "I'll be fine."

"Yeah, right."

"Damn it, Gage, I said I'm fine."

"Okay, you're fine. But I still don't like it. I have the feeling you're hoping whoever or whatever did this is out here."

Joan said nothing.

"Is that it?"

Silence.

"It is, isn't it? You would welcome a visit from whoever did this, wouldn't you?"

Joan thought about that very question as she glanced at Kiersten's lifeless body. She then turned and glared at Gage. She said nothing.

"I don't suppose there's any way of me talking you out of this is there?" Gage asked.

"Not even remotely."

"I thought not." Gage handed back the radio she had dropped.

Joan's glare turned to a false smile. She put her radio back in place and put hands in her back pockets, saying, "Thanks, and I'm—I'm sorry about the way I snapped at you."

"Don't give it another thought. And just for the record, I still don't like this."

"Noted." Joan replied.

Just as Gage was about to turn and leave, Joan stopped him and asked him that if by chance he were to run into Marie, not to tell her anything. She said she thought it would be best if Marie heard the news from her. Gage nodded and took off.

Ten steps away, Gage turned and watched Joan for a moment. "Joan, if for any reason you change your mind," he said, holding up his radio, "Just give me a holler, and I'll turn around in a heartbeat."

She nodded in response.

After Gage was out of sight, she stood there alone desperately thinking of how she would break the news to Marie. She knew it would be a heart-wrenching task. How do you tell someone that their child, the embodiment of innocence that they brought into this world, had been murdered, killed by a sadistic piece if shit with nothing better to do? In her line of work, this was something she had been trained to do, and it would most certainly not be the first time in which she had to dispense such disheartening news. But in most cases, the husbands, wives, parents, and kids, had all been strangers. This, however, would be the first time she would have to tell a friend, her best friend. In all those times, however, the tradition of life had never seemed more tainted or more ignored then they did at this very moment. By no means was Joan a person unopened to change, but when it came to death, a parent should always pass before a child. In that respect, she was traditional.

Chapter 12

1

Joan sat on a hollowed out log. She was leaning slightly forward with her elbows resting on her knees; her chin resting on her interlocked fingers. As she waited, Joan's thoughts ranged from despair to hatred, and her mind shouted, *I should have done more.* But how? *What?* Everything that could have been done *had* been done. One thing was certain, however, she would make it her life's mission to find whomever or whatever took this precious girl's life.

As she glanced at Kiersten hanging by the neck, Joan could not help but want to get home as fast as she could, snatch up Caitlin, pull her close and tight, and hug her with no thoughts of ever letting go. She could not wait to look her daughter in the eyes and say I love you. Tears sprung from Joan's eyes as she thought about the limited time Marie would now have left with Kiersten before putting her to rest.

Joan wiped her eyes dry. She knew she had to steel her emotions; she had to get back into the game, back into police mode. With that in mind, she reached down and started to pick up sticks she could use to cordon off an area approximately fifty yards in all directions. After walking the perimeter, it was hard for her to believe, and even harder to understand why she was unable to find a single footprint that would serve as an entry point into the crime scene.

While Joan was walking the perimeter a second time, she heard what sounded like a truck pull up and come to a stop somewhere off to her right. A few minutes later, Gage and Barbara emerged from the dense trees.

"There's actually a road that leads up here?" She asked.

"If you want to call it that," Gage replied, "I think it was used a long time ago when the mines were still running. It was a tight squeeze, but we're here."

"Joan," Barbara asked, "How you holding up?"

"You know, fine one second, breaking down the next." There was a slight quiver in her voice.

Joan took a moment. She needed to non-personalize the crime scene; to clear her head for the task at hand. "Okay, Gage, I want you to follow me in towards the body, Barb, you follow Gage. Make sure you stay as close to my footprint as you can. Barb, you know your job, Gage and I will start processing the area. I want no leaf unturned. If you aren't sure of something, ask. Gage, you'll be working the left side while I will work the right. Barb, when you're ready to cut the body down, let me know. Any questions?"

They nodded no and slipped on their latex gloves.

"Then let's get moving, daylights burning."

Barbara followed Gage and Joan carefully. Once there, she sat the body bag and her C.S.I. kit on the ground next to the tunnel wall. She pulled out a digital camera and photographed the clothes and Kiersten's lifeless body from head to toe.

After snapping off the needed pictures, she placed the clothes in an evidence bag and labeled it. Under the clothes she found a gold necklace and a charm in the shape of half a heart. Barbara was sure that the other half was around Todd Chandler's neck. She photographed the necklace and placed it in a separate bag, labeled it, and placed it inside the larger bag with Kiersten's clothing.

Later, when Barb was ready to cut down the body, she asked Gage to retrieve the step ladder from his truck. As Gage carefully backed out of the crime scene, Joan kept processing the area around the body. She found nothing.

While Barb waited for Gage to return, she placed paper bags over Kiersten's hands. Next, she wrapped a clean plastic sheet around the teen. When Gage returned with the step ladder, he placed it in close proximity to the body so that he could reach the rope and cut it about eighteen inches above the noose. Joan and Barbara caught the body and gently placed it in the black body bag. Within the confines of the plastic, Barbara loosened and removed the rope and placed it in a separate evidence bag. She then looked the body over thoroughly before giving the sheriff a brief account of what she thought might have caused the teen's death.

"Well, first impressions would suggest asphyxiation due to the obvious, but these ligature marks around the neck aren't sufficient to indicate that she struggled while the son-of-a..." she paused. "While her killer placed a rope around her neck and left her to hang, which I find highly unlikely.

"You mean highly unlikely unless she were, what, already dead?" Joan asked.

"Well, there's a contusion mark here around the temporal region along with some swelling which could have rendered her unconscious or, if hit hard enough, could have killed her instantly." Barb paused again. "It's possible that she could have been dead prior to being hung, which I have to say, makes no sense whatsoever, but if she were dead prior, there'd be less bruising then there is. I'll know more after the autopsy. I also found no trace of seminal fluid, and there are no signs of forced entry. She wasn't raped. As far as T.O.D., judging from the bodies' temperature and the lividity in the arms and legs, I'd have to say sometime this morning between six-thirty and seven, near sunrise."

Joan nodded and stepped away. "Gage," she said, "Let's go." As Barb finished processing the body, Joan and Gage reemerged in their efforts to finish processing the area that had been previously staked out. Joan was determined to find evidence that would pinpoint the perpetrator's entry point into and his exit point out of the crime scene area. There was none. In fact, the only thing she did find was a slight indentation in the desiccated creek-bed along with what appeared to be a few droplets of dried blood. Joan called Barb over for a second opinion.

"Here," Joan said, kneeling down as she pointed to the disturbed area. "That's blood, right?"

"Let's find out."

Barb photographed the area around the impression in the leaves. She then removed a tube that housed a moistened cotton swab treated with Tetramethybenzidine from her jacket pocket and rubbed it on the suspected dried blood. It immediately turned a blue-green.

"Blood it is," Barbara replied.

But who's?

Next Barb took a small shovel and scooped up the dirt that encircled the dried blood and placed it in a small evidence bag and labeled it.

Joan stood with a perplexed look on her face. "I'm almost positive that something has been dropped here, something heavy." Joan paused. "I'm thinking it was Kiersten, and that blood is hers, probably from the contusion on her head."

"Okay," Barb said, "But do you notice anything else?"

"Yes," Joan said matter–of–factly. "And it's starting to piss me off."

"Why?" Gage asked, "What's pissing you off? What are you two seeing that I'm not?"

"Nothing. That's just it," Joan replied.

"Okay, I'm lost. I don't suppose one of you would mind clueing me in on what it is that I'm not seeing."

"Footprints," Joan said. "Logic would dictate that there would be—should be—footprints. Other than the ones we made, there are none. And if she was dropped here, that means he had to carry her to this point. If that were the case, there would be two sets of the perp's footprints; one coming, and one going. The ones coming would be more prevalent than the ones leaving."

"Why's that?" Gage asked.

"Weight," Joan replied. "Kiersten weighed about hundred and ten pounds. That, plus the weight of the perp should have…"

Silence.

Chilled by what *wasn't* present, Joan looked over the area again. She was looking for signs that the crime scene may have somehow been staged, and then cleaned to hide any indication that anything had taken place; that is, except for the sixteen year old hanging by the neck. She was looking for a plausible explanation as to how someone could have entered the area in question while carrying a hundred and ten pound girl, drop her, pick her up again, hang her, and leave said area without the hint that anyone had been here at all. She saw nothing.

"This is wrong. We're missing something," Joan stated. "No one can be that illusive, and yet, the son-of-a-bitch sure as hell can't walk on water, or in this case, on air."

"What about the bridge?" Gage asked. "Couldn't someone have lowered her down from there?"

"You were up there," Barb replied. "Did you see any evidence to support that? Any rope burns or abrasions on any of the trusses, traces of rope fragments, footprints, anything at all?"

Gage thought about each question as it had been asked. "No to all of the above. And now that I think about it, even if there were, someone would have had to come down here to place the clothes under the body, right? I mean, I can't think of any other way to put them there so neatly, so precisely."

"Good point Gage." Joan said.

"So where does that leave us?" Gage asked.

"Well, let's put it this way," Joan replied, "I've never had a crime where I couldn't find a clue of some kind, so either this guy is a pro and knows forensics, or the son-of-a-bitch can walk on air."

There was a short pause.

"One thing's for sure though," Joan said.

"And that would be?" Gage asked.

"Whoever it was sure as hell wasn't worried about covering up the fact that he dropped the body here, and that's what I can't wrap my mind around. Why cover everything else up but leave this? It makes absolutely no sense.

2

Joan felt a wave of repulsive anger looming within her at what she must now do; tell Marie Shae that her only daughter was dead. She summoned the memories of her own tragic losses, hoping that they would bestow upon her the strength and sensitivity to carry out the task.

They carried Kiersten's body to Gage's truck and laid her gently in the truck bed. Joan sat next to Kiersten's body all the way back to the main road where they had left Barbara's car.

On the trip back, Joan thought about the crime scene. She had the feeling that she was somehow being taunted and mocked by the perp. She couldn't help but think that the answers she needed were right in front of her, hidden in plain sight—unseen—but there nonetheless.

When the truck came to a stop, Joan jumped off the back. "Where's Marie at now?" She asked, her stomach churning.

"When she woke up," Barbara answered, "she wanted to go home, so I drove her there. I hope that was alright. I gave her a mild sedative to take later in case she had trouble resting."

"Its fine," Joan said, flicking her eyes to Gage. "That's where I want you to drop me off."

"Are you sure you want to tell her alone?" Gage asked. "I don't mind hanging around for support if you want."

"No. I need you to make sure Charlie made it back. Barb, you don't mind if we take your car, do you?"

"No, that's fine. You should know," Barbara said, "That the autopsy is going to be done at the Dixon City Hospital. I've already made arrangements for transportation to take her there, and I called in a favor from an old friend. She's one of the best. She'll be waiting for me when I get there."

"Thanks," Joan said, smiling gratefully. "Just make sure those photos, the clothes and the rope get to the forensic lab in Richmond, today. Have Ed drive them if you have to. Make sure they check the clothing for sweat. The bastard carried her in from quite a distance. He may not have left foot prints, but he damn well had to have worked up a sweat. Tell them I would appreciate it if they get back to me as soon as you can, day or night."

Barb nodded in concurrence to Joan's requests, and then signed for and took the forensic bag full of Kiersten's belongings.

Chapter 13

1

After being dropped off at Marie Shae's house, Joan found herself standing in the driveway. She felt completely frozen and awkward in knowing that her own daughter was home safe and sound, yet, she found comfort in it. She found herself wishing she were anywhere but there, or at the very least for any other reason than the one she had come with.

She cast her eyes on the front door and then to the picture window. Nothing seemed to move. Silence had pooled so deep that she not only felt her heart pounding hard and rapid, she could actually hear it. *Thump thump. Thump thump*, beating faster and faster.

She walked toward the front door, slowly at first, then, like her heart beat, more rapidly.

Joan knocked on the door and waited. A tear sprung as she thought of the helpless feeling Marie was about to face, the heartbreak and grief that was about to be thrust into her world.

Marie opened the door with full anticipation of seeing Kiersten standing on the porch. But as the door swung open, all she saw was the mournful look on Joan's face. "Where's Kiersten?" She asked as a wave of uncertainty coursed through her body. "Where's my daughter?" She turned her head quickly toward the driveway, but Joan's truck was not there, and the hope that darted through her mind that Kiersten had been, for whatever reason, arrested and was sitting in Joan's truck, faded. She glanced back to Joan looking for answers.

It was difficult for Joan to look her best friend in the eye. She could see that the hope, however slight, that Marie displayed as the front door opened, had quickly disappeared.

Marie eyes glazed with tears "Well, where is she? Where's my daughter?"

Joan lifted her tear-filled eyes to Marie's. Marie started trembling. "Joan, you're scaring me. What is it? Is she hurt? What? What the hell happened?"

"Marie, there's no easy way to..."

"No! I don't want to hear that you can't find her, or that you're giving up. That's not what I expected from you, Joan," she said tersely. "I thought you were the kind of person that didn't give up—on anything."

"Marie, I need you to listen to me now," Joan said. "I hate to have to be the one to. . ." She paused momentarily in an attempt to draw upon her inner strength. *Dear God, help me,* she pleaded silently. "We did find Kiersten, this morning, but we didn't get there in time. I'm sorry. God, I'm so, so sorry."

Marie's tear filled eyes widened. A cloud of disbelief racked her mind. *Surly this can't be happening,* Marie thought, *not to my Kiersten, not to me, not to our family.* Her lower jaw gaped open as if she was about to let out an ear splitting scream, but nothing came out. To Joan, it was like looking at her friend in a soundproof room.

Then the scream came. It was one of sheer, heartbreaking pain. Her knees buckled, but Joan caught her and held her steady.

"How could you let this happen?" Marie asked. "You were supposed to protect her. You're the police for crying out loud!"

Then, out of nowhere, a sudden change took over Marie. "No! No way. I don't believe you. Where is she, really? Did she put you up to this? She did, didn't she? Always trying to be clever."

Joan grabbed Marie firmly by the arms as she continued to rant and rave.

"I'm sorry Marie, but she didn't put me up to anything. She's dead. Your daughter is dead. I'm so sorry."

Joan walked her into the kitchen and sat her down at the kitchen table.

"How?" Marie asked, her voice cracking, "How did it happen? How did my little girl die?"

"I don't think this is the right time to..."

"Will there ever be a right time? Tell me. Tell me now, damn it. I have a right to know how my only child died."

Joan walked away from the kitchen table. She hadn't wanted to get into the particulars until Marie had more time to absorb the devastating news. To tell her now that her daughter was murdered could quite possibly throw her over the edge. But as Joan thought about it; she knew that if the roles had been reversed, she would want to know.

"She was hung."

Marie's eyes widened further. "Are you—are you telling me she committed suicide?

"No! You know she would never do that. Kiersten was murdered."

"Oh God," her hands briefly covered her mouth. "Where?" Marie asked, sobbing hysterically, "My God, where?"

"About a quarter-mile from the coalmines, under the old train bridge."

"Why the bridge? Why that place?" Her questions were underlined by a short pause, "Please tell me you know who did this. Tell me that you'll catch the son-of-a-bitch. I want to see him burn in hell for what he's done."

Joan knelt down beside Marie. She wrapped her arms around her, and held her friend close. She wanted so desperately to tell her that they had a lead; that they did indeed know who the killer was. But she would only be lying, and that she didn't want to do—not now—not to her best friend.

"All I can tell you Marie, is that we, that I, will personally use every resource available to catch and punish the person or persons responsible. I don't care how long it takes."

"I just, I just don't understand," Marie stammered, her head leaning on Joan's shoulder. "I used to tell her never to play around up there. I had always told her that it was too dangerous."

"She wasn't playing around up there. Whoever did this, abducted her, probably from where you and Todd found her handbag."

"I know. I know she wouldn't have gone up there, not alone anyway. It just seems odd that the one place I told her never to go is. . ." Marie took a ragged breath, "is the place she was killed."

"Why would you say that, Marie? Had something happened to her there before?"

"No. I just didn't like her playing that close to the mines, so I used a story that I got from Charlie Malloy. He told me about the place five, maybe six years ago."

"Told you what, exactly?" Joan asked, trying to downplay hearing Charlie's name.

"He said something bad had happened there once, and that…" She paused.

"And that, what?"

"He said the place was haunted."

"Haunted? Haunted how? Haunted by what?"

"I don't know, just haunted," Marie said, her voice wavering. "Of course, I didn't believe him, but, like I said, I didn't much like the idea of her playing around up there anyway, so I told her the story. It worked too because she never went back, at least not that I'm aware of."

Silence filled the room as Joan comforted Marie. As Joan held her, she started thinking about Charlie and what his role was in all this. She knew he wasn't the party responsible for Kiersten's death, but he certainly knew something.

"Marie," Joan said, releasing her hold so that she could look at her face to face, "I don't want to overstep my bounds here, but would you like me to contact your ex for you?"

Marie grabbed a paper towel to dry off her tear-streaked face.

"Do what you want," she replied in anger. "I haven't heard from the son-of-a-bitch in eleven years. I kept track of him though, for Kiersten's sake. Go ahead, call and tell him. Tell him he doesn't have to worry about child support any more, not that he ever did, but I'm sure it will make him happy just the same. He probably won't remember that he even had a daughter."

Marie left the room abruptly and returned carrying an index card with her ex-husband's phone number on it. She handed it to Joan, saying, "If you think the bastard would want to know, then you can go ahead and call him. As much as I hate him, he was her father."

Joan took the card and slipped it in her shirt pocket.

"Joan," Marie asked, "Can I see her? I need to see her. I need to see my baby. Please?"

"Are you sure you're ready for that?"

"I have to be. I never got the chance to say goodbye. You think you have all the time in the world to say things, and then you don't. It's taken away from you." Marie paused and looked up at Joan. "I really need this Joan. I need to tell her that I loved her, will always love her, and to say goodbye. Please don't deny me this. I'm begging you." Joan knew better, but she also knew that Marie had a right to I.D. the body.

"Let me make a phone call. I'm not making any promises, but—I'll see what I can do," Joan said.

"Thank you, Joan. Thank you."

Joan called the hospital in Dixon to find out how things were going. Much to her surprise, Barbara told her that they would have the preliminary autopsy done in about an hour. Joan then called Gage at the Sheriff's office to find out if Charlie Malloy had made it back. Gage informed her he had. "Where's he at now?" Joan asked.

"I saw him staggering out of Jackie's. The waitress, Faye, had to help him out. She said he was fighting with a bottle of Captain Morgan's Rum, and the rum won. I'm holding him for being drunk and disorderly; he's sleeping it off in one of the cells as we speak."

"All right then, sounds like you have things under control."

"I try."

"Have you heard anything from the crime lab yet?"

"No, but I'm sure it won't be much longer."

"Call me when you do."

Joan hung up the phone and returned her focus to where it was needed most, to her friend. She was still debating over of the idea of letting Marie see her daughter's deceased body. At least it wasn't a decision she had to make right away; the coroner said it would take another hour.

Joan glanced over to Marie, "Well, we won't know anything for a while yet."

"I don't understand why I can't see her now."

"Because the coroner hasn't finished with her yet. What I want you to do until then is lie down and get some rest."

"Rest? You tell me that my daughter has been murdered, and you expect me to rest?"

"I expect you to try. Barbara said she gave you a mild sedative to take if you had trouble falling asleep. Where is it?"

"On the counter."

Joan retrieved the pill, a glass of water, and followed Marie into the living room. Marie took the sedative and sat down on the sofa. The sedative didn't take long to work. Marie was already exhausted and the extra push of the sedative was all that was needed. She drifted off into a restless sleep.

2

After arriving home, it didn't take Ed long to fall asleep. He didn't even make it to his bedroom; he walked through his front door and sat down in his recliner for a second. That second ended four hours later when he woke to a grumbling stomach. He had not eaten since the night before at Jackie's. He poked around the kitchen for something to eat. All he could find was an overripe banana, which just about melted in his hand as he picked it up, and two slices of leftover pizza from three days ago. The pizza won. Ed washed the pepperoni and cheese pizza down with a glass of milk. He wanted a beer, but he knew if he had one, another would follow.

After eating, Ed called the sheriff's office to find out how things had progressed since he had left. Gage informed him of Kiersten Shae's death. After all the time Joan and Todd had spent looking for her, to think that she was less than two miles away from the area they had searched, and only a mile away from the Zachary residence.

Ed hung up the phone and collapsed back into his recliner. His first thought was of Marie and how she was going to handle the tragic news. His next thought was of Todd.

Had he been told?

Ed picked up the phone and called the office back. Gage answered again. "No, don't think he knows yet. Joan's with Marie now, the poor thing. I sure wouldn't want to be in Joan's shoes right now, I can tell you that."

"Better hers, than Marie's."

"You got a point there."

"Anyway," Ed said, "Someone ought to tell him."

"Are you volunteering? Because I sure as hell don't want that detail either. Besides, Joan just called and asked me to keep an eye on Charlie Malloy."

"I guess that leaves me." Across the phone line, Ed sighed. His heart was heavy with sorrow. "I'll—head over in a few," Ed said solemnly and hung up the phone. He went to his bedroom, took off his uniform and threw on a pair of jeans and a Harley Davidson T-shirt, jumped into his truck and took off.

The sun radiated golden rays across a clear blue sky that offered a perfect day to do just about anything—anything that is, except telling someone a loved one is dead.

Ed parked in front of Todd Chandler's house. His palms were sweaty. As he walked up the cobblestone walkway, he saw Todd's mother, Vanessa, come out onto the porch to greet him.

"Hi, Mrs. Chandler," Ed said. "How's Todd doing today?"

"Still sleeping, I hope," she turned to look through the screen door.

"Have you got news on Kiersten?" she asked.

"I'm afraid so, and it's not good."

"Is she hurt? Is she in the hospital?"

"I'm afraid it's worse than any of us could have imagined."

"God no, don't tell me. . ." her voice faded.

"Joan found her around 11:00 a.m. I haven't seen her yet, but Deputy Gage says that it looks like she had been beaten up pretty bad, and then, for whatever reason, the bastard hung her by the neck out at the old Train Bridge."

A loud thump came from inside the house. Vanessa and Ed rushed in and found Todd on his knees.

"No! No!" Todd yelled, shaking his head. His tanned face had turned white as if all the blood in his body had just vanished, leaving behind an empty white shell. "Oh God, please don't let this be happening." Todd's teary eyes turned toward his mother's, "Mom, please tell me this isn't true."

Vanessa knelt down and wrapped her arms around her son, bringing him close. "I'm so sorry, sweetie," she said as she stroked his hair. Todd threw up his arms and scrambled to his feet.

"She's not dead, she can't be. I—I can still feel her—I. . ." his voice trailed off as he glanced at the deputy.

"I'm very sorry, Todd," Ed said. "You know you and the Sheriff did everything humanly possible last night to find her, you have to believe in that. Her death is not your fault."

Todd dropped his head. "But it is. If I'd only been there on time," he said, tears tracking down both sides of his face.

"Todd, you don't know that. For all we know, if you had been there, you both might be dead."

"It's just that, that. . ." Todd wiped the tears from his eyes and said, "I want to see her. I need to see her. And I'm not taking no for an answer!"

Ed hesitated monetarily, "Okay, I don't like it, but if it's alright with Mrs. Shae, then I'll take you. Fair enough?"

Todd thought about it, and then nodded.

Ed put his hand on Todd's shoulder. "We'll get the bastard responsible for this, Todd. I can promise you that."

3

Joan continued to watch over Marie as she slept, just as she said she would. She still had doubts about taking Marie to the Dixon City Morgue. To Joan, it was the last place and yet, the first place she needed to be.

While Marie slept, Joan wandered around the house from room to room looking at all the pictures of Marie and Kiersten; her eyes filled with tears as she felt the closeness the two had shared.

Joan vowed that when this mess was over, things would change. She would spend as much time with her own daughter, Caitlin, as possible. She would make the time; take more time off if need be. Whatever it takes, she would be there for her.

Marie's house was spacious and full of light. Outside, the three-bedroom rancher was surrounded by impeccable flower gardens. Joan wondered how a single woman could run a business in town, raise a sixteen year old, maintain a house, and still find time to plant and weed a flower garden.

Joan turned back to the sofa as she heard Marie stirring. She walked to the Queen Anne chair across the room and sat down. As she continued to watch over Marie, her mind turned back to Kiersten's murder, and back to Charlie Malloy.

She asked herself the question, *who could have done it and why? And why was it that Charlie Malloy's name kept popping up?* She did not think that he was directly involved with the killing, but he knew something. There was just something about Charlie's immediate change in demeanor at the mere mentioning of the name *Bunnyman*. He became fidgety and out of sorts. It was a name that meant nothing to her, or to her deputies. But it obviously meant something to him.

Joan's eyes turned to Marie as she laid there sleeping. She was tired herself and laid her head back in the chair. Her eyelids felt as though they were anchors ready to be dropped at any moment. Several times she jolted her body awake as it tried to slip into a restful sleep. Finally, however, she succumbed to fatigue.

When Joan opened her eyes, she was no longer in the living room watching over her friend. She was still sitting in the Queen Anne chair, only she was in the middle of the woods.

The sun was out and shining as bright as it ever had. The sky was as blue as she had ever seen. A gentle breeze blew from the east, sweeping with it, the heat of the sun off her skin.

From the moment she had opened her eyes her attention had been drawn in the direction of the incoming zephyr. Something was calling to her in unsaid words, trying to lure her, bidding for her to move towards the source of the soft, alluring, wordless invitation. For whatever reason, she did.

4

A few minutes after five that evening, Caitlin came in from playing outdoors. She had spent the better part of the afternoon with Renee Hoberton, her best friend from school who lived just down the road about a quarter of a mile. Caitlin had been trying to teach Renee the intricacies of the modern day water gun fight. They both lost.

Renee was not much to look at; sporting a lanky build that even for a nine-year-old was shapeless. She had shaggy red hair and freckles to match. In fact, she was downright homely.

For such a young, unattractive girl, however, she displayed a very pleasant and happy disposition.

That wasn't always the case, however. It wasn't until Caitlin moved to the area that Renee seemed to transform. Caitlin could do that for people, unknowingly of course, but there was something that just seemed to rub off of her and onto the people around her, giving them a serving of self esteem or whatever was lacking in their lives.

Renee's mother picked her up at five. Caitlin waved good-bye and headed for the house as they pulled away.

Jessie laughed at the sight of her granddaughter when she entered through the front door. She was dripping wet from head to toe. "I didn't know it was raining," she said smiling. Caitlin smiled. Her perfect dimples lit up a drenched face.

"Grandma," she said, "you're just being silly."

"Maybe so, sweetie, but I'm an old woman, and I'm entitled. What I'm not entitled to," she continued as she wrapped her arms around Caitlin, "Is having you look like a drowned rat when your mother gets home." Jessie leaned down and kissed the top of her granddaughter's head and added, "Now run along and take a long warm bath." She patted Caitlin on the fanny as she scooted off down the hall. "And don't forget to wash behind the ears!"

Jessie heard the bath water running. Gentle splashes told her that Caitlin had gotten in the tub. That was why she was startled when she looked back towards the bathroom to find Caitlin standing right in front of her. "Oh, gosh," she exhaled, "I thought you were in taking a bath."

"I am," she said in an almost trance-like state. "When Mommy calls, tell her I'm fine and that I'm glad she found the girl."

"What?"

"She will call, and when she does, she'll be worried about me."

Jessie turned to the phone and then back to Caitlin, only Caitlin wasn't there, and then she heard the familiar splashing in the tub.

5

Before Joan knew it, she was deep into the woods. The sky was no longer blue, and the woods were dark, dense, and haunting. A tempest wind buffeted past her body, but the trees around her lay as motionless as sand in an hourglass whose time had run out. As she continued, everything around her seemed to be swallowed up by the darkness, yet, she did not need a light to see her way; it was as if she knew every step to take to avoid tripping.

Joan kept moving in the direction of the voice, a voice that now seemed to demand her presence. It ultimately led her to a light. The light itself was enticing and was perched on the center trusses of an old rusty, moss-covered bridge that lay against the backdrop of shear blackness. The light seemed to change to a shadow as she moved nearer to it. The shadow seemed to have a feeling of familiarity about it, and she was unable to remove her eyes from it. Not once did she blink.

Joan moved closer, and at ten feet, as if on cue, the shadow began to change to something that now looked three dimensional, and real to the touch. *It must have been real all along,* Joan thought.

The true shape of the form revealed a half-naked body of what appeared to be a young girl hanging by the neck, facing in the opposite direction in which Joan had been walking.

But why was she dragged out here to find it?

What force gave her the sight to see into the blackness that surrounded everything around her except the bridge, the body, and herself?

What was it that demanded her presence?

And whose body was it?

Joan reached out her hand to touch the right arm of the body. She stopped as she realized the skin looked almost transparent. She inched her hand forward and felt the skin. It was cold, damp, and felt like it had been there for weeks. It also felt like her finger would go through the decaying flesh if she poked it too hard.

The air around her had suddenly filled with the stench of death. She spun the body around to reveal the face of the young teen. The first thing she noticed was that the girl was with child. The skin around the abdominal area was so stretched out it was like looking through a gossamer fabric sack. Inside lay a motionless baby whose facial definitions were so detailed that Joan had known straight off whose baby it was. It was like looking at a picture of her deceased husband John right after he had been born. The baby was hers, hers and John's. *But how could that be? And who was this teen that carried it in her womb?* When she saw that it was her best friend's daughter, she dropped to her knees. Then came the voice, a voice that was all too familiar—a voice that sent shivers flowing down her spine.

Joan looked around, but saw no one, she looked up at Kiersten's face, but it hung there motionless. She then looked at Kiersten's womb, to the baby inside. In the blink of an eye, the facade of the baby's face changed from her unborn child, to that of her adopted daughter, Caitlin. Joan was just about to scream, when the baby's eyes flared open and the words, "Mommy," murmured out of the baby's lifeless, purple lips, "It's just a dream, Mommy. Don't be afraid."

At that moment, a sensation buffeted past Joan which startled her awake. She sat up quickly in her chair, safely back in the living room across from her friend. She was not quite sure of what had just taken place, only that she must have had a dream, one that caused the hair on her neck to stand on end, leaving her with a strange and deep sense of unease.

She fought to try and remember the contents of the dream, but the images were cloudy and distorted, as if they were hidden deep in her mind.

As she stood, the room was suddenly overwhelmed with the scent of shampoo. She looked around the room for a scented candle, or a potpourri dish, but could see nothing that would have given off the smell. The scent was strong. It was as if she had a bottle of shampoo in her hand and had it positioned perfectly beneath her nose. And it wasn't just any shampoo. The scent was familiar—it was the same scent that she had always bought for Caitlin, *Johnson's Baby Shampoo*.

Her hands shook as she reached for the phone. After two misdials, she finally reached her own house. Her mother Jesse picked up the phone in a controlled nothing is wrong tone. "Where's Caitlin?" Joan asked, willing her hands to stop shaking.

"Whoa, this is weird," Jessie said, "Caitlin said you would call. She said you'd be worried about her. Joan, is everything all right?"

"Where is she now?"

"She's taking a bath. Why? Is there something wrong? Did you find the girl?"

"Girl?"

"Yeah, Caitlin said you would find the girl near an old bridge. I'm afraid I don't know what she's talking about. Do you?"

Joan hesitated, knowing this wasn't the time or the place to discuss this matter. But question after question popped into Joan's mind as to how her daughter could have possibly known that she would call her, not to mention how Caitlin knew about the dead girl, let alone that she would be found at a bridge. "Mom, would you please just go and check on her for me?"

"Yeah, sure sweetie. Just hold on a sec."

The wait seemed endless.

Jessie's voice came back on the line, "She's fine. She's taking a nice long bath."

A feeling of complete relief rushed through Joan's body, and the shaking stopped, but the questions did not. It wasn't, however, until Marie stirred again on the couch, that Joan's thoughts broke free of Caitlin.

6

By the time Joan finished preparing the toasted cheese sandwiches and perked a fresh pot of coffee, Marie had awakened from her nap and walked sluggishly into the kitchen. Joan poured a cup, and handed it to her.

"Have you heard anything yet?" Marie asked wrapping both hands around the hot coffee cup, cradling it as if to absorb the warmth.

"I'm afraid not," Joan replied, "but it shouldn't be much longer."

Marie spotted the sandwiches sitting on a plate next to the stove. "Joan, I hope you didn't make those for me. I feel like I'd throw-up if I ate anything."

"Can you at least try?"

Marie didn't know how she'd ever be able to eat anything ever again. At this point, she didn't care whether she lived at all.

Chapter 14

1

Frankie Kaminski and his two brothers, Eric and Ryan, had been playing in the woods for hours. A teacher's conference gave them the day off from school. And what a beautiful day it turned out to be. What more could three rambunctious kids ask for?

Their mother, Jean, wanted nothing more than a little peace and quiet, which meant that her three crumb-snatchers, as she lovingly called them, needed to get out of the house.

"The three of you are getting on my last nerve with all that noise. Take all the energy outside. I don't want to see you till dinner." Their mother had told them.

So they did.

The boys immediately began a game of Hide and Seek. Always fighting as to who would be the first seeker, they decided to draw sticks. Frankie lost and was designated the first seeker.

Boundaries had been set. No crossing the street, which was more of a Mom rule than a boundary, Mrs. Zachary's barn to the east, the creek to the south, and the Smith's place to the west.

Frankie leaned his face up against a tree with his forearm between the tree and his head. Sixty seconds was what he had to count to before tearing off after his siblings. Upon reaching ten, he peeked under his arm just to see which direction they were heading in.

"Fifty-eight, fifty-nine, sixty. Ready or not, here I come." Frankie shouted at the top of his lungs.

They played for hours, each taking a turn as the seeker. As the afternoon whizzed by, they continued, ignoring the time until the sun started setting behind the tree line to the west. "We've got time for one more game before Mom calls us for dinner." Frankie said. "I'll be the seeker."

Once again, he leaned against the tree and started counting. Ryan and Eric took off. This time they headed for Mrs. Zachary's place.

Ryan had trouble keeping up with his older brother, but every hundred or so feet, Eric would duck behind a tree to look back, trying to see if Frankie was coming. When the coast was clear, and just as Ryan had caught up, he would take off again.

When Eric reached Mrs. Zachary's barn, the first thing he noticed was the bright yellow tape stretched out across the entrance. It stood out prominently against the weather beaten barn. Though he could not yet make out the wording on it, he had an idea of what it was and what it was used for.

"Look," Eric said, pointing toward the barn as Ryan caught up with him. "Something has happened here. That yellow tape looks like the stuff police use on TV"

"Cool," Ryan said as he darted toward the barn. He stopped, however, as he passed by Mrs. Zachary's house. He had noticed the same tape across her back door.

Eric walked up behind him a few seconds later. "Man, what do you think happened?" he asked.

"I don't know," Ryan said.

In the awe of the moment, they took no notice that Frankie had all but caught up with them.

"I see you!" Frankie yelled, coming to a stop, waiting to see which way the two would bolt. But they didn't. They turned around and motioned him to come over. Frankie, however, wasn't biting on the possible trickery he thought the two might have scammed up.

When Eric saw that he wasn't coming, he waved him off and darted toward the barn. That's when Frankie noticed the tape and realized that the two weren't up to anything.

Frankie jogged toward them and caught up with his two siblings in no time. The three scampered to the rear of the barn, cautiously looking for police who they suspected wouldn't like them playing around the area. With no cops in sight, they inched toward the front. When they reached the two large barn doors, they saw that they had been chained and locked shut. There was no possible way they were getting in to see why the police had to seal off the area. Ryan expressed his unhappiness by kicking the barn doors.

He just had to know why it was taped off.

His wheels were spinning in overdrive, trying to figure out what was inside that the police didn't want anyone else to see.

"Wait," Ryan said, remembering the window on the side of the barn, "Follow me."

His two older brothers did as he requested. "Maybe we can get in from there," he said, pointing up to the window that was every bit of five feet off the ground. "Or at least have a look inside."

"It's too high, idiot," Eric said sharply.

"No, it isn't," Ryan countered as he thought about the bales of hay behind the barn Mrs. Zachary used for her rabbit pen. He walked to the rear of the barn and stopped. "We can use these," he said, pointing. Frankie and Eric both walked over to see what their punk brother was talking about.

When they saw the hay, at the same time, they both said, "You ain't half as dumb as you look." Ryan flipped them the bird, and then tried to pull the first bale of hay around into position under the window.

"Come on, Eric," Frankie said, "let's give this girly-boy a hand."

Ryan stopped, scowled at them, and then continued.

Within minutes, three bales were in place, two bales in front of the window, and the third stacked on top of the first to form a makeshift staircase. Eric and Ryan tried to get up at the same time. Eric, being bigger, of course, won and knocked Ryan down onto his tiny rump.

"I'm first," he said, glaring at his younger brother.

"You're first, all right," Ryan spouted. "You were first in line when God was passing out brains too, but you thought he said trains and passed, you big dork."

Frankie stood back, shaking his head as the two exchanged comebacks. Eric continued his glare. He wanted to jump down and smash Ryan in the mouth, but he was just as intrigued about why the barn was surrounded by the yellow tape as Ryan.

He turned his head away from Ryan. He put his hands up against the glass to shade the sun from his eyes. Inside, the barn was dark, but after a few seconds, his eyes became acclimated to the low light within. He began to see a reddish color staining the floor near the rabbit pen.

And as his eyes continued to adjust to the light, he saw pieces of what looked to him like rabbit parts thrown all over the place.

"Oh crap!" He said, his eyes widening."

"What?" Frankie asked. "Come on, Eric, what do you see?"

Eric jumped down with a stunned look on his face.

"What?" Ryan asked.

"I think you should have a look for yourselves," Eric said peering into the woods—for what, he didn't know.

Ryan jumped up next. He had to stand on the tips of his toes to see. "Cool, there's blood —like everywhere."

"Let me see!" Frankie yelled.

Ryan jumped down and Frankie took his place. "Man, that is gross," he said, and then jumped down.

For the first time all day, the three were not fighting with each other; they were fighting with their imaginations, scaring themselves in the process.

"I think it might be a good idea for us to get the H-E- double toothpicks out of here, and fast," Frankie said.

"What about the blood?" Ryan asked.

"What about it?" Eric fired back.

"What if it's…," Ryan paused, swallowing hard, and finished his question "What if it's Mrs. Zachary's blood?"

"If it is," Frankie said, "The police already know about it." There was a short pause, then, "I still vote we scramble out of here," he added looking around the area. "Anyone want to argue?"

"Nope," the other two brothers said in unison.

"Good. On the count of three, we turn and we run as fast as we can. We don't stop for nothing. Got it?"

"I'm scared," Ryan said.

"Me too," Eric added.

"Then that makes us the three scared Musketeers." Frankie said

As the sun gave in to a broodingly dark night sky, Frankie started the count, "One."

Lurking in the woods among the dark shadows of the tall spruce pines, a dark shrouding presence moved across the sloping forest floor. The stealth presence moved in on the three boys like a lion moving in on its targeted prey.

"Two."

On the count of two, the three turned and faced the direction in which they intended to run.

Around them, unnoticed by the three young kids, the sounds of the forest had vanished, replaced by almost complete silence. The robins and cardinals singing, gone—the chirping of crickets, gone—the croaking of bullfrogs from neighboring ponds, gone.

To an adult, it would have seemed strange, but to a nine, ten and a twelve-year-old, things of importance usually went by unnoticed, especially after seeing the gruesome scene inside Mrs. Zachary's barn.

What didn't go unnoticed, however, was the foul, wretched smell that seemed to have come out of nowhere.

One hundred yards away, a presence moved in closer and closer to the three kids, staying within the boundaries of the shadows as it moved with swift agility.

Then Eric saw something. What it was, he didn't know. "Did you guys see that?" He asked, his heart beating faster than before.

"See what?" Frankie looked around nervously.

"I, I don't—I don't know what it was, but it was big."

A sudden movement in the bushes caused all three to jump back. Ryan lost control of his bladder, but didn't even notice.

And then they all saw it. Something big and dark darted across the deer path in front of them. Fear took hold of the three boys like frost on warm breath.

"Three," Frankie yelled, and they bolted forward.

Suddenly, the large man shaped presence was upon them, towering over them, leaving them with nowhere to run.

They screamed at the sight of the large figure. They tried to bolt in different directions. But as fast as they moved, it moved faster. It did not matter in which direction either of them moved as it seemed, whatever this thing was, could be in three places at the same time.

There was nowhere to run, nowhere to hide. They were pinned between the barn and the tall, dark, human-shaped figure whose body reeked of death.

Ryan tried again to outmaneuver their assailant, but again, the speed at which it moved surprised him. In an instant, Ryan was picked up by the scuff of his neck and thrown hard, headfirst, against the barn. He fell limply to the ground. Frankie and Eric could do nothing more than watch in horror as their younger brother laid there on the ground, motionless, blood gushing from his lips.

"Ryan? Ryan, wake up," Frankie yelled, not once taking his eyes off the dark presence. "See? See what you've done? He's hurt. Why? Why would you do that? What is it you want?" He yelled. But the intruder just stared at them with black, inhuman eyes.

"Help. Help us, anybody, please help." Eric yelled.

The dark presence continued to stare, never changing eye contact from one to the other. Eric, as did Frankie, had the distinct feeling that this man, this putrid smelling thing standing before them was only staring at him, as if being singled out for some demented reason.

Each boy was scared beyond the limits of their own imaginations. They were each clueless as to what or why this imposing, figure wanted with them.

They tried to think of what to do next. With an *'I could shit a Twinkie'* look of fear in their eyes, their brains impulses told them to run, and run fast. But they were mindful of what had just happened to their little brother for doing that very thing, and they felt compelled not to move. They were immobilized by the shear horror of the situation.

Conversing with the dark figure was out of the question, they had already tried, but it said nothing. All they could hope to do was stand there and wait for the intruder to make his move, and then try and attempt another escape.

A few horrifying seconds later, the assailant did just that, and they both tried one last time to bolt in two different directions. The presence that smelled and looked of death, descended upon them faster them they could run. It grabbed the two by the collars of their T-shirts with great speed and agility. With inhuman strength, it picked them up by the throat, one in each hand until their feet dangled in mid air and applied pressure until unconsciousness set in, and their squirming bodies stopped all movement. He then swung them over his shoulder and headed back into the woods.

Left behind, still lying on the ground, was Ryan. His breathing was very shallow. But he was alive.

Chapter 15

1

Jack Helmsley sat at his desk at F.B.I. headquarters in Washington D.C., sipping on a bottle of diet soda. He had just returned from a stakeout that proved to be as useless as a bottle of Viagra in a morgue full of dead men. Jack, to say the very least, was pissed off. Getting bad intelligence via informant was something he could not tolerate, would not tolerate. He was Jack Helmsley, and nobody, nobody, gave Jack Helmsley bad information without facing the consequences. He felt his time could have been better spent thumping some slug on the head, making a bust, maybe pocketing a little cash to throw into one of his offshore accounts. He knew, however, how to contact his drug-induced informant, knew how to entice him to a secret meet so that he could personally thank his pill-pushing friend.

The office was quiet. Most of the agents had gone home for the night. Jack liked it that way. He found solitude in the peacefulness of a large uninhabited office.

In the background, he could hear the echoing of a TV bouncing off the walls. When the name of the town, Milford, Virginia came out of the reporter's mouth, the soda bottle seemed to stick on his lower lip. And when he heard the words, missing teen, he swung his chair around and listened intently to the rest of the reporters story, but it was over, just a quick blurb. All he got was a town name, Milford, and the fact that a teenager named Kiersten Shae was missing.

Jack turned back to his desk and checked the bin marked incoming. There was an inch worth of various reports and memos, but nothing that mentioned the situation at hand. "Damn it," exploded out of his mouth. He then checked his email. He had 76, but none of them seemed to interest him and were deleted with an enraged poke at the Delete key, each more furious than the next. A few heavy fingered strokes on the keyboard put him on the FBI's NCIC database, a system used for the simplest of crimes to the most vulgar. With a few more strokes on the keyboard, he instructed the database to do a search for a specific crime in a specific time period in a specific area. If anyone from anywhere had put information into the database that met the criteria he was looking for, the system would find it, and give the particulars of the case.

Jack got two hits and printed them out. One, he had just heard about on the TV—the other took place over thirty years ago. After looking at the two, he said softly, "These can't be related. Too many years have passed. Coincidence is all, has to be."

Jack shredded the reports and left the office; he could not, however, get the town of Milford or the missing teen out of his mind. And he sure as hell couldn't forget the dirty S.O.B. scumbag informant that had him sitting in his car for ten hours on a stakeout that produced nothing more than a sore back and a flattened ass.

After reaching his car, a BMW that once belonged to a former informant, Jack grabbed his cell phone from his belt, dialed and waited.

"Yeah," a voice answered. The voice was desperate and raspy, as if the voice itself was saying, "Quick get me a line of coke to snort, or give me a needle of anything."

"You alone?" Jack asked.

"Yeah."

"Meet me in the alley off Hudson in ten. I've got a little something for ya."

"Yeah? Really? What do yah got, huh, Coke, Meth? Come on, which is it?"

"Ten minutes." Jack hung up, started the car and pulled away.

Minutes later, Jack arrived at the agreed upon destination and waited. He sat there, his mind reflecting back to Milford, back to the missing teen, back to a chain of events that took place thirty-two years ago. His thoughts trailed off as a ragged looking man stepped out of the shadows.

Jack had positioned himself well within the shrouded alleyway and went unseen. He slipped out of the car and took the guy by surprise. He knocked him down with a hard blow to the head with the butt of his gun. After the guy fell, Jack was on top of him in seconds checking for weapons. He found a .44 Magnum and a cell phone. He put the phone in his pocket and held the gun in his right hand.

"Now, now, that's a mighty big gun for such a little prick like you. A lying little prick at that," Jack said, the fierce look on his face easing some as his eyes rolled from his left hand that was holding his .38, to his right hand. As he glared at the .44, a menacing smile came to his face. "That's not a gun," he said flicking his eyes back to his .38. "This," he said, returning his menacing glare back to the .44, moving his hand up and down as if getting the feel of its weight, "this is a gun."

He continued looking at the .44 like a child on Christmas Day who had just opened a Red Ryder bee-bee gun. "Now tell me, what's a lying little prick like you doing with such a big gun, huh?"

"Pro… protection," the guy stuttered, then "wha, wha, what do you want?"

Jack's mind was again on Milford.

"Hey?" the scumbag said.

"What?" Jack yelled, and then, "Get up fuck face."

Jack walked around the guy and said, "What do I want? I'll tell you what I want, but you will almost assuredly—not like the answer. I want to wrap things up. You know, clean house so to speak." He paused to let his words ricochet around in the scumbag's meth-fried brain. "What I want," Jack said finally, raising the .44, "Is you, fucking dead." Jack pulled the trigger without hesitation. The bullet slammed through the scumbag's lower jaw sending teeth and bone fragments clear out through the back of his head. The scumbag stood there momentarily with a surprised look in his eyes, the rest of his face was all but gone, and then, as if in slow motion, fell limply to the ground. Jack walked away with Milford and the missing teen still on his mind.

2

Barbara met her friend, Judy Willingham, outside the Dixon Memorial Hospital. "It's been what?" she said, giving her a quick hug, "Almost a year now?"

"Thanksgiving," Judy replied.

Judy leaned in and gave Barbara another hug. "It's so good to see you."

"It's good to see you too." Barbara's facial expression turned serious. "Listen, I wish I had more time to chat and catch up on gossip, but. . ." Barbara's voice halted briefly as the ambulance pulled up, her eyes fixed on it until it came to a complete stop. "But unfortunately there's work that needs your professional expertise."

"You did say you had a special case."

Two EMT's opened the rear doors of the ambulance, and together pulled out an aluminum gurney. On top laid the black bag that housed Kiersten's body.

"So, what is it that you have for me?" Judy asked as they watched the two men wheel the body bag toward the emergency entrance. "What's so important that would bring you here in person, not to mention, keeping two old friends from reminiscing?"

The two EMT's stopped and glanced back toward Judy as if waiting for orders. She, in return, held up the peace sign indicating the #2, which told them where to take the body.

"A sixteen year old girl," Barbara said, her voice hardening. "The mother is a close friend of the sheriff's, which is why I asked for you and why I'm here in person. You are one of the best, and I need to make sure this gets done right and done today."

"Well, I don't know about being one of the best, but I can certainly make it a priority." Judy put her arm around Barbara and led her toward the hospital entrance. "Come on, I've made arrangements for you to assist. Hope you don't mind?"

"Not at all," Barbara said. "I was counting on it."

After several hours, the autopsy had been completed. Kiersten's brain had swollen substantially on the right side causing the veins carrying oxygenated blood to the brain to be pinched. Though she would have eventually died over a short period of time without immediate medical attention from the blow, the cause of death went down on paper as *Asphyxia due to Hanging.*

Judy finished up the report while Barbara called Joan at Marie's house to fill her in on their findings.

3

It was nearing 6:30 in the evening when Joan received the call from Barbara.

Marie was physically calm when the phone rang, but inside, her heart was crushed.

Joan took the call in the kitchen. "I'm listening," she said.

"She died of asphyxia," Barbara replied. "With what Judy and I found during autopsy and what I told you happened at the crime scene are pretty close—with a few exceptions."

"And they are?"

"Well, it's a little odd, but according to the M.E., she was alive while she was hung, yet there were no defensive wounds or bruising to indicate that fact."

"Go on."

"We know that she didn't jump because other than her trachea being damaged, nothing else was, and from that height, her neck would pretty much look like a jumbled mess of fragmented bone and muscle."

"So why didn't she fight back?"

"Well, it appears that that bruise around her temporal was caused by a substantial blow by the perp. From what we can tell, he used the back of his right hand."

"How many times?"

"We could only find evidence that she was hit twice. Once on the back of the head which probably knocked her out during the initial abduction, the second one though…"

Joan could sense hesitation in Barbara's voice. "What?" Joan asked."

"I think we're dealing with a very strong and powerful man. That single blow could have killed her immediately if the blow had been made directly to the temple, but it wasn't. Impact took place about two centimeters from the temple, just above her left ear. A hard hit like that could cause momentary confusion, a little dizziness, maybe even paralysis. It's very probable that she could have seen and heard everything that was happening to her, but was unable to do anything about it. Normally I would think that a weapon of some sort was used, but the bruising reflects a single backhand blow. Like I said, whoever did it was very strong."

"I see. Well do me a favor and tell Marie that she didn't suffer" Joan glanced at Marie whose hands still clutched the coffee cup. "And can you prep her for a positive I.D.? Don't ask. A simple yes or no will do."

"Yes of course. She'll be ready when you arrive."

"Thanks, Barb. Oh, and one other thing, I know this is highly irregular, but I want you to make sure everything is done tonight, and when I mean everything, I mean send her body over to a mortician after we leave. Marie would like to have the funeral the day after tomorrow. She has already called the local church and they're digging the plot as we speak. I know its short notice, but..."

"I'll see to it personally."

"Thanks." Joan put down the receiver.

"I have to see my daughter—her body. I have to, Joan."

Joan glanced at Marie whose eyes looked like a body of water waiting to overflow.

"I know it's not going to bring her back, and I know it's going to be hard, but it's something I have to do, for me, for Kiersten."

"Okay," Joan said, hugging her.

Joan retrieved a jacket for Marie from the closet and the keys to Marie's car, and walked with her out the front door.

As they drove in silence toward the hospital, Joan thought more about what Marie had said earlier about the bridge, and about good ole Charlie, whose name for some reason, kept coming up. Joan knew that asking Marie to tell her the story that Charlie had once told her, might be asking too much too soon. But it might take the edge off the inevitable thought of seeing her daughter's body during the drive.

"Marie, can you tell me the story that Charlie had told you, the one about the bridge."

Marie wiped her eyes, blew her nose, and started talking. "At the time, I thought it was nothing more than an old wives' tale. At least, that's what Charlie had made it seem like. I'm sure it doesn't mean anything," Marie replied.

"I'm sure you're right, but if you don't mind, I'd like to hear it anyway."

Joan listened as Marie repeated the story, trying to stay as close to what she remembered Charlie telling her as possible.

"He said that about, I don't know, I guess it would be almost thirty or so years ago now, a man hung around that bridge, and that any kids that he caught playing around that area, he would uh..." Marie started sobbing again as she remembered a horrifying detail to the story, the detail that was now a dreadful reality. She slowly regained enough composure to finish. "He would string them up by the neck."

"Oh God, Marie," Joan said. "I had no idea. I'm so sorry I put you through that."

Marie went on, "He called it the strangest thing, the bridge I mean."

"And what was that?"

"Bunnyman. He called it *Bunnyman Bridge."*

Joan stared blankly at Marie, and asked, "Why that? Why name it Bunn…"

"I don't know, damn it!"

"Marie, I know this isn't easy, and I'm sorry. But this is the second time today that the name Bunnyman has come up. And both times Charlie's name has been connected to it."

Joan could feel Marie's eyes on her.

"No," Joan said, "I don't think Charlie had anything to do with any of this. I just want to get to the bottom of this as quickly as possible." Joan glanced at Marie. "I want this bastard as much as you do."

"I know." Marie said, her voice breaking. "I'm sorry, I am. It's just that I feel as though I lost my whole world today." Marie swallowed the lump that formed in the back of her throat and continued, "All I remember is that Charlie said it had something to do with rabbits, but I can't remember what."

"Is there anything else you can remember about the day Charlie told you that story? Anything at all?"

Silence.

"I know it was a long time ago, but even something that may have seemed trivial at the time, might be of use," Joan said.

Marie thought for a long while. All was silent except for the humming of the tires rolling over the pavement. "There was one thing," Marie said.

"What?"

"I'm sure it's nothing, but I remember Charlie being really anxious, scared even. But he had been drinking at the time."

"I know that wasn't easy, but I promise you that it will help, and I will catch the bastard."

They drove the rest of the way in silence.

4

In the parking lot outside the Dixon City Hospital's emergency room, Marie sat stiffly upright in the seat. Her eyes were staring straight ahead and her face was expressionless.

"You don't have to do this," Joan said, slipping her hand over Marie's, squeezing gently.

"Yes, yes I do. I don't know how to explain it, but I do."

"Marie, I…"

"Let me finish," she said, pausing and wiping her nose. "I know that's my daughter in there. I know she's dead, but unless I see her with my own eyes, there will always be the *what ifs? What if it isn't Kiersten? What if it's only someone that looked like her?* I have to know, even if I already do. I know this must all sound crazy to you, but…"

"No, I don't think it sounds crazy at all." Marie fell into her arms, seeking support. "Just let me know when you're ready and we'll go inside."

A full sized truck with an extended cab pulled up and parked next to Joan as they were about to get out of the car. Inside were Ed and Todd.

Todd sat with his head tilted forward with his hand spread out across his forehead, his elbow resting on the door side armrest. Marie got out of the car and walked over and lightly tapped the glass window. Todd opened the door and stepped out. Marie reached out and hugged him to her. "Everything's going to be alright, Todd," Marie said in a tender voice.

Todd clung to her for several minutes, repeating the same thing, "I'm sorry, I'm so sorry."

Twenty minutes later, the four were standing outside of the medical examiner's room, waiting for word that the body was ready for viewing. Barbara took Marie aside, and explained what they had done and why. She then led her into the room, escorted her to the table and pulled the sheet down just past the neckline before leaving her alone.

Marie wept in silence as she reached under the sheet and grabbed hold of Kiersten's hand. She prayed that God would take her sweet beautiful child to heaven, and in the same breath, prayed that they find the bastard that killed her, and send him straight to hell.

Several minutes passed. Marie stepped out and asked Todd if he wanted to go in alone, or if he wanted her to accompany him inside.

"If you could just walk me in, Mrs. Shae, I'd appreciate it."

Without hesitation, she grabbed his hand and walked with him to the table. She turned to leave and added, "If you need me, I'm just outside the door."

Todd stood there alone. He placed his hand on her cheek. A chill ran down his spine as he felt her cold, damp skin. He gently caressed her face, leaned forward, and kissed her forehead.

He spoke to her, apologizing to her for his ignorance and poor judgment. In his mind, he was responsible for her being here, for her being dead. He could not shake the feeling.

He dropped to his knees, and in a poignant whisper, said, "God, I'm going to miss you, I love you, Kiersten Shae, I always have, and I always will, even in death, I will always love you.

Chapter 16

1

On the way home, Joan insisted that Marie spend the night with her. Although Marie would have rather spend the night in her own home and sleep in her own bed, she was too exhausted and emotionally drained to fight, and accepted Joan's offer. Not to mention that deep down the thought of spending the night alone in her empty home would seem unbearable. It was a feeling that she knew she would eventually have to overcome. But it wouldn't have to be now, not tonight.

Once home, Joan gave up her room to Marie, insisting that she would sleep on the rumpled old couch. After seeing to all of Marie's needs, she called Gage at the police station to check in, and to make sure Charlie Malloy would be there for her morning interrogation. She was pleased to hear that he was still there, still locked up sleeping off the booze.

It was good that Charlie was sleeping, she thought; he would need it. Once Joan had started interrogating a potential suspect, there would be no stopping until she had all the information she could get. She already believed that he knew something relating to Kiersten's murder, and she was bound and determined, no matter what it took, to find out what that information was. Although Joan liked Charlie, she didn't much like the fact that he was keeping something from her. In fact, it pissed her off even more so because she was a friend to him when no one else would give him the time of day.

After taking a quick shower, Joan joined Jessie in the kitchen and asked about Caitlin's whereabouts. She was surprised to hear that Caitlin had felt tired, and had gone to bed early, and that wasn't like her. "I think I'll just peek in to make sure she's feeling okay." Joan said.

As the door to Caitlin's room opened, a fresh scent of shampoo billowed out. It was the same scent, Johnson's Baby Shampoo, that she had smelled earlier at Marie's house during her dream. Baffled by the strong scent, Joan closed the door and glanced towards the kitchen. She wanted to ask Jessie if Caitlin had somehow spilled the bottle of shampoo in her room, but no sooner had she closed the door, the scent dissipated as if it had not been there at all. She opened the door again. Nothing. Her nose was met with a small blast of air that smelled of nothing more than the clean linen that Jessie had placed on Caitlin's bed earlier that morning. Joan thought about the dream; it had all the right ingredients; her daughter, the scent of shampoo, and the fact that at the moment she called the house, Caitlin had been taking a bath and would have more than likely, washed her hair. *That's got to be it,* she thought, the power of suggestive thinking. Joan eased the door closed.

The scent of shampoo, however, only added to the things she was going to ask Jessie about in the morning, but now felt compelled to ask right this minute, questions that could not be explained away as easily as the shampoo, or if Caitlin had indeed washed her hair or not. Joan wanted to know how Caitlin knew she was going to call. How her daughter knew that she would find a missing girl? Better yet, how did she know there was a missing girl at all? Joan's mind scrambled for answers, but could find none.

Joan turned and headed for the kitchen for another chat with her mother.

"I made you a ham and cheese sandwich, dear," Jessie said as Joan entered the kitchen.

"I don't want a sandwich," Joan replied. "I want to know how Caitlin knew everything that was going to happen today—the call, the missing girl, that I'd be the one that would find her. How on earth could she have possibly known all that?"

"I don't know," Jessie, said, "I thought something was strange this morning"

"Strange? Strange how?"

After thinking for a second, Jessie said, "The first thing she said to me this morning was that you wouldn't be taking her to see Mrs. Zachary's rabbits, but I figured that she heard you leave this morning, or maybe she overheard your phone call this morning. But then, as she laid there in bed, somehow knowing beforehand that she would be seeing no rabbits today, she said the oddest thing."

"And that was?"

"She said, 'Grandma, its O.K. I know Mommy's busy trying to find her.' When I asked who she meant, she said she didn't know, but that you'd find her by a bridge. The only other thing that seemed strange was when she asked me if I'd ever seen red rabbits. That's all I really know. But if you ask me how she knew, I couldn't even fathom a guess."

Swimming in questions, Joan stared at the wall in front of her. On it was a picture of Caitlin taken the day the adoption had been final. As Joan reflected on that moment, she recalled how Caitlin had reacted to the news. Joan remembered her being genuinely happy, but somehow, she didn't seem all that surprised that a court of law would award sole custody to a single woman—a single woman who was a gun-toting police officer. The more Joan thought about it, the more she was certain that Caitlin had already known. *But how?*

2

Charlie Malloy fumbled around on the police station cot, reaching for a blanket that was not there. When he sat up, he realized that he was not at home. In fact, he had no recollection of where he was or how he came to be here, wherever here was. Everything seemed a blur.

He glanced around the room. Three of the four sides were solid brick walls. One of them had a barred window. The fourth wall, made out of iron bars, encased him in a space that was no more than eight feet by eight feet.

Gage flipped on the lights to the cell as he heard Charlie stirring around.

"Finally woke up, I see," the deputy said, approaching the steel bars holding a tray containing the Milford Diner's Special: a deluxe cheeseburger, fries, and a 16 oz. Coke.

"Where the hell am I?"

"Well, it isn't the Ritz."

"Asshole," Charlie muttered under his breath.

"What was that?"

"Nothin. What's yah got there?"

"Well, like I said, this isn't the Ritz, but if you're hungry, it's called dinner. I ordered it an hour ago. Had no idea you'd be out so long." Gage sat the tray on the floor outside the bars. "Jail," Gage said, "I gave you the best cell in the house. Look, you even have a view." Gage motioned his hand to the barred window.

"Jail? How'd the hell did I get here?"

Gage opened the door, picked up the tray, and walked in. He sat the tray down on the cot. Charlie squinted at him, his brow furrowed, nose stuck up in the air.

"You're here because I brought you here, about four hours ago," Gage replied.

"Well let me the hell outa here."

"I'm afraid I can't do that Charlie."

"Why the hell not?"

"Now Charlie, you woke up surrounded by three brick and mortar walls, and a forth made of wrought iron bars, then, you asked me, a deputy in uniform standing on the other side of said bars, where you were. In my opinion, that would indicate that you're still inebriated. If I were to let you out, that would be a blatant irresponsibility of my civic duties as a deputy, to protect and serve the greater population of our humble little town. Besides, with that bunnyman thing running loose, don't you think you're safer in here with an armed lawman?" Gage shot him a brief smirk. "Now, do you want this or not?"

Just as Charlie took the tray of food, a woman came bursting through the front door of the police station screaming hysterically at the top of her lungs. Gage recognized her as Jean Kaminski.

"My boys. My boys are missing." she yelled. "Someone please help me. Please, God, can someone help me find my boys."

Gage rushed out of the jail cell, locking the iron door behind him, and ran to Mrs. Kaminski. He arrived just in time to catch her as she started to faint.

"Stay with me now, stay with me," Gage said, escorting her to his desk chair and helping her sit. "Now then, tell me exactly what happened."

Jean Kaminski struggled through the events that had brought her to the police station screaming.

Gage gave her a glass of water and said, "Now-now, they're probably just out playing and lost track of time. Maybe they went a little deeper into the woods then what they're used to. You know how kids are."

"No. I went looking for them when they didn't show up for dinner, but they were nowhere to be found. I hollered for them as loud as I could, but they didn't answer. They never miss dinner. Something's wrong, I can feel it. I'm their mother, I know something's wrong. Please help me find them." She burst into uncontrollable sobs.

Gage went back to the jail cell, stared hard at Charlie, and then spoke softly, "You'd better listen up, ole pal, and pray that her kids are fine, and that we find them, alive. If they end up like Kiersten, God help you if you're trying to cover something up. You do know something. I know you know something, I can see it in your eyes."

Jean moved toward the cell behind Gage.

"Did you do something to my kids, you old bastard?" She asked.

"No!" Gage said, pulling her away, back over to his desk. "He's been here most of the day. Now I know this isn't easy, but I need you to just sit here for a few minutes while I call the sheriff. Can you do that?"

Jean nodded.

3

Ryan woke up sprawled out on the ground a few feet from the barn. He had been lying on his right arm and felt a strong tingling sensation running through it.

He had no idea as to how long he had been there, nor what time it was, but as the grogginess wore off, he started remembering everything that happened. The thought of his two brothers and their whereabouts worried him. He shouted out their names as loud as he could and winced in the effort, but his words went unheard. Fear claimed his pain and he tried again. Still, he heard nothing.

His side ached with each breath he took. He winced as he took his right hand and reached for the source of the pain. It hurt the worst on his lower left side. Almost unbearable to the touch, he raised his t-shirt and saw a small bulge on his left rib cage. He pressed on it, and winced again in pain.

Ryan turned his head from side to side, but saw nothing but the dark looming trees, and the blackness behind them.

In an attempt to find his two brothers, Ryan ignored the pain and filled his lungs full of air, and cried out both their names, but again, only silence answered back. The night was cold, dark, and lonely, and to nine-year-old Ryan, terrifying beyond words.

4

Frankie and Eric lay back-to-back, their hands and feet tied to each other. When they regained consciousness, they had no clue as to their whereabouts, only that they were sheltered from the elements of the night. They felt no wind, saw no light, and heard nothing but the faint echo of each other's muffled sobs.

They could only guess that they were somewhere deep within a cave, in someone's dug out crawlspace, or a basement with a dirt floor.

"Frankie," Eric managed to whimper out, "Are you O.K.?"

"Yeah, I think so," his voice breaking. "You?"

"I'm scared. Why are we here? What's going to happen to us?" Eric asked.

"I'm scared too, and I don't . . . Oh, shit." Frankie yelled and kicked his leg outward, taking Eric's with it. "What was that?"

"What was what?"

"I don't know. I felt something move across my left leg." But there was nothing there, just the frayed end of the rope shifting as the two shivered in fear.

It was then that they noticed that their clothes had been removed. If it weren't for their socks and underwear, they'd be completely naked. They started weeping and trembling in horror as this discovery made its way to their brains. They had no recollection of their clothes ever being taken off, or where they were now.

"Eric?" Frankie said in a broken voice, "I'm going to try and untie our hands, help me."

"Okay."

They struggled for twenty minutes and finally could feel the ropes loosening, but their arms were tired from the effort. Their wrists were stinging from the ropes rubbing their skin raw to the point of bleeding.

"Frankie," Eric said, "I'm so scared, and I, uh—I think I've crapped myself. I'm sorry." Eric started to cry.

"It's not your fault. And if we get out of here, I won't tell a soul."

"Promise?"

"Promise," Frankie replied reassuringly, "But let's get these ropes off before we start worrying about that."

Chapter 17

1

Joan laid on the sofa in her living room. Her eyes had finally grown heavier than the weighted questions she had about Caitlin. Just as her eyes closed, the phone began to ring, and even though Jessie had been sitting in the chair next to her, Joan jumped to answer it before it had a chance to ring twice. She did not want Marie disturbed from getting the rest she needed.

Gage was calling to tell her of the three missing boys.

"Give Ed a call," she said, taking in a deep breath. "I'll be there in twenty."

"Joan. My God, what is it?" Jessie asked.

"I don't believe this," Joan said, and then thought briefly about waking Caitlin up to see if she knew where they were. "The Kaminski boys are missing. Apparently their mother hasn't seen them since early afternoon. I'm going to need you to watch Caitlin for me, and to make sure Marie has everything she needs. God, I wish I knew what the hell was going on around here."

Jessie gave her a reassuring smile. "You'll figure it out. And as for Caitlin and Marie, I've got it covered. Don't worry."

Joan left the room to get dressed. She returned five minutes later, wearing a pair of old worn-out jeans, an Indian motif flannel shirt with a black T-shirt underneath. Tucked in the back of her jeans, was her .38 caliber pistol. "Keep an eye on Marie for me too, please. Get her whatever she needs. And, Mom," Joan said, "Make sure Caitlin's windows are shut and locked. In fact, check every window in the house. And check in on her every now and then."

Ten minutes later, Joan arrived at the station to find Gage and Ed waiting for her. Jean Kaminski was slumped over at Gage's desk, her head resting on her forearms.

The three of them moved across the room to Joan's desk. "Five years," Joan said, keeping her voice at bay. "Five. And in all that time we've had nothing more than a few break-ins, barroom brawls, an accident here and there, and a few other incidents that aren't even worth mentioning. And now, in a span of about forty-eight hours, we've managed to have a murder and three more kids disappear. If I didn't know better, I'd swear I was back in homicide in New York." Joan raised both her hands and rubbed her temples, as if to rid herself of an annoying headache.

"I think we should all take a deep breath," Gage said. "We'll get to the bottom of whatever's happening. We just need to keep our heads."

Joan looked at Gage and then flicked her eyes to her other deputy. "Ed," Joan said, "Take Mrs. Kaminski home in case her kids show up, and stay with her. Gage, you're with me. If you need to call your wife, you'd better do it now."

"Thanks, but I've already taken care of that," Gage replied.

Ed nodded and escorted Jean out to his truck and took her home.

The drive took ten minutes. Joan and Gage had followed Ed and pulled up to Jean's two-story colonial. They exited Joan's truck and watched as Ed escorted Jean into her home.

"Well," Gage said, "Where do we start?"

Suddenly, as if the thought had been transmitted into her brain, Joan said, "Mrs. Zachary's place, it's a straight shot that way," she said, pointing towards the woods. "Can't be what, more than a mile, right?" She said this with such assuredness that she surprised herself. "Come on, let's move."

The night was clear and the moon was full, spreading its wealth of light over the entire area. A slight northern breeze whisked through the branches of the leafless oaks and tall pines. Though the moon's light was helpful, Joan and Gage enlisted the aid of two healthy flashlights that sported new batteries.

As they moved east, Gage saw movement in the brush that hid a shallow ravine twenty feet away. He stopped in mid-step, his right foot still in the air. "What was that?" he asked, feeling a little edgy, fear evident in his tone of voice.

"What was what?" Joan asked.

"You didn't see…" Gage's next words eluded him as the movement in the brush occurred again, only this time it was closer. Whatever it was, was now less than fifteen feet away and closing in on them fast. "There." he continued, "Did you see that?"

"Yeah, I did." Joan pulled the .38 from the small of her back and flicked off the safety. Gage followed her lead.

Everything got quiet. Even the wind seemed to hesitate momentarily. Another movement in the bushes put Joan and Gage in a shooter's stance, fingers on the trigger. Both sighed in relief as a raccoon came out into a clearing; a mother raccoon with her three little ones tagging along behind her. She was rather small, but the light from their flashlights made her eyes look as if they were possessed.

As they continued to scurry across the deer path, Joan thought the animals looked confused, scared even. Whatever was running through their tiny raccoon minds, didn't let the light from the flashlights or the presence of humans divert them from the direction they were heading. Joan and Gage could do nothing but watch the animals scurry past them.

"Like I need this shit tonight," Gage said. "I nearly pissed my pants." Joan rolled her eyes. "That's strange though," Gage said in continuance, "Them running at us that way. I don't think they were afraid of us. Maybe they were pets or something."

"That, or maybe they were more afraid of what was behind them."

Gage shot Joan a look. "Why did you have to go and say that?"

Joan said nothing.

Gage stepped toward her, "Seriously, do you think that's what it was?"

"Only one way to find out." Joan moved onward.

"Shit," Gage said in a sigh.

A few minutes later, she stopped.

"What?" Gage asked.

"Sshh, quiet," Joan whispered, and then without warning, dashed toward the bottom of the ravine and veered to the right out of Gage's sight.

As she took off, she could hear Gage behind her. He had stopped running and was hunched over, gasping for air.

"Stop," he yelled, in between breaths. "I need to rest for a few."

"You need to stop smoking," she yelled back as she continued running.

Seconds later, Joan yelled, "Here, over here."

Gage started running toward Joan's voice. He rounded a large stump, and saw Joan kneeling down beside a small boy. He was conscious and complaining about his ribs. Gage knelt down beside them just as Joan was gently lifting up his shirt.

"Jesus, that's a nasty fracture," she said.

"Frankie, Eric, where are they?" the boy asked.

"I bet you're Ryan, is that right?"

"Yeah," Ryan said, grimacing in pain, "But my brothers, where are they?"

The moon ducked behind a cloud and darkness spread across the night sky like an oil freighter spilling its black gold into a running body of water. With it came wind and specks of cold rain.

"Don't you worry about them right now," Joan said, feeling anxious herself about the whereabouts of the other two boys. Joan looked up at Gage as she took off her flannel shirt and spread it out over the boy.

"First things first," she said. "We need to see about getting you some medical attention."

She turned to Gage as she retrieved keys from her pocket and put them in his hand. "Take my truck and drive back to town; go to the town clinic and grab one of the folding stretchers and a few blankets and get back here as fast as you can."

When he left, Joan sat with the nine-year-old, his head lying in her lap. She ran her fingers through his hair. Ryan got quiet, and for a moment, closed his eyes as if to sleep. Joan's experience in traumas told her that was not a good idea. Not knowing the extent of his injuries, she needed to keep him awake, alert, and talking.

The rain began to fall harder, the wind gusting.

"So," Joan said, "What in the world did you boys do today?"

Ryan opened his eyes and answered saying, "Played—hide and seek." He stopped and screwed up his face in pain. Again, he tried to close his eyes and drift off.

"Ryan, I want you to stay with me," she said. "Don't you dare fall asleep on me. Finish telling me about your day."

Ryan batted his eyes a few times to gain focus. "Then we saw the blood in Mrs. Zachary's barn through the side window." Ryan's eyes squinted again in pain before continuing. "Is she O.K.? Mrs. Zachary, I mean. Did she get hurt along with all her rabbits?"

"No, honey, she's doing just fine."

What else could she tell him? That the old woman was lying in the Dixon City Hospital in a coma? He was stressed out enough already.

"So, what did you do next?" she asked, trying to change the subject.

The rain began to fall harder, and she desperately wanted to move Ryan to the hollowed out tree twenty feet away, but did not want to risk a more serious injury in doing so. She sheltered him the best she could with her own body.

"Then, we tried to outrun the man."

Joan's eyes lit up as Ryan spoke of an unknown intruder. "What man?" she asked, "What did he look like?"

Was the man Ryan spoke of the same man that had killed Kiersten? A feeling deep in her bones told her it was.

"Dark, big, and he smelled really bad…." he winced.

Joan continued stroking the boy's hair. She could feel his body seizing in pain. "I'm sorry, sweetie," she said tenderly. "I know it hurts, but help's on the way." *Where the hell is Gage?* She thought.

A few minutes later, Gage returned with the stretcher, blankets, and Barbara Williams, who had arrived back in town right before Gage arrived at the clinic. She gave Ryan a quick look over and said, "Well, other than the broken rib, you don't look too much worse for the wear." She smiled and rubbed his head. "I think you'll make it." She gave him a shot of Demerol to ease the pain and moved him onto the stretcher. They carried him back to his house just long enough to let his mother know he would be fine before taking a ride to the Dixon City Hospital by way of an ambulance that Barbara had called before leaving the clinic.

Jean Kaminski was relieved to see her youngest son, and to know that, other than the broken rib, he would be fine. But she still had two missing boys, and that was not O.K.

"We're not giving up," Ed told her, hoping that Kiersten's death, though tragic, would be the only one, that they would find the Kaminski boys before they met the same fate.

As the ambulance took off, the skies opened up and unleashed torrents of rain. At times, the wind blew so hard that the rain moved more horizontally than what nature had intended.

Twenty minutes later, sitting at her desk at the police station, Joan was on the phone to Ben Stevenson in the State Trooper's Office. "We have two more kids missing. I need as many men as you can assemble, and maybe a couple of bloodhounds, though with this weather, I doubt they would do much good."

"You'd be surprised what these dogs can do," Ben replied. "You want them out there tonight? It could take a few hours to assemble enough men and to contact Mr. Creedy about the use of his bloodhounds."

"Yes, as soon as you can. Just give me a call when you're on your way."

2

Frankie and Eric had struggled for hours to free themselves from their bindings before finally succumbing to sleep.

While he slept, Frankie began to dream. He dreamt of good things at first—things he enjoyed. Baseball was at the top of his list. But the dreams had abruptly changed to images of Ryan. In his dream, Ryan's head was a baseball, and the pitcher was the tall dark presence that appeared out of nowhere. He had the ball in his hand, and he released it with all his might towards the barn. The ball hit the barn with a dull thud, sending splinters of bone, splatters of blood and brains everywhere. When he looked down, he saw his brother lying on the ground, dead and headless. He woke in a cold sweat, screaming Ryan's name.

Eric was dreaming as well, much the same way as his older brother, but when Frankie yelled, Eric awoke startled and disoriented. At first, Eric thought that the whole terrifying incident—the kidnapping, Ryan being hurt, he and his older brother being taken to God knows where, was nothing more than a bad dream. Tears filled his eyes as he realized it was not.

The tears, however, were short-lived as he and Frankie realized that the time spent struggling to free their hands before drifting off to sleep had, indeed, paid off. When they moved their hands innocently after waking, they felt the looseness of the ropes and finished removing it from their wrists, and then reached down and untied the ropes around their ankles.

The room or cave or basement, whatever it was they were in, remained as black as the devil's eyes.

"What do we do now?" Eric whispered.

Frankie replied, "We get the hell out of here, that's what. We move very slowly and we try to find a light switch or a door or something that will help get us out of here."

Shuddering in fear of what laid before them, hiding in the blackness, they inched forward on their hands and knees. It was a slow process; moving one leg, then a hand, the next leg, and then Frankie would reach out in front of himself as far as he could, hoping he would touch a wall that would indicate they were indeed in some sort of room. And if they were in a room, there had to be a door, there had to be. And the door had to lead out of this frightening nightmare, and back to their home, back to their mother.

In their minds, they pictured monsters, madmen, boogiemen, and psychopathic killers that they had seen at the movies and on TV. Frankie wanted to cry, but he was determined to be strong for Eric, and though Ryan wasn't with them, he wanted to be strong for him as well.

Three minutes later, Frankie's hand touched some kind of object on the ground in front of him. If felt smooth and linear.

"What is it, Frankie? Why did you stop?"

"Sshh, I'm not sure yet."

He reached out a little further and found a round odd shaped object that was of the same smooth texture as the first piece.

"Bones," he whispered to Eric, "I think I've found bones, but I'm not sure." After picking up and feeling the odd shaped object, turning it blindly in his hands, his fingers explored the smooth surface. When his fingers sunk in to two shallow dents, and then glided over a ridged opening that felt like teeth, he dropped the object to the ground and said, "I think these are human bones, and I just found the skull." His voice started breaking. "I bet this is what he has planned for us."

"What do you mean?"

"I mean, he thinks he's going to leave us here to die, just like this person. But he doesn't know the Kaminski boys, cause were getting the hell out of here, and I mean now!" At that moment, Eric felt Frankie start to stand and he followed suit, making sure he kept hold of his brother the whole time. Frankie started moving at a much faster pace, his hands out in front using them as a guide.

After taking several more steps into the unknown, Frankie tripped and fell. Eric fell on top of him. Frankie's hands touched the cave floor. "Bones," he said, "I fell on top of more bones."

They moved forward again, faster this time. Ten steps later, his hands ran into a wall that felt like solid rock, rough and jagged, like a cave. Frankie and Eric followed the wall for what seemed like forever. The wall felt as though it led them through constant turns. Finally, after an unknown number of turns, they found a solid wooden door.

Frankie felt around and found the door handle and prayed that when he turned it, it wouldn't be locked. It wasn't. But then Frankie stopped and let go of the doorknob. He was plagued with uncertainty as to whether he should open the door or not. Suspended in fear of the unknown, he pressed his ear up to the door and listened, waiting, expecting to hear something from the other side of the door. Nothing, not even a hint of wind could be heard, but still he was afraid to open the door. He stood there in stark terror thinking that the thing, that incredibly strong, nasty smelling thing that had hurt, or worse, killed their little brother, could be less than a door's width away, listening, waiting for them to come bursting out, keeping silent to give them a false sense of hope, taunting them.

"Come on," Eric yelped, his palms sweating.

"What?" Frankie said in as loud of a whisper as he dared.

"The door," he replied anxiously, "Let's open it already, and get out of here."

"What if," Frankie hesitated, swallowing hard, trying not to vomit, "What if that—that thing, is on the other side of the door, just waiting for us to open it?"

"What if he isn't?"

"What if he is?"

"Come on, I don't want to argue, I just want to go home."

"O.K. O.K."

Frankie took a deep breath, let it out, and again reached for the doorknob. He started to turn the knob slowly, quietly, and when he couldn't turn it any further, he pushed the door forward. As the door cracked opened, fresh air greeted them. He opened it further, stopping a few times to see if he heard anything, but did not. When the door was opened enough for him to stick his head out, he did, and was relieved to see nothing but light. He threw open the door the rest of the way. Then, out of nowhere, the dark intruder appeared. He grabbed them by the hair, slung them up, one under each arm; they were kicking and screaming as they again felt pressure on their small bodies; felt the air being squeezed out of their lungs. They passed out.

When Frankie woke, he felt pressure again, but it was different than before; it felt more restricting, more painful. The pressure he felt was no longer coming from his mid-section as before, but from around his neck. Eric too felt the same pressure. And for a brief moment, their vision was less blurred; each was able to see the other strung up by the neck. They raised their hands in an effort to loosen the rope, but their struggles only made the rope tighter.

Tears ran down Eric's face.

"Eric," Frankie said in a constrained whisper, "I'm sorry."

Then, for both, everything became clouded and faded into an eternal darkness.

Chapter 18

1

Joan woke around 5:00 a.m. surprised Trooper Stevenson hadn't yet called. She slipped out of her Nautica jeans and black T-shirt and changed into a clean uniform. Just before heading out the back door, something beckoned her to look in on her daughter Caitlin.

Slowly, she opened Caitlin's door and was surprised not to find her in bed. She was instead sitting on the floor at the foot of her jumbled bed. Caitlin had seven of her favorite stuffed rabbits sitting in front of her, all lined up as if she were conducting a tea party. Joan watched as Caitlin put small bunches of wildflowers between each of her stuffed rabbit's legs, calling them each by name as she rested the flowers on their paws, "For Kristine and Frank and Eric and Michael and Kimmy and Becky and Alan. There, that should help Todd."

She could not make out everything that Caitlin was saying, just a few names she called her rabbits. But for a moment, the harried events that had plagued her the last two days, seemed to vanish as she watched Caitlin play. She was entranced at the simplicity of a child playing with her toys, at how simple life could be, how life should be.

A child playing.

A mother watching.

She was sure it was how things were meant to be. Life shouldn't be filled with the madness of people murdering people, or stark raving lunatics killing kids. Not always having to look over your shoulder, watching for something bad to happen. *Damn Eve for eating that apple,* Joan thought.

Just as she was about to shut the door, her mind flashed back to the vivid, horrifying picture of Kiersten hanging by the neck. It was a scene that would forever be etched into her memory. *How fragile,* she thought, *life really is, and how fast it could all change—in the blink of an eye—at the drop of a hat—at the pulling of a trigger of a gun aimed at her husband.*

But she at least had Caitlin, the one joy in her life, the person that brought her out of despair and back into the life of the living.

Joan could only hope that for her friend Marie's sake, she could find a ray of hope, something that she could cling to. Joan, of course, would always be there for her in the months of hell to come. But would that be enough?

As she drove to work her head filled with the questions she so desperately wanted to ask Charlie. And for his sake, he had better not try and bullshit his way out of spilling whatever it was that he knew. Joan would be ready for that. In her mind, she had a brief image of her stringing him up by the balls if he were to try and weasel his way out of answering her questions. The more she thought about it, the more she was convinced that he would play ball. She had an odd feeling that he wanted to spill his guts; that he had wanted to do so for years, and all that seemed to be missing, was opportunity, which had never surfaced, until now.

2

Todd awoke abruptly at 5:00 a.m. from a night of restless sleep—a night of horrible dreams and images. The last one, the one that woke him, was an image of Kiersten hanging by her neck just above his bed. He scrambled out of bed so fast that he nearly fell as his feet hit the floor.

He crouched down with his hands and arms wrapped around his legs with a grip so strong that he could feel the circulation in his legs being cut off. Beads of sweat trickled down his face and off his chin, dripping down onto his plaid pajamas. He sat there horrified. Of what, he did not know, as he could no longer remember the context of his dreams. He could only remember how real they had seemed, and sensed that they were about Kiersten.

But as fast as the paralyzing fear took over his body and mind, it vanished as though it had never existed. As the fear left, a sudden feeling of calmness filled his senses, as if he just had an epiphany that, in the end, everything was going to be fine. The sensation came just as the room was deluged with the fragrance of wild flowers, a scent that reminded him of a special place that he and Kiersten had recently found and shared their first real kiss. The grip around his legs loosened as he inhaled the aroma. He felt a welcomed calmness take over his body as he crawled back into bed and fell off into a deep peaceful sleep.

3

For Charlie Malloy, the night had seemed extraordinarily long. With the darkness of night came haunting images, noises, and the terrifying screams that took place thirty-two years ago. They were presented in perfect color and sound in his mind. He glanced at the clock and knew it was just a matter of time before Joan came busting through the door wanting answers to questions that only he could answer.

For a little over thirty two years, Charlie had kept a secret bottled up deep inside him. For him, the secret seemed like a ship lost out at sea looking for a port in which it could berth and set anchor; a secret that only a privileged six knew. And now, using Kiersten's death in the same way that a long ago sailor would use a beacon of light from a lighthouse to find its way through treacherous waters, Charlie could see that secret now having the opportunity to come to port. The name of the port was Joan Fortune.

Out of the six men that were involved in the events of that ill-fated night, he knew of two that were for sure still alive. Those two consisted of the ex-deputy of Milford, Henry Turner, and himself. Sheriff Henderson, died five years ago in a car accident, Koelmel had died in a home fire, and Neely had died in a hunting accident. Each died under rather mysterious circumstances, leaving Charlie to feel as though they were being punished for taking the law into their own hands. He often wondered what ill-fated death God had planned for him. The one person unaccounted for was JP, who seemed to have vanished after that night thirty-two years ago.

Charlie Malloy hated what he had once been a part of. Hated it because he was a Christian man and he knew it was wrong. But given the intense situation of his daughter, Rebecca, being killed at the hands of a psychopathic madman, his mind had become frail and easily influenced by those with lesser moral values.

4

When Joan pulled up in front of the police station, there were three state trooper cars, two TV station vans equipped for onsite live feed transmissions, and a black Oldsmobile blocking where she would, on an ordinary day, park her truck. But this was no ordinary day. She maneuvered her truck to the side of the building and exited.

As she rounded the corner, two reporters peppered her with questions. "No comment," was the only response she was ready to commit to until she had a further grip on the situation.

"Is it true that you knew the victim personally sheriff?" Michelle Davis from the NBC News team, asked.

"What part of no did you not understand?" Joan fixed her eyes on the female reporter. "You're a woman, surely you know that no means no."

She then turned abruptly and walked into the building with but one thing on her mind, dealing with Charlie Malloy.

As she made her way upstairs, she wondered how the media had gotten wind of Kiersten's story so quickly.

As her foot hit the last stair, it came to her. The person or persons from the State C.S.I. lab that had been assigned to examine the collected evidence from the case at some point must have had to make a report to their superiors. And of course, any report, especially one involving the death of a young teen would be worth money to the right reporters. Joan knew it was common practice for reporters to pay cash for information. She, however, despised any cop taking bribes of any kind.

She reached the police station and opened the door. In doing so she was again disappointed at what she saw. All but two of the eight state troopers were young. Joan's first thought was that the six looked like rookies fresh out of the academy.

God, how I hate rookies, she thought.

She reached up and felt the scar on her right cheekbone as the memory of how she received it flashed inside her head.

Rookies had an air about them, a cocky attitude accompanied with the thought that they knew everything. Not to mention that they thought they were somehow invincible and that they would go unscathed by the person or persons they would one day be pursuing.

At times, their experienced partners would brunt their arrogance; the scar on Joan's right cheek was a perfect example.

Standing at the far end of the room were two more men. Joan knew straight away from the way they were dressed that they were from the F.B.I. They wore black suits, white button-down collared shirts, ties, and shiny black loafers. And if there was anything that Joan hated worse than rookie cops, it was the F.B.I. They always seemed to show up right as a case was on the verge of being solved, and when it was, they'd be right there taking full credit.

Just the thought of them being here infuriated her. Their presence made her feel as though someone didn't think she was pulling her own weight. That maybe, her being a woman, she couldn't handle the current situation. Probably the same jackass that spilled his guts to the reporters, she thought. Joan, however, proved them wrong in New York, and she had her mind set on proving them wrong now.

As she approached the two men, she concealed her contempt for them as best she could.

O.K.," she said, glaring at one, then the other, "Would one of you two special agents like to let me in on why the F.B.I. is out here in the middle of nowhere? No one's been kidnapped, there's been no ransom request, at least not that I'm aware of, and I'm aware of everything that goes on in my town."

The older of the two stood a little over six-feet and weighed nearly 220 lbs. He was a formidable looking man even though he carried a good portion of his weight in the mid-section. He had dark brown eyes and a head full of graying hair.

"Special Agent Jack Helmsley's the name," the gray haired man said in a deep and hollowed voice, "And this here is Special Agent Tim Rollins, my partner."

"Credentials, if you don't mind," Joan said eyeing the gray haired man.

"No, not at all," Rollins said, reaching into the pocket of his black suit jacket. Helmsley glared at him as if he had spoken out of turn, and then reached in and pulled out his own badge.

Without a glance at either of the two pieces of identification, Joan said, "Well, I guess you are who you say you are."

As they put the badges back in their jackets, she again saw the look of displeasure ole' gray hair shot at his partner.

"So, Timmy was it? Joan asked as she flicked her eyes to the other agent, flashing a smile as she did.

"Timothy actually, but I prefer Tim, if you don't mind."

"So tell me Tim, where did you dig up this old fossil?"

Tim was a pleasant looking light skinned black man who dwarfed in comparison to his aged partner. He stood five feet eleven inches tall and weighed 180 lbs. He sported a bald head and a set of gray eyes that seemed to change colors depending on the situation he was in at the time. His eyes seemed to have changed two shades to the darker side as the question was put to him.

"He was assigned, I mean, I was assigned to work with Agent Helmsley late yesterday afternoon."

Sensing a little tentativeness in his voice, Joan pressed, "Right out of the blue, just like that, boom, here's your new partner. I mean really, is that how they do it in the big time? They just hit you with a new partner right before you go home for the evening?"

"Tim," Jack said in a harried tone, "You don't have to answer that. In fact," he added, staring down at Joan, "We don't need to answer any of your questions."

Joan smiled and said, "Well, unless I woke up this morning in a different country other than the good ole' U.S. of A., or unless you have orders dictating that you have jurisdiction over this case, you sure as hell do have to answer my questions. Now, why are you two here, really?"

Tim looked at Jack, as he felt Jack's eyes glaring at him, and Jack at Tim, as if to say keep your pie hole shut.

"Listen, boys," Joan added, "Why don't I just call down to the Roanoke Office and speak to the resident Agent in Charge? Maybe he…"

"Training," Jack finally replied in an authoritative tone, cutting Joan off.

"Training? What kind of training?" Joan asked, her voice edging on sarcasm. "I hope it wasn't on how to look inconspicuous, because you two stick out like two roaches in an ant farm."

"You're funny," Jack Helmsley said with a narrowed, forced grin. "But really, we are just here to watch and observe, and of course to lend you any assistance you might need. You see, Timmy here has only been with us for a little over six months, and I thought this would be good experience to watch a pro, such as yourself, in action. He's going to be working in the National MP division at the bureau. That's missing persons..."

"I know what it is, Special Agent Helmsley." *And you're really good at flattery and brownnosing,* Joan thought.

"And, well, that's what you have here, so here we are."

"In that case," Joan replied, "I'm always obliged to help those in need."

She sensed somehow that they were here for another reason, though her suspicion fell more toward Helmsley. Rollins seemed quite pleasant and forthcoming; a quality Joan admired. It was something that she hadn't been afforded in her prior workings with the F.B.I. *Maybe they're not all bad,* Joan thought, *but Helmsley was as full of shit as was a cow pasture.*

Maybe it was the way his eyes always seemed to be on the defensive, or that cocky grin that she didn't like. Whatever the reason, she did not trust him, and that was that. In her mind, there was a sense of foreboding about him that hit her like a blow to the head. She could not explain the feeling; she only knew it was there.

She knew she had no real basis on which not to believe their story for being there. And then, a thought popped into her head out of nowhere. It was a thought that was as clear to her as if someone had whispered it in her ear. *Was Helmsley using Agent Rollins as a decoy to manipulate his getting assigned here—unofficially? Helmsley would have the best of both worlds. He would gain points with his superiors for showing interest in the tutelage of a fellow agent and at the same time, he would be able to satisfy his own agenda. Yet, he would not have to worry about reporting in. Clever.*

Right now, however, Joan had no more room on her plate to deal with unsolicited and unwanted help from the F.B.I. She had bigger fish to fry. Charlie Malloy was the fish.

"Well," Joan said looking past the two agents into the cell where Charlie sat in wait, shuddering, "If you really want to help, why don't you give your buddies down at the Hoover building in D.C. a call and see if anyone in your B.A.U., that's, Behavior Analysis Unit."

Helmsley furled his brow and glared at Joan through squinting eyes. "I know what that is Sheriff," he replied in a harried tone, cutting her off.

"Good, then see if they can scrape up a profile on the type of sick bastard that might be responsible for stringing up a sixteen-year old girl by the neck."

"We can do that," Rollins said.

Agent Helmsley gave his partner another hardened stare.

"Yeah, I know just the guy. I'll get right on it." Helmsley said in a tone that reeked of sarcasm. "And if there's anything else I, I mean *we* can do to help, you know, like run a fingerprint or blood work, just give me a holler." He handed her a business card. "I'm just a phone call away."

Joan noted that Helmsley finished up his last two statements with *'me'* and *'I'm'*, instead of *'we'* and *'were'*. "Glad to hear *you* say that, Jack," Joan retorted. Upon saying that, Joan felt a sudden urge to look straight into the eyes of Agent Helmsley. She had not a clue as to why, only that the urge was so overwhelmingly powerful that she had no choice but to do so. And when she did, he was staring right back at her with an intimidating smug look. But she would be having none of that and met his stare with the same resonance as was being given.

She then added, "As I stated before, this is *not* a kidnapping, and therefore it is not a federal offense. We also know that, though tragic, the murder of a small town girl isn't going to make your R.A.'s *must solve list,* therefore you have no jurisdiction here. I'd advise you to remember that. You say you're here to observe and assist, stick to that and we won't have a problem. Are we clear?"

"Absolutely," Helmsley replied.

Jack did his best not to show it, but Joan could tell he was getting hot under the collar. *Might as well throw one more at him,* she thought. "I think I'll call your boss to thank him in advance for any assistance that you will no doubt be giving us. You wouldn't have any objection to that now, would you?"

"No, not at all, sheriff," Rollins replied with a grateful smile.

"Thank you, Agent Rollins," Joan said, knowing that if she did make such a call, Helmsley would no doubt have his bases covered. She then walked past the two agents, acknowledged Rollins with a nod, and continued on as if Helmsley had not been there at all.

The next thing on Joan's agenda was to have Ed coordinate the search parties. She told him to concentrate on the area around Mrs. Zachary's place and around the bridge. She also told him to explain how they might encounter dead, and/or mutilated rabbits, and if they did so, to keep track where and of how many.

"And Ed," she said in a whisper, "If you don't mind, can you take the two feds with you? I can't quite explain it, but I..." She stopped and thought better of passing off her personal concerns to anyone else. "Just take them with you, okay?"

"Sure, no problem," Ed replied.

Chapter 19

1

Joan unlocked the cell door and watched as Gage carried in a small oak table; she followed with two chairs and placed one on each side of the table. As she glanced at Charlie, she could see that he seemed genuinely frightened. By *what,* she wasn't sure, but she was determined to find out.

Gage left and returned with a pitcher of water and two glasses. He put the glasses down, one on either side of the table, poured each glass half full and set the pitcher in-between the glasses. Gage then took position outside the cell door as Joan started.

"Take a seat, Charlie," she said.

Hesitantly, he did.

"So, Charlie, where would you like to start?"

"Not sure what you're referring to," he said nervously.

"You're awfully timid for someone who doesn't know what I'm referring to."

Silence.

"Okay, then," Joan said, "Let's start by you telling me exactly who or what this Bunnyman person is, and what you know about him, or it, whatever the case might be."

Right away, Joan could see Charlie tense up. "You see. I bet your pulse rate just jumped 20, maybe 30 beats a minute at the mere mention of that word. Now, what does it mean to you?"

Silence.

"Charlie, I'm not in the best of moods. In case you haven't heard yet, Kiersten Shae is dead. She was found hung by the neck at an old bridge. The same bridge, coincidently, that several years ago you told Mrs. Shae she should keep her daughter away from. You told her it wasn't safe, that someone killed some kids there once a long time ago. Now cut the crap and tell me what it is you know."

Charlie stared past Joan to the wall behind her. His eyes were fixated on a small stain and did not waver from it. They looked like two black holes filled with water, ready to overflow.

"Charlie?"

"The son-of-a-bitch killed my daughter—killed my Rebecca," he shouted.

"Talk to me Charlie. I promise it will do you good. Just tell me what you know."

Again, silence.

"Who killed your daughter Rebecca?"

Charlie looked briefly at Joan and then resumed his stare on the wall.

"It was a Monday, October fifteenth, way back in sixty-nine." He said, his voice filled with fatigue and fear, "A day just like any other day—you know—normal, people chatting in the halls, gossiping. I could hear kids playing outside through my office window for crying out loud, I mean everything was. . ." He broke off as his bottom lip started to quiver. He attempted to hide it by wiping his mouth with the sleeve of his shirt, and then continued, "Then my wife, Ruth, called a little after 6:00 p.m. I was working late and would have normally already been home, but elections were nearing. I was a town congressman, you know!"

Joan nodded.

"When she called, I could sense somethin was wrong. Her voice was tense and full of worry. She wasn't one to go and get all upset and all, but she was, and she called to tell me that our sixteen-year-old daughter, Rebecca, hadn't made it home from school. Like I said, I knew straight away that somethin was wrong, not only by how she sounded, but because Rebecca, well, she weren't exactly the type that had many friends. She always came straight home from school. And when she was gunna be late, she knew to call. My first thought was that someone done kidnapped her. What, with me running for a second term, I thought it might have been a political ploy, you know, to get me to back out of the race."

"Go on Charlie, what happened next?"

Charlie continued staring at the spot on the wall. His stare was beaming, penetrating, almost like he wasn't looking at the wall at all, but through it, looking into the past. "But then I remembered about the other four kids that had been taken, and my hands started shaking." Charlie hesitated for a moment, picked up the glass of water and downed it, poured another glass of water and took a sip. "All of them were found dead over a two week period. Three of them were from right here in Milford. The other, a boy, he was from down in Dixon."

"You're doing fine," Joan said, "Go on."

"But that wasn't the end of it. There were two other girls that had disappeared the same day as my Rebecca. They had been reported missing earlier that morning. You'd think that the Sheriff's office would have done more, like watchin the school as the kids were let out, or maybe askin the parents to pick up their youngins. They shoulda done more then what they did."

"And what happened to them?"

"I—I'm trying my best to tell you," Charlie stammered.

Joan said, "Come on now Charlie, I have two boys missing as we speak. They're out there somewhere scared half out of their minds. Give me something to work with here."

"I'm trying, I really am." He took a deep breath and continued, "I got scared, like any father would. I was horrified in thinking that my daughter could be a victim of some half crazed fuck.

"Ruth, my wife, was my wife; she sounded so scared on the phone. I guess she had a right to be. She knew about the other missing kids, the first four anyway, and she knew how they were killed."

"And how was that, Charlie?" Joan asked, leaning closer, resting her hands on the table, "How were they killed?"

Charlie shifted his gaze from the wall to Joan, and with a cold sounding sense of reality, said, "The three kids from Milford were found hung by the neck off that damn bridge. The fourth one, the boy from Dixon, I'm not sure about. Supposedly, they never found the body."

Charlie's eyes returned to his spot on the wall and he continued,

"The one thing that no one could understand is why he did what he did. I mean, the girl hadn't been raped, neither were the two boys. Again, I don't know too much about the boy from Dixon. But when they were found, all of their clothes exceptin for their undies and socks had been removed, folded, and placed underneath each of the bodies. He just left them there—swinging by the neck."

Joan knew that none of the information about Kiersten's clothing had been given out. Only those directly involved in the case were privy to that.

"Okay then, Charlie, were these kids killed by this Bunnyman? Is that why the name sends shivers down your spine?"

Charlie fell silent.

"Come on now, Charlie, you're doing fine so far, let's not put a damper on it. Who the hell is this Bunnyman character and why does he scare you so much?"

"I'll get to that," he said. "I just want to make sure I tell you everything." Charlie sat there for a moment, his eyes still peering at the wall.

"Okay, fine. What happened next?"

"I called Sheriff Henderson—as much good as that did. I told him that my daughter was missing. He became extremely agitated at the whole situation. He couldn't believe that he had let four teens die, one of which was his own son, and now, had another three missing, all at the hands of some lunatic that supposedly escaped from the mental institution outside of town."

She wondered if he had meant the old burned down building that had once housed the worst of Virginia's criminally insane.

"The sheriff," Charlie continued, "was having trouble believing that anyone, let alone a patient from that place, could have outwitted him. I think it's what eventually drove him to look beyond the boundaries of the law, to do something not quite in the law books of today's modern society."

Silence filled the room. Joan saw in her mind the photos of the two dead men, the two punks that had been responsible for killing her husband John. They had caught them three weeks after John was laid to rest. She, if given ample opportunity, might have killed the shooter, might have killed them both. After all, they killed everything that was right in her life.

"So, what you're saying then, is that this Sheriff Henderson's kid had been one of the kids killed, and he wanted an old fashion lynching?"

"His son was the first of the kids found dead. I guess he wanted retribution on his own terms."

Joan started getting a bad vibe about the way Charlie's testimony was heading, but she felt compelled to continue. She had to know everything.

"What happened next?" she asked.

"He told me to get home to the wife, so I did. The next day, the sixteenth of October, after a night of no sleep, I had to go to the office to finish up some work. At least that's what I told my wife. Truth was, I couldn't bear to look at her—at Ruth, I mean. Every time I did, I'd see Rebecca staring back at me, and I just couldn't take it. They looked so much alike." He hesitated a moment as he looked for his wallet. "I'd show pictures, but I don't have my wallet."

"We have it, don't worry. Go on."

"Anyway, I called a neighbor to stay with Ruth, and then took off. Next thing I knew I was sitting in my office trying to sleep, but couldn't. Every time the phone rang, I nearly jumped out of my skin. Scared to answer it. Scared not to. I mean, what if it had been Rebecca calling, or Ruth to tell me that our little girl was home? God, how I wished that had been the case. But it was only Sheriff Henderson. He wanted to see me in private. He wanted to tell me that he had found my daughter, and the other two girls. They had been hung, their clothes folded and placed under the bodies just like the others.

"He had already told Ruth. Thank God she wasn't alone."

As Charlie talked of the death of Rebecca, his lower lip quivered and tears streaked down his tired and wrinkled face.

"I cried. Man, how I cried. I mean—my little girl was dead. I was half-crazy. I think that's why Sheriff Henderson brought up the plan when he did, to catch me at a time when I wasn't quite right in the head, a time when he knew I'd be seeking retribution of my own. It was a plan he had cooked up to catch that psycho bastard and give back a little of what he'd been dishing out."

Charlie's eyes narrowed to a squint. "After I agreed to the plan, he done called the other four men to tellim it was on. All but one of us had reason for goin with the sheriff."

Joan's bad vibe grew beyond the point of further interrogating Charlie. She needed to talk with her deputy and called for a break.

After stepping outside, she grabbed Gage by the arm and pulled him aside. "Gage," she asked, "Did you read Charlie his Miranda rights? Please tell me you did."

Gage stared at her with a blank expression, which clearly told Joan that he had not. "Damn it, Gage. You knew we were going to be questioning him today."

"What's the big deal? We both know there's no way in hell that he had anything to do with Kiersten's murder. Besides, I arrested him for being drunk and disorderly. I highly doubt that he would have understood any of it anyway."

"Still," Joan replied, "I have a bad feeling about what he's getting ready to tell us. And if I'm right, he's not only going to need those Miranda rights, he's going to need to expand on those rights and obtain a court appointed attorney."

Gage looked at Joan with a baffled stare and replied, "An attorney, why? For what? He hasn't done anything wrong to need a lawyer. Miranda rights, yeah, maybe I should have read them to him, but a lawyer?"

Joan glanced back into the cell at Charlie. He was still sitting, still staring intently at the wall. "I don't know," she said. "I just have a very bad feeling about. . ." Joan paused. "Gage, I want you to grab the recorder out of my desk and go back in there, turn it on, and tell Charlie what you're doing."

"Which is what, exactly?"

"You're going to read him his rights. I'll be there in a minute. I want to check in with Ed."

Gage went to do what was asked of him while Joan grabbed the two-way radio. "Ed, this is Joan, over." Ed responded back, but had nothing to report. He gave Joan the positions of the search parties. They were scattered throughout the forest surrounding Mrs. Zachary's property, and were moving east toward the coalmines. Joan marked them on the map hanging behind her desk.

"The way we're going," Ed continued, "we'll be at the bridge in about an hour. Don't want to miss anything. Over."

With a bad feeling still fluttering around in her head that stemmed straight from Charlie's story, Joan replied, "Ed, you and two other men break off and make a bee line straight to the bridge and," her thoughts broke off as she thought of something. She had no idea how or why this information came to her, but felt oddly justified in using it as if it were from a good source. "And Ed, make your move when you're sure the two feds aren't watching. Over."

"Roger that, over and out."

Joan returned to the cell where Gage was just finishing. Charlie looked up at Joan and said, "I don't want any damn lawyers. I just want to finish this; get it off my chest."

Joan glanced down at the recorder to make sure the reels were turning.

"Then go ahead, Charlie, finish."

"All of us, except for Deputy Henry Turner, had a beef with this guy, whoever he was. All I knew, all any of us knew at that time, was that this all started when one of those lunatics from that nut house escaped and killed two of the nurses, a security guard, and three of the doctors that worked there. They were high ranked doctors too. Top brass, if you know what I mean. Anyway, I didn't get the impression that Turner was too keen on the idea, but he went along with it because the sheriff had clearly forced his hand."

"What do you mean he forced his hand?" Joan asked.

"I'm not saying he did, I'm just saying he might have. Turner liked to drink, see, a lot. Sometimes, a lot of the times, he'd drink on the job. I think the sheriff was going to fire him if he didn't go along with him, but again, that's just my opinion."

"What about the other three men? Who were they?"

"Daniel Koelmel, Ted Neely, and a guy from Dixon who said he was the older brother of the boy that was killed. He didn't give us a name, just told us to call him J.P."

"Go on." Joan wrote down the names.

"I can still hear it as clear as day—the words the sheriff spoke to us before we commenced with his little campaign. He said, 'There's a fine line between the law and justice. And what we're going to do tonight is justice, plain and simple, and I dare any of you to ever say otherwise. This sorry excuse of a man, this inexcusable waste of flesh and blood, killed my son Alan, and Ted, he killed your son, Eric.'

"When the sheriff was finished, Daniel Koelmel spoke out and told us that this madman killed his daughter, Kristine. Then I spoke up and told everyone that he had just killed my little girl that very morning, along with the other two girls, Cheryl Deysher and Kim Lipman.

"But that wasn't all. That evening, before we all got together, two more girls, twins, turned up missing. I didn't get their names, least I don't remember hearing them anyway. They were taken from a couple of travelers that just happened to be passing through, supposedly on their way to Richmond. Guess they stopped for a bite to eat or somethin. The sheriff put them up in the Milford Lodge, and told them he was going to organize a search party. He didn't mention a word to them about the other children that had turned up dead. I'm guessen that he didn't want the story gettin outside of town cuz of what he was about to do, what we all were about to do."

Joan was taking her own notes to back up the tape recorder. "So you, the six of you went looking for him after the meeting, is that right?" she asked.

"No," Charlie replied as tears began falling again. Each tear followed the same path down his weathered face, shimmying through his shaggy beard and falling to his lap. "I went home first. We hoped that the killer would stay with his pattern."

"Pattern?" Joan asked. "You told me the guy hung them from the bridge and folded their clothes. What other kind of pattern was there?"

"He didn't just hang them. He always took them somewhere first; least that's what the sheriff told us. The sheriff said he never could track him to that location though. Anyway, this guy always waited till the morning. He'd hang them between the time the sun first struck the pines and noon. Again, that's according to the sheriff."

How, exactly, would he know that? Joan asked herself. How would he know unless he had been there to witness the murders firsthand? And if he were there, why in the hell wouldn't he have put a stop to it right then and there?

"So, let me get this straight for the record. All this information came directly from Sheriff Henderson, is that correct?" Joan asked.

Charlie nodded. "He told us that the MO for the first three murders was the same; he said he played a hunch and went to the bridge the morning after my Rebecca was taken. By the time he got there, two of the girls, Kim and Cheryl, were already dead. He found them just like the others, hanging by the neck. When I asked about Rebecca, his poise seemed to change, he got reluctant to finish, but he did. He said he waited to see if the bastard would show up with her, with my Rebecca.

And he did, about an hour after sunup. But Sheriff Henderson said he didn't have a clear shot, that if he had taken one, he would have been taking a risk at hitting Rebecca. He also said that there was no way that the man could have seen him, or could have known that he was there, but somehow he seemed to know, and it didn't bother him. The sheriff said he just went about his business, like it was nothin.'"

"Why didn't he do something, *anything* for Christ's sake?" Joan said standing, her voice flaring with anger. "If he didn't have a shot, why didn't he at least rush him, take him down?"

"Personally, I think he was scared," Charlie said. "They say you know evil, feel it even, when you see it firsthand. I think that's exactly what the sheriff witnessed that day, pure evil, and it scared the hell out of him. I think he was scared beyond the normal sense of the word. So much so that he was unable to take the shot. He just froze, and he just sat there and watched my little girl die." Charlie wiped the tears from his eyes, the snot from his nose, and took another sip of water before continuing.

"Anyway, I went home. Ruth was a mess as you could imagine. But when I told her what we were planning, she got mad. I'd never seen her so mad. I told her this was an opportunity to right a wrong for the death of our daughter, for the death of all the kids. It wasn't like she wasn't in grief, or didn't want to see justice; she just didn't want to see this kind. 'Wrong is wrong.' she said. She said that if I went through with it, she wouldn't be there when I got back, but I couldn't, or wouldn't see that she was right. That's when I ran out of the house and met up with Sheriff Henderson and the other four men at the bridge.

"When we got to the bridge, I remember there being dead rabbits, lots of them, torn all to hell they was. It was weird though."

"Weird in what way?"

"Cuz not a one of them had a pelt left on their mangled bodies. They had been ripped clean off, and we never found a one, not a single damn pelt. Some of them had been freshly killed, and some had been there for days, rotting, maggots eating away at the carcasses. The sheriff said that he had been receiving reports of people finding dead rabbits all over the forest for a couple of weeks. He said that even some of Mrs. Zachary's rabbits had been slaughtered." There was a long pause, and Charlie's brow furrowed again as if his mind had stalled and needed a push.

"Go on, Charlie," Joan said.

"Huh, oh, sorry. We had been there for hours, waiting. The sun was about an hour away from comin up when a fog started rolling in. I hate the fog. Can't see…"

"Don't know why," Gage muttered, cutting Charlie off, "You spend most of your waking life in one."

"Damn it, Gage!" Joan barked.

"What?" Gage replied.

"Charlie, I'm sorry," Joan said. "Please continue."

"When the sun came up, we saw him coming, the fog didn't get all that thick, least it didn't stop us from seeing him carrying one of the young girls.

"Anyway, the girl was barely conscious, but alive. He just dropped her down to the ground from off his shoulder."

Joan recalled Kiersten's crime scene, the indentations that were left.

"We weren't close enough to see her breathing," Charlie said, "But when the poor thing hit the ground, she winced in pain. That's when we all jumped him. Three of us were armed with ball bats, two others with crowbars, and the sheriff had his gun out, but he didn't fire it—not once. We hit him and we hit him and we kept on hittin him. I hit him so hard, that my bat busted in half. I didn't know what to do then, so I just started kicking at him as hard as I could. We kept it going for a good ten minutes or so. But we didn't stop there; we took the rope he had intended to use on the girl, and strung him up as he had done to those poor kids, to my Rebecca."

"Then what?"

"Then we all sat down. We were all of us exhausted, both physically and mentally. I checked on the girl, made sure she was O.K. She was alive, only had a few bumps and bruises. What I didn't know was how she would be in the head. I can still see the fear in her eyes, the look on her face; the same fear that my little girl must have had. Poor thing looked as if she stared death in the face, and she probably did.

"As the bastard swung by the neck, I took notice of what he was wearing, rabbit pelts. He was covered with them from head to toe. Some you could tell were fresh, some looked older than me.

"That's why I guess you could say, that I named the bridge *Bunnyman Bridge* and him *the Bunnyman*. It was obvious that he'd been doin all the rabbit killin.

"Next thing we knew, the girl uttered a single word—*sister*. That's when it dawned on us that there was still a sweet innocent little girl out there somewhere, and we had just killed the only person who knew where she was."

"Did you ever find her?" Joan asked.

"No." Charlie replied.

"After we cut-em down, we took him to an old abandoned coal mine, busted down the wooden blockade that was a sealin it shut, and carried him about a hundred yard or so. Then we blasted it shut with five sticks a dynamite.

"The next day, the whole town got involved in the search for the missin girl, but like I done told ya, we never found her."

"What about the other girl, the one you saved, how was she the next day? Did she remember anything?" Joan asked.

"Nah, she went into some kinda depression. So far as I know, she ain't never said another word to no one, not even her kin. And I'm sure the sheriff didn't mind either cuz he didn't want nuna this mess gettin out. In fact, he had me burn everythin: all the records, reports, files, anythin haven to do with the case. He spent the whole night gettin it all, and then he gave it all to me. I burned it the same day in my fireplace—the fireplace in my empty home. Ruth had gone."

"Well, did he ever find out who the bastard was?" Joan asked.

Charlie stared into Joan's green eyes. "Turns out, the son-of-a-bitch was a local, lived right here in Milford. He had a job working for the Milford Coalmining Company. He went and got himself arrested a year earlier for killing his whole family. Never knew what his name was, other than the name I gave him, *Bunnyman*. I kept that pretty much to myself, except for Mrs. Zachary. I told her the whole story one night after the sheriff retired and you took over. And that's all I know."

"So you didn't recognize this man at all? Never saw him around town or at public meetings?"

"Nope. Even if I had known him, I don't think I would have recognized him anyway."

"Why?"

"His face was smeared with dirt and blood, and he had a scruffy beard, couple-a week's worth of growth as I recollect. But I didn't know the bastard anyway, and I didn't care to. Don't get me wrong, I was glad the S.O.B. was dead, but at the same time, I was sorry that I hadn't listened to my wife. It wasn't worth losing her over." Charlie paused for a second before continuing, "Knowing the guy's name would have made it harder for me to forget about what we had done, and afterwards, after I knew Ruth had left me, that's all I wanted to do was forget."

"What about the others, the ones besides the sheriff and the deputy?" Joan looked down at her notes. "Daniel Koelmel and Ted Neely, how well did you know them?"

"Knew them both well, had beers with them right regular. Course, that all changed after what we done. We kind of made it a habit to avoid each other. I only saw them once a week at church, and then we didn't speak."

"And what about this JP character, had you ever seen him before that night?"

"Nope. I don't ever recollect ever layin eyes on him before. All I can tell ya was that he was a mean cuss, did most of the hitting. The sheriff had to pull him off. I couldn't blame him though; the bastard had killed his younger brother. Said it was the only family he had left."

"Did this JP guy say what his brother's name was?"

"Yeah, and I remember it cause it was similar to what he wanted us to call him. It was JC."

"Seems strange though," Joan said, "that he wouldn't tell you his real name. I mean if no one else gave their name, then it would be different."

Joan turned to Gage. "Why don't you call down to Dixon, make some inquiries about any kids that might have died by hanging or by any other means back in sixty-nine, say between August first and October sixteenth."

"Will do!"

Chapter 20

1

The sun's rays reached through the tall pines like shards of glass. The rain front that moved in the previous night covered the entire east coast, the aftermath of which left behind a rather sloppy trudge through the woods.

As requested, Deputy Ed Cross and two of the state troopers broke off from the main search party and headed toward the old bridge. Their path, however, had more than sloppy puddles and drenched foliage in which they had to navigate through. Shortly after they had parted ways, they happened across more rabbits whose torn and ripped bodies were strewn about the forest floor. The stench of death was all around them, and they welcomed the southern breeze to help keep the smell tolerable.

Fifteen minutes later, the bridge came into view, and with it, the hopes of finding the two boys alive, vanished. The scene was only more hideous than that of Kiersten's because there were two bodies—two dead children. The M.O., however, was the same; all the way down to the clothes being folded neatly under each half naked body.

2

Charlie raised his free hand and wiped away tears. He knew he had done wrong. He had always known it. And he was happy to have the 32 years of guilt lifted from off his chest.

But what if they didn't believe me? Oh, God. What if they thought that I had made up the whole story? These questions waded through Charlie's mind. "They have to believe me," he said silently to himself.

Slowly, Charlie turned his head away from the wall toward Gage who was conversing with someone on the phone at the far end of the office. As they talked, Gage turned and glanced at Charlie with a couple of Yeah, right looks, looks that made Charlie feel as though his suspicions were warranted.

Sweat started pouring down his forehead and into his eyes, causing them to burn. His heart thumped hard and fast against his breastbone. Charlie knew that at least three of the six men who had been a part of that horrid night were now dead. That left himself, Turner and J.P., and who the hell knew where they were. That left essentially no one with which they could corroborate his story. They have to believe me, he thought again. They have to.

"Charlie," Joan said softly, grabbing his hand. It was shaking. He was desperately in need of a beer or something stronger, a shot of Jack Daniel's. "I am truly sorry about the loss of your daughter. And I'm sorry that your wife felt as though she had no other alternative than to leave you at a time when you probably needed her most."

Charlie glanced at Joan, but said nothing.

"Charlie," Joan continued, "I just want you to know that I'm truly grateful that you came forth with this information, but I am an officer of the law, you know that. You refused to have counsel present, and you've just revealed to me that you assisted in the taking of another man's life. You helped kill someone, Charlie. It doesn't matter that it took place thirty-two years ago. There is no statute of limitations when it comes to murder."

Joan released his hand and stood up. She paced the cell floor, thinking of the legal ramifications that was about to be thrown at her friend. "Charlie," she said, "I want you to know that I'm also your friend, and I will personally stand by you in every way possible. I won't leave you hanging out to dry. I'll make sure you get a good attorney. With your age and the fact that you're cooperating with the proper authorities now, and given the circumstances behind the incident, you should do O.K. I can't promise you anything, mind you, but I can sure as hell stand up for you, and I will."

Chapter 21

1

The two-way radio blared as Joan locked the cell door. The sound of her deputy's voice told her something was wrong. She was right. The two boys had been found.

She picked up the radio, paused, and spoke into it. She told her deputy that she would be out there as soon as possible, and for them not to do or touch anything except to make sure the original cordoned off area was still intact.

The office went silent. There were no words that could be said that would make sense of what was happening in their small tourist town, a place where families came for long weekends or for an entire week on vacation. Joan shuddered at the thought of what her small town looked like just two short months ago when men, women, and children lined the streets and filled the hiking trails.

Thank God for the timing, Joan thought to herself.

She called Barbara and filled her in and asked her to get out there as soon as possible.

Joan walked to the window and looked outside. When she had arrived this morning, there were just two reporters. Now, there was a brood of story hungry TV stations with their best reporters hovering outside the building, waiting to be the first to get an exclusive story at the expense of someone else's misery.

It's a sick world, she thought.

When Joan opened the doors, the reporters dropped their coffees, and grabbed their microphones. Leslie Tatterson, of Channel Six Action News, got to the sheriff first. Joan shot her a 'you heartless bitch' look before speaking. "First of all," she started, "I will not, repeat, NOT, be taking any questions, so don't bother wasting my time or yours, because it isn't going to happen." She paused for a moment. "As most of you already know, yesterday we found the body of Kiersten Shae. I'm sure you all know I can't divulge any particulars of the case. What you don't know was that three more kids ranging in age from nine to twelve turned up missing yesterday some time after three in the afternoon. We found one of them last night out in the woods trying to get home. He has a broken rib, a few bumps and bruises, but for the most part, he is doing fine and is currently at the Dixon City Hospital with his mother. His two brothers," Joan swallowed hard and continued, "The other two have just been found. I'm sorry to say that they did not make it. Their names are being withheld until their family has been notified. Now I'm sorry, but that's all I can say at this time, except that the Sheriff's Office is asking all parents to make sure their kids have a ride to and from school. If they don't, please keep them home, or contact my office and we'll make sure that they have a ride. We'd also like to ask all of you here in town and on the outskirts, to report anything or anyone that looks out of the ordinary. I'd like to further ask that if anyone has any information pertinent to this case, no matter how trivial it may seem, please call my office at 1-804-603-1989. Thank you, that's all I have to say at this time." Joan turned away from the lights, cameras, and microphones, and went back inside.

2

Brandon Nelson was taking the last sip of his morning coffee as he reached for the remote to turn off the T.V. He would have to leave now or be late for a noon house call with one of his patients. Just as his finger was ready to depress the off button he heard mention of his hometown again in the news. Staring intently at the screen, he listened.

"*We are breaking away from our regularly scheduled programming to give you an update on the missing teen, Kiersten Shae. Here with us now is our on the spot reporter, Leslie Tatterson.*"

"*Thanks Bob, I'm here live in Milford, where minutes ago Sheriff Joan Fortune gave us an update...*"

Brandon watched the interview with the town's sheriff. His thoughts raced back in time as he listened to the fact that there were now three kids dead, and he wondered how they had been killed. As his mind reflected back thirty-two years into the past, the images that formed in his mind were of kids being hung by the neck, a detail he was almost, no, a voice in his head whispered, *positive*, that the good sheriff had left out on purpose.

Brandon sat back on the oak bar stool. "Just go see your patient, and forget about it," he said to himself. But he couldn't. The proverbial seed had been planted. That seed being the voice somewhere in the back of his head saying that there was indeed a connection between what had happened all those years ago to what was happening now. He tried to repress it, but the voice was *most* insistent.

As the story was finishing, a phone number scrolled at the bottom of the screen for anyone having information. Brandon fumbled around for the pen in his shirt pocket, retrieved it, and scribbled it down.

Before placing a call, he wanted to try and recall and jot down as much information as he could remember about the murders that took place all those years ago. He wanted to remember specific details about the case, details that would confirm or deny whether the two cases were indeed related or not.

He reached for the phone after jotting down a few notes on the edge of a newspaper. When the phone started to ring, he suddenly felt self-conscious and foolish for thinking that there could be any relation between the two cases that were separated by a generation. On the third ring, just as he was about to hang up, a male voice answered, "Milford Police Department, Deputy Jensen speaking."

3

Joan walked up the stairs to the police station. Behind her, she left a barrage of questions from the mass of reporters that lined the front of the municipal building. Comforting solitude hit her as the doors to her office closed, but it didn't last long. As she entered she saw Gage standing at her desk with the phone pressed to his ear, "Hold on a sec, Dr. Nelson, the sheriff will be right with you." Gage covered the speaking end of the receiver, "Someone calling about the case."

Joan went to her desk and took the receiver from her deputy.

"This is Sheriff Fortune, how can I help you?" For a span of about ten seconds, she heard no voice from the other end of the line. She could, however, hear breathing. "Hello?" she said with authority, "Can I help you?"

"Ah, hmm, well, I'm not sure," a male voice replied.

"Hey, you called me, remember?"

"Yeah, I know I did, and to be honest, I'm feeling a little foolish about it."

"Well, why don't you give me your full name, tell me why you called, and let me be the judge of that."

"Well, I guess it couldn't hurt. The name is Dr. Brandon Nelson." As Joan wrote down his name, she detected a certain uneasy feeling in his voice. A voice, she thought, that sounded rather masculine and educated; a voice that would normally sound confident and self-assuring, but now sounded like someone out of his element.

"Okay Dr. Nelson was it? What do you want to confess to?"

"Confess," Brandon said, confused. "I don't have anything to confess, I just wanted to…" He stopped. The silence unnerved Joan.

"You just wanted to what, Dr. Nelson?" Joan finally said.

"I just wanted to confirm some information about how you found the bodies of the three kids. I just saw you on the TV, and, well, I was just curious, that's all," Brandon said feeling more foolish than ever.

"I'm not at liberty to disclose any of that information, but if you know anything, about the crime scene, I mean, feel free to enlighten me."

"O.K., let's say I tell you what was at the crime scene. Can you confirm it if I'm right?"

After careful consideration, Joan replied, "If you tell me something that's accurate, I'll confirm it."

"They were found hanging under an old train bridge out near the coal mines."

"I'm listening," Joan said, sitting up in her chair; he had officially caught her attention.

"Were they found wearing nothing but their under garments and their socks?"

"Go on."

"The rest of their clothes were found folded neatly and lying on the ground beneath their feet."

How could he know that? Joan thought.

Silence.

"I'm guessing by your silence that I'm right on at least part of what I just said. If that is the case, I don't want you to get the wrong impression of how I know about the particulars of the case," he said, feeling a little uneasy. "I don't want you thinking that it was me, I mean that I…"

Silence.

"Why should I get the wrong impression? Are you feeling guilty?" Joan asked.

"Guilty, maybe, but not for the reasons you're thinking."

"And what reason would that be?"

"With what I've told you, you probably think I had something to do with the murders, but let me assure you, I did not."

"What did you say your name was?" Joan asked.

"Dr. Brandon Nelson. I'm a psychiatrist and a professor at the University of Virginia in Richmond."

"Well, why don't you just ease my suspicions by telling me how you just happen to know so much about this case."

Brandon said, "I think it would be better if I just came out there and talked to you in person, one on one. I can be there tomorrow by noon."

Joan wrote a note down on paper and motioned Gage over.

"No," a female voice said from seemingly everywhere. "There's no need for that." The voice was soft and weak and sounded as if it had traveled many miles before landing in Joan's ears. Joan looked around the room for the source, but could not find one, and ignored it. She again motioned for her deputy.

"You can trust him," the voice said. "Trust him."

"Trust who?" Joan said aloud as Gage arrived at her desk.

"Huh?" Brandon Nelson said on the phone.

Gage shrugged and looked warily around the office, then flicked his eyes back to Joan. "Me?" Gage said as if asking a question. "Yeah, you can trust me."

Joan then remembered the feeling that she had earlier that morning. It was the feeling that she was somehow being fed information by some means other than the normal channels of communication. And she was having the same feeling now, only, she was *hearing* the information, not feeling it as was the case earlier.

For a second, Joan's mind spun around in circles. She was listening to three people talking to her all at the same time: a mysterious caller who accurately described Kiersten's and the Kaminski boy's crime scene, her deputy, and a strange voice that seemed to be present only inside her head.

"Dr. Nelson, can you hold on a second?" she asked and removed the phone from her ear before he had a chance to answer. "Gage, did you just hear that?"

The puzzled look on his face told her that he hadn't.

"Hear what?" Gage asked.

"Nothing." She said, "Here, see what you can find…" Her voice trailed off as the voice spoke again, "Trust him, trust him." There was something else in the voice too, something she didn't expect, not that she expected to be hearing voices in her head; there was a depth of feeling that came with the words that went straight to her heart, as if the words themselves had been spoken by some quintessential being, or maybe, a loved one.

"Joan? Joan?" Gage asked, "Is everything alright?"

"Yeah, fine, "Joan replied looking anything but equanimous.

"What did you want? That guy on the phone giving you a hard time?"

Joan flicked her eyes toward the note in her hands, and then to Gage. "Um, files," she said, the note crumpling in her hand. "I'm entrusting you to get your hands on the personnel files of all the employees that worked at the Milford Coal Mines. Look for people who had local addresses. Charlie said this guy was a local."

"And where would I get records from thirty two years ago?"

"It's called police work."

"No, that would be called secretarial work," Gage said.

"Fine, you're hired, now scoot."

Gage smiled half-heartedly, and started to walk away when Joan said, "Try the Social Security Office. If they can't help, try upstairs in the attic. I think this building was used as the Milford Mine's headquarters."

"Okay," Gage said and then turned and headed for his desk.

Joan glanced around the room again, half expecting to see the person responsible for the voice, but did not. She than glanced down at the phone cupped in her hands.

"Dr. Nelson, I'm so sorry," she said, trying to think quickly. "I was checking my schedule." The line was quiet. "Mr. Nelson, are you still there?"

"Hold on," he said, "I'm actually checking mine too. I do have a session with a patient, but I think I can get a colleague to fill in for me."

"I actually have a funeral to attend in the morning." Joan replied.

"Yeah, I was sorry to hear about the girl—Kiersten, I think her name was."

"Yes, Kiersten was her name."

At that moment, Joan felt as if someone had just wrapped their arms around her, hugging her. What the hell is happening to me, she wondered.

"Maybe after—the funeral I mean, say around three?" Brandon said.

Silence.

"Sheriff?"

"Yeah, yeah," Joan finally said, "That ah—that sounds good. There's a diner in the center of town. You can't miss it."

God, she thought, *what the hell am I doing?* And even as the words left her mind, a memory of her father embraced her. *Follow your gut, sometimes, that's all we have,* she remembered him saying.

But just in case, she thought, as she remembered something else her father always said, *always have a back-up plan.*

"I guess you know that I've traced this call and now know where to find you in case you don't show up," Joan said, knowing that she not only didn't have a chance to run a trace, but also lacked the tools in her small office in which to do so. But he didn't have to know that."

"That's fine, I have nothing to hide. I'll see you tomorrow at 3:00."

"Looking forward to it, Dr. Nelson."

Chapter 22

1

At about 1:00 p.m., Joan met Deputy Cross at the crime scene. Barbara Williams arrived shortly thereafter. As word spread about the two dead kids, the rest of the search party assembled at the scene.

Agent Jack Helmsley was furious about not being notified immediately upon the finding of the two kids. He felt as though he was intentionally being left out of the investigation, and expressed that fact to Joan.

"Yeah," Joan said, "I can see that you're all busted up inside at the death of these two kids. It's written all over your face."

"Why do I get the distinct feeling that you're trying your best to purposely keep me out of the loop here?" Agent Helmsley asked, his words smothered in animosity. "We are only here to try and help."

"Which is it, Jack—I or we?"

"What in the hell are you talking about?"

"Simple question, really. First, you said that I was keeping *you*—as in you alone—personally out of the loop. Then the next thing you said was that *we* were only here to help, meaning, at least I'm assuming that meant you and your *new* over the counter partner. Now, which is it?"

"Look," he said, "We're all here for the same reason—to catch whoever it is that's terrorizing your town and killing innocent children, and of course to provide a novice agent with some technical training."

Joan wanted to respond with a *Yeah, right* remark. She had always hated the F.BI, but this guy, to stand here in front of her and patronize her, well, it didn't bode well in his favor. She knew, or—was it more of a feeling— that he was here for a purpose. But what purpose? She thought, and who was he, really? He had the look of an F.B.I agent, the clothes, the dark reflective sunglasses, and the credentials, but there was something about his demeanor, the way he carried himself. What secrets was he carrying around with him?

"Well, if what you say is true," Joan replied, "Then you shouldn't consider the time you and the others spent away from the crime scene as being wasted just because I didn't call off the search party. There is still a killer on the loose. Who knows, maybe you could've run into him while you were out there. If you did, that would have been a hell of a lot more helpful to us than you standing around here with your hands in your pockets wondering how on earth this killer can move in and out of here, seemingly at will, not to mention that he's doing so without leaving behind a single shred of evidence.

"Fine. Whatever you say. I mean, you are, or should I say, were, the one in charge," he replied. His tone remained civil, but in his mind, he so desperately wanted to clench up his fist and smack it right on the bridge of her nose, shattering the nasal bone, sending the splinters into her brain. It was something he had wanted to do since the first time he had met her at the police station.

So smug, Helmsley thought. *So tough. Pretty little thing like you should be popping out babies, not playing cops and robbers.* The very thought of seeing the blood gush from her nose and mouth gave him a sincere feeling of joy and calmness.

"What the hell are you talking about—*were?*" Joan asked harshly.

"One dead mate, it stays in State, two or more dead, it goes to the feds."

"You sick. . ." Joan stopped as she realized she had an audience.

"Hey, you're the one who wanted to play by the rules. When two or more people die with the same M.O.—that tends to constitute a Serial Killer, and when asked, the F.B.I. just loves to jump right in and take over. It's out of my hands. By this time tomorrow, this place will be swarming with Federal Agents from the Behavior Analysis Unit."

"Help? I didn't ask for any help." Joan replied.

"Oh, I didn't mention that? Please forgive me, but I took the liberty of doing that for you."

Joan looked smartly at him, turned and walked away. "Don't expect any cooperation from me," she said over her shoulder.

Jack, of course, had no real intentions of calling in any additional help. The last thing he wanted was a bunch of feds walking around sticking their noses into his business, at least not until he had accomplished his goal, which was to find out who the perp was copycatting a 32 year old murder spree and eliminate him. And maybe that bitch, he thought.

2

Hours had been spent looking for evidence that was no more visible now than at Kiersten's crime scene. Joan became irritated and angry. She was standing at the foot of two dead kids that had their whole lives to look forward to. The very thought of seeing the two boys placed in black body bags as Kiersten had been, made Joan turn away. Hearing the zippers closing the bags made her cringe.

She wiped the tear from the corner of her left eye, took a deep breath, and looked around the area. *So hard to believe,* she thought, *that this type of hideousness has descended upon my town, on my watch.*

She had left New York to rid herself of the horrors of big city life. She left to get away from the drug dealers, the mobsters, and the drive by shootings of gang members aiming their guns at other rival gangers, leaving behind the innocent dead in the streets. Now, as she looked around the crime scene, she felt as though she would almost welcome back the crimes of the city. At least there, she would be able to find some evidence to go on: a witness, bullet casings, a serial killer's calling card, the last words of a rival gang member telling her who or at least what gang it was that shot him, something. Here, however, there was nothing except three dead kids between ten and sixteen years of age, and not one damn clue as to who did it.

What kind of monster does this? Who kills kids just for the fun of it? Who? Who?

Joan turned and glanced down at the body bags at her feet, took another deep breath, and asked the state troopers to head to the school to escort any kids whose parents hadn't heard the news, or couldn't get there in time to pick their kids up.

As the night draped over the waning sun, Joan felt dumbfounded. All she had to show for two days worth of police work was three dead kids and the testimony of what amounted to the town drunk. Maybe, she thought, the feds would come up with something she had not.

3

When Joan arrived home, she spent the entire evening with Caitlin in her arms watching Beauty and The Beast on DVD. Caitlin was fast asleep in her mother's lap by the time the movie was over. Joan felt like staying there on the couch the entire night, holding her daughter, stroking her hair, watching her chest rise and fall as she breathed, feeling the puff of breath caress her face. At that moment, it felt as if everything was as it should be. Joan wished she could make this feeling last forever by holding on to the most precious gift ever given to her, Caitlin. She knew, however, that she had a psycho killer that needed to be stopped. The question remained, how?

As Caitlin snuggled in her arms, Joan noticed she was turning and twisting more than normal, as if she might be having a bad dream. She didn't, however, want to wake her. Caitlin had her arms, regardless of her movements, wrapped around Joan tightly. That feeling, Caitlin hugging her, felt not too far from the feeling that she had experienced earlier in the day while talking to Dr. Nelson; that feeling of warmth and caring, a feeling of complete trust. The feeling was so close to what she was feeling now, that it made her wonder. As she looked down at her daughter, she whispered, "Was that—you?" And then dismissed the idea entirely, feeling foolish for even thinking it.

For the next hour, Joan held her daughter, but the time came when she needed to get her own rest for the day to come.

Joan carried Caitlin to bed, tucked her in and kissed her on her nose. Caitlin did not stir.

When she reached her own room, she undressed and slipped her naked body in between the sheets. She reached for the book she had been reading, Dean Koontz's, *Watchers,* that she had sitting on her nightstand. *Yeah, just what I need,* she thought, *a book about a creature after a man and his new genius dog friend.*

Joan laid the book back on the nightstand and got out of bed. She moved to the window that faced her rear yard and the vast dark forest beyond. She stood in the window watching the wind as it blew, rustling through the branches of the tall blue spruce pines that lined her back yard. The wind gusted and shook free the dried autumn leaves from the two large oak trees that stood sentinel on each side of the house. The wind carried the leaves across the yard like waves across an ocean.

When the gust was over, the rolling leaves fell silent, like ocean water on a beach after a crashing wave, silently seeping through the sand.

Rays of moonlight shifted around the yard through the numerous cirrus clouds that flooded the night sky. Outside, the night seemed quiet and peaceful; inside, Joan's mind was spinning from the events that had transpired over the last forty-eight hours.

It was then that she saw it.

No, it was her imagination.

Blink, she thought, *just blink and it will be gone.* But it wasn't. The shadow within shadows resembled the outline of something—a man or some creature, a bear on its hind legs maybe. Joan didn't know what, but something was definitely standing just inside the tree line of the woods. Joan closed her eyes, rubbed them, opened them, but it was still there.

Watching.

Waiting.

But who or what was it watching? Why was it watching at all? It didn't appear to be her that it was looking at, the angle was wrong. It was looking further down her house.

It was looking at Caitlin's room.

Joan ran across her room, down the hall and into her daughter's room. Once there, Joan saw that Caitlin was fast asleep, stirring, but asleep. Her whole body was turning from side to side, not convulsively, but enough to let Joan know her daughter had carried the bad dream with her from the couch.

Talking. She was talking too, not full sentences, but she was saying words. "*Push left… fall right,*" and she repeated them over and over, "*Push left . . . fall right. Push left . . . fall right.*"

Joan had no idea what to make of it. She moved toward the window. She saw nothing outside.

No outline of a man

No outline of a creature.

Except for the fact that Caitlin seemed uncomfortable in a dream she was having, everything appeared to be normal. Joan started to think that what she saw outside was nothing more than a figment of her imagination—just an involuntary thought brought on by the book laying on her nightstand. *That has to be it,* she thought.

Joan looked down at Caitlin. She was no longer talking, only sleeping, peacefully and quietly; no bad dreams happening now.

She moved toward her daughter's bed. She listened to the deep, slow, rhythmic sounds of Caitlin's breathing; she was indeed sound asleep. Joan reached down and retrieved the covers and pulled them back up gently, being careful not to wake her. *Odd though,* Joan thought, *the covers looked as if Caitlin, at some point during the night, had actually tossed them aside and had gotten out of bed.* Joan then remembered something that happened the other morning, something that at the time had caught her off-guard as she peeked in on Caitlin. She had been sitting on the floor at the foot of her bed; her stuffed rabbits placed carefully in front of her as she played with them, but when asked later that evening about it, Caitlin had no recollection of ever doing so.

Sleepwalking, Joan thought, as her mind pulled back the memory. *Sleepwalking, and now sleep-talking.*

A smile came to Joan's face as she glanced down at her daughter. With no more thought on the matter, Joan made sure the window was locked, then leaned over and kissed her sleeping daughter and went back to her own room.

As she reached for the light switch on the bedside lamp, she glanced at the book that had invaded her mind with unwanted thoughts. She shook her head and smiled. She couldn't believe that she let a book get the better of her. She flipped off the lamp and fell asleep.

4

Caitlin's sleep-talking, on the other hand, had only just begun. The moment Joan had left the room, the dreams returned, this time, however, they were more intense than before. Caitlin's small body again began to squirm under the covers; her head turning from side to side as she dreamed. Her eyelids were shut tight, but underneath that thin layer of skin, rapid eye movement was taking place. Her eyes moved fast, darting from side-to-side, as if watching the ball on a tennis match at high speed.

Caitlin had had dreams before—scary ones even—but never so profound. The screams she heard had sounded so frightening and real, as if the person screaming had been standing right next to her. Moreover, the scenes showed to her were so vivid and lifelike to the point that the stench of the blood she saw cascading across an unknown kitchen floor swirled up through her nostrils as she breathed.

In her dream, she saw a husband. A husband that was kind and caring. A hard working father who had seven, no wait. Yes, she could see more clearly now, it was soon to be eight, he was to be the proud father of eight beautiful kids.

And then she saw his wife.

And, like her husband, she was loving, and full of life, both externally and internally. She was pregnant and due any time.

And the kids were all good kids, brought up to respect their elders.

Names, she saw names—no—*heard* names.

Kristine.

Frank.

Eric.

Michael.

Kimmy.

Becky.

Alan.

Then she saw a dark blur; it was the baby, the pregnancy had gone terribly wrong.

Backwards. Breached.

What was breached?

The baby.

She saw blood—*Oh, God, the blood.* So much blood. The floor was covered with it.

Caitlin woke and sat upright in her bed. Sweat trickled down her angelic face, but it did not derive from fear, at least—not her own. The fear she felt belonged to the person within her dream. The fear belonged to the father, the mother, and all of the children. She did not understand the dream, or why she was even having it to start with. *Why would I have a dream like that?* She wondered. Her grandmother would say that people have no control over what they see in their dreams, and for the most part, she would be right. But her grandmother would also say that dreams are just that, dreams, stories conjured up in a make-believe world, stories that were not real. But this, Caitlin knew, was not the case, at least not this dream.

Caitlin had questions with no one to answer them. But then, out of thin air, a woman appeared in front of a picture of Joan that hung on the wall facing her bed. The woman came in the form of an apparition, fading in and out, blurry at times. She was a very attractive woman wearing a simple, but pretty flowered dress. And though the image was translucent and without color, Caitlin knew the dress was purple with yellow and white flowers. If anyone else had walked in the room at that very moment, they would have seen nothing more than Caitlin sitting up in her bed, staring at the picture of her mother.

Then the woman spoke. She told Caitlin that she was a very special young lady with very special powers far beyond that of which most people could comprehend; powers that would grow stronger as she grew older, powers that could aid the stopping of the horrible deaths that had not yet taken place. And as Caitlin listened, she realized that she somehow knew every word that the woman was going to say before she said it.

As the woman continued to talk, Caitlin saw an image of the next girl that was to be taken. Caitlin remained calm; she now understood the dream, knew what had to be done, and she knew who to contact for help. But the contact wouldn't be made by ways of any conventional means.

Chapter 23

1

In the corridor outside the police station, a pair of eyes looked furtively in from the door window.

Gage moved a cart that contained an old fashioned black and white TV out of the storage room, turned it on and adjusted the volume to his liking. He was just about to jump into a box of files sent to him by Tom Parker from the Social Security Office.

Parker, a jolly ole' soul that could pass for any Mall Santa at Christmas, had spent a better part of his day looking for the information that Gage had requested. He found what little there was and called for a courier to have it taken directly to the Milford Police Station that same day.

Gage had just removed the lid from the cardboard box that looked every bit as old as it was when the phone rang. The eyes of Charlie and of those just outside the police station door watched as Gage walked over and picked up the receiver.

"Milford Police Station, Deputy Jensen speaking, how can I help you?" Gage answered.

"Deputy Jensen, I'm Jed Ottman here from the Dixon City Sheriff's office. I have that info that you requested the other day."

"Oh, is that right?" Gage replied, turning his head toward Charlie to meet his stare.

"Yeah, sorry it took so long, but you know what it's like digging through old records by hand, especially things that took place thirty some years ago."

"Yeah, as a matter of fact, I do, or rather I will by the time this night ends."

"Thank God for computers, right?"

"You'll get no argument from me. So, what is it that you found?" Gage asked still eyeing Charlie.

"Not much, really."

"What do you mean, *'not much'?*"

"Just what I said. I pulled all the murder cases for that entire year. Had eighteen in all. But nothing in the time frame you mentioned. I even expanded the search to cover a five-year time period. Seems the only hanging we ever had, was a suicide. Some poor bastard lost his wife and job in the same day. File says he hung himself with his belt from a rafter in his attic. Hell of a way to go out, don't you think?"

"Yeah. What was his name?"

"Tomas Arden."

"Nothing else?"

"Nothing that matches the M.O. you gave me. I did find a gal named Julie Patterson which matches the initials you gave me; she was killed in 1970 though, hit and run. The driver was never caught. I doubt it's related to the case, but it's the only J.P. I could find during that specific timeframe."

"Well, hell, I guess that's a dead end."

"Sorry to put a damper on your night."

"You didn't. I just hate a dead end that's all. Anyway, thanks for your time in this matter. I'll let Sheriff Fortune know first thing in the morning."

Gage hung up the phone and glared at Charlie who was clinching the cell bars so tightly that his knuckles had turned white.

"So, some guy with the initials J.P. from Dixon lost a brother at the hands of the same person that you say killed your daughter Rebecca, huh? I mean that is what you said, right?" Gage asked.

Silence.

"Are you sure you wouldn't like to change your story there Charlie ole boy?"

"No! What I told you is the truth, I swear it. I swear it on my daughter's grave."

"Let me guess, that's your story and you're sticking to it, right?"

Silence.

"Just what I thought," Gage said.

"I'm telling you the truth, that's what J.P. told me, told all of us."

"Well, I surely do hate to be the bearer of bad news, but it seems that no one from Dixon died hanging from that bridge thirty–two years ago. Hell, from any bridge for that matter."

Again, silence.

"I imagine," Gage said, "that your poor daughter's turning cartwheels in her grave knowing that her own father won't help us save more kids from the same fate that was handed to her. No wonder your wife left you."

"No! No! Stop saying those things. I've told you everything I know. I loved my wife, and I loved my daughter. I'd do anything to help. I did do everything, even murder. Why won't you believe me? Why?"

Outside the office door, the eyes still watched.

Chapter 24

1

In Champagne, Illinois, twenty miles outside of Chicago, a dark-haired woman left her two-bedroom apartment at 8:45 p.m.

Her apartment was small and modest and was located in an upscale neighborhood. She had lived in this apartment for the better part of three years. At times, she worked out of her home, not a lot, but enough so that she kept a second set of files for all of her teens.

She worked for the State of Illinois as a Teen Prevention and Intervention counselor, specializing in drug rehab.

On this night, the seventeenth of October, she entered her silver, two-door light gray Volvo and pulled out of her driveway. She maneuvered through her borough and onto Roosevelt Boulevard where she proceeded to head east toward Interstate 80. Her destination was the Chicago O'Hare Airport.

Forty minutes later, she parked her car in the long-term parking lot and got out of her car. She shut the car door leaving the keys in the ignition and the doors unlocked. She walked to the United Airlines ticket counter carrying nothing but the clothes on her back, her driver's license, and a credit card in the left rear pocket of her Nautica jeans, and a memorized dream. A dream of which only small bits of information were unfolding, one frame at a time—a dream that if she demonstrated patience and followed through to the end, promised to answer all the questions that were forming in her mind.

2

Charlie finished his dinner and drifted off to sleep. He was unaware that Gage had even left the office, let alone the building.

He woke suddenly to the calling of his name.

"Charlie," a male voice called out in a playful tone, "Oh, Charlie boy, you've been telling secrets that you vowed you would never tell. And we just can't have that."

"Who's there?" Charlie cried out.

"Now, Charlie, there you go, hurting my feelings. That's not a very nice way to treat an old pal."

After a few seconds of silence, Charlie had to stand up and face the man whose voice he thought he recognized, a voice from his past. Scared, Charlie turned slowly as he stood. The figure moved to the front of the jail cell just as Charlie turned around.

"Oh, it's you," Charlie said in a relieved tone. "You scared me half to death."

The familiar face glared at Charlie. "Scaring you wasn't *quite* what I had in mind."

"Then, why are you here after all these years? Have you heard about the recent killings? Do you think that the killer could have survived what we did to him, and now he's come back?"

"You mean your—what was it you called him—*Bunnyman*—wasn't it? Yeah, that was it. I doubt that anyone could have survived all that," the man said with a menacing smile, "Not after that beaten we threw him."

"Well, why did you come back then, J.P.?"

"Because it appears that someone knows what happened here all those years ago, and whoever it is—has decided to do a little—copycatting of your *Bunnyman*. So, I thought I'd come back and deal with the problem personally. And," the man said, his voice turning cold, "I have come to resolve a problem that I should have taken care of a long time ago. A mistake that I can assure you—I will never make again."

"Problem? Wha—what kind of problem?"

"Witnesses, Charlie, ole-boy, witnesses. I shouldn't have left any back then, and I sure as hell can't, no, let me rephrase that, I won't leave any behind this time. I want to put an end to all this *Bunnyman* bullshit once and for all."

J.P. pulled out a gun, slid it between the bars and squeezed off one round. Charlie's eyes widened in a blur of pain as his hands went to his chest. He stumbled backward towards the wall. The bullet went clean through. He glanced down at his bloodstained hands, and then back to his ole pal, sighed, and said "Why?" with a gurgled breath.

"I just told you," J.P. said, "No more witnesses." He then squeezed off two more rounds, another to the chest, and one to Charlie's forehead. He watched as the old man's legs gave way to his lifeless body, his arms collapsing to his side as he slumped backwards against the wall and slid to the floor leaving a wide streak of blood on the wall. Charlie's head slouched forward. J.P. watched as Charlie's skin turned ghostly white as the blood oozed out through the two holes in his back, and gushed out of the hole in the back of his head that was three times the size of the one in his forehead. The blood crept along like a slow moving river to the center of the jail cell, and pooled.

Charlie's ole pal removed the silencer, turned and exited the room as if nothing had taken place.

3

At thirty-six thousand feet, the dark haired woman sat in the second row, seat A in the first class cabin. Her eyes were closed, but her dreams told her what to expect next on her journey.

When she landed at Reagan National Airport, she was to go to the Hertz Rent-A-Car counter and pick up the car she had reserved the night before. From there, she would drive southeast to La Plata, Maryland, and check into her hotel room at the Comfort Inn, room 34, again reserved the night before, though she could not recall doing either. From there she had no clue of her final destination. She did know, however, that more dreams would follow with more direction, and that all would be known at precisely 8:00 p.m. the following day.

4

Gage returned to the station a little after midnight. He threw a blanket and a pillow that he had brought from home onto the cot on the far right corner of the room.

Before retiring for the night, he moved quietly to the cell to check in on Charlie.

Gage's eyes focused on the pool of blood in the center of the cell. He ran to Joan's desk and retrieved the keys.

After unlocking and entering the cell, he checked Charlie's carotid artery for any sign of a pulse. He found none. "Damn-it!"

5

Joan woke to the ringing of the phone. For only having slept an hour, she felt amazingly refreshed. Throwing aside the sheet and blanket, she yawned, rubbed her eyes, and reached for the phone. As Gage told her of what he found upon returning to the police station, she felt nauseous, weak, and sad. Not only had she known Charlie since her arrival to Milford, he had been the first to welcome her to his humble town. He was a friend, but more importantly, he had been the only lead she had to the murders that took place thirty-two years earlier, and consequently, to the ones taking place now on her watch, and that pissed her off.

"Damn it, Gage! Where the hell were you when all this happened?"

Gage replied, "I went home for a quick bite and to grab my pillow and a blanket. He was sound asleep when I left, and the office was locked. I didn't know anything was going to happen."

"Yeah, well, something did. Charlie is dead." Her anger was underlined with a long pause. "Did you call Barbara yet?"

"No, thought you'd want to get here first."

"Go ahead and make the call. I'll be there in a few."

Joan hung up and went straight to the master bath, threw cold water on her face and toweled it dry. The refreshed feeling that she had prior to answering the phone, was now a distant memory.

After throwing on some clothes, she went to Caitlin's room and quietly peeked inside. The room was somewhat dark with only a Beauty and the Beast nightlight glowing behind the chair in the far corner. It appeared that Caitlin was still sound asleep, or at least in her bed as she could see the outline of her body tucked under the blanket. Good, she thought, then whispered, "Sleep tight sweetie," and closed the door.

Chapter 25

1

As the dawn's light washed over the night sky, Marie Shae lay quietly in bed. Her eyes were closed, but her mind was wide awake; she was tortured with thoughts of having to bury her beloved daughter. With her eyes closed she could at least pretend that Kiersten was still alive, she could pretend that she was sleeping peacefully down the hall, that everything that had taken place over the past forty-eight hours had been nothing more than a terrifying nightmare. *God, if only,* she thought. But she knew otherwise. She knew that at the very moment when her eyes opened, she would be entering the most challenging day of her life. This day would be the last time she could gaze upon her daughter's face. This would be the day she would have to speak the words of permanency that no parent should ever have to say, *Goodbye.*

As Marie laid there with her eyes still tightly closed, a smile crept onto her lips, as reflections of Kiersten's childhood flashed through her mind: Kiersten running through the tall, grassy fields in their back yard; she could see her daughter squirm as she watched the baiting of a hook with worms before fishing; she could see the tall black oak in whose shade they laughed together and where they had shared many mother-daughter talks. Those reflections faded and the smile crept away as the grandfather clock echoed from the living room seven times. She knew it was time to get up and start the disheartening day.

She sat up in bed facing the picture window that overlooked the back yard. She felt numb. She never figured to be one of the unfortunate parents that would have to bury a child before they, themselves, passed on.

Oh God, why? Why?

Marie's eyes wandered over to the black dress that hung from the back of her closet door, a dress that she had not worn in over three years. The simple black, yet elegant looking dress represented another horrible time in her life. It was the same dress she wore when she laid both her parents to rest after a fatal car accident took them from her.

Marie stared at the dress as if somehow using it to summon comfort from her deceased mother. *God, how I miss you, Mom,* she whispered silently. How she could have used the comfort of a motherly hug at this heart-wrenching moment in her life.

Just then, the sun's rays pierced through the tall pines, and like a warm hand, caressed Marie's tear drenched face. It felt as if her mother had heard her plea and reached down from the heavens to comfort her, and to say, "Everything's going to be all right dear. I'm here with you now." Marie knew it was only her imagination, but somehow, she now felt the courage to do what must be done, for her daughter's sake.

Marie glanced toward the window and in nothing more than a silent whisper, said, "Thank you." She rose up from the bed and made her way to the bathroom.

2

The rising sun cascaded down over the town of Milford. A southern breeze warmed the air, sparking off a beautiful Indian summer day. It would have been, on any other day, perfect. Today, however, was the day Kiersten's body would be laid to rest. It would also be remembered forever, in Todd's eyes, as a day filled with unspeakable pain that would be felt deep down to the core of his heart and soul; a day of wretchedness and misery spawned skillfully and scornfully by evil.

After wrestling with his mind as to whether or not he would attend Kiersten's funeral, he decided not to go. He wanted to say goodbye, but in the end, he knew that he could not bear to sit in a church wearing the black suit that his mother had laid out for him and look at the girl he had always cared for and loved lying in a coffin with her eyes forever closed. He simply couldn't bear the pain.

Instead, he sat on the hood of his car with his two best friends, Mike McVain and Chad Williams, who had shown up around ten that morning to check in on their grief-stricken friend.

Though Todd's greeting was somber at best, he was glad to see them.

"I know were supposed to go to Kiersten's funeral, but I can't

Todd knew he needed to say goodbye, but not from the edge of a six foot deep hole in the earth. "I don't know if you guys will understand this or not, hell I know I don't, but I need to say my goodbye's from the place she died. I need to tell her I'm sorry, and I need to do it at that bridge."

"Let's go then," Mike replied. Chad nodded.

"We'll go wherever you want," Chad said. Mike nodded.

Now, it was noon. Todd's car was parked thirty or so yards from the bridge. The three passed around a bottle of Southern Comfort that Todd had taken from his parent's bar before leaving the house. They drank, and mourned, in silence.

3

Joan came to the fence on the far left corner of her backyard. Sweat glistened off her forehead, and dripped from her chin. She wiped the beads from her brow and gulped the last of her water. The forest behind her lay silent, not a stir of air could be seen in the trees above, let alone be felt. Her morning run did little to clear her mind, or to provide answers to the questions running wild through her head. *Why were these kids being killed, and why hadn't I found one lousy clue that would expose the killer? Who was this mysterious man, this Brandon Nelson, and why had I felt such strong feelings of trust and honesty toward a man I had never met? Why had Charlie been killed?*

Reality seemed to be slipping from her as she could not wrap her mind around the reasons for the murders, or why they were killed at the same bridge where kids were supposedly murdered in the same fashion thirty-two years ago.

She went inside her house, showered and got ready for the funeral.

4

Caitlin watched her mother return from her run from her bedroom window. She looked sweaty and upset. She knew her mother's routine well: run, take a shower, and go to work. Only, on this day, it wasn't to work she would he heading off to, it was Kiersten's funeral.

After her mother entered the house, she left her room and went to the front porch to wait for her.

Knowing what she knew, Caitlin felt that her mother would not yet understand how an eight-year-old girl could possibly know that though Kiersten had died a senseless and tragic death, her soul was at peace. Caitlin wondered herself where she could have possibly gained the knowledge of knowing that Kiersten was not only at peace, but was in the loving arms of her deceased grandparents, Lisa and Ed; that they were there waiting with open arms for their granddaughter to enter that final passage just beyond the bright light. They were waiting to help guide her from this life to the next, to a place where only happy thoughts occurred, a place where there was no sadness, no pain, and no senseless tragedies. How could Caitlin know all that? And how could she expect her mother to understand that knowledge?

"Mom?"Caitlin asked before her mother left the house.

"Yeah, sweetie, what's up?"

"Would you tell Mrs. Shae, that I'm sorry—you know, about her daughter?"

Her mother knelt down and gave her a big hug and kissed the tip of her nose.

"It's going to mean a lot to Marie that you're thinking about her," Joan said. "Maybe in a day or two, we'll swing by and say hi. Would you like that?"

"Yes. I'd like to tell…" Caitlin hesitated, took a breath and swallowed the words she had in her mind. She knew that now was not yet the time to reveal to her mother her new ability, an ability that she had not yet come to fully understand herself, or why it was given to her in the first place. And how would she be able to explain her ability to see things that shouldn't be seen, communicate with people with whom she should not be able to communicate with?

"I'd like to tell her in person how sorry I am."

"Then, that's what we'll do," Joan said. She then kissed Caitlin on the forehead and headed for her truck.

5

Though engulfed in grief, Marie finally managed to get dressed. She wiped the tears from her puffy eyes and moved down the hall to her daughter's room. She paused and reached for the doorknob. As her fingers touched the cold brass, she hesitated and leaned her forehead against the door.

Before she knew it, the door was slowly opening. Out of the room came a blast of air that encapsulated the very essence of her daughter. The scent was strong, as if at that very moment, her presence was somewhere within the room. After being momentarily frozen by confusion, she hurriedly pushed the door open. Marie hoped beyond hope, that time had been recalled, that Kiersten would be sitting on her bed waiting to greet her as she entered. But as the door fully opened, reality trumped hopeful thinking. Inside the room was nothing more than the backdrop of Kiersten's life emphasizing her absence, everything unmoved and untouched. Everything was just as she had left it, like footprints on a beach that an ocean's wave would never again touch.

As Marie gazed into the room, she saw her daughter's favorite white shawl draped across the back of an old rocking chair that sat in front of the window overlooking the front yard. Slowly, she moved toward the chair and picked up the shawl. She nuzzled it against the right side of her face. She breathed in deep; her sallow eyes wept more tears as Kiersten's scent was all over it. Placing the shawl over her shoulders, she took a seat in the rocking chair. It was here that she felt Kiersten's presence the strongest.

6

Standing outside Marie Shae's door and after having knocked three separate times, Joan breathed a sigh of relief when the door finally opened.

"Joan," Marie asked with glazed-over eyes, "Why are you in uniform? Are you expecting trouble?"

"No. It's more of a formality than anything."

"Formality? We're burying my daughter today. What do we need with formality?"

"Well, it's very unlikely, but sometimes the..." Joan's reply trailed off in hesitation. She cleared her throat, and continued, "Sometimes the kil...these people like to show up at their victim's funeral. I just want to be prepared. Okay?"

Marie did not answer; she just nodded and closed the door behind her.

As Joan and Marie pulled up in front of the church, Marie said, "I want to see her. I want to be with her—alone."

"Are you sure?"

"Just for a few minutes—please."

7

Caitlin slipped off to sleep after she went to the sofa to watch a video. As she slept, her subconscious immediately reached the same complex and bizarre dreams as the night before. Only in this dream session, the images that were being revealed were more harried and rueful. In this dream, she saw a baby and she saw the baby's father, felt his guilt, his madness. Then she saw rabbits—dead rabbits, mutilated rabbits, hundreds of them.

As the dream continued, the images she saw became even more morbid. These images, though brief, were the worst of all that she had been shown so far. Her ears tuned in a deafening silence. Then, she saw it—a bridge. The bridge appeared to be old and rundown, hovering over a dried up creek bed.

Next, she saw, one by one, the disheartening images of kids being hung by the neck. Seven kids in all, hanging, swaying in the breeze. When it was over, when the last child had been strung up, and his last breath taken, she heard the father's cries, and knew they had only begun.

But, who was the family she was seeing in her dream, and whose nightmare was she visiting?

8

Joan entered the church and found Marie standing in front of her daughter's coffin. "Marie, it's time," she said hesitantly.

"I know."

"Can I get you anything before we start?"

"You can get Todd. I think she'd want that, a moment with Todd."

"I'll get him," Joan replied.

Joan went to the front of the church and cracked open the door. She saw Ed standing on the stairs, and asked him if he would mind locating Todd.

"Not at all," he replied.

9

Caitlin woke and sat up on the sofa. This time there was no apparition, no female form floating in mid-air to explain what she had just seen, as if the eight-year-old should now understand. And in an eight-year-old way, she did. As she sat there trying to figure out how and when to tell her mother, she had a feeling that completely overwhelmed her. *Todd, Mike, and Chad were all in danger.* One more than the others, but they were all in mortal danger.

She began to say, "The bridge, the bridge," over and over. "The bridge, the bridge. Please, go to the bridge."

10

Ed saw Kiersten's family, friends, and neighbors flooding the front lawn of the church. He did not, however, see Todd. He walked among the bereaved guests for several minutes checking vehicles as they pulled into the parking lot, but still, no Todd.

Joan joined in the search when Ed did not bring Todd into the church as quickly as she would have thought. It was then that Gage drove up in front of the church, tires screeching. He jumped out and quickly moved toward Joan. "I know this isn't the place or the time, but after what happened to Charlie last night, I got to thinking about the crime scenes."

"What happened to Charlie?" Ed asked.

"He went and got himself shot. Three times over," Gage said. "But I think we're dealing with two different killers."

"Why would you say that?" Ed asked.

"The M.O.s, they're different for one. I mean, the kids, they were hung, but ole Charlie, he was shot."

"And?"

"And think about it. Shooting a gun in the middle of the woods is one thing, but in the middle of town; in the middle of the police station, a locked police station, I mean even with a silencer, that's pretty ballsy."

"I must be tired," Ed said, "because I'm still not following."

"What I think he's trying to say," Joan replied, "Is if it was the same person, it would have made more sense to shoot the kids and hang Charlie, and I have to agree with him, not that killing anyone makes any sense. Then there's the M.O.s. Killers, serial or not, don't generally change their pattern in midstream. They tend to stay with what they're comfortable with." Joan's eyes raked through the crowd for Todd again, and for anyone that looked out of place. "No," she continued, "Someone else killed Charlie because he knew something."

"Which was what exactly?" Ed asked.

"I'll fill you in on that later," Joan replied

"What about the Dixon Police, did they find anything?"

"Nothing!" Gage replied.

"Nothing on the initials J.P. either?"

"Nope, not one damn thing, which leads me to believe that Charlie Malloy, God rest his dead drunken soul, was feeding us a line of bull."

"Don't be too sure," Joan replied.

"Why?"

"He's dead, isn't he? He had to know something. And that's what we need to focus on. In fact, let's focus on just that. Gage, I want you to give the F.B.I. a call, see if they can run a check on those initials and all the other names Charlie mentioned, including Henry Turner."

"Why call? We have two agents here already," Ed said.

"Let's just say I don't like judging a book by its cover."

"You don't trust them?"

"I wouldn't say *them,* but where agent Helmsley is concerned, about as far I as can throw him. In fact, while you're on the phone with F.B.I. Headquarters, see what you can find out about our Mr. Helmsley. See if they know why he's really up here."

"Where's Todd?" Gage asked. "I thought he'd be here for sure."

Joan shrugged as she continued to scan the crowd. She still did not see Todd. "Maybe it was too much for him. I just hope he hasn't gone and done something foolish."

"Foolish, as in what?" Gage asked.

"Foolish as in…" Joan's voice trailed off, then, "Did you guys hear that?"

Chapter 26

1

Todd, Mike and Chad continued passing the bottle of Southern Comfort around, each taking small hits as they had never hit the hard stuff before. Todd took the bottle back from Mike and chugged down several healthy gulps on this round. The booze warmed him and made his throat feel as though it was on fire. His eyes watered as he gritted his teeth and labored to get the last gulp down. "Wow," he said trying to catch the breath the Southern Comfort had just taken away. He passed the bottle back to Mike who chugged a bit and then passed it to Chad.

They sat there for almost twenty minutes in silence, passing the bottle back and forth.

Todd glanced at his watch and saw that it was nearing 1:00 p.m. He scooted off the hood, and took several paces toward the bridge that would normally look like any other bridge that old. But now, having been tainted with the death of three young kids, it also looked cold and ominous. Todd suddenly had the feeling that he—that they should not have come up here at all. The feeling was as strong as his love of Kiersten, yet he could not, would not drag himself away until he said what he had came to say. "Well, guys," he said with a slight slur, "In about a minute or so, it will be official, Kiersten's funeral will have started, and then... and then, they'll bury her." Todd held up the bottle high into the air as if to offer a toast. "I'm so sorry Kiersten Shae," he said, slurring every word, more so from grief than the booze. He wiped the tears from his eyes. "Just know how much your mother loves you, how much she will *always* love you. And though I also never got the chance to tell you Kiersten, I love you, too." Todd then threw the half empty bottle against the bridge. It shattered. Shards of glass exploded

194

of the bridge and flew to the ground in the exact spot where Kiersten's clothes had been found.

Mike and Chad watched as Todd fell to his knees. They jumped off the hood of the car and knelt beside him, one on either side.

After ten minutes had passed, the three stood up.

"Thanks," Todd said, "For coming out here with me. It means a lot."

"Where else would we be?" Chad said, "You're our bud. We couldn't let you go through this alone."

As the three boys huddled together, their arms stretched out across each other's shoulders as they had done so many times in the past during a football game, not one of them had an inclination that lurking in the shadows of the tall pines, was Kiersten's killer.

Watching.

Waiting.

Anticipating his next kill.

And though the dark figure was eyeing all three, he sought only one.

The question was, which one did he want? Why not all three of them? Which one of the boys enraged his anger at the very sight of him, igniting an aggression and a passion so deep to make him want to end yet another life?

2

Joan pulled the hair back away from her ear. "Are you two sure you didn't hear that?"

"Hear what?" Gage asked.

"Have either of you seen Todd yet?" she asked.

"No, why?" Gage asked.

"Chad or Mike?" she asked hurriedly.

"No. Joan, what's going on?" Ed asked.

But Joan knew she didn't have time to explain, let alone, be able to give a reasonable explanation as to how she knew they'd find Todd, Mike and Chad at the bridge where they had found Kiersten and the two Kaminski boys.

"Gage, you stay here, look after Marie. Keep your eye out for anyone that looks out of place."

"Yeah, sure, but, where are you two going?"

"To get Todd."

Joan and Ed jumped into Gage's truck and took off. Ed drove.

"Since I'm driving, would you mind if I ask where we're going?" he asked.

"I told you, to get Todd."

"Yeah, but from where?"

"The bridge."

3

Todd, Mike, and Chad looked at each other, and at the same time said, "Man, I've got to piss." The synchronization of words was followed by a brief chuckle.

Mike broke the huddle to leave first. As he turned, a hand came out of nowhere and knocked him backward. He landed hard on his back several feet away. Todd and Chad saw Mike as he landed and turned to see what had hit him. Within seconds, two hands reached out and grabbed both Todd and Chad by the neck and raised them up off the ground.

Mike was dazed, but managed to get to his feet. When his eyes fully cleared, he saw Todd and Chad struggling to get free from the grasp of the figure that had just hit him. Mike lunged toward the dark figure. The man tossed Todd aside, and while he was still holding up Chad, slammed Mike across the chest. Todd got up and ran to Mike who now lay on the ground unconscious, breathing very shallowly. He looked to Chad, who was no longer struggling, no longer moving. This man was too strong to try and overpower, but Todd thought that maybe, if he could somehow knock him off balance…He was up and running toward the man before he had finished processing the thought. As he neared their attacker in a full-out sprint, he ducked at the last second as he saw a fist heading for his head. Todd tried to hit the man shoulder first in the mid-section, just like he was taught in football practice, but seemed to have passed straight through him as if he hadn't been there at all. Todd fell forward and hit the ground hard. The man's hold on Chad, however, had been released, and he fell to the ground like a wet rag and lay there, motionless.

Before Todd could recover, the man grabbed him with both hands and effortlessly threw him ten feet through the air.

Todd clawed his way back to the car, using the bumper as leverage to help him up. The dark figure again moved in on Todd. He picked him up by the back collar of his shirt. The dark figure then spun him around in mid-air, releasing his hold as Todd rotated 180 degrees only to be caught again before his feet had a chance to hit the ground. Todd was now face to face with the man who was tossing him around like a rag doll.

"What the hell are you?" He gasped, staring into the man's black emotionless eyes. Eyes that looked glazed over with nothing behind them, nothing but shear, unrelenting evil. It was then that he knew he was staring at the man who had killed Kiersten.

He raised his right fist and threw a limp punch that landed short of the man's shoulder and then fell limp to his side. "You sick freak! You killed her, didn't you? *Didn't you?* You freak!"

The raunchy smelling man raised Todd up further off the ground and tossed him through the windshield of his car. Todd's head split open as it hit the glass, shattering the windshield on impact. The momentum carried him halfway through the window, half of his body laid inside on the dashboard, the other half, on the hood. He was unconscious and had blood streaming down his face and down his left side from a jagged cut to his lower abdomen.

When Todd came to, his mouth was thick with the coppery taste of his own blood; he had no idea how much time had elapsed, or where his friends were. As he turned his head slowly toward the bridge, he could see Chad approximately fifteen feet away lying on the ground on his right side facing him. Todd could tell that his friend was still alive; he could hear his labored breathing. He also saw blood drooling out of his mouth.

In the time it took Todd to blink and refocus, their attacker appeared. He was standing under the bridge dangling Mike out in front of him two feet off the ground. His friend's body was motionless. He watched in horror as the inhumanly strong man slid a rope over the head and around the neck of his now half naked friend Mike and let him go to swing freely.

"No! No! This can't be happening. Please God, don't let this be happening," Todd yelled. Mike was dying right in front of him in the same manner as Kiersten, and there wasn't one damn thing he could do to stop it.

Now, as Mike hung from the bridge, the dark figured freak moved toward him. Todd tried to move, but pain seared through his left side as the three inch gash stretched open at his attempt to sit up; it was unbearable. He closed his eyes and waited for the inevitable.

4

Joan was out of the truck almost before Ed had it fully stopped. Beaten down brush, bark ripped off trees and broken limbs told her she had been right, or the voice in her head had been right. Todd had indeed come this way.

Halfway down the car-made trail, Joan and Ed came to a sudden halt. A guttural scream raged through the air. They both grabbed their weapons and clicked off the safeties, and ran toward the bridge.

5

After several gut-wrenching minutes had passed, Todd opened his eyes and found himself still laying half in and half out of the car, and Chad still lying in the same spot on the ground. The dark figured man that had hung Mike was now walking away from them.

At that moment, Joan and Ed came running through the trees, guns out. They stopped in between Todd and Chad, both yelling at the same time, "Freeze!" But the man just kept walking.

"Freeze, you son-of-a-bitch, or I'll shoot!" Joan yelled again. He had paid them no mind whatsoever, as if they were of little or no concern to him at all.

Joan fired twice. The blast of her .38 was almost lost in the boom from Ed's .45. All they saw, however, were puffs of dust after the bullets went straight through the dark figured man and into the embankment that rose up toward the train tracks. The dark figure just kept walking and disappeared into the shadows at the far end of the tunnel. Joan ran after him, but by the time she reached the tunnel, the man was nowhere to be found. It was as if he had vanished into thin air. *Not possible,* Joan thought. Yet—he wasn't there.

They scrambled hurriedly to cut Mike down, but by then, it was too late. Mike was dead.

They then ran over and helped Todd and Chad. Todd was hurt badly with a gash to his head and another to his abdomen. Chad, on the other hand, had a broken rib, and was bleeding internally; he barely had a pulse, but he was alive.

Later, after Todd and Chad had been admitted into the Dixon City Hospital, Joan and Ed looked at each other as if both had the same thought running through their minds, the shooting at the bridge.

Joan could still not believe that both she and Deputy Cross had missed with all four shots that were fired. She had, after all, been given the award of *Best Marksman* in the handgun competition at the academy, and Deputy Cross was a decorated army vet with fifty-eight kills to his credit, many with his Army issue .45.

"How's that possible?" Joan asked.

"We must have just missed. We were running beforehand. Maybe— we were, I don't know, shaky."

"No! They hit him, all four shots hit him," Joan replied.

"I doubt that anyone could just up and walk away with two bullets in their back from a .38. Crawl maybe. But I can damn well guarantee you that they wouldn't walk away with two bullets from my .45, especially since I've been using hollow point shells."

"Hollow points?"

"Hollow points. I didn't tell you because I knew you'd disapprove, but after what happened to Mrs. Zachary and her rabbits, and not knowing exactly what we're dealing with, well, let's just say I wanted to make sure that whatever I hit—went down."

Ed had been right about one thing. On any other occasion, she wouldn't have approved the usage of hollow point shells, but in this case, she was half-tempted to ask him if he had any that would fit her .38.

"I'm telling you, we hit the son-of-a-bitch," she replied.

"Didn't you see the dust from the bullets hitting the bank?"

"Yeah, exactly, that's how I know we hit him. The puffs of dust came from in front of that S.O.B. If I didn't know any better, I'd swear the bullets passed right through him. Don't ask me how, because I sure as hell don't have any answers for you, but I know he—*it*—was hit."

"So what are you saying then, that we were shooting at—what, a ghost? I think Todd and Chad would beg to differ."

"I don't know, damn it, I just don't know."

Silence.

"Then there's the stuff Todd was saying," Joan said, "I mean, I don't know how much of it was exaggerated, he was pretty out of it."

"What exactly did he say?" Ed asked.

"Something about the man's eyes looking expressionless, like there was nothing there, nothing behind them, something weird like that."

"That is weird."

"Yeah, but you know what bothers me even more?"

"What?"

"Footprints, other than the ones we made, there were none. And there was no blood either, but I swear to you, we hit him. Damn it, I know we hit him."

"Are you sure about the footprints?"

Joan gave Ed an icy stare.

"Okay," he said, "I believe you. There were no footprints."

Joan then walked over to Ed, reached for and retrieved his .45. "Hollow points, huh?" she said, remembering that she still had her late husband's .45 Sig Sauer stowed away in her closet. "Have any extra ammo for that thing?"

"How many rounds do you need?"

"I think the magazine holds eight. It belonged to my late husband."

"What brand?"

"A Sig Sauer?"

"Same as mine," Ed said walking to his desk. "Your husband knew his guns." He unlocked his bottom drawer and pulled out a red and black box. He pulled out 16 shells and an extra clip. "Here," he said, after handing Joan the shells. "Take this too, you know, just in case you need to reload quickly."

The heavy artillery should have made Joan feel more at ease, and normally, it would have. But for the first time since the loss of her husband and unborn baby, she felt completely powerless. Four kids were dead, and all she had to go on was a culprit that had seemed to disappear right before her very eyes. That thought haunted her. The one thing she did know was that whoever it was that killed those kids, was a dead man walking.

Chapter 27

1

From the moment Brandon Nelson walked into the Milford Diner, Joan couldn't resist the urge to stare. There was just something about the way he carried himself. He walked like a man with confidence with his long, yet, casual strides. He was tall and she could tell that he kept himself in more than reasonably good shape. He was in superb shape.

His hair was long and black with just a hint of gray setting in. He wore it pulled back and braided into a neat ponytail that extended just past his belt line. He had light tanned skin that seemed to glisten in the morning sun as it pierced through the diner window.

Intriguing, Joan thought, *and handsome.*

"Is it the hair?" he asked as he came to rest beside Joan's table.

"I beg your pardon?" Joan replied, feeling now, the same way the State Troopers must have as they realized that they had come to the wrong conclusion about her appearance.

"The hair," Brandon said again, "You were staring. I'm guessing it's the hair."

Joan felt a blush creep up on her face and could only hope that what was left of her summer tan would hide the burning redness.

"No! Yes! I mean, I'm sorry," Joan stammered. "Yes, it's the hair. I have to admit, I wasn't expecting to meet someone whose hair is longer than mine."

His eyes were every bit as blue as the sky on a clear day over Greece. He had a square chin and a chiseled nose and cheek bones. His voice was clear, concise, and masculine. To Joan, his voice sounded like a mix of Alec Baldwin's rasp and Sam Elliot's deep-distinguished tone, twanged together with a natural Virginian accent. *An honest voice,* she thought.

"I, for some reason, get that a lot," Brandon said, and smiled showing a near perfect set of teeth, and would be, except for a small chip on his lower left incisor.

"You have to admit though," Joan said, "That not many psychologists, or any other male doctors that I know, have hair as quite as long as yours."

"So, I don't exactly fit the typical stereotype of a clinical doctor, is that it?"

For a second, Joan found herself speechless, embarrassed even. Coming from a big city such as New York where diversity is everywhere and everything, there was no room left for stereotyping, but it seemed she had.

Brandon broke out in a slight chuckle. "I'm just kidding," he said as he pulled out a chair. "May I?"

"Yes, of course," Joan said. "Please."

Brandon took a seat and continued, "I really do get that all the time. In fact, I had to talk my way into my first real job because of my hair. One that, when I look back now, I wish I never would have taken. Nevertheless, my hair is part of my heritage."

"Your heritage?" Joan asked, again staring.

"Yes, Native American. I'm a direct descendant of the Rappahannock Indians from right here in Virginia, in fact. But," he hesitated as he caught her stare, "I'm sure, Sheriff Fortune, that my hair or my heritage is the least of your concerns."

"Sheriff Fortune isn't necessary, please, Joan is fine," she said. "And I hope you can forgive me for staring. It's not something that I usually do. It's just that—well—somewhere beneath all that hair, you remind me of someone."

"Someone good I hope," Brandon replied.

Joan felt a tear forming, but steeled herself from the urge. She wasn't prepared for dealing with memories of her deceased husband. She cleared her throat and said, "Don't worry, it is."

Now was the time, the time to break out of the uncomfortable feeling she was having, *or was it that she was feeling too comfortable?* Since the loss of her husband, Joan had stayed clear of men. Losing her husband was an unbearable pain that she never again wanted to experience.

"So, Dr. Nelson, let's get right to the gist of it. How is it, exactly, that you came to know about the clothes?" Joan asked, wanting to jump right in to the reason for his visit, "That information wasn't given out."

Joan watched Brandon's face, that only seconds ago was brimming with a smile and cheerful eyes, turn in a flash to one that looked somewhat haunted.

What did he know?

"Before I start," he replied, his eyes narrowing to reveal a serious look, "I just have two requests."

"And they are?"

"First, that you call me Brandon. And second, promise me you'll do your best to keep an open mind on what you're about to hear," he took a deep breath, and continued, "And an open mind about me as well. Can you do that?"

Joan gazed at him quizzically for a few moments before answering him.

"Well *Brandon*, that's actually three, but, whose counting."

Brandon's seriousness eased for a moment.

"What I can promise," Joan continued, "Is that I'll do my best to try, on all three accounts."

"Good enough for me. Problem is—where to start?"

"At the beginning is always good. And if you want my trust, I think I should hear everything."

"Fair enough." He took another deep breath and started. "What I'm about to say never happened, which is to say that it did, but you won't Find any paperwork, reports, or anything like that to back up what I'm about to tell you."

Joan's attention went immediately to the files that Deputy Cross said were missing from her office, and to what Charlie had said about the files he destroyed per Sheriff Henderson's request.

"Which is why I asked for an open mind," Brandon said. Then, "Joan? Sheriff?"

"I'm sorry," she replied. "Did you say something?"

"Not really, but judging by the look on your face, I can see that I have already struck a chord with you, something that perhaps you may have already noticed."

Just then, Myrtle Ashton, one of the diner waitresses', rested her elbows on the edge of their table, and her eyes on Brandon's strong, good-looking face.

"Morning, Joan," she said. "Who's your good looking friend?"

Joan glanced up at Myrtle, feeling slightly embarrassed. "Just a friend," she replied raising her eyebrow to show a slight displeasure of the remark.

"Too bad," Myrtle replied back, and at the same time, gave Brandon another good once over. "So, what's it going to be handsome?"

"Just coffee, decaf please," Brandon answered

"Make that two," Joan said, glaring at Myrtle.

"Two decafs coming up." Myrtle smiled and winked at Joan as she turned away to place the order.

"I'm sorry about that," Joan said. "She's a bit flighty, if you know what I mean."

Myrtle wasn't really that way; it was just that she, along with all the other patrons who knew Joan on a personal level, were thinking the same thing. Who was this guy? After all, it had been a long time, if ever, since they had seen her having coffee, or anything else for that matter, with a man other than her deputies.

"Don't worry about it. I'm not." Brandon announced. "In fact, I'm rather flattered."

"Anyway, you were saying," Joan said.

"Huh? Oh yeah, right. I was saying that it's probable that you won't find anything to back up what I'm about to tell you."

"And why is that exactly?" After a slight hesitation, Brandon narrowed his eyes as he began to speak of the experiences that he had during his internship at a psych ward.

"The government: politics, the greasing of the greedy palms, who knows for sure. The facility that I interned for before graduating college was the Virginia Mental Institute for the Criminally Insane.

"The power of the mind had always fascinated me ever since I was a kid growing up. I was what you would call—nerdy. You know, real smart, the kid all the other kids hated, and loved to pick on."

"Here you go," the Myrtle interrupted. "Two decafs."

"Thank you," Brandon said.

To Brandon, Joan said "Go on,"

"As I was saying," he said continuing, pouring a little cream into his own cup. "From that point on, I had a deep seeded need to know what made the mind tick. What better profession to do that in than psychology, right?" Joan nodded as she sipped her coffee.

"Anyway, I breezed through med school, and took the intern at V.M.I.C.I., which I'm sure you know, is only about ten miles from here."

Joan thought for a second, remembering that Charlie had spoken of the place.

"You mean that old burnt out building just outside of town?"

"That's the one. Thank God it's closed. The things that went on in that building I swear would make Ted Bundy squirm.

"I know this all happened a long time ago," Brandon continued, "But I remember it like the back of my hand. It was Wednesday, September 13th, the day in which my life changed forever." Brandon was looking past Joan to a time over thirty years ago.

"Why that day in particular?" Joan asked.

"That's the day that I first saw evidence that there was another level to the building. A sublevel some forty feet down from what I could tell. I stumbled upon the door by chance. I took off half a day to meet an old girlfriend for lunch. As I was leaving, I happened to catch a glimpse of what appeared to be an elevator behind a highly secure door. They were escorting a man that looked familiar, but at that time, I was in a bit of a hurry and didn't get that good of a look at him.

"That door stayed on my mind through lunch, which you can imagine, pissed off my date. Yet, I was so engrossed with the possibilities of that elevator, and where it went, and why all the secrecy. I knew it didn't go up. My office was in that exact location on the second floor."

Joan listened intently as his story unfolded.

"When the opportunity presented itself, I took it," Brandon said with a subdued look. "I just couldn't believe how easy it was. I mean getting the plan together was harder. I had to get the code, get the guard's routine down, and pick the perfect time in which to make my move. Doing all that without being caught wasn't easy, but executing the plan turned out to be quite simple."

Brandon watched the sliding paneled door for weeks, each time witnessing the security involved. Just to the right of the door, was a ten-digit keypad. A seven-digit code was needed.

For days he watched which of the Institute's top psychiatrists had clearance to enter the secured area in what he hoped was an inconspicuous manner.

He wrote the names down on a small tablet he kept in his shirt pocket, hidden from view by his white smock.

Getting the seven-digit code proved harder than he thought as each of the cleared personnel had their own individual code. But he wanted to know what the big secret was all about: he had to know what exactly was going on down there, and because of that, his persistence paid off, he got the code.

"It took me five days to procure one set of seven numbers that would open the sliding door.

"I kept a record of all the security guards, their schedules, what they were doing, and when. I kept track of the routes they took, the time it took them, all that sort of stuff. And then I did the same with the nighttime nurses. It took me two weeks, but I got it all."

"It would seem that you went through an awful lot of trouble."

"I'm not going to say it wasn't, but it was worth it, at least I thought it was at the time."

"Why? What'd you find?" Joan saw a distant look in Brandon's eyes. It was as if he were trying to recall every detail.

"Well, after I pretended to be working late for a couple of weeks as not to raise any suspicion—you know, make it seem routine, I decided to make a trial run to see how things would go.

"Before leaving my office, I changed shoes from the black oxfords I wore in to a pair of moccasins so that I could move about as quietly as possible on the Institute's hardwood floors.

"Once I made it past the nurse's station, and then the guard's desk, I was able to slip over to the secured door and enter the password. When the door opened," Brandon said, his eyes intensifying as if he were there at that very moment, "Everything had seemed to go so well, I just—kind of—stepped in." He hesitated, taking a sip of lukewarm coffee.

"I have to tell you," he said continuing, "I don't think my heart had ever raced so fast in my life. I was so hoping that there weren't any more passwords needed. Thank God there weren't. I don't think that I would have had the nerve to try anything like that again.

"Anyway, after the door slid shut, I felt a little relieved. Scared out of my mind, but relieved all the same. I found myself in a small room staring at an elevator. I hit the only button there was, a down arrow, and the door opened right up, so I went in. Inside the elevator, there were two buttons to choose from, one up and one down. The choice was obvious, so I made the selection and down I went.

"It was then, as I started to descend, that I started to wonder whether or not I really wanted to go through with it. Even as I think back on it now, it still seems like an insane judgment call on my behalf. I mean here I was, an interning clinical psychologist doing something I knew to be absolutely crazy, but I figured I was already there, so what the hell.

"Once I was at the bottom, the door slid open and I exited the elevator. It didn't take long to find out what the place was all about."

Joan leaned back in the chair, engrossed.

She knew however, that she would now have to check the place out for herself. She wanted to leave right then and there, but could not seem to find the strength needed to break free from Brandon's verbal documentary of his accounts he claimed were related to the recent death of three kids, and supposedly, the death of some kids thirty two years ago.

"So, what was it you saw?" She asked, almost dreading the answer.

"To make a long story short, I saw barbaric things," Brandon answered in a disturbed tone. "Once I stepped out of the elevator, I must have tripped a switch or a motion sensor that turned on the lights. Everything lit up, row by row, and as they did, these things, these freaking weird looking instruments jumped out at me. Not in the real sense of the word, but hypothetically speaking. There were things that in all my years of school, I had never seen before, I didn't know what to make of them."

If it had not been for the torment in Brandon's eyes, and the honesty in his voice, Joan more than likely would not have believed him. He described medical instruments that sounded like they were way before their time, yet in the same breath, he described things that sounded medieval.

To the left, he told Joan, were two large glass encased carts that appeared to be refrigerated units. Inside the first unit were four small round glass jars that had within them, human brains. Each brain seemed to be at a different point of decay.

In the second unit, there were three shelves, each of which had twenty or so vials of different colored liquids.

To the right of the room was what appeared to Brandon as some type of staging area that consisted of a stainless steel counter and was filled with medical supplies: gauze, needles, boxes of rubber gloves, and various medical drills, scalpels, and a few different types of saws.

At the center of the room was a large table. On it was nothing more than a standard lab set-up. Also on the left side, though further down the wall, there were two hydrotherapy tubs. On the wall on either side of the tubs, were valves and gauges.

"As I looked around the room", "Brandon continued, "I felt stupid for thinking the worst, I mean other than the weird instruments, the place seemed to be nothing more than a mere laboratory. Yet, they chose to keep it a secret. Why, I didn't know, until I heard the first of several loud screams. The sound was coming from the far end of the room, but there was nothing there. As I moved closer, the sound grew louder, but still, I saw nothing. I walked all the way to the wall. That's when I noticed that the wall was nothing more than a set of doors constructed in a way as to not look like doors at all, unless you were looking for it. I wouldn't have noticed it myself if I hadn't help build houses for the poor during a summer break in college. The wall was simply built as a diversion, to conceal yet another room; a secret room within a secret room if you will.

"As I reached out to pull the door open," Brandon said, wide-eyed, "My heart was beating so fast and hard that I thought the damn thing was going to bounce right out of my chest."

Joan couldn't help but smile.

Brandon couldn't believe at how easily everything came back to him, especially given the fact that he had tried so hard to forget that haunting part of his past. He, at times, even blamed himself for the events that took place after his departure.

"What was behind this mysterious secret door?" Joan asked.

"The worst thing you could imagine," he replied. "There were five medical tables, four of which were occupied with male patients strapped down with thick leather straps. Their ankles, waist, and foreheads all strapped down as tight as they could get the leather to stretch. I'm telling you," Brandon said, looking her straight in the eye, "I've never seen such brutality in all my life.

"Against the back left corner of the room was another medical table. Attached to the table with chains were devices that resembled police styled handcuffs. Next to the table was a small stand with a black box sitting on top. I started walking towards it when all of a sudden, the man harnessed down to the far right, hollered out, "Watch out for Satan," and in the same breath, whispered, "Watch out for the rabbits."

Joan wanted then to say something about the recent slaying of rabbits, but Brandon seemed to be almost mesmerized as he told the story, and she didn't want to break his concentration.

"I jumped at the sound, I mean, I almost came unglued. It took all I had not to just turn around and leave right then and there. But then everything went quiet again, which, when I think back now, didn't make matters much better. Silence can be quite scary in the right situation.

"After settling down, I continued toward the rear table. As soon as I saw it up close, I knew it was used for some kind of barbaric electrocution. There were rods leaning up against the wall. The rods were plugged into the back of the black box, and the box was plugged into the wall. The tips of the rods had a mesh of metal strands reticulated into six-inch oval balls. On the floor next to the stand was a metal bucket half-filled with water.

"It was then," Brandon said in disgust, "that I knew why they had it all hidden some forty feet down. They hid it all so no one would hear the screaming."

2

Gage and Ed dove into the boxes that contained files of everyone that had worked for the Milford Coal Mines. Gage had done as Joan had asked after the SSN administration's efforts had proven to be of no help. He checked the attic, and in doing so, found boxes upon boxes of records. After nearly three hours, he had found the ones he was looking for, and carried them down.

After an hour of going through boring files, the sound of the phone was a welcomed relief. Ed picked it up and identified himself.

"I need to speak to Sheriff Fortune please," a nasally male voice said.

"May I ask whose calling?"

"My name is Rodger Klein. I'm with the board of directors for the Department of Health. Is she there?"

"I'm afraid she is not in the office at this time. Can I help you?"

"I'd prefer to speak directly to the sheriff. Do you know where I can reach her?"

"Well, if it's that important…"

"It is," he said matter-of-factly, cutting Ed off. "At least she made it sound as if it were."

"In that case, why don't you try calling back in say—fifteen minutes. I'll see if I can't get a hold of her and…"

"Thank you, sir," he said and hung up abruptly.

Joan had called the Department of Health yesterday after her conversation with Dr. Nelson. After some friendly persuasion, and a few misleading threats involving the use of the F.B.I, they had caved. "That alone," Joan had told the head of the Health Department, Rodger Klein, "could lead into unwanted investigations by the I.R.S., not to mention the press. Oh man, once the press gets hold of what I'm looking for and why, who knows where it will end."

With some hesitance in his voice, Rodger Klein asked, "What exactly are you looking for? Surely you know we have a strict and legal obligation to protect our patients?"

"Most of those patients are more than likely dead, and all I need right now are names," she had said. "I don't see a need for their clinical whatever's. Then, there's the fire. I would, of course, like to see any and all police and fire marshal reports about the fire. I know I can get that from the State Police Headquarters, but I'm more than sure that your insurance companies did their own investigations, and I'd like to see both reports."

After a brief moment of silence, Rodger Klein agreed to her requests.

"Thank you, Mr. Klein," Joan had said. She smiled, proud that her bluff had worked. "I hope that you can make this happen quickly. We are, after all, trying to solve the murders of three kids."

"Of course," Rodger said and then hung up.

3

Ten minutes after Ed stepped out of the office, Gage fumbled around for the phone, trying to answer it while trying to manage the files he had in both hands at the same time.

"Milford Sheriff's Office, Deputy Gage speaking, how can I help you?"

"This is Rodger Klein again, is the Sheriff in yet?"

Just as Gage was about to say no, Joan walked in the office along with Ed and a man Gage had never seen before.

Gage handed the phone over to Joan.

"This is Sheriff Fortune speaking."

"Hello, my name is Rodger Klein, I spoke with you yesterday."

"Do you have what I asked for?"

"I wish I was calling to say yes, but unfortunately, no, I do not," he hesitated, and then hurriedly added, "But it's not for the reasons you may think."

"Tell me then."

"It seems that when the fire broke out, it destroyed all our patient files."

"There were no backups?"

"I'm told they were destroyed as well, along with our employee files."

After a brief hesitation, he added, "I will say that I find it hard to believe that a Government run facility would have kept their back-up files in the same location as the originals, but, again, that's the official word I received.

"No computer files stored anywhere?"

"Not back then."

"Is there anyone you know that worked there at that time that's still around, an old colleague, maybe?"

"Not that I know right off-hand. I mean, I had friends that worked there, Jacob Palmer, in particular. We went to high school together, but he died in that damned fire along with most of the other employees, along with all the patients."

"I'm sorry, did you say—all the patients?"

"Yes. I sent you the police report and the Fire Marshal's report, via messenger service. I also included our insurance company's findings. You should be getting that today."

"Sorry to hear about your friend," Joan said. "If you happen to think of anything or anyone that can further assist in this investigation, you'll get back to me, right?"

"Of course."

"Thank you, I appreciate your looking into this for me so quickly."

"I'm sorry I wasn't more helpful." He still sounded hesitant.

"Don't worry. It seems you did your best." Joan thought silently about the name he had just dropped into her lap, Jacob Palmer, J.P. — the very initials Charlie had given her before his death. "Actually, you may have helped more than you know."

"I hope so," Rodger said, sounding rather relieved, and hung up.

Just as Joan rested the receiver in its cradle, it rang again. It was the C.S.I. tech, Tanya Fucus, who had been examining the evidence of the four dead kids, and that of Charlie Malloy. She had just received the ballistics on the bullets that had been retrieved from the wall of the cell that Charlie had been shot in. She informed Joan that the shell casings came from a .44 caliber handgun and that it looked like a silencer may have been used.

"I'm running the ballistics through the F.B.I.'s, N.C.I.C. database, but the bullets were pretty well damaged, so I wouldn't get your hopes up."

"Anything on the clothing of the kids: hair, sweat, particulates that might tell us where the perp held them? Anything at all?" Joan asked.

To Joan, Tanya said, "All I was able to pick up from the clothing were minerals that are associated with the mines in that area. I also found traces of coal dust which also derives from that region. I have to say that after reading the file I was very surprised that there wasn't any sweat from the perp. That's quite a hike through the woods from where the abductions took place. I can't imagine the perp not sweating at some point. The only thing that makes sense is that he must have worn a serious moisture wicking suit of some kind, or water proof gear."

"Anything else?"

"Nope, but if I catch wind of anything, I'll give you a call."

"Thanks," Joan replied and hung up.

Joan sat at her desk, her mind still running with the initials J.P., and the name Jacob Palmer.

After several minutes passed, Joan looked up and saw three men staring at her. "I'm sorry," she said. "It's just that we might finally have a link to this J.P. character." Her eyes went straight to Brandon Nelson. "Brandon," she said, and then remembered that he had not yet been introduced. "Dr. Brandon Nelson, these are my two deputies, Gage Jensen and Ed Cross. Gage, Ed, meet Dr. Nelson."

They shook hands and gave appropriate acknowledgments.

"He used to work in the mental institute down the road, the one Charlie told us about." Her gaze turned back to the Dr. "Did you ever know anyone that went by the initials J.P.?"

"No, can't say that rings a bell."

"What about the name Jacob Palmer?"

"Jacob Palmer?"

Joan nodded.

"Oh yeah," Brandon said. "I knew him. I knew him real well. He was the security guard on duty the night I snuck down to the secret room. Why?"

"According to Rodger Klein from the Department of Health, he died in the fire."

"Listen you two," Gage said. "Secret rooms, dead security guards, what's all this have to do with our investigation?

"It's a long story Gage, and right now, I don't have the time to get into it." Joan's eyes flicked back to Brandon. "What were you about to tell me right before Ed came into the diner?"

"I believe I was about to tell you the name of one of the four bodies I saw that night."

"Can you pick up from there?"

"Sure. If my memory serves me, I walked over to the first table and looked at the three drip bags hanging down off an IV cart. Each IV bag had a tube that ran down to a central port, merging into one. From there, it ran into the left arm of some poor bastard I've never seen before. The first IV bag was all I needed to see. I mean, this guy was being given dosages of adrenalin and steroids that far exceeded the F.D.A. When I saw that, I pulled the chart that hung down from the foot of the bed to find out why this guy was there and why he was being given those drugs to start with.

The man's name was Ted McCormick. The first page was pretty standard with normal info: name weight, height, marital status, and next of kin. The second page gave a brief description of the reason he was there to start with. In his case, he had exhibited excessive interest in child pornography.

"Now, don't get me wrong, the guy was a sick S.O.B., but he had been brought there to receive help, not be tortured."

"Tortured?" Joan asked.

"That's where the third page came in," Brandon said, continuing. "It gave two lists: the first was of what was already done, the second, was of what was going to be done. As I read through the list, I looked at the patient to find where on his body the test had been performed. The man had holes drilled into his skull for God sakes. He'd also been given all kinds of experimental injections of medicines that, at the time, I had never even heard of, and have yet to. God only knows what they were and what it did to the man."

"Who did these people think they were?" Joan sounded off in anger. She had seen some pretty sick things in her life, but nothing she could remember had quite affected her in the same way she was feeling now.

"Wanna-be Gods, narcissistic bastards, take your pick." Brandon replied. "I'm all for research for the betterment of mankind, but this, this wasn't research. This was someone's sick and blatant irresponsibility of pretending to be helping mankind, when all they were really doing was destroying it."

Joan, at that point thought she had heard just about enough for one day, but was still uncertain how this all fit in the scope of what was happening now, and pressed him to continue.

"What about the other tables?" she asked.

"I checked them too, however, the next two men were dead, so I went to the last table. I took one look at him and thought he looked familiar. I immediately grabbed the chart, and sure enough, he had been one of my patients, a man named Carl Saunderson."

"Why was he there?" Gage asked.

"I only had a few sessions with him. He had only been in the facility for about three weeks. I saw him twice during his second week and once during his third. Then, after he missed his next appointment, I inquired about him and was told that he had killed himself. Presumably, he just couldn't bear to face the demons that he claimed were inside of him. The note that I was told he left, said something to the effect that in killing himself, he would be killing the demons that were ultimately responsible for the death of his family. Yet, here he was—harnessed down and readied for someone to do God knows what to him."

"Did you get to see the note?" Joan asked.

"No."

"Why not? You were one of his doctors. Interning or not, you had a right to know."

"What can I say? I was outranked. Cased closed."

"Did this Carl ever mention demons to you?" Joan asked.

"No, but at the time, it didn't really matter what he said or didn't say."

"Why not?"

"The man was caught, arrested and found not guilty for reasons that fell under the term, 'reasonably insane'. He was then brought to the institute. He was obviously mentally disturbed. The time I spent with him, he never uttered a single word, which is common. In these types of cases, patients would seem totally coherent and responsive one second, and then be talking total gibberish the next. I didn't see that in Carl Saunderson's case. That's not to say that another doctor couldn't have had a break-through session of some kind. But if you ask me, he wasn't there long enough for anything like that to happen. In fact, I'd have to say that he wasn't there long enough for there to have been any real attempt at even finding out what went wrong with the man's mind, let alone time to help him come to terms with what he had done. There just wasn't enough time."

"So, what, you think he tried to off himself and because of that, they decided to take him down to their little lab?" Joan asked.

"At the time, that very question baffled me too."

"What do you mean?" Joan asked.

"The whole suicide thing, it didn't make any sense when I was first told about it. But that night, in the lab, it made perfect sense."

"Why? What changed? Gage asked, "I mean, don't suicides happen all the time in those kinds of places?

"They do happen, yeah. And I'm sure they happened more back then than now, but there are usually signs."

Joan turned back to Brandon, "Signs? What kind of signs?"

"You know, like signs of recession, an increase in hostility towards themselves, the avoidance in taking their medications. I mean there are all kinds of little tics that we're trained to watch out for so that we can try and prevent them from hurting themselves. And when we see those signs, the patients are put on a suicide watch. Now, it's true that we didn't catch every possible tic, and suicides did occur. There are flaws in every system. But the flaw in this case, was that there was simply no flaw."

"O.K., you lost me there, Doc." Joan replied.

"Yeah, me too." Gage said.

"I'm sorry," Brandon replied. The moment of silence that followed stretched on as if he were trying to recall a distinct rule that described the formulaic practices of the institute.

"If I remember correctly," Brandon finally said, "When a new patient was brought in, he or she was put on an immediate suicide watch until the patient had been deemed non-suicidal. That information would then be dispensed to all doctors and nurses within the facility. I personally never received that memo. It was like I wasn't privy to that information. I don't know why unless it was because I was just an intern at the time."

"Well, you said it yourself; there are flaws in the system."

"Yeah, but the flaws were the suicides themselves. We simply couldn't see, or in some cases, didn't want to see the warning signs of those that ended up offing themselves. But once they're on the list, they were watched very carefully. At least that's what I was told upon my indoctrination into the institute."

"Well, what can you tell us about him, this Carl Saunderson? Who was he, and what was he like?"

Brandon took another minute to recall the important details of Carl's medical transcripts.

"His medical file said that he was a local miner. He lived right here in Milford. He worked for years in the mines. Raised a family with his wife—Sandy or Sandra, something close to that. They were supposedly good Christian people that stayed pretty much to themselves. You know—quiet people. They had seven kids, four boys and three girls. If I remember correctly, his wife had been expecting their eighth child a few months before he was brought in."

"Sounds like quite a brood," Joan replied.

"You got that right. But back then, big families were commonplace. Anyway, from what I read in his file, his wife went into labor on Easter morning. There wasn't time to get her to any hospital. The file said that something went wrong, but didn't give specifics. I remember thinking it may have been a breached pregnancy. Anyway, the poor woman died right there on her own kitchen floor giving birth. I could only venture a guess that she hemorrhaged, and bled out.

"As you can imagine, it freaked her husband, Carl, out. He must have thought he did something wrong that caused her to die.

"At that point, the image of his wife lying there with blood all over the place was more than he could handle. I mean, try to imagine that scene replaying over and over in your head. To him, the blood must have looked as if it were just pouring out of her. That's what I think caused him to go into P.T.S.D."

"O.K., hold on there," Joan interrupted. "Let's back up a few lines, only this time, let's keep it in layman's terms."

"I'm sorry," Brandon replied, "Sometimes I get to talking clinical analysis with someone and forget they're not doctors.

"Post Traumatic Stress Disorder," Brandon said. "It's a mental illness that occur when someone is confronted with, or experiences firsthand a traumatic event. In some cases, someone who saw or felt intense fear or someone who felt completely helpless in a horrifying situation can fall prey to this type of illness. I think that when Carl Saunderson saw his wife bleed out and die on their kitchen floor, his mind broke. It's just that kind of horrific situation that can cause this type of stress disorder."

Joan knew that feeling, the feeling of helplessness, the feeling of not being able to help the one you love in their time of need. She knew what that bitter taste of no longer having control of your life and the feeling of wanting to end it all tasted like. *Who knows what would have happened to her if Caitlin had never come along?* That thought had crossed her mind many times over the years. Yet, she always told herself that she would have made it anyway; sometimes believing, sometimes not.

"You mentioned the word caught." Joan said with a touch of confusion in her tone. "Why would they have to catch him?"

"That's the part that I'm not positive on," Brandon replied, sounding hesitant. "There had been a few different accounts of what actually happened after he put his wife to rest.

"It seems that he followed what we call a standard pattern for P.T.S.D., that being, flashbacks that persistently made him re-experience that ill-fated morning along with nightmares bearing that same fate. The patient starts to adamantly avoid stimuli, avoiding any and all things that were associated with the tragic event. At the same time, they start to experience an emotional numbing and can have panic attacks and/or disassociation. If that wasn't enough, they can even start to hallucinate, not to mention they can start to develop patterns of aggression and violence.

"From reading Carl's police report, which accompanied his psychiatric evaluation, it appears that he started having bad days at work, seeing things that weren't there, having panic attacks every time he'd see a rabbit."

"Why would he do that?"

"He correlates rabbits with Easter, thus another reminder of the incident."

"So you think that could be the reason for all the rabbit mutilations that we have been experiencing around here of late?" Gage asked.

"What? You've had recent accounts of rabbit killings?"

"Yes. Quite a few of them," Joan replied.

"Starting when?" Brandon asked.

"I'm guessing it was about a day or so before Kiersten turned up missing," Ed said.

"Interesting."

"Why's that?" Joan asked.

"According to a few witnesses, Carl Saunderson slaughtered his kid's pet rabbits. If I'm remembering the statement correctly, a neighbor had said Carl hadn't been around for days, that he went off into the woods and left the kids to fend for themselves. Then one day, out of the blue, he shows up, butchers the rabbits, skins them, and takes off again. The kids came home from school, saw the bloody mess, and got scared that something happened to their father. The next morning, the two older kids went to look for their father who, by now, had more than likely become completely disassociated and unattached to reality, which in the long run, wasn't good for the kids."

"Why?" Joan asked.

"They unfortunately found him."

"Unfortunate how?" Joan asked.

"Unfortunate in that when they found him, he killed them."

"Where?"

"At your bridge!"

Joan's eyes lit up as a thought raced through her mind. *She knew Carl Saunderson was dead, Charlie testified to that, but did Brandon know?*

"You don't think that…"

"Carl was Kiersten's killer?" Brandon said, finishing her question. "I don't see how. All this took place over thirty years ago. Not to mention he wasn't looking too good that night I saw him in the lab. So, I would definitely have to say no."

"What about one of the surviving kids? Do you think that…"

Again, Brandon cut her off and finished her thought, "That it could have been one of them? Not possible. They're all dead."

Joan's eyes widened.

"You're telling me this Carl Saunderson killed his own kids—all of them? How? Why?"

"It all comes back to P.T.S.D." Brandon hesitated a moment and then spoke, "Listen, what I'm telling you is nothing more than sheer speculation, but it's the only thing that makes any sense."

"Go on," Joan replied with a sense of urgency.

"Yeah, please do," Gage said.

"He must have gone into some kind of rage and grabbed the two kids and strung them up by the neck using vines as a makeshift rope. From what I remember reading, he returned to his house, grabbed some rope, and then led his remaining kids, one by one, to the same bridge. When he was done, seven of his kids were left there hanging by the neck for days. Some hunters happened along and saw what had to be a horrific scene. The report said that he was just sitting there under the bridge. When he saw the hunters, he rushed them. They had to wrestle him to the ground and drag him into town to be arrested. The state took over the case, and after a quick trial, he was brought to us at the Institute.

"The odd thing, and the one thing that brought me here today, was the way that each body was left. There were pictures of the scene in his file, and the image has never really left me. They were all half-naked, nothing on but their under-garments. The rest of the clothes…."

"Let me guess!" Joan said, now finishing his thought. "Were found neatly folded, lying on the ground under the respected bodies."

"You got it."

Joan now fully understood the reason why Brandon had wanted to meet. Questions permeated her mind from every direction. But one stood out more than the others.

"Seven," she said. "You said seven. Carl put his wife to rest, and then sometime later, he killed seven of his kids, right?"

"From what was pieced together, yeah, I'd say that about sums it up."

Joan's eyebrows narrowed as her mind strung together the words needed for her next question.

"What happened to the baby?"

After asking the question, Joan saw a slight smile emerge from Brandon's face.

"What?" she asked. "What'd I say?"

"It's not what you said, it's just that you don't miss very much do you?"

"I try not to," she replied, then, "So, what about that baby?"

"Well, that was another oddity. They never found the baby. No one knows what fate was handed to that precious child. Everyone just assumed that the baby either died at birth along with the mother or that Carl killed her too."

"So, it was a girl? The baby I mean. Mrs. Saunderson gave birth to a baby girl?"

"Well, that's what was in the reports, but to be honest, I don't know how anyone would know that information if they never found the baby's body. The reports never said anything about blood samples being taken prior to the burial of the mother. For all we know, the baby died at birth and was buried with its mother."

Joan glanced down at her watch. "God, I can't believe what time it is."

Brandon brought his wrist up to view his watch.

"It is getting rather late," he said. "I guess I'd better check into the hotel before they cancel my reservation."

Joan was glad to hear that he would be staying the night, though she would never admit it, not even to herself.

"I'd offer you a room at my house, but, I'm all out of rooms, and my ah—my sofa isn't what you would call comfortable," she said, trying not to sound forward. "But after you check in, how about dinner? I have no idea what my Mother is cooking, but you're more than welcome to join us if you'd like. Besides," Joan continued, with a slight smile, "I'd love to hear how you got out of that lower level."

"What about the rest of us? Any offers heading our way?" Gage asked.

"You have a wife waiting at home for you."

"I don't," Ed exclaimed, "But I'm already spoken for. I'm going to see how Barbara's holding up, and check in on Chad."

Brandon stood, threw a glance at the two deputies, nodded, and said to Joan, "I'm all yours."

Chapter 28

1

Joan waited in her truck. As she watched Brandon walk over to the Milford Lodge, a thought entered her head. He looks as good going, as he does coming. It was a subconscious thought, one she didn't purposely seek, but a thought all the same. "What the hell is it about that man?" she asked herself in nothing more than a whisper. "He's an attractive man, and I'm not blind, that's what." she said, answering herself. She had been fighting the urge to stare at him all day.

Another time, another place, she thought.

After checking in, Brandon followed Joan to her home. There, he met Joan's mother, Jessie, and Joan's pride and joy, Caitlin.

The introduction didn't quite go as Joan had planned. Caitlin surprised everyone by taking over the event.

"Hello," she said extending her right hand, so politely, so grownup, as if she were already seventeen; eighteen even, "My name is Caitlin."

Brandon looked down and saw a beautiful young girl standing in front of him with a tiny hand extended outward. Grabbing it gently, he said to Caitlin, "Well, hello to you, too. My name is..."

"Dr. Brandon Nelson," Caitlin replied, interrupting him.

It reminded Joan of a credit card commercial she had seen.

Taking your daughter to the movies: thirty dollars.

Taking your daughter out to buy a new dress: eighty dollars.

Having your daughter spurt out a person's name that she had never met, had never had contact with, and whose name she had never heard before: PRICELESS.

"Is—there a problem I should know about?" Brandon asked seeing a perplexed look on Joan's face.

"No, no problem."

Joan's mother shrugged her shoulders as if to say she hadn't a clue.

"It's just that I don't remember bringing up your name in front of my family before," Joan said. "But I guess at some point, I must have."

Dinner, as it turned out, was spaghetti with Jessie's one-of-a-kind homemade secret recipe of sauce and meatballs, a recipe that she vowed never to reveal until the time of her departure from this world.

The dinner conversation was light and cheerful, something that Joan had missed over the past few days. Just spending a quiet evening at home was a treat. Even though Joan knew that more serious chat would intervene the moment that Caitlin went to bed, it was still nice to sit and have an adult conversation with someone other than her mother, work related or not.

Brandon found it equally as nice and was quite taken with Joan's little family. He found them to be kind, down-to-earth people, and all in all, he found them to be delightful company.

Caitlin fascinated him, not by her charm, although she had plenty of that, too. He was more fascinated with the intellect in which she displayed. He also knew she was hiding something, nothing bad, a secret. He had no way in which to explain how or even why he knew this about Caitlin, but he did, and he did so from the moment he met her as he shook her tiny hand. It was as if the information had been somehow passed off with an unfelt electrical charge, or transmitted by mind waves. By whatever means, he just knew. He also knew that she would display that secret this very night. Maybe not in the next few minutes, maybe not even in the next hour, but some time before he left, it would happen. And when it did, it would once again put a look of dismay on the face of her mother.

At the diner, Brandon had noticed Joan's attractiveness, but steeled against his normal flirtatiousness and tried to act in a professional manner. But as the evening went on, he realized that she was not only attractive in her looks, with her green eyes and her cute nose, and a figure that was as much of an arousing promise as were her full lips. But she was attractive in her intelligence and mannerisms as well. She intrigued him. And he could sense that somewhere underneath all that beauty, there was a tiger lurking, waiting to pounce on anyone that offended or offered any harm to her family. He sensed in her a very strong, positive, and determined woman.

Brandon had really only loved one woman in his life, Nancy, the mother of his son Thomas. She was a free spirit and at the time of her pregnancy, had told him she was not ready to settle down. Even after the birth of their child, she displayed no interest in perusing a relationship, nor did she display the motherly virtues that would usually follow giving birth. She, in fact, signed over sole custody of Thomas to Brandon prior to leaving the hospital. Thinking back now, he confronts his rational thinking as to how he could have fallen for a woman that could so easily give up a child in order to follow her free spiritedness. The one thing that he will always be thankful to her for, is, and was, her selflessness in agreeing to have the child, and maintaining a health lifestyle during the pregnancy.

Thomas was now twenty-one and well on his way to following in his father's footsteps in the study of psychology at Yale.

After dinner, Caitlin excused herself and went to the sofa in the living room to watch one of her favorite new shows.

In the kitchen, Brandon talked his way into helping with the dinner dishes. As Jessie washed, he dried and handed the clean dry dinnerware off to Joan to put them in their proper places. And all the while the dish-fest was going on, somewhere in the back of Brandon's mind, was Caitlin, and the thought of her saying something that would shock them all.

2

Joan checked in on her daughter and returned to the living room where Brandon sipped at a fresh cup of coffee that Jessie had just poured.

"Is she asleep?" Brandon asked as he sat his coffee cup down on the saucer.

"Soundly."

Brandon did not want to tip his hand to the fact that he still felt as though there was more to Caitlin than met the eye. Something special that Joan apparently had no clue about. As he thought about that, he wondered how it was possible for Joan not to have known. She was way too observant, a personality trait that Brandon had picked up on during the course of the afternoon. And if Joan didn't know about it, then there was the chance that Caitlin herself didn't know, or at least, didn't understand it. All he knew was that sometime before he left, they would all know.

"You know," Brandon said as Joan took a seat, "You have a precious little girl on your hands."

"Yes, I do," Joan, replied, looking down the hall to her daughter's room with a big gleaming smile. "She's my life, my whole world."

Joan picked up her coffee, sipped it twice, looked at Brandon, and said, "So, are you going to tell me how you managed to get out of that place or not?"

"Well, a deal is a deal," Brandon, replied, offering a soft smile that suggested warmth and kindness in a way that Joan had not felt in a long time.

"You kept your end of the bargain by providing dinner, and what a great dinner it was. So, I guess you're entitled to, as Paul Harvey would say, '*The rest of the story*'."

Brandon took another sip of coffee. As he started, his face, that only seconds ago, radiated a phenomenal smile, disappeared behind a mask of seriousness once again. Joan recognized the look from that which he displayed at the diner, and again at the police station.

"Let's see," Brandon said looking straight ahead, as if to somehow place himself mentally back in the basement of the institute, "You wanted to know how I got out of there, right?"

"Yeah, I believe that's where we left off."

"Well, the fact is, I was escorted out by your now-dead security guard, Jacob Palmer."

"That doesn't sound good. How'd he know you were there?"

"It was the one thing that didn't cross my mind, security cameras. I was standing over Carl Saunderson, mortified at how tight the leather straps were around his wrists, ankles, and forehead. His eyes were open and staring straight up at the ceiling. The whole thing gave me the creeps. After I looked at his chart, and the charts of the other three men, I noticed that they all had one thing in common."

"And, that was?"

"On the charts under next of kin, read, NONE. Right then I knew why they had been chosen. I mean, think about it, if for some reason they happened to die during one of their barbaric experiments, there would be no one to answer to."

"Are you suggesting murder?"

"I'd be hard pressed to find a better word. From what I saw, those so-called doctors make murderers look good."

"So, what did they do with the bodies?"

"Good question. The woods maybe?"

"No," Joan replied, "If they were so cautious that they would build a facility some 40 feet deep, and keep it hush-hush, I don't think they'd be that careless with something as critical as the disposal of a body. Burying it in the woods would be way too risky."

"Why, as long as it's buried?"

"Animals," she said matter-of-factly. "Coyotes for instance, can smell blood and rotting flesh up to six feet down, and once they smell it, they won't stop digging until they get it. If that happened, that would leave bones exposed for someone to find. No, they would have had a plan in place. We just need to find out what it was."

"You think that's still possible after all this time?"

"We'll know more tomorrow when we get to the institute, but for now, let's finish this story of yours."

Brandon finished the last of his coffee and set the cup and the saucer on the end table.

"Anyway," Brandon said, continuing, "while I was making a mental note about the men not having any next of kin, this guy Carl moaned again, something about the devil coming. His words were full of garbled gibberish. It was hard to make out exactly what he was trying to say." Brandon's piercing blue eyes started to glaze over, and he stared blankly at Joan as he continued, his body tense and rigid. To Joan, he seemed as though he might have been mournful and somehow spooked from the remembrance of the past. "I felt, I don't know," Brandon continued, "I guess I felt sorry for the man, anyone would have, even if they had known what he had done to get himself there. I don't believe in the death penalty, and I sure as hell don't believe in what I saw down in that facility."

"I agree that no one deserves to be tortured, Brandon," she said, "But in my business, seeing what I've seen, not just in the past 72 hours, but in New York, as well, I can't help but believe in capital punishment, as long as the crime fits the bill. What you've just described to me is not just sickening, it's cruel. I truly am sorry that you had to relive that part of your life."

"And I'm sorry I had to put it in yours. I know where you stand as far as capital punishment goes, but if we catch this guy, I would like to be the one to treat him, find out what made him do these hideous crimes."

"Can't promise you that, Doc, Joan replied, "I've put too many away that ended back out on the streets doing the same damn things I put them away for. And all because, and I don't mean any offense, someone like you thinks he can fix them. Well, you can't fix what isn't broke. You need to understand that some, maybe not all, but some, just like killing."

"Well, I do appreciate your candor. We may not agree on everything, but I do understand where you're coming from. I just wish I could have done something about what was going on down there."

"Well, you must have raised a hair up someone's backside, because from what you've said, it wasn't that long after you left that the place was torched and closed down."

"Thank God for that."

A comfortable quiet crept through the room as they exchanged warm glances.

"So," Joan said, ending the silence, "Why don't you finish up with your story, I have a feeling it's going to be another long day tomorrow, and it's starting to get late."

"Well, after I heard Carl's moan, I started to loosen the straps on his arms, not all the way mind you, I had no idea what all had been done to him or what he was still capable of doing. I loosened them just enough to allow proper circulation. It was while I was loosening the strap on the left arm that the guard grabbed a hold of me and spun me around. Man, the look on his face, I mean, if looks could kill. Anyway, he escorted me back upstairs and locked me in a room until the next day. I was then read the riot act and was given my walking papers."

"They let you go, just like that, after everything you saw?"

"It wasn't that easy, believe me. I think the only thing that kept me from being sent back down to the lab for God knows what, was the fact that I did have some good old kin folk, and the fact that I lied and told them that this wasn't the first time I had been down there. I told them that I had pictures and video. Let me tell ya, they looked none too happy, but I guess they couldn't take the chance on whether I was lying or not. They made me sign some legal documents."

Joan raised her eyebrows. "What kind of documents?"

"Let's just say it fit the same criteria as would a doctor/patient confidentiality agreement. God forgive me, I signed."

3

In Caitlin's room, soft whispers echoed through the eight-year-old's mind as she tossed and turned in her sleep. Caitlin opened her eyes at a little before midnight and sat up in bed. She glanced around the room to see where the whispers were coming from. She stopped at the picture of her mother. It was the same picture in which she had seen something before—a woman. Caitlin hadn't been afraid of her then, and she wasn't now. She knew the woman meant her no harm. The woman had wanted nothing more than to help her. This was something that Caitlin had known from the very moment that she started having the dreams and hearing the whispering voices.

As she stared at the picture, no woman appeared, but the unshakeable sensation of her presence was there, vague, but there. The feeling was as formless as it was real. Caitlin kept staring at the picture. She was positive the woman would return, and she did. The woman's lips were silent, but Caitlin knew it had been her whispers that had awakened her. The woman just hovered in front of the picture as before, transparent and colorless.

Caitlin looked at her. *So pretty*, she thought.

To Caitlin, the woman said, "It's time," and then disappeared. But it was all that needed to be said. Caitlin knew what it was that Ruth Saunderson meant, and she knew what she must do to prevent another senseless and tragic death.

4

Joan stood and paced the floor. She circled the living room three times trying to absorb the story that Brandon had just told her. "You made mention about some similar murders having taken place soon after you left the institute. Can you elaborate a little?"

"It was a story I read in the *Richmond Times* shortly after I received my walking papers. Not for one second did I believe the story was true, but supposedly two of the patients escaped and killed a few nurses, a guard, and three of the top doctors. Then they released as many of the other patients as they could before disappearing into the woods. The papers said that all the patients had been caught and were accounted for, except for two. Some guy named William Todderman and…"

"Let me guess, the other was Carl Saunderson."

"You got it. They found Todderman, however, five days later hanging from that old train bridge. He had been stripped of his clothes just as Carl's kids had been. His clothes were lying on the ground in the same way too, folded neatly under the body. And now it's happening all over again, just as if," Brandon hesitated momentarily, knowing what he was about to say would sound nuts, crazy even, "As if Carl were back from the dead."

"Watch it Doc, you could lose your license with talk like that."

Brandon couldn't help but smile. "Can we change the subject, please?"

"Yeah, sure," Joan replied, "Let's talk about the rabbits. You mentioned something about rabbits being killed back then as well."

"That's what makes this whole thing so—eerie. I mean, everything that happened all those years ago seems to be happening now, in the present, all the way down to the mutilated rabbits. The papers back then said that it was the most bizarre act of animal cruelty they had ever seen. The rabbits weren't just killed; they were ripped apart, mutilated, and stripped of their pelts in much the same way as what you described."

"Anything else that you can remember?" Joan asked.

"Two things actually," Brandon replied. "First, I never heard whether or not they had ever caught or found Carl Saunderson after the fire. And secondly, and what I found to be highly coincidental was that about a week after the Big Escape, the institute mysteriously caught fire. Supposedly the fire destroyed everything. Not one patient made it out alive, not to mention that all the pertinent files of the patients and the employees were conveniently destroyed. Nothing left but a brick and mortar shell."

"I heard about the files. I was talking to Rodger Klein earlier, the phone call that Ed came to get me for, he told me the same thing."

"Rodger, I know him, a bit tight in the drawers, but he's a good man."

A moment of silence passed between the two as if both were thinking the same thing.

"So convenient," Joan said. "Fires."

"Tell me about it. The whole thing stunk of governmental cover up."

"Did you ever hear anything more about the place?" Joan asked.

"No."

"Hmm."

"What?" Brandon asked, leaning forward.

"Probably nothing, but doesn't it strike you as odd that you didn't hear any news about someone finding the sub level. I mean, if the place burned down, and someone, a fireman let's say, found the lab, don't you think that would have made headlines? You know," Joan continued, "Secret lab found in burning mental institute, details at ten."

Joan watched as Brandon stood and walked to the picture window that looked out over her front yard. She joined him. Outside, the tall oaks across the road from her property cut the moon's cascading white light into long flanking beams. Fallen leaves tumbled across the yard. Everything looked so calm, so peaceful.

"Yeah, that is a little odd," Brandon finally said. "I can't believe I let that detail escape me. I guess I was just glad to see it all come to an end."

"But did it?"

"What do you mean?"

"In light of everything that's been happening around here, can we say beyond a shadow of a doubt that it has—come to an end, I mean?"

The room grew silent again as they sat back down. Brandon searched his memory one last time to make sure he hadn't forgotten any important details. But to the best of his recollection, everything he knew, or could remember, was now out in the open.

Joan put Brandon's story together with that of Charlie Malloy's. Everything seemed to fit all the way down to the timeframe of when it all started.

"Well," Joan said, breaking the silence, "You don't have to worry about Carl Saunderson."

"Why's that?"

"You said that you never heard whether or not he had ever been caught. Well, he was, and now he's dead, has been for a long time now."

"How? Who?"

Joan's expression told Brandon she had information, but was hesitant in bringing it out. "You know," Brandon said, leaning forward with an almost teasing smile, "I am a doctor, and anything you say would have to be held in the strictest of confidences." She smiled.

"What you probably don't know," Joan said, her voice taking a serious tone, "Is that after Carl escaped, he continued his killing spree of young kids."

"Oh God."

"Yeah, tell me about it. I had Charlie Malloy who was one of the fathers whose child was abducted and killed by Carl locked up in my jail."

"*Had*, as in past tense?"

"Had, as in he's now at the Dixon City Morgue with three bullet holes in him."

"How'd that happen?"

"I'm guessing it was a professional hit, I mean, whoever it was had brass ones, if you know what I mean. The bastard waited until my deputy went home for a bite to eat, then walked right into a locked police station, capped him, and walked out. No one saw anything. Anyway, before he died, he pretty much confessed that he had some part in the murder of Carl Saunderson. It seems that he and five others wanted vigilante justice. Charlie said that they beat him short of death and then hung him under the same bridge as he did their kids." Joan stood and paced the floor again, "To cap off the evening, they took his body, placed it deep into one of the coal mines and blasted it shut. Everyone involved was ordered to keep their pie holes shut."

With shock-filled eyes, Brandon asked, "By whom?"

"That's the interesting part," Joan replied. "It seems that the sheriff at the time, a man by the name of Henderson, lost a son at the hands of Carl Saunderson. He's the one that organized a group of grieving fathers whose lives had been torn apart by that lunatic."

"Lunatic is a strong word, Joan. Surely you don't condone what they did, I mean the man was mentally ill, granted, but he was that way for a reason."

Joan thought about the question for several minutes, thinking back to the weeks after her husband's funeral. The time spent roving the streets of New York in search of his killers, wondering if she had found them, would she have pulled the trigger as easily as they had when they shot her beloved John.

Across the room at the beginning of the hallway, a voice answered, "No, Mommy, you wouldn't have."

Joan and Brandon turned to see Caitlin walking toward them. She was in her PJs, carrying her favorite stuffed rabbit.

"Hi sweetie," Joan said, surprised. "What are you doing out of bed, and what did you mean just now?"

"You wouldn't have, you know that, don't you, Mommy?"

"Wouldn't have what, sweetie?" Joan asked again.

"Shot the men who killed John."

Joan sank into the chair. The room became silent. *How could she have known he had been killed? Better yet,* Joan thought, *how did she know what I was thinking just now?* Her mind became empty, unable to find any type of response. Her thought process was at a standstill. All she could do was sit there and stare blankly at her daughter.

Brandon broke the silence, "Whose John?" But he got no response. Brandon cleared his throat and tried again, "Ah, can one of you tell me who John is?"

Joan, after several attempts, found the words, and turned to face Brandon, "He was my husband."

To Caitlin, she said, "How did you know what I was thinking just then, and how did you know John had been killed?"

Caitlin eased forward. She said to Joan and Brandon, "I know lots of things that I shouldn't. Things about people—things about events that have happened—and things about events that will happen."

"What do you mean by that?" Brandon asked. "What is it that you think you know, and how is it that you think you know about these—these people—these events?"

Sometimes I see things in my sleep," Caitlin replied, "Sometimes I hear voices. They tell me things."

"Those are just dreams sweetie, dreams—that's all."

"No, Mommy, it doesn't just happen while I'm sleeping. Sometimes all I have to do is touch someone, or look into someone's eyes. And sometimes," Caitlin said, now staring directly at her mother, "All I need is to be in the room when someone is thinking about something. A few moments ago, you were thinking about whether or not you would have killed the men that shot your husband. And I know, and I think deep down that you know, no matter how angry you would have been, you would not have done it. That's not who you are."

And she was right. Joan had searched the far reaches of her mind, every nook and cranny of it. She knew that she would have more than likely pushed the envelope beyond legal limits by beating the crap out of the murderous bastards, but killing them, that would have put her in their league. That, she would not have done.

At that moment, however, Joan did not know how to feel. *How could one person feel so excited, yet so afraid of what was happening right before their very eyes?* Her eight-year-old daughter was standing in front of her, telling her that she could read people's minds, see the future, the past. Surly there had to be a reasonable explanation for this. Joan had just not seen it yet. But there had to be.

"I also know about Carl Saunderson." Caitlin said, now staring blankly through the picture window. Her voice was calm and steady, but the more she talked, the more adult-like she sounded. If Joan had not been present in front of her daughter, she would have sworn someone else was speaking.

"I know that he thought he somehow killed his wife, Sandra, during the delivery of their eighth child. I know he suffered a mental breakdown, and that he killed his seven kids and their pet rabbits. I know he was caught and tortured by scientists. Cruel things were done to him." Caitlin flicked her gaze from the picture window to Brandon. "But it wasn't your fault Dr. Nelson, you were the only one who wanted to try and help him, but they didn't give you a chance."

Caitlin turned her gaze back through the window outside and beyond.

"I know that he escaped and resumed living in the memories of his past by stalking and killing kids he thought to be his own. He was caught, beaten, and hung. And when they thought him to be dead, they threw him down a black hole and sealed it. They thought he was dead, but he wasn't. He crawled his way back through the blackness, back to the entrance. For days he tried to dig his way out, but he was too weak. He died right there—his eyes open, staring into the darkness. I know that though his heart no longer beats, and that his lungs are no longer filled with air, and though his physical body was drained of life, his spirit remains in your world, waiting in want."

Joan asked, "In want of what?"

"To go home. He wanted then what he wants now, to be with his family. To be reunited with us. But he has lost his way, and his spirit believes that by retracing his former life, his former actions, he will find his way back to me, to our children."

Both Joan and Brandon noticed the context of the words used. 'Our', and 'me', but said nothing.

"You talk about him as though he were alive," Brandon said.

"His life form is dead, but his spirit lives between this world and the next, and so do those that wait for him."

"What else can you tell us, Sandra?" Brandon asked, experimenting with the name.

"I can tell you that five of the men who killed Carl Saunderson, are now dead. Only J.P. remains, and he is in the area."

"J.P.? Can you tell us who this J.P. is?"

"All I can tell you is that he is a very bad man. He's the one that killed Charlie."

Caitlin yawned, "I'm going back to bed now."

"But there's…"

"Questions," Caitlin said, interrupting Joan. "I know, and they will be answered in time. Some will be answered tomorrow when you and Dr. Nelson go to the institute. Just remember to push left and fall right." Caitlin yawned again as she turned and headed for her room. As she reached the beginning of the hall, she stopped, turned, and said, in her own voice, "There is one other thing,"

"What's that?"

"Sometime tomorrow night, around eight, you'll be having a visitor."

"Who?"

"You will know who she is when you see her," Caitlin replied, as she turned and continued toward her room.

5

When Caitlin entered her room she closed the door and walked to the window. She looked out across the back lawn and into the blackness of the night towards the tree line. And though she could not see Carl Saunderson, she knew he was there. She grabbed her robe and fixed up her bed to make it look as if she were in it, sleeping. Next, she opened the window and climbed out onto a ladder she had placed there earlier in the day, though, at the time, she had not known why. As she climbed down the ladder, she stopped long enough to close the window behind her, climbed down the last two rungs, and walked to the end of the yard.

As she peered into the intimidating darkness, the woods gave off a strange sense of foreboding. But Caitlin was not threatened nor scared of the eeriness that lay before her.

She saw what she was looking for thirty feet away, the tall dark figure of Carl Saunderson. He moved away as her eyes fixed on him. With the moon hovering above, she thought she could see him almost squinting just before he raised his hands in front of his eyes as if shielding himself from an intense light.

She tried to enter his mind with her own, tried to feel what he was feeling, but all she saw was fear. He feared her.

"Carl, don't be afraid," she said. But her words went unanswered as Carl turned and disappeared into the dense trees. And though she could no longer see him, she knew where he was going, and she followed.

6

With Caitlin back in bed, Joan suddenly felt exhausted.

Questions, she thought, *I should have asked more questions. I should have known. What kind of mother have I become? How could Caitlin have possessed such a mind-bending trait, and I be none the wiser of it? And what kind of trait was it anyway? How could someone have the power to tap into someone else's mind, to see someone else's thoughts?*

To Brandon, she said, "What in God's name just happened here?

Brandon reached out, and wiped her tears.

"I just want to understand what's happening to my little girl," Joan whispered.

"We've all had a very trying day, and I think what we all need is a good night's sleep. We can let this go until tomorrow when we both have clearer heads."

"Just answer me one question before you go."

"If I can."

"Is there anything wrong with Caitlin? I mean, I've seen TV shows and watched movies and…"

"No!" he said. "There is absolutely nothing wrong with your daughter."

"Are you sure? Because I don't know what I'd do if anything ever happened to her."

"I'm positive." A few seconds of silence passed. "I will tell you this though," Brandon said, "Your daughter is a very remarkable young girl with a very extraordinary gift."

"Brandon, let me ask you one last thing."

"Ask away."

"Why didn't you seem all that surprised when Caitlin came out and told us what she knew, and how she came to know it?"

"Truthful answer?"

"Of course."

"Well, truthfully, I don't have the slightest inclination as to why. All I can tell you is that earlier, when I first shook your daughter's hand, I felt what I can only describe as a sort of—vibe, a psychic transfer if you will. Other than that, I don't know what to say."

"But she's okay, right? You're sure of that? Joan asked.

"I'm quite positive that there is nothing physically wrong with your daughter. Other than the fact that she can, well, do what she did tonight, and even that might be a onetime occurrence. Now get some sleep."

"Brandon, thanks for being here."

"Actually, I should be thanking you." He paused at the front door, "If you happen to have a sledge hammer handy, bring it along tomorrow. I have no idea how well they boarded up the building."

Joan closed and locked the front door. She turned and saw Jessie leaning against the wall next to the kitchen entrance. Joan could tell immediately that her mother had something weighing on her mind.

"Mom, what is it? Is there something wrong? Is Caitlin okay?"

"Caitlin's fine," Jessie replied, "It's just that I overheard everything that Caitlin said, and—and…"

"And what?"

"I didn't put two and two together until just now."

"Mom, you're not making any sense. Put what together? Has she said anything to you about her—psychic ability? Has she?"

"I'm not sure," Jessie replied. "Remember the other night, when we got back late from shopping?"

"Yes."

"Right before we pulled into the driveway, she asked me whether or not I thought you would take her to see Mrs. Zachary and her rabbits, and in the same breath, she said she knew you would."

"And?"

"The next morning after you called and told me not to take her up there, I went to her room. I thought she was sleeping so I stayed and was looking out her window. Suddenly out of the blue, she sat up in bed and said she knew that you weren't going to be taking her to Mrs. Zachary's. Then she asked me if I'd ever seen red rabbits." Jessie paused a moment, "As it turns out, it seems that she knew everything that was going to happen that day, with a child's mentality that is. I mean, she didn't express names or details of how you would," she paused again, "of how you would find the girl, Kiersten, I'm guessing; she only knew that you would."

"Why didn't you say anything?"

"At the time, I thought it was just a dream she had. Later, when you told me about Kiersten, I thought it nothing more than a coincidence. You were distraught enough already, and I didn't want to bother you with it."

Joan sat on the sofa, her eyes fixed on the wall. She was seeing Caitlin in a new light. She started remembering the countless times she had misplaced her keys and Caitlin knew right where to find them, and the times when they were out shopping and Caitlin would remind her to pick something up. But then, the big one hit her. She remembered the first time Caitlin had called her Mommy. She had said it emphatically, before anyone knew how the outcome of the adoption would turn out. It was as if she had already known that the adoption was a done deal.

Chapter 29

1

Dark shadows filled the forest, but Caitlin managed to move swiftly through the darkness, never once tripping on a stone, or the many tree roots that stuck up through the ground. It was as if she knew every obstacle in her path.

She still had no clear visual on Carl Saunderson but she knew where he was, and where he was going. Once they arrived, Caitlin knew what had to be done. She had seen inside his mind; she knew he was afraid of her, and that was an insight she planned on taking full advantage of. She knew that she would have to send him out to take a life, in order to save three.

2

Joan had climbed out of bed at 5:00 a.m. before the sun was up. The night had seemed unending as she tossed and turned, unable to capture the sleep her body craved. Instead, thoughts scrambled around inside her head. *Who had killed Charlie? Caitlin said J.P. did. But who was this J.P.? Was he Jacob Palmer,* she thought, *but he's dead. But then again, so is Carl Saunderson, for thirty-two years and he seems to be up and about. Or is he? God, this is nuts! I need to verify that. I need to see for myself whether or not he's dead,* she thought.

But those weren't the only thoughts. Her most intriguing thoughts were those she had of Brandon Nelson. For whatever reason, no matter how hard she tried, she could not get the man out of her mind. Even with all the other unpleasant thoughts swimming in her head, his presence was always there. He had unpacked emotions in her that clearly needed dusting off. At this point, she didn't know what to fear more: Caitlin's gift, a thirty-two year old ghost, or the feelings of passion that she had truly believed would never find their way back into her life.

After she got dressed, she looked quickly in on Caitlin. She looked as if she were fast asleep, nestled tightly under the covers.

She closed Caitlin's door, and went out to the shed in the back yard and removed the rusted sledgehammer from off the wall, and returned to the house.

Joan gathered two flashlights, two pairs of work gloves, two sections of climbing rope, each about forty yards in length. She had hoped that the strength of the rope had not diminished since the time she and John had last used them on a weekend vacation during the summer before he had been shot and killed. She also grabbed the repelling gear and her .38. Next, she went to her closet and retrieved her deceased husbands .45 cal Sig Sauer, extracted the clip and pushed in the hollow point shells that Ed had given her. After sliding the clip back in and popping it in place with the palm of her hand, she pulled back the loading mechanism to put a bullet in the breech, put the safety on, and slipped it into the waistband of her jeans at the small of her back. The extra clip was stuffed in her rear pocket. She wasn't worried about it seizing up on her; she fired the gun now and then, and always kept it clean.

3

Joan found Brandon waiting in the outer lobby of the Milford Lodge. He jogged to the passenger side and hopped in.

Brandon's hair was pulled back and braided. He wore a pair of loose fitting Levi's, a black button down shirt, and a brown leather jacket.

"How'd you sleep?" he asked.

"Not too well. You?"

"Good. Well, I did have some thoughts that kept me awake at first."

Joan raised an eyebrow, but said nothing.

"I'm guessing that pretty much of your night was spent thinking about your daughter." Brandon said.

"Among other things."

"Like?"

God, she thought, *if only this were another place, another time.*

"Like the plausibility of us chasing after a ghost for one thing," she said, holding Brandon's gaze for a moment before turning away. "This whole thing is just so—it's all just so unbelievable. I mean, Carl Saunderson is dead, yet we're being told he's out wandering around the woods abducting children and killing them just as he did all those years ago. It's ludicrous, and I need to be sure he is in-fact dead before we head to the institute. I need to see where he was buried. I need to see his bones."

Joan's statement was wrapped around a moment of silence.

"Maybe it's just that I can't believe in the living dead," she said, continuing, "Or any variation of the whole zombie-ghost thing. What about you? You're a man of science. What do you make of all this craziness?"

Brandon took a long, deep breath before answering.

"Do you know to what extent a man or woman can shut down their bodies?"

"What do you mean '*shut down*'?"

"I mean, that it has been said that humans have the capability to slow down their heart rate and breathing to the boundaries that a normal educated person would think them to be dead, yet they are alive and well."

"No. I didn't know that. But even if I did, we're talking thirty-two years. Thirty-two years of silence from a man you believed to have P.T.S.D. Thirty-two years of no one dying, at least not of the same M.O."

"I know. I'm just trying to get you to understand that if we, as mere humans, can manipulate someone into thinking we're dead when we're not, who knows what the human soul is capable of outside its physical body, and to what extent its capabilities can stretch. Who knows for how long a spirit can lay dormant before returning because of some unforeseen event stirring up its former remains."

A long moment went by. Joan's eyes seemed to be wandering. She then said, "Oh God."

"What?"

"An event—stirring things up, you mean like an earthquake or maybe a tremor?"

"I was thinking more in the terms of an archeologist digging up the remains of Egyptian Pharaohs, but sure. We are, after all, talking about the realm of implausibility, so sure, why not? Why?"

"We had a tremor here three days before Kiersten was reported missing."

"Three days, are you sure about that?"

"Positive. Why?"

In the silence after Joan's question, Brandon repositioned himself in the seat of Joan's truck and leaned back. He took another deep breath and let it out. "In my profession," Brandon said, "I tend to read a lot of books. I even read the goofy ones including—well, let's say the *implausible* ones. I've found that if I have some knowledge on the subject that the patient is having a problem with, I have a place in which to start, which in return, makes me feel as though I have a better chance of having them come to terms with what brought them to my office to start with.

"In this case, we're talking about ghosts, the living dead, and I've read plenty of books on this anomaly, believe me. I'm not claiming to be an expert, far from it, in fact. But from what I've read, three days from the time of disturbance seems to be the amount of time that it takes for an entity to gather its strength and return as a lost soul, if you believe in that sort of thing. Just as an example, even the Bible says it took Jesus three days to rise from his death."

Joan tried to shake off images of corpses lying in their coffins in the middle of a funeral, and then suddenly their eyes open and they sit up; they try to speak, but they can't because their mouths are sewn shut. She shuddered.

"It's still hard to believe that we're talking about ghosts for crying out loud," she said, "But you're right as far as the knowledge we have on life after death, or should I say the lack there of, but what about Caitlin? How do you explain that?"

"Well, I'm glad you asked. Last night, after retiring to my lonely room," Brandon, said, with emphasis on the word 'lonely', "I set up my laptop, and did a little research on what we experienced last night. From what I—what we—saw last night, I believe Caitlin is both telepathically and clairvoyantly gifted. I also believe that she can use those gifts from either side of the lifeline."

"Which means what exactly?"

"Well, simply put, it means that we, meaning you, Caitlin and I, should hop on a plane and head off to Las Vegas. With her talents, we should be able to own the town by, say mid-week." Joan gave a quick smile and wiped a tear from her eye.

"I take it then you're just here to use us."

"Of course."

Joan gazed into Brandon's piercing blue eyes and said, "I don't believe that for a minute. You're a good man. Don't ask me how I know this, I just do."

"Caitlin, maybe?"

"I think *probably*, would more fit the bill."

As Joan put her truck in gear and drove out of the hotel parking lot, she asked, "If you were doing research, and I'm assuming you were on legitimate websites, then there really are people out in the world like my Caitlin. I mean, people that can read someone else's mind, read the future?"

"Not just that, but there are people that claim they can contact the other side, that being the deceased.

"There is a tremendous amount of controversy on the subject." He paused, and then said, "Have you ever watched *Crossing Over* with John Edwards?"

"Yes."

"Then you know his thing is to connect with the other side."

"Yes."

"I won't presume to know how far Caitlin's ability goes, but when she said '*They told me*', I was under the impression that she was talking about an entity that was, as they say, stuck between worlds, unable, for whatever reason, to release themselves from this world and move on to the next, to rest in peace if you will. And later, when she used words like 'our,' and 'me,' I was under the impression that someone, Carl's wife, was speaking through her, I mean it didn't even sound like your daughter's voice. I even called her Sandra just to get a reaction, but she answered my question as if that were in fact her name."

4

After taking a shower, washing her hair, and slipping back into the same clothes she had worn the previous day, the brown-haired lady checked out of the hotel and jumped back into her rented Mercury. Her final destination had not yet been revealed. The silent voice that only she could hear, had told her to head into Virginia by way of Route 301, through Port Royal, and then Bowling Green.

From there, she knew she would be given her final instructions on where to go, and when.

5

Gage called Joan on the two-way radio just as she and Brandon pulled away from the Milford Lodge. The Clark family had just reported their daughter, Kimberly, missing. She had been taken sometime during the night.

"Great," Joan replied angrily. Just what we need, she thought.

"What?" Brandon asked.

"Another child, Kimberly Clark. Damn it, she's only five years old."

Joan hesitated for a second, as she remembered something Charlie Malloy had mentioned during his interrogation. She keyed the microphone. "Ed, call the state trooper's office. Tell them we have another missing girl. You might as well let that asshole Helmsley know as well, but as soon as you do, you and Gage, get over to that bridge before the sun rises. You got it?"

"Roger that. What's your twenty? Over."

"A few minutes from the coal mines."

"Why the mines? Is something up?"

"Curiosity more than anything else. I want to verify what Charlie told us about the remains of Carl Saunderson."

"Copy that. Oh, and Joan, be careful at the main mine shaft. There were signs that the massive amount of rocks sealing the mine is unstable."

"How's that?"

"When we were out there the other day, after we split up, I noticed a hole in the top left of the mine shaft. Not big, but it could become bigger if you catch my drift."

"Copy. Thanks for the heads up.

As Joan put down the mike, she pulled up to the fence that she and Gage had walked through the day they had found Kiersten.

Walking toward the mines, Joan saw the train tracks that had led her to Kiersten's body. She shuddered at the memory.

The sun was just edging over the tree line as they reached the main mineshaft. At the top, on the left hand side, was the small opening Gage had warned her about. Joan climbed the mound of rocks with the agility of a cat. Brandon followed, but used a little more caution as his weight shifted the loose rock beneath him. He immediately understood why Joan's deputy had given her the heads up.

At the top, Joan peered into the hole using the 6-inch flashlight she retrieved from her rear pocket.

"See anything?"

"Not from here. I need to get inside."

"Do you think that's wise?"

"I didn't come out here to look at a hole."

Joan put the flashlight back in her rear pocket and entered the small diameter hole, feet first. She thought it best to take a little more caution going down as her body dispelled what little light penetrated the twenty inch diameter hole. After several slips and a near complete fall, she reached the bottom with only a few minor scrapes and bruises on her elbows, and a small bump on the head from a falling stone.

After grabbing the flashlight from her rear pocket, she flicked it on. It didn't take long for her to see that Charlie had indeed been telling the truth, at least partially. The body wasn't where he said they had left it. Instead, it lay on the ground right in front of the fallen rock.

There was little light in the mine; just an opaque glow coming from the hole she had just crawled through. The light from her flashlight was restricted to where she pointed it.

Either Charlie was wrong about the placement of the body, she thought, *or the guy wasn't as dead as they thought, as Caitlin had said last night.*

The air was less than desirable. It was damp, stale, and smelled of sulfur and death.

"You okay down there?" she heard Brandon ask.

"Yeah, fine," Joan replied, "I think Caitlin was right last night. I found a set of bones right at the foot of the collapse."

"Do you think it's Carl Saunderson?"

"I won't know that for sure until I get a C.S.I. out here."

The flashlights beam followed the outline of the skeletal remains. Joan could see grooves in the dirt that started at his feet and led off into a deep black tunnel.

Using the grooves as a sight line, she brought the beam of light back to the bones that had long ago been stripped of flesh. She was no pathologist, but judging by the look of the two femur bones of the alleged Carl Saunderson, they had both been broken, several times. One of the breaks looked as though it would have ripped through the flesh.

Moving the flashlight upward, she saw a fracture on the pelvic bone near where the man's testicles had once hung. The rib cage was severely damaged as well; the sternum was no longer attached. Both arms were outstretched above the head. The ulna bones in each arm showed signs of multiple fractures. In her mind, she pictured these as being defensive wounds in an effort to protect his face, but as the beam of light reached the head, she knew it had been a worthless effort. The empty eye sockets looked like dark hollow caverns. The empty space between the eyes made it look as if the man had been born with a disfiguring cleft. As she looked further, she knew this not to be the case. The bridge of the nose lay smashed inside the fractured skull.

As she looked over the bones for a second time from head to toe, she wondered how this man, who might very well be Carl Saunderson, could have found the strength after such a beating to somehow crawl back from where they had originally dumped the body. Then she remembered what Brandon had said about the amount of adrenalin and God knows what else that had been pumped into Carl's body while in the Institute's secret lab.

Faintly, she could hear the baseball bats, the crowbars, and the boots thudding against the man's body. She could actually hear his cries and screams that went unheard by his vigilante killers. She could feel the anguish that he must have felt in his last waning moments of life, not in dying, but in dying alone. *Death, he deserved*, she thought, *but not like this.*

She turned suddenly as she felt a presence behind her. The beam from her flashlight darted across the black rock wall and then down what could only be described as a horizontal pit of blackness. She felt undiluted fear seeping through her body, like water through a breached dam.

"Hello," she said, her words reverberating back to her in a hollowed tone as if they had traveled for years through the mines and were just now getting back. "Is anyone there?" Again, all she heard was her echoing words stretching through the blackness.

Then, "Joan." Her whole body shuddered. "Joan, are you alright?"

Relieved that it was Brandon, she answered, "Yeah, I think."

She scurried back up the rocks taking little caution. She exited the small hole gasping for air.

"You alright?" Brandon asked again. "You look like you've just seen..."

"Don't even go there, please," she said in between breaths. She took a minute to steady herself. She then said to Brandon, "Whoever that was down there, didn't die without pain."

6

Joan requested Tanya Fucus from the C.S.I. team out of Richmond because she was already familiar with the case. She also requested some lighting, and a Mining Engineer that could assist in determining the structural integrity of the mine before they let anyone else inside.

The reply was that they would have all they needed by noon on Tuesday.

Before heading to the institute, Joan cordoned off the area with standard yellow police tape.

Twenty minutes later, they arrived at the entrance to the Institute. She pulled up into a weed-infested parking lot, and parked.

The building was barely visible through the now untamed trees and bushes around it. Joan reached into the truck, and grabbed the gear that she had gathered earlier that morning. She handed Brandon the sledgehammer, threw the rope over her head and shoulders. The rest of the gear was in a knapsack which Brandon slung over his shoulder. They made their way through the bushes and thickets to the base of the brick building. The sun was now in full view, and Joan hoped that Ed and Gage had already found Kimberly Clark, *alive.*

To Joan, the building looked bigger than she had initially thought. It was an impressive looking structure with advanced architecture. She tried to picture the building as it might have looked in its prime, *beautiful,* she thought. Now, it looked dark, almost Gothic. The brown brick had been chard black around the base of the doors and windows which have since been boarded up and had been decorated with years of graffiti.

After a quick survey, Brandon said, "I think our best chance to gain entrance would be from the back. There used to be a solarium back there, and it might be easier getting in by breaking the tempered glass than this, that is if there's any left." He began knocking on the plywood-covered windows.

"I'm convinced," Joan replied.

They inched their way down the right side of the building, and as Brandon had suggested, there was a glass-enclosed solarium.

7

At eight a.m., the brown haired woman entered the town of Bowling Green. She had no sooner crossed the town's border when the voice she had been hearing, telling her what, when, and where to go, had filled her in with the rest of her itinerary. The final phase that she knew she must follow was now quite clear to her.

8

Joan and Brandon rounded the rear of the building. Brandon had been right about the ease of gaining access to the Institute. The intense heat of the fire, and some of the firefighters themselves, had shattered most of the panes of glass. Those windows had been sealed up with the same three-quarter inch plywood as were the doors and windows in the front. Several panes of glass, however, had not been damaged in the fire, and were subsequently not covered with plywood. They were instead, covered with graffiti, and cracked. Several large stones lay in front as though they had been tossed at the tempered glass, but it had held its own.

"This looks as good a place as any," Joan said.

"Don't we need some kind of search warrant or something?"

Joan grabbed the sledgehammer, held it waist high, and said, "When there's a girl and three boys dead, and another girl missing, this is the only warrant I need." She smashed the glass.

After thirty-two years of being sealed, the solarium smelled of must, mold, and burnt wood. Years of fallen leaves, overgrown foliage and a coating of bird droppings covered the remaining glass walls and roof, making the inside of the solarium dark and gloomy. Long shadows in the corners gave the room a feeling of evil.

Guided by the beams of their flashlights, they crept down darkened halls, turning right then left. As they walked further into the decaying building, Brandon's memories reared up unwanted voices of the deranged and mentally challenged criminals that these walls had once held within. It was a disturbing memory, one that he did not feel he would have after all this time.

After gaining his perspective of the buildings layout, Brandon said, "There's the security desk, or what's left of it anyway. Only, something's not right."

"What is it?"

"The door should be right over there." Brandon pointed to the far end of the lobby. "That wall's not supposed to be there."

"Are you sure? It has been a while."

"I'm absolutely positive," Brandon assured her. "The main entrance is right there," Brandon flicked the flashlights beam 40 or so feet to the left. "My office was on the left side of the building as you walked up the front walkway."

"Then that leaves us with only one explanation."

"They concealed the door."

"If you're sure that's the right spot, then yeah. And judging by the discoloration of the wall, I'd be willing to bet it was put there pre-fire," Joan said. "No wonder we never heard anything about a secret lab. They knew they were going to torch the place, so they put up this wall so that no fireman or the police would ever see it. And judging by the damage caused by the fire, my guess is that it started in one of the hall offices just past the solarium."

"That would be right around where the patients rooms were. No wonder none of them made it out." Brandon said in disgust.

They both thought about that for a moment.

"Clever little devils, weren't they?" Brandon said.

"Murderous evil bastards is more like it!"

"Can't argue that."

"I haven't read the Fire Marshal's report yet," Joan said, "But I bet they came to the same conclusion." She paused, looked around, and then to Brandon, she asked, "Where is the patient and employee file rooms located?"

Brandon had to think about that for a moment as he tried to recall a mental map in his mind. "Down the first hall on the right as we exited the solarium, third, no, fourth door on the left," he said. "And from what I can tell, that's the area that took the brunt of the fire."

"Ten bucks says it's the place of origin."

"I think I'll keep my ten bucks, thank you." he said, staring off into a darkened hallway.

Joan could tell by the look on Brandon's face that he was having a reflection of his past, and waited a moment to speak, taking the opportunity to study the area around her. The building's interior architecture had been as impressive as that of the exterior.

Brandon made his way to where Joan was studying the massive front doors. "Sorry," he said, "I didn't think I'd have any old feelings about this place, but…"

"No apologies needed," she said in an understanding tone. "I do have a theory on the reason for the fire, if you're interested."

"You mean, now that I'm back in the present?"

"Are you?"

"Yeah, I guess I just needed a moment to reflect. And yes, I am interested in your theory."

"If you think about it, the fire does make sense if the right people were involved. I mean, if a Senator or the F.B.I. or some other alphabet agencies for that matter, were to catch wind of an internal investigation, that alone would give them motive. If the investigation was being conducted by some eager beaver state official looking to make a name for him or herself, they would see to it that the courts would have issued warrants for unadulterated access to anywhere in the facility."

"Like I said, you don't miss much."

"I have to admit that if it were me, I'd do the same thing. And I'd probably start the fire in the exact same spot too."

"Okay, you have my full attention," Brandon replied. "Why?"

"The wall. It was obviously put here for a reason. And I think that reason was so they could torch the place and not have to reveal what lies beneath. If the fire was started far enough away, like the file room for instance, that would have given the fire department time to gain control of the fire prior to reaching this point, eliminating the possibility of them having to breach the wall to contain the fire while at the same time, making sure all files and records were destroyed."

"Yeah, but why did they feel the need for a fire to start with? Why not just put up the wall and call it quits?"

Joan had to think about that for a moment, and then it hit her. "They couldn't chance it. She said. "If I were the investigator, the first thing I'd do would be to obtain a copy of the original blueprints. And of course, they wouldn't have shown the wall, and that would have raised suspicion right off the bat. But, if someone had set the place on fire, and closed the place down prior to the investigation, there'd be no reason for one. The case would have been closed."

A slight smile traced the rim of Brandon's lips. It was hard for Joan not to take notice.

"What?" Joan asked. "Why the smile?"

"I'm laughing at myself. I always took myself to be reasonably smart, but now I just feel like an idiot that I didn't think of that."

"Don't. I think like a cop. You, you think like a doctor."

9

With everything going on, Jessie's first instinct after getting up was to look in on her granddaughter. She slowly opened the door and peeked in. *Poor thing,* she thought, *she must still be exhausted.* Jessie closed the door and went to the kitchen to make breakfast. She whipped up a batch of pancakes, scrambled some eggs, and fried six strips of bacon. After laying plates out on the kitchen table, she went back to Caitlin's room. The girl hadn't moved a muscle in the thirty-minutes it took Jessie to prepare breakfast. *How odd,* Jessie thought. It was almost 8:30. Caitlin never slept past seven, always wanting to watch her morning cartoons. Jessie walked softly to her granddaughter's bed and sat on the edge. "Caitlin dear," she whispered. "Breakfast is ready. I made all your favorites."

Caitlin did not move.

"Caitlin?"

Again she did not move and Jessie drew back the covers. A pillow had been put in place where Caitlin's body should have been. Jessie shot up from off the bed and went to the bathroom across the hall, she was not there. Fear ripped through her body. She went to Joan's room, but she wasn't there either. She searched the entire house, from one room to the next at a frenzied pace, but Caitlin was nowhere to be found.

The back yard, she thought, *maybe she's in the back yard*. But she wasn't there either.

Unadulterated fear, like a vise, squeezed at her chest.

She stared out the window. Almost instantaneously, a calming sensation immersed her body and replaced the horrid squeeze that had a hold on her heart. The urge to call Joan was also abated. She still had no idea as to the whereabouts of her granddaughter, but she somehow knew that she was safe and unharmed. She also knew that it was Caitlin who was somehow trying to remove the anxiety that had gripped her body and mind.

Jessie sat on the sofa and reached for one of the embroidered pillows that Caitlin had helped her make. The fear was now gone, but concern lingered. She gripped the pillow and put it against her chest and squeezed it as if it were Caitlin sitting on her lap.

10

A realm of blackness encapsulated Carl Saunderson's ghostly frame, Caitlin, and five-year-old Kimberly Clark. It was through this blackness that Caitlin and the ghost of Carl Saunderson glared at each other, visible only to each other, as if they were sitting across from one another in a lighted room. Carl, however, could still not look directly at her, for the light that was Caitlin, was too intense. Looking at her, if only for a moment, served only as a reminder of that which he craved for, and could not have. And if he did so, he might have been devoured by it before reaching his goal. That he could not do. So for now, he did nothing.

Caitlin sat next to Kimberly, holding her hand, wet from wiping away her tears. Caitlin had untied the girl's hands and feet the moment she found her lying on the floor of the cave. Carl had been unhappy with that. Caitlin knew this, but didn't care.

Kimberly could not see Caitlin, but her warm soothing touch calmed her, and she stopped crying. Caitlin had spoken softly to Kimberly after untying her. She told her she no longer had to be frightened, that the man who had brought her to this dark place would not, and could not harm her, and that soon, very soon, it would all be over.

Caitlin's eyes cut straight through the blackness, straight through to the core of the dark figure's soul. There, she saw pain and anguish. She could see that he had not always been a bad man, but a beloved father and husband, as in her dream. But like skin on all mere mortals, his soul was covered with pure malevolence. And no matter how hard he tried, he could not break free from it.

She could tell that the dark figure was somehow disturbed by her presence, fearful of her existence.

"Mr. Saunderson," Caitlin said, "Please, don't be afraid. I'm here to help you. But before I can, you must help my mother." Caitlin's voice had changed. She had no recollection of it, but she was speaking with a mature woman's voice. "She's in danger from the same man that hurt you years ago. Please, Carl, you know what you must do. I know there's good in you. Show me your worthy of what it is that you seek most, to rest in peace with your family. You know where she is, now go. Help Joan."

11

Joan and Brandon stood for a second looking at the brick wall. Brandon said, "What do we do now?"

"Knock it down," Joan replied, "But I think it would take a little more force than I can muster up." Joan handed Brandon the sledgehammer and he put it to quick use. On the fifth blow, he broke a hole large enough to stick a flashlight through.

"I can see the elevator door," he said.

Brandon enlarged the hole further, and they both climbed through.

They pried open the door to the elevator with a fire ax that had been hanging on the wall next to the elevator.

"This is convenient," Joan said as she broke the glass case that housed the ax.

The elevator was at the bottom of the shaft some forty feet down. "Not afraid of heights are you?" Joan asked, looking downward.

"Why?"

"Because we're going to have to repel down."

"No, not really. I would, however, prefer it if we had a little more light."

"Where's the fun in that?" she asked as she tied one end of the rope to a U-bolt, and then threw the other end of the rope down the shaft.

"Fun? Is this your idea of fun?"

"No, but it's better to look at it like fun rather than looking at it as if it's going to kill you, don't you think?"

"Well, if you put it in that way."

Joan pulled out the .38 from her holster and handed it to Brandon.

"Have you ever used one of these before?"

"Just point and shoot, right?"

With a slight smile, Joan replied, "Yeah, just point and shoot. Just be sure of what you're pointing at."

After attaching the rope to the climbing harness, she jumped and disappeared into the darkness. After dropping what she believed to be about thirty feet, she slowed her pace. And although Brandon was shining his flashlight down the shaft, the bottom was still hard to see. When she reached the bottom, she grabbed her flashlight and turned it on. She was standing on the top of the elevator.

"Joan, you alright?" Brandon yelled.

"Yeah, now it's your turn," her voice echoed back up from the pitch-black hole.

"Yeah, now it's my turn," he said unsteadily, not loud enough for Joan to hear.

From the top of the elevator, Joan and Brandon lifted the emergency door, and jumped down into the elevator.

They pried open the elevator door using the ax and stared for a few seconds as the door opened into an abyss of darkness.

Brandon pulled the .38 out of his front waistband.

"Not the best place to have the barrel of that gun pointing," Joan said, "I hope you put the safety on."

"Safety? There's a safety?"

Joan smiled.

Together, they stepped out into the unlit room cautiously, flashlights in hand. As their feet hit the floor, a few ceiling lights came on.

"That's what happened the first time I was down here," Brandon said, "I'm surprised they still work."

"Must be a dedicated power line separate from the rest of the building," Joan replied.

"Kind of makes you wonder why, doesn't it?"

The room had seemingly been left untouched by the fire above except for the slight lingering smell of smoke.

They moved toward the center of the room. At that moment, one of the lights sparked and blew out. "Hope that's just a coincidence," Joan said.

"Me too, but just in case, we better get what we came for before all these lights blow out. This place gives me the creeps as it is. I can't imagine what I would feel like with just a flashlight to see with."

"I'm with you," Joan replied.

"I think I remember seeing file cabinets in the second room," he said, pointing.

Brandon found the seam on the wall and opened the hidden door. Once in, it didn't take Joan long to spot the medical tables that Brandon had mentioned. On them, were three sets of human skeletal remains. *Probably the men Brandon spoke of,* she thought.

"God," Joan sighed, "Those poor bastards. They didn't deserve to die like that."

Out of the corner of Joan's eye, she saw a spark, then, another light went out and the room grew even darker and more eerie.

"Come on, the files are over here," Brandon said. Joan gave a quick nod as she moved toward Brandon. As she moved past the first of the skeletal remains, her eyes focused on the holes that had been drilled into the skull and a wave of nausea swept over her. For a few brief seconds, she thought she was going to throw up. When Brandon called to her again, his voice calmed her stomach, and the nausea quickly faded.

Brandon had pulled the file marked *Carl Saunderson* and started scanning the contents.

"This is it," he said, "But most of the contents have been removed." He pulled another file. "Damn it." The file was the same. He pulled another, the same, another, and again, the same. "Someone has pulled out all the pertinent information. Yet another convenience," Brandon said with obvious disgust in his voice. "There's nothing here but a bunch of nothing. My guess is that on the mishap of the firefighters not gaining control of the fire in time, they minimized the damages by removing any discriminating evidence." Brandon slammed files to the floor.

As Brandon protested his anger at the files, Joan's eyes had focused on something odd on the wall behind the file cabinets.

"Brandon," he heard Joan say. "Remember that hidden door that we just came through?"

"Yes. Why?"

"Didn't it look something like that?"

"Yeah. As a matter of fact, it looked exactly like that."

"Then I think we have another hidden room."

She moved her flashlight beam from the floor to the ceiling. What she was looking at was a seam that upon first glance would seem normal, but there was nothing normal about this creepy chamber of horrors.

Joan pushed aside the file cabinets, and pushed on the panel. It opened enough for her to get a hold alongside the edge of the door and pull it open. Brandon reached in to try and locate a light switch, but came up empty. Joan moved past Brandon into the room. Inside, flanking the room on both sides, were two more doors. The door on the far left was of normal size, but the one to the right was four feet wide and four feet tall. The bottom of the strange door was about four feet from the ground.

Joan moved to that one first. The door was heavy, and was constructed out of solid iron. With a labored tug, and a disgruntled squeal, the door opened. They could do nothing but stand there and stare in disbelief. They were looking at what appeared to be an incineration chamber.

Joan moved closer and stuck her head inside the door. She looked down between the iron grates and with the light from her flashlight, saw mounds of dust and bone chips. Moving the flashlight up, she saw two rows of burners that stretched the full seven-foot length of the grates.

"We wanted to know what they did with the bodies, well, here's our answer. They tortured them to death and then burned the bodies. And I'd be willing to bet my pension that that door," Joan flicked her flashlight to the other side of the room, resting its beam on a metal door, "Leads to a tunnel that takes you out to the woods where they dumped the ashes."

It was then that all the lights went out, and all that was left was the two flashlights that now were beginning to fade, as the batteries were dying, which didn't make sense because Joan had put in fresh batteries.

"I think that's our exit call," Brandon said.

"I think you're right."

And as they started back, a sudden chill filled the room, and with it, a quick burst of air that smelled of death buffeted past them.

"Did you feel that?" Joan asked.

"Yeah, I think that was our second call."

Joan tripped as they hurried forward. She released her flashlight to free her hand to help cushion her fall. She landed on her hands and knees unhurt.

Her flashlight, however, did not land. The twelve-inch Mag-light spun in mid-air as if someone were using it as a baton. Joan rose to her feet, her eyes glued to the light show. She grabbed hold of Brandon's right arm.

Then, the flashlight stopped spinning. It instead, hovered over the floor, the beam of light pointed directly into Brandon's face. Brandon pointed his own flashlight at the one that appeared to be hovering, only, there was nothing holding the flashlight up.

The beam of light started to move again from side to side as if what or whoever was holding up the flashlight was trying to taunt them.

With great speed, the flashlight rushed toward Brandon, stopping an inch from the tip of his nose.

"Brandon," Joan asked, "What the hell?"

"I don't have a clue," he responded. "I have a feeling that whatever this is, for some reason, is fighting itself over whether or not it should kill me. I'm pulling for the not."

Suddenly, the flashlight fell to the floor with a dull thud, flickered a few times, and went out.

"I'd say that that was our third and final call to get the hell out of here," Brandon said with fear oozing from his words.

"I agree."

Joan followed Brandon back to the files where he retrieved the Saunderson file, and then headed for the elevator.

Twenty minutes later, both were out of the elevator shaft, and out of breath. They sat side by side with their backs braced against the brick wall opposite the elevator doors. "I hope we don't have to go back down there. The place gave me the heebie-jeebies," Joan said, her breath slowing to normal.

"I don't relish the thought either, but you should have seen it thirty-two years ago."

"No, thank you. I can only imagine. On second thought, I don't even want to put that image in my head. What I just witnessed was bad enough."

12

Joan and Brandon navigated their way back to the solarium where they had initially entered the building. A human shaped figure standing in the opening that they had created brought them to a sudden halt. The shape was vague, but it was definitely human. The figure stayed in the confines of the shadows, not moving, not saying a word; it just stood there stiffly, and watched them. Joan grabbed Brandon's flashlight and raised it to the face of the shadowed figure. As the light hit his face, the figure said with an arrogant smile, "Sheriff Fortune, how nice to see you again." A nickel-plated .44 hung from his right hand. "And if my memory serves me, like it always does, you must be the infamous Dr. Brandon Nelson."

Joan said, "Agent Helmsley, what the hell are you doing out here?"

Brandon said, "Agent? Helmsley? What—are experiencing some kind of amnesia oriented power trip? You feeling the need to boost your ego a little more?"

"You two know each other?" Joan asked.

"Oh my," Agent Helmsley blurted, "A badge, a great bod, a pretty face, and to top it all off, she has a brain to boot. Who knew?"

Joan's face displayed anger, and her eyes narrowed. She had never wanted to point a gun at anyone that wasn't pointing one at her, but...

"Knock it off," Brandon said.

"Or what? You'll try and psychoanalyze me, put me on Lithium, or maybe some Prozac. Oh, please, you're scaring me," Helmsley said, "The last thing I need is for you to stand there and try to insult my intelligence with your psycho-babble. I went through counseling while I was growing up. And this, I can tell you without reservation or hesitation, you, the three jerk-off's that tried to run my life back then, and all the other so called psychiatrists, are nothing but a bunch of egotistical assholes who don't know jack-shit about nothing."

"You're the only asshole I see." Brandon said angrily.

"Oh my, have I struck a nerve? You don't have to answer that. I can see by the look on both your faces that I have. I'm so sorry. And to answer your question," Helmsley said taking a few steps closer, "Dr. Nelson and I go way back. Don't we, Brandy ole boy?"

"Joan," Brandon said, "Meet Jacob Palmer, the dip-shit security guard that busted me in the lab thirty-two years ago."

"Come on, Nelson, no need for name calling. I was just doing my job."

"I thought you died in the fire," Brandon said.

"Wouldn't be standing here now if I did, now would I? Course, one might be surprised what good ole' Uncle Sam will do for you if you do a little dirty work for him."

"The fire, the missing documents from the files. That was you?"

"Holy shit, Sheriff, you've got a keeper. He's nearly as smart as you."

Joan played with the initials in her head, and instantly remembered the conversation she had had yesterday with the head of the Department of Health, Rodger Klein. She quickly committed them to the story Charlie Malloy had told her. J.P.

With the links now connected, she asked, "The same J.P. that lost a brother at the hands of Carl Saunderson thirty-two years ago?"

"I had a feeling that ole' Charlie boy couldn't keep his mouth shut. Oh well, I guess he will now. And for the record, I had no brother. I just made it up as a way to have the local yokels help me find the dumb son-of-a-bitch."

"You're the one who put three bullets into Charlie Malloy?" Joan asked.

"Yes I am. And I must say that I took great pleasure in closing that drunken idiot's mouth. And now, I'll be handing you two half-wits the same fate, only, I'm going to make it look like the good doc here is the guilty party. Then he shoots himself. You know the routine," Helmsley said, with an eerie calmness in his voice. "You just couldn't deal with the guilt of killing all those kids."

"You've got everything all figured out don't you?" Brandon asked.

Joan's hand twitched as she thought of pulling her gun and blowing away the piece of shit standing twenty or so feet away. Her hand moved slowly toward the small of her back, toward the .45.

"Joan. Oh J-O-A-N," Helmsley said. "I don't think that would be a very good idea."

He took a step closer and eased back the hammer of his .44.

Brandon tried to move in front of Joan. She pushed him back.

"That's not an F.B.I. issued weapon you have there, Agent Helmsley," Joan said, holding Brandon back with her left arm.

"But it is a hell of a gun, don't you think?" he replied. "I like to think of it as my—American Express Gun, I never leave home without it."

"So, what's next?" Joan asked.

"I've already told you, I'm going to finish you two off, and then I'm going to head home. I mean, I'll probably stop off somewhere and have a steak and a beer. I might even sip on a cup of coffee afterward, but other than that, I have nothing pressing to do."

"You say that like killing is of second nature to you," Brandon replied.

"What can I say Doc, I'm good at it."

As Agent Helmsley finished speaking, he sniffed the air around him. A putrid aroma funneled into the solarium, and with it, a bone chilling breath of air. "Where in the hell is that stench coming from?" Helmsley asked, clearly agitated.

"What are you babbling about now?" Joan asked, and then smelled it too. Brandon did as well, but didn't let on to it. Nor did they let on to the sudden change in temperature that followed.

"That smell, where the hell is it coming from?"

"Well, they say that assholes smell like ass, so..." Joan said to Helmsley.

"Shut up, bitch," Helmsley shouted. "You know, from the very first moment we met, you've been pushing the envelope closer to the edge with that smart-ass mouth of yours. Carrying a gun and a badge doesn't make you tough."

"Drop the gun and we'll see about that," Joan replied, her temples pulsing, the veins in her neck flaring. "If I were you though, I practice falling down first."

"I said shut up. Don't make me have to tell you again." As each word left his mouth, Agent Helmsley seemed to become even more distracted by the smell around him, and Joan noticed the sudden uneasy look on the agent's face.

This would be a good time for a mental distraction, she thought. "Since you're going to kill us anyway, Jacob, or jack-off, whatever you're calling yourself today, why not tell us what the big secret is—*was*? What really went on in that lab?"

Agent Helmsley glanced toward Joan. Her remark had clearly pissed him off, but he ignored it knowing she'd be dead soon enough. After a long pause, he said, "Nature is pitiless in a pitiless universe, and is certainly not concerned with the survival of Americans. So, up till about the time that *fuck* Saunderson started wreaking havoc at the institute by killing three of our best scientists, the institute had been trying to find a way to take those scumbags that came into the facility, and make them a viable part of society. Sure, they were men willing to forego the proverbial red-tape, but at least they were trying."

"You mean they were trying to make them a part of a viable *military* society."

"Does it really matter? They were scum."

"And what does that make you, *Jack*?" Joan asked.

"I told you twice now to shut up, and it seems as if you can't, or won't. So, I guess I'll have to give you a hand," Helmsley said, raising his gun higher.

"You're nothing more than a ruthless killer," Joan said.

"You see, I totally disagree with you. In today's world, it's kill or be killed, as I'm sure the Doc there—oh, you don't mind if I call you Doc now—do you?"

"As a matter of fact, I do."

"Oh well, in that case, *Doc*, with you in the shrink business and all, I'm sure you can explain better than I ever could to your pretty little whore that the character of any act, good or bad, depends solely upon the circumstances behind the reason in which it was done."

"On the contrary," Brandon said, "'It's a kill or be killed world', that's a pretty good clinical diagnosis."

"Don't pull that sarcasm bullshit on me there, Doc. I'm smarter than that."

"I know. I heard. You've just rendered my profession useless. No more need for psychiatrists, just give your local schizophrenically deranged F.B.I. agent a call, only—you should be prepared for a 24-7 operation."

Joan could tell by the narrowed eyes and the furrowed brow that it was Brandon that had now gotten under Helmsley's skin.

"Shut the fuck up," Helmsley said, his voice clearly agitated. "That's it; I've had all I'm going to take from you two clowns." Helmsley raised the .44 to eye level.

At that moment, a dark figure moved in behind the agent. At the same time, the words Caitlin had said in her sleep a few nights ago, flashed through Joan's mind, *"Push left, fall right."*

The dark figure grabbed the agent by the head, and with one quick and violent thrust, twisted his head to the left.

Joan pushed Brandon to her left and then fell to her right just as Helmsley's gun went off. She heard the sound of bones snapping. What she had just witnessed was the ghost of Carl Saunderson bringing Jacob Palmer, AKA, Jack Helmsley's pathetic life to an end.

She watched the agent fall to the ground like a giant rag doll, lifeless. In the time it took for her to blink, Carl's ghostly presence had disappeared, and with it, the ghastly smell and the chilled air.

Brandon stood and extended his hand to help Joan up.

Joan stopped for a second as they neared the dead body of Agent Helmsley. She reached down and retrieved his wallet and badge and stuck them in her back pocket, and then headed out of the building.

13

Carl Saunderson paced the dark cave from one side to the other. When he stopped, Caitlin said, "Thank you, Carl." But Carl just stood there, gazing through the abyss of darkness towards the bright light that was Caitlin.

When he had returned to the cave, he had noticed that the light that was Caitlin had dimmed. This excited him, for he was sure that when the light was completely extinguished, he would have his final kill. He could feel the excitement building, for this would be a special kill of a special girl, the likes of which he had never seen. And he was sure that this special offering would offer atonement for his past. But for now, all he could do was continue to watch as the light that was Caitlin—grew dimmer, and dimmer—and wait.

14

Brandon and Joan raced back to the truck leaving behind the body of Agent Helmsley. The power behind the evil force of Carl Saunderson's ghost had left the agent's head twisted so badly, that as he lay on his stomach, his head was positioned as if he were looking up at the ceiling; his eyes still open. Under normal circumstances, Joan would have done the right thing and closed the eyes of the deceased. But in this case, she made an exception.

As they neared the truck, Brandon noticed the blood dribbling down Joan's left arm, and said, "You got shot?"

"Just grazed."

Brandon glanced at Joan's left arm. The wound was above her bicep.

"Joan, you took that for me. If you hadn't pushed me out of the way, that bullet would have gone right through my heart."

"What kind of sheriff would I be if I went around letting our visitors get all shot up? I couldn't let that happen, not in my town anyway." Joan grimaced as she applied pressure to stop the bleeding.

"I'm serious."

Joan could hear that he was.

"You saved my life. How do I thank you for that?"

"I think you just did. But you should really be thanking Caitlin," she said, grimacing again. Though the bullet had grazed her, shearing off an eighth of an inch of skin, it felt like a hot poker had just been placed on her arm. "She's the one that put the thought in my head to push left and fall right."

"Well, whatever. The fact remains that I owe you. I'll start by taking a look at that when we get back into town. I'm sure the hotel has a decent first aid kit I can use."

"That's not necessary. It's not as bad as it looks. It's not the first time I've been grazed, but God willing, it will be the last."

"Look, you're bleeding, and to you it may be a scratch, but to me, it looks deep, and you may need stitches. Just let me look at it, that's all I ask."

"Alright, you win," Joan said, smiling at the prospect of being pampered by a gorgeous man like Brandon.

Brandon stopped by the Milford Lodge reception desk to retrieve the first-aid kit. She followed him to his room.

"Sit here," he said, maneuvering the lampshade to direct the light toward her arm.

Innocently, Brandon asked for Joan to remove her T-shirt. She did.

"That's going to leave a cute scar," he said as he reached across her for the gauze and a foiled alcohol pad from the nightstand. He suddenly felt tingly at the close proximity of their two bodies.

"Just to let you know," Brandon said in a sensitive tone, "This will sting." After removing the alcohol pad from the foil wrapper, he eased it to her wound. He felt her arm tighten, heard a hiss from her mouth. He glanced at her lips, at the hiss sound seeping through, and though he had noticed her beauty when he first met her in the diner, and again at dinner, as he looked at her now, he saw an entirely different beauty; beauty with strength and a raw sense of fearlessness that one wouldn't find on the cover of any Playboy magazine. The magazine would show curves and fullness, yes, exotic beauty, definitely, but strength—no, *but she fit the bill for all the above, and then some,* he thought.

As Brandon worked on her arm, Joan felt Brandon's eyes upon her. *It was a professional glance,* she thought, but hoped otherwise. She wanted to meet his gaze, felt the need to, but didn't.

There was something about him though, something that just made her want to crawl up inside his shirt and press herself against him, feel the warmth of his skin against her own.

She was smitten with him, had been from the moment he walked up to her in the diner with a confidence that few men have and yet, still able to remain modest. She also knew that whatever it was about him, stretched far beyond his good looks. She had only known him for a little over a day and a half, yet feelings that had been foreign to her for a long time, fluttered about her body. His piercing blue eyes made the blood in her veins heat up at an erotic pace. Her heart thumped harder and louder. She wondered if he could hear it, if he could feel it.

After Brandon taped a clean gauze pad to her wound, he again reached across her body to put the tape back on the nightstand. As he did, she leaned in and lightly brushed his lips with hers.

"What was that for?" he asked.

"For taking care of my arm."

"Not that I'm complaining, but...."

Before Brandon could finish, Joan kissed him again, winding her right hand in his hair.

"And that?"

"That was for me." She then grabbed Brandon by the shirt and pulled him to her. She kissed him again. He didn't resist.

"I hope I'm getting the right message here."

"What? Would you prefer I put you in handcuffs and arrest you first? Read you your rights?"

"For now, this is working just fine, but maybe later."

"Good, then shut up and come here."

They kissed passionately. He reached for the lights, never letting go of her lips as she unbuttoned his shirt.

Their love making was slow and tender. The silence of the room was cast aside as groans of desire floated out of them.

Joan desperately wanted to take over and devour this near perfect specimen of a man. But she let him take her in his own way. And she was glad she did. It felt so good to have him fill her with such a hard exotic passion, stirring emotions in her that she had held at bay for longer than she cared to remember, feelings she had not felt since John.

For Brandon, he too had emotions stirring deep inside him. Sure, he had dated many women over the years since Nancy, but this, being with this incredibly strong, fit woman, being inside her, he could barely find the words. Her supple lips tasted like sweetened jam. Her body was soft and smooth, yet firm and muscular, and he left no part of it unexplored.

Later, as the redness of the setting sun washed across closed curtains, they laid cuddled together. Brandon played with her hair as it sprawled across his chest. She thought for a second about how she had ended up here, in bed, with a man she had just met. She knew deep down however, that the how's and the whys weren't important. At that moment, his hand caressing her hair was all that mattered.

"You know, I could stay here all night," Joan said in an almost playful tone.

"Why don't you, then?"

"Because. I have...."

"I know. You have a visitor stopping by. Want me to come along?"

"I think that I should meet this person alone."

Joan saw the immediate disappointment on Brandon's face, and added, "Not that I don't want you there. I'm just not sure who or what we're dealing with. And after everything that's happened today, I just don't want to put you in harm's way. Not again. Not ever."

"So, what happens now?"

"I go home, take a shower, and wait."

"I meant with us."

With that, Joan rose. A ray of sunlight captured and caressed her naked body as she crossed into the darkness on the other side of the room.

Brandon watched as she moved. *So smooth and elegant,* he thought, *so strong, yet feminine.* He admired her with a deep sense of appreciation for all that she had to offer, not just for him, but for anyone around her.

"Joan, what just happened here?"

"I don't know, but it probably shouldn't have."

"Why?" he asked.

With all that has happened, she thought, in such a short amount of time, the murders, finding out your daughter is psychic in every sense of the word, could all be chalked up to be an inability to facilitate clear thinking, hence, making love to a virtual stranger.

"No," she heard a voice say, a voice that sounded more like a whisper; the same voice that had been falling on her ears for the past two days. But the voice had been right on all accounts, and she knew it was right now; her body said so as she stretched languidly, feeling the tenderness of muscles not used often enough, protesting.

"Because it felt too damn good, that's why. But that's not..."

There was an awkward moment of silence, and then she added, "I'm not sorry about what just happened, it's just that—I'm the sheriff of a small town with four dead kids and another one missing. And to make matters worse, it seems that the only suspect I have is a dead man's ghost. I don't have time for this."

"And what, you're not allowed to take a break, clear your head, free your mind from what's been happening around you?"

"No."

"That's ridiculous Joan, and you know it."

"So, now I'm ridiculous?"

Brandon threw back the sheets and crossed the room. She was only half dressed. He could see goose bumps forming as he drew closer to her.

He brushed his hand across her breast and felt her nipple respond instantly.

"Joan?"

"Whatever this was, I can handle it. I'm a big girl."

He took her chin and lifted it slightly so that he could look her in the eyes. "I felt it too—the heat, the passion. I needed this, and so did you. My rising body of evidence should tell you that whatever this is, I want to pursue it." He caressed her face. "Let me put it to you this way, if I had a choice between never having met you at all, or getting hit by that bullet, I'd choose the bullet every time."

She smiled, the playful tone returning, "Well, at least we're on the same page, except maybe for that whole bullet thing."

"So, what are you doing tomorrow?" he asked.

"Besides trying to catch a ghost, I'm all yours."

"I hope you mean that."

He felt her lean against him. "I do," she whispered, and then playfully kissed him. "I really do need to get going, though. No more play time."

"Don't forget about our date tomorrow."

"Not a chance in the world."

Chapter 30

1

After taking a quick shower, Joan threw on a pair of old blue jeans and a worn out T-shirt, and met Jessie in the living room at 7:55 p.m.

Jessie had a beleaguered look on her face as she spoke, "I'm still not sure why you seem so calm. Your daughter is missing."

"It's like I said, I feel, no—*I know* she's fine, I can *sense* it. I don't know how, but I know she's fine, and so is Kimberly Clark." Joan flicked her eyes towards the window for a quick glance out into the night, and then flicked them back to her mother. "You felt it too, you said so yourself after you discovered her missing. You said you had an overwhelming sense of calmness take over your body. Even now, you don't feel that she's in harm's way, do you?"

"No."

"That was—is, Caitlin. I know it's hard to understand. I'm having trouble understanding it myself. She has the uncanny ability to transmit thoughts, and I'm starting to think she can do the same thing with feelings."

The doorbell rang at exactly eight.

"I'll get it, Mom."

2

The woman standing on the porch looked to be around forty years old. She had shoulder length brown hair. Joan had never seen this woman before, but for some eerie, but explainable reason, she knew who she was staring at, just as Caitlin had predicted she would.

"Samantha?" Joan asked.

"Yes, but how'd…. Never mind. And you must be…."

"Mrs. Fortune. Mrs. Joan Fortune, the sheriff here in Milford."

"Joan, is it? I guess I shouldn't be surprised."

"Why's that?" Joan asked as she motioned the woman into her home.

"That's the last thing Caitlin said to me before I left her in that church, 'Don't worry Mommy, I remember her saying, 'Joan will take good care of me.'"

"How did she know it would be me? How did she know that I would be the one that adopted her?"

"You should know by now that Caitlin is a remarkable young lady, and that she possesses a rather extraordinary talent for knowing things she shouldn't. But, at that time, I had asked her that very question myself."

"What'd she say?"

"She just said she knew."

The room filled with silence and tension as Samantha studied pictures of Caitlin on the mantle. "She's beautiful, isn't she?" Samantha said, "And she's smart too, I can sense it, and she's charming, and caring. I love the way that she, even at such an early age, always puts others before herself."

To Samantha, Joan said, "Yes, yes she is, does, to all of that."

How could she possibly know, Joan thought, "that the child she had abandoned a little over five years ago so well? But she was, after all, Caitlin's mother. Maybe she possessed some of the same traits.

"I can't blame you for thinking what you're thinking," Samantha said as she saw a somewhat astonished look on Joan's face. "I do—I did have a lot of the same abilities Caitlin has, only my parents, my step-parents, thought I was some kind of a witch or something; a spawn from hell if you will. They thought of me in much the same way as they thought of my biological father."

"Carl Saunderson?"

"So you know then." Samantha asked.

"I think I knew from the moment that I opened the door to find you on my porch."

"Caitlin didn't say anything to you about it, about him?"

"No. But that doesn't surprise me. Maybe she thought she was protecting me, like you said, she always thinks of others before herself. I only wish I could have known sooner."

"You have my father's file with you now?"

"Yes, but…" Joan stopped and shrugged. Caitlin, she thought, nibbling her bottom lip, that's how Samantha knows about the file.

"You mind if I have a look at them?"

"No. No, of course not," Joan said, reaching for the file she had placed on the end table. "But it's really of no use."

"Why?"

"They, whoever they are, took all the pertinent information out. All it really gives us is the fact that he was actually there at the institute, and a timeline." Hesitating, she continued, "But I've seen things, things that you may never want to know about."

"I know about the torturous things that were done to my father, to all the men. Deep down I've always known. But now, holding this file, it's as if I can see mental images of what was done to them; I can feel their pain. This file makes everything seem so—unbelievably real."

"I'm sure it does." Joan took the file out of Samantha's trembling hand and opened it. "I'm sorry about your father, what he went through, losing his wife, all of it. I'm truly sorry."

"Thank you," Samantha said, as her eyes glazed over.

In the file, they came across some old pictures of Carl's family, pictures of each of his seven kids, and of his wife, Sandra.

"You know, it's funny how I never met any of my brothers or sisters, yet I know all their names."

There was a short pause, and then, "This one," Samantha said, "is Kristine. She was the sixth born. She looks so much like Caitlin."

Joan picked up the picture for a closer look. It was true. The resemblance was uncanny. Joan then picked up a picture of Sandra Saunderson, Carl's wife, and held it up to the left side of Samantha's face. "And you, you look just like your mother." Another short pause, "She was a beautiful woman, your mother."

"Thanks. I only wish I could have gotten to know her."

"Again, I am sorry."

Samantha stood and roamed around the room, stopping now and then as she looked at the photos that Joan had displayed throughout the living room. She picked up some of them for a closer look. "You know she's O.K., don't you?" she asked looking at a picture of Caitlin taken only a few months earlier.

"Yes, I keep hearing a voice inside my head telling me not to worry. I mean, I know she's okay, I feel it, but until I see her with my own eyes, how can I not?"

Samantha roamed from picture to picture, as if trying to memorize each one.

Joan said, "Feel free to take any pictures you like, I'm sure I have the negatives around."

"Thanks, I would like that very much."

Joan's eyes followed her around the room. Thoughts crept in of Samantha wanting Caitlin back. Surely she didn't think she could stroll in here out of the blue and just take Caitlin away from her. She had to know better, had to know that Joan would put up a fight.

"So, what happens now?"

"Just keep listening to that sweet innocent voice, and try not to worry. If you can do that, I can tell you what she wouldn't."

"What? Tell me what?"

"She, Caitlin, is in control right now, but I don't know for how long. Let's just say that it would be best for all of us if we get to her in the morning, the earlier the better. I have to be completely honest with you, I can't promise anything. Unlike Caitlin, I can't see what will be."

"And Caitlin?" Joan asked, a trickle of fear in her voice.

To Joan, Samantha said, "My visions aren't that clear. Like I said, I can't promise anything, and I'm not going to lie to you either; we need faith, love, and a lot of luck on our side."

"Then why wait till tomorrow? Why not go now?"

"Because Caitlin has control of him, and the longer she does, the more the evil that is now a part of him, will diminish. We need for him to see her for who she really is, his granddaughter. If all goes according to plan, I hope by the end of the day tomorrow, Caitlin will be back in your arms."

"So, you're not here just to try and take her back?"

"God, no. I mean, I admit that I would love nothing more than to have a second chance with her, a chance to get to know her and raise her as my own, but I know it's too late. She loves you. You're her mother now. I can't, I won't take that away from her, or from you. You've done a wonderful job raising our—your daughter."

"*Our* daughter," Joan replied with a warm smile.

"Thank you for that. I know I don't really deserve it."

After a long moment of silence, Joan asked, "So why exactly is it that you're here? I mean, if not to take Caitlin, then why?"

"To make sure that she does return to you, and to stop my father."

"What do you mean by that?" Joan asked. "I don't want to sound cruel, but he's a walking pile of bones capable of killing in the same fashion that he did while he was alive. I mean, how does one go about stopping something like that? How do you stop a ghost?"

"You can't."

Joan's mind was being told to remain calm, that everything was fine. *Everything wasn't fine,* Joan thought, feeling worried and fearful for the first time since she found out that Caitlin was missing. But at the same time, Caitlin was working just as hard telepathically telling her not to be.

"But one of us," Samantha continued, "can lead that non-physical being, that ghost as you call him, into the light—to a place he has sought for so long. One of us can lead him into the loving arms of his family who are waiting for him on the other side. And whoever does…" The last three words were underlined by a long pause, and the room again grew thick with tension.

"What? Whoever does—*what?*" Joan asked, feeling the hairs rising on the nape of her neck.

"Whoever does it, whichever one of us has the chance to guide him through the light to the other side, won't be coming back."

"And when you say us, you mean Caitlin or yourself?"

"Yes."

"And you're willing to give your own life for that of Caitlin's?"

"What mother wouldn't? But it's not a certainty. Like I said, we need a lot of luck on our side."

Joan became even more uneasy.

"Don't, Joan," Samantha said. "Don't fight the peace that Caitlin wants you to feel. She's growing tired. The harder she has to work at it, the more tired and weak she'll become."

Samantha paused and looked at her selected picture and rubbed her thumb across it. "She'll need her strength tomorrow. If she has any hope at all, she'll need her strength."

Taking Samantha at her word, not wanting to wane away her daughter's ability, Joan wanted to change the subject, and did so by returning the conversation back to Samantha.

Joan took notice of the high-end clothing she wore, Ralph Lauren, the way her hands were perfectly manicured, and her hair shimmering as though done by a professional.

"You look like a woman who has her head on straight," Joan said. "Why is it that you decided to give up Caitlin?"

"It's a long story," Samantha replied. "So, if you don't mind, I'll cut to the chase."

"I don't mind at all."

"While I was growing up, I would get into trouble, not anything bad, at least not right away. But every time I did, my folks, or should I say care givers, would tell me stories of my real father, and what he had done. They told me how he murdered his wife and hung his own children. I didn't want to believe them of course, but deep down I knew what they were saying was true, at least for the most part. I mean, I knew he didn't kill my mother, not on purpose anyway. Every time they started, they would go into greater detail and then, they would tell me I was just like him."

"That's unconscionable," Joan replied. "And it certainly isn't something a parent, or any adult for that matter, should be telling a child at any age."

"Anyway, I ended up using drugs, and started selling myself just to pay for them. Next thing I know, I'm pregnant. I knew I couldn't take care of her. I tried hard for three years, but I realized I was doing more harm to Caitlin by keeping her, so I chose to put her in God's hands. After that, I got clean and managed to put myself through college. I was determined to make something of myself just to prove that I wasn't my father's daughter. I now work for the State of Illinois as a Teen Prevention and Intervention counselor to try and help kids from following down the same path as I had. I didn't want other mother's to feel as though they had no other choice but to give up their children."

"Well, I think you've done Caitlin proud, and I hope you realize that your father was in a frail state of mind, unable to recognize or establish right from wrong when he took the lives of your brothers and sisters. He was in a great deal of pain due to the loss of his wife. It is my understanding that she knew you were breached, and though she told your father to cut her open and take you. Ultimately, he felt he killed his wife. Forget about the fact that all he had to use was a standard kitchen knife; he believed he killed his wife and that drove him over the edge. He closed himself off from everything and everyone that reminded him of that day."

"How is it that you know this and I don't?" Samantha asked.

"I didn't know until just now. Caitlin just told me, *telepathically*, I mean. My guess was that she wanted to spare you the pain of believing that you were the reason your mother died, when in fact, your mother knew that by telling her husband, your father, to cut her open, she was in fact, giving her life for you." As the words faded from Joan's lips, the Stephen King saying came back to her, '*Everything's Eventual*'.

Near midnight, as tendrils of moonlight maneuvered through the thickening slate gray fog, they both fell off into a deep dreamless sleep, Joan in the high-back chair, Samantha on the couch.

Chapter 31

1

With morning came a thick fog. Joan and Samantha awoke at the same time, alert to all of the horror that had taken place in the town of Milford, and to all that was said between them the night before. Joan looked at Samantha, "It's time."

Morning routines of washing their faces, brushing their teeth and their hair, were as far out of their minds as was going to the movies, or what they would eat for dinner. They knew that time was of the essence.

2

Brandon woke and felt as though he had just gotten the best night's sleep in years. He also felt, however, that he needed to be at a certain place at a certain time. He could not explain why he had the feeling, only that it was there, and that it was important. He quickly threw on some clothes, shoes and a light jacket, stepped outside into the gray murky fog and walked to the end of the hotel's parking lot to Route 512, and waited.

3

Carl Saunderson watched all night as the bright light that was Caitlin, dimmed to a mere glow, barely the strength of a single candle. For the first time, behind the glow of light, he could see her for what she was, nothing more than an eight year old girl.

Is this what he had feared all night, a child, a mere mortal child?

In the dark, Caitlin could still see and feel Carl nearby. She could feel his presence. She could feel the evil that filled his thoughts, but not like before. He was angry, yes, but only because he felt somehow tricked.

He rushed the two girls. But Caitlin stood and moved in front of the frightened five year old before he reached them.

"Carl? Carl Saunderson." She yelled in a voice that was not her own. Upon hearing the voice that to him seemed overwhelmingly familiar, he stopped within an inch of Caitlin. She stood her ground and looked straight up at the six foot two inch man and said in her own voice, "Grandfather…"

4

As Joan was passing the Milford Lodge, she saw a man waving at her from the end of the parking lot. The fog concealed his identity, but she knew it was Brandon and stopped to pick him up.

"How'd you know we'd be passing by?" Joan asked.

"I don't exactly know. I just had a feeling that I had to be standing there at exactly that time. I can't explain it."

Joan and Samantha glanced at Brandon, and then to each other and said, "Caitlin."

"What?" Brandon asked.

"It's Caitlin. She is with Carl Saunderson as we speak, has been all night."

"Oh God, Joan…"

"Don't worry. She's fine; at least she's telling me she's fine. I think she has some kind of power over him."

"For now anyway," Samantha added. "I sense that some of his evil has gone, but she's growing weak."

"And who might you be?" Brandon asked.

"I'm sorry," Joan replied as she pulled away and continued down Route 512, "This is Samantha Smith, Caitlin's birthmother."

"This was the guest Caitlin spoke of the other night?"

"Yes," Samantha answered. "My real name is Samantha Saunderson, Carl Saunderson's daughter."

"That can't be. He killed all his kids."

"Yeah," Joan said jumping in, "But you said it yourself, Carl killed seven of his children. They never found the baby that he helped bring into this world. Turns out that Carl's wife was somewhat psychic as well, and knew what was going to happen, but was in no condition to stop it. She must have told one of her kids to take the baby to a neighbor's house, the Smith's. She must not have had time to tell the other kids to watch for their father." Joan paused for a moment and then continued, "And even if she did have time, what would she have told them, to run away because Daddy's going to kill you? They would have thought her to be crazy. They would have thought she didn't know what she was saying."

"Wow, this is a bit intense," Brandon said, looking back toward Joan, "Not to mention a little mind-boggling. I mean for all of you to be here—at the same time—in the same town—the very town where all the killing started."

"And where it must end," Samantha said determinedly.

As they approached the abandoned institute, the wind picked up and created mini tornados of dead leaves, pine needles, and small twigs. The already darkened sky grew even darker before their eyes, and the fog that enveloped them became even denser and began to grow eerily cold. But as Joan's view of the road ahead decreased, it only increased in her mind, and she knew why. She knew that Caitlin could see all around the truck, she could see what Joan saw, and in doing so, displayed the image of the road clearly in Joan's mind.

5

Carl Saunderson reached out to grab Caitlin, but in doing so, received a paranormal shock through his ghostly frame. He stepped back, and for the first time, he spoke in words, "It's only a matter of time, little one. Then I'll have the both of you."

Caitlin said nothing. She knew she had to concentrate on projecting the image of a clear road for her mother. Her power over her grandfather was fading due to exhaustion, and she was well aware of the time she had left before she would no longer have control over him. And though his evil had diminished, she knew the inevitable outcome if both her mothers' didn't arrive on time. She knew he would not be able to resist the taste of his past and kill again. She knew her grandfather would kill both Kimberly and herself.

6

Joan pulled into the parking lot of the Institute. She was surprised to find both Gage and Ed waiting for her. Also there, in the passenger side of Ed's truck, were Kimberly's parents sitting side by side, their hands interlocked; their faces full of worry and despair. That look was all too familiar to Joan. It was the same look that her friend, Marie Shae had displayed when Joan arrived on her doorstep to break the news that they had found her daughter Kiersten.

"Gage, Ed?" Joan asked. "What are you two doing out here?"

Gage and Ed exchanged glances.

"You called and told us to meet you here," Gage answered, "or should I say your daughter did."

"Yeah, Caitlin said you were indisposed at the time, which was why you asked her to call," Ed said.

"And the Clark's, I suppose I asked you to bring them as well?" Joan asked.

"Yes."

Gage moved closer to Joan and put his hand on her shoulder and pulled her aside several feet away from all the unfamiliar faces and asked, "Joan, what the hell is going on?"

"I don't have time to explain everything, so listen up. First of all, I didn't have Caitlin call you. Secondly, I don't know how exactly she could have called, because she's been missing all night. My only guess is that she put the thought into your heads while you were sleeping."

"What? Joan, you're not making any sense."

"I know. I'll explain everything to you and Ed later, but for now, please, just trust me."

"What do you need me to do?"

"Tell Ed to stay here with the Clarks. Then I need you to come with me and the others."

"I can guess who the guy is, but who's the chick?"

"Gage, please, I don't have time for questions, just do what I ask. And one last thing."

"What's that?"

"No matter what you see out here today, keep an open mind."

Gage shot her a disturbed nod and said, "Sure, fine, but I hope you follow through with that explanation."

Joan and Brandon walked down the side of the institute to the rear of the building. Gage and Samantha trailed anxiously. Yellow police tape had been put across the broken glass, and the corpse of Jack Helmsley had been removed.

They proceeded past the building and straight into the woods, towards Caitlin, towards the ghost of Carl Saunderson. And as they walked, the fog that surrounded them grew thicker, and if it were at all possible, the sky seemed to grow even darker than it was upon their arrival. It was as if an eclipse was taking place at that very moment. The wind suddenly picked up and began to whirl more violently than before; the intensity caused the trees to lash out with madness, as if a tornado had reached down and brushed its violence against the branches. The tree limbs clashed together creating a haunted moaning sound. It reminded Joan of the voices of the dead from an old zombie movie.

Small branches and leaves rose from the ground and funneled around them. As they moved slowly forward, the debris behind them fell innocently to the ground as if it had never been touched. Ahead of them, more wind, more debris, a darker sky, and an even denser fog. Joan knew where she was going in spite of the turbulence around her.

Five minutes later, Joan reached a clearing, and within the clearing, there was no fog, no flying debris and in fact, there was no wind at all. The air within the clearing seemed motionless.

They could all see the cave entrance with a clarity that had eluded them as they marched to this point, to this twenty-foot clearing.

"This is it," Joan said.

"Yes, this is the place," Samantha said in agreement, and this is where we must separate. This is where I go on alone."

"But…"

"No buts, Joan. I need to do this for Caitlin." Samantha reached out and grabbed Joan's hand, "I will do everything I can to bring Caitlin out of this, alive. That—I can promise you." Joan wrapped her arms around Samantha and hugged her. Samantha let go and walked into the blackness of the cave.

7

Carl Saunderson looked down at Caitlin. The light around her was gone. He reached for her cautiously. She looked as she did before, innocent and young—a normal child. When his ghostly hand felt the chilled skin of Caitlin's right arm, he felt no shock, no fear. He only felt the urge to kill. He grabbed her by both arms with a firm grip and lifted her up until he was face to face with her, his granddaughter.

He glanced toward Kimberly as he placed Caitlin under his left arm, and then reached down for her.

Kimberly, who had not been scared all night with Caitlin by her side, now felt horrified as she felt Caitlin wrenched from her grasp. She screamed. Her high-pitched shrill echoed through the cave, bouncing off the walls until it was set free outside the cave entrance.

With both girls under his arms, he turned to exit the cave. As he did so, a voice came out of the blackness. It sounded somehow familiar.

"Carl," the voice said, "It's time for us to go and join our family." Carl looked into the darkness and could see a woman with shoulder-length brown hair. He knew he had seen her before, but he could not remember from where. He reached back into the depths of his memory, trying to pull up images of people he had known from his past. As he did so, the hold on the two girls was weakened, and Caitlin and Kimberly slipped out of his grasp.

"Walk away," Caitlin said to the frightened girl. "Close your eyes and walk away slowly. Follow your mind's path out of here. Go. Now."

Kimberly closed her eyes. In a slow pace, she maneuvered her way through the twists and turns to the cave's entrance, where she then opened her eyes. And as any scared child would do, she ran to the first person she recognized. Joan hunched down and wrapped her arms around the terrified girl.

"Gage," Joan said, "I think there's a couple of people that would love to see their daughter. Would you do the honors?"

Back in the cave, Carl continued to search his memory, scrambling for the answers that eluded him. His mind was filled with pain, guilt, ugliness, and death. Finding the image he was seeking was not an easy task. Silence stretched on through the blackness, finally, an image of his wife Sandra appeared. "Sandra?" he asked in a muffled moan. "Is that you?"

"No," Samantha said moving closer to Carl, "It's me, father, Samantha. I'm your daughter. You delivered me, father, remember? Mom died giving birth to me and you believed it to be your fault that she died. I'm here to tell you that it wasn't your fault. It was no one's fault. It was just her time. God called for her, and it was just her time to go."

It was then that a bright light appeared; one brighter than that which Caitlin had displayed most of the night. But this time, Carl, Samantha, and Caitlin could see through the brightness and beyond. It was like a hole connected to a path that led straight to the sun, only magnified tenfold. Out of the light, eight shimmering figures appeared. A woman and seven children. The children ranged in age from five to fifteen. It only took Carl a matter of seconds to recognize them as his family, his beautiful loving family. They were what he wanted most and had tried so hard to get back to, but could not, until now. They were there, right in front of him. God, how he longed for them.

8

Outside the cave, Joan hung onto Brandon's arm as a bright light beamed out of the cave opening. Around the clearing, the wind picked up more speed and continued to whip through the branches of the trees. The sky changed to a color darker than night. The area just above the clearing, however, remained a constant blue.

With their eyes focusing on the cave entrance, they saw formless shapes emerge in and out of the light. At times, they appeared to be human shapes, but as fast as they would take the form of a human, they'd change back to something unrecognizable. For a brief second, Joan would have sworn one of the shapes took on the appearance of her husband, John, waving to her, and another, her best friend's daughter, Kiersten. At that moment, Brandon saw a figure of a man that brought tears to Joan's eyes. *Her husband John*, he thought. He suddenly felt guilt associated with the feelings he had for Joan. But as that thought crossed his mind, the ghostly form of John Fortune came face to face with him, and then whisked straight through his body. He immediately felt a chill followed by sudden warmth that enveloped his entire being. And with that warmth, came the feeling that he had just been given John's blessing for the relationship on which he was about to embark.

"Now I understand," Joan said in a whisper.

"What?" Brandon asked. "Understand what?"

"The reason why Caitlin needed her biological mother here, I now understand why."

"Mind clueing me in?"

"Caitlin, even with all her unique abilities and strengths, still wouldn't have been strong enough to open the door to the other side, let alone be able to control all the spirits that would be there lying in wait for their ultimate chance to get out one last time."

Brandon glanced at Joan in utter amazement at how calm she was with Caitlin still inside the cave.

9

Carl's family drifted closer to him and then stopped. He could feel their forgiveness radiating from deep within their souls and their hearts. He felt Caitlin's small gentle hand grab hold of his. He felt a slight tug as Caitlin started walking toward the family he had sought for so long. A few steps later, Samantha reached out and grabbed his other hand, and together, they walked him further into the light, closer to his family.

The closer he got, the more his appearance transformed from the gruesome and haunting apparition of what he had become, to the good-looking man, husband, and father, that he had once been.

As he continued to move forward, he started to resist, and his pace slowed.

He took a few more steps, and slowed even more. After two more steps, he stopped and jerked both hands away from Caitlin and Samantha. They both looked surprised as they felt Carl's hands being jerked out of theirs. Everything had been going so well, and now it was as if he didn't want to go.

Had the evil that had been locked inside the lost soul of Carl Saunderson spoiled forever the goodness of his former self.

Could he no longer see or remember the good times he had once shared with his family before all the heartbreak, tragedy, and cruelty took over his life?

It was at that moment that Carl returned to his monstrous appearance. As he began to back away, he snatched Caitlin by the throat with a grip of death. Caitlin knew that at any moment, with even a slight squeeze of his hand, she could be killed. Yet, she did not scream, she only looked to her biological mother and mouthed, "I'm sorry."

10

Outside the cave, Joan saw the bright light change from a brilliant white to a dark blood red. She knew something was wrong. Without thinking, she sprinted into the cave and yelled for Brandon to stay put.

She entered the cave and saw Carl with his hand around Caitlin's neck. Samantha was standing a few feet away in front of the ghostly images of Carl's deceased family.

Joan stopped, and reached for her gun, but then realized it would be of no use, and even if it were, she couldn't take the chance of hitting Caitlin no matter how good a marksman she was. She lowered her gun and holstered it.

"Carl, Carl Saunderson." she yelled at the top of her lungs. "Please think about what you'd be giving up if you harm your granddaughter. For God's sakes, think about your family that's here, now—waiting to take you home. You're just not able to see them through all the hate and anger that's been filling up deep within you."

All Joan could think to do was to plead with him, and she did just that, and she did it with as much compassion and humility that she could muster up. "Carl, please, think back to the times before all the bad things happened. Remember all the times you spent with your wife Sandra, with your seven kids: the trips to the lake, Sunday picnics, playing catch with your boys, watching your wife teach your daughters how to cook. Remember, Carl, please God remember. It's all there waiting for you," Joan said motioning toward the light, toward his family.

"And you won't have to go by yourself," Samantha said. "I'm here to go with you, to make our family complete once more, as it was thirty two years ago. Father, please come with me."

The light gradually started turning back from blood red to the brilliant white. Carl released Caitlin and she fell to the ground. She stood, coughed, and rubbed at her throat. Joan ran to her and scooped her up and hugged her tighter than she ever had.

"Go, I can take it from here," Samantha said.

"Thank you, thank you so much."

"It is I that should be thanking you, but if you really want to thank me, then get her out of here, and…" Samantha stopped, looked toward her father, then looked to the rest of her family, and continued, "And Joan, please make sure Caitlin knows how much I love her. How much I will always love her."

"I will, I promise."

Samantha then grabbed her father's hand and without any further hesitation, walked with Carl into the light. Joan and Caitlin watched as the family of ten reunited. The light began to dim, and as it did, Joan and Caitlin both saw Samantha lying on the floor of the cave.

Joan put Caitlin down and started the walk out of the cave.

"I'm sorry it had to end this way sweetheart, but it was either your mother, or you, and this is what she wanted. She loved you so very much."

"I know," Caitlin said as they exited the cave, "I just wish that…"

"That you could have gotten a chance to know her better?"

"Yes."

"I do to." Joan replied softly, "She was an amazing woman."

Outside the cave, Joan and Caitlin joined Brandon and they walked together back towards the truck. Caitlin walked in-between Brandon and her mother, holding their hands.

To her mother, Caitlin said, "Mom, how'd you know?"

"How'd I know what, sweetie?"

"That I wished I could have gotten to know my birthmother better."

"I—uh—I don't know. Maybe a little of you is starting to rub off on me."

"Maybe," Caitlin replied.

As they made their way past the Institute toward Joan's truck, Caitlin asked, "Mom?"

"Yeah, sweetie, what is it?"

"Will I rub off on my little brother, too?"

The End